SCAPEGOAT

PART ONE

FRIDAY 22ND OCTOBER

CHAPTER 1

23:48 City of London

'What you lookin' at?' the sallow-faced youth yelled angrily at the old man.

Huddled under a sheet of cardboard in the doorway, the disheveled tramp didn't say a word as he shifted uneasily, struggling to sit up under his bedding, his unfocused eyes searching for a way out.

There was none that he could see; the grey London back street was deserted at midnight.

He might have called for help, but the buildings around were home to people during the day, not at night when the absence of the bankers, accountants, stock brokers and oil-traders who populated this part of the City made it the perfect place to go unseen – dark, quiet and far away from prying eyes.

Not only perfect to hide, but also perfect for this feral youth and his two drunken companions to prove their manliness by picking fights with the weak and the vulnerable.

The youth - red-haired, wiry and in his early twenties - stepped closer and with the right toe of his purposeful boot, prodded the near-empty bottle of cheap cider lying beside the befuddled old man.

'I'm fucking talking to you!' the youth shouted, the veins in his sinewy neck pulsating with anger as he wildly kicked the bottle and sent it thudding into the old man's chest. Bouncing back onto the pavement, it spun around like the pointer in a game of truth or dare before coming to a stop - the neck pointing straight at the frightened old man.

'God, he fucking stinks!' said another youth stepping forward to join the first.

This one - thicker set, bald and with a spider's web tattooed on his neck - wrinkled his nose in disgust as he contemptuously examined the old man.

'Just give him a kicking,' he said, tugging on his mate's leather jacket to emphasise his point, 'he's not even worth pissing on.'

Hoping Red would take his friend's advice, the old man's dark brown eyes moved from the red-haired youth to the bald one and then to the greasy fair hair and angry blotches of acne on the flushed cheeks of the third.

Three of them.

Each strong, in their early twenties and spoiling for a fight - an uneven contest if ever there was one.

Red bent close to the man's face and shouted, 'I asked you a question – what do you think you're staring at?'

The tramp looked back at Red impassively, his focus not moving away from his protagonist's face even when the thick gobbet of spit Red let fly hit his left cheek, ran down over his upper lip and splatted onto the cardboard bedding.

Buoyed by the cheers from Baldy and Acne, Red strutted arrogantly before stopping to unzip his trousers.

The old man stiffened imperceptibly as he guessed through his drunken haze what was coming next.

Although the cider-infused tramp lifted his left arm to shield his face, Red's steady stream of pungent urine ran down it to soak his chest and the cardboard, before forming a gently steaming puddle on the pavement.

Shaking the last drops off the end of his manhood so they splattered at random, Red zipped his trousers back up and did a small victory dance.

'Oh look,' he said triumphantly to his laughing companions, 'the old cunt has wet the bed!'

Red's momentary jocularity turned back to anger and he bent forward.

'How do you like that old man?' he said, straightening and - determined to have the final say - stepping forward on his left leg to unleash a ferocious kick with his heavy right boot.

Seeing the leg coming swiftly towards his solar plexus, the old man reacted surprisingly quickly, thrusting out his left arm in a short, straight, jabbing motion.

The cracking sound as Red's kick connected with the tramp echoed round the darkness of the deserted street. Baldy and Acne cheered encouragingly as Red shifted his weight to his right leg, locked eyes with his target and prepared to launch his next salvo.

At that moment the focus was between just the two of them.

The old tramp and the obnoxious youth, each experiencing very different emotions. One confused and in pain, the other composed and ready to strike.

Before he could launch his next kick, Red's eyes glanced down at his right leg then darted back to the old man - understanding dawning somewhere deep in the primal part of his brain, even as the echo from Baldy's and Acne's cheers faded.

Red's right leg trembled and began to buckle sideways - not from the knee, but halfway between the knee and the ankle where the old man's blow had broken clean through his tibia and fibula.

Struggling to gain his balance, Red threw his arms up and wide - like a hapless goalie diving to save a penalty - as his right leg folded beneath him like a piece of rubber.

No longer full of youthful bravado, Red writhed on the pavement.

'My leg! My fucking leg! He's broken my fucking leg!' he yelled, trying to straighten his useless limb.

Ignoring the wailing youth, the tramp rose unsteadily to his feet and looked from Baldy to Acne until he was satisfied that neither was intent on revenging their fallen hero.

Electing to discard the sodden cardboard, the tramp

wiped the piss-splattered bottle on his sleeve and began shuffling up the street, leaving Baldy phoning for an ambulance; Red writhing on the ground in pain; and Acne surveying the scene with bewilderment.

The mantra from his training echoed in Branigan's head as he pretended to stumble drunkenly away from his protagonists.

'Never break cover.'

CHAPTER 2

23:58 City of London

'Fuck, fuck, fuck!' Branigan muttered, shaking his left hand and trying to work some feeling back into it.

They might've taught him everything he needed to know about putting an opponent out of commission at The Academy, but their lessons stopped short of telling him either how to stop it hurting when you broke someone's leg, or keep your dignity when some drunken fool pissed all over you.

Still, Branigan reasoned - his strong lithe body still mimicking the awkward stumbling gait of a drunken old down-and-out - the odds were his mission wasn't ruined.

Unlike Red's leg.

They called the strike he'd used to break the bones "Iron Palm," and there was a time when he practiced the move daily.

But then, of course, that was before he broke The Rule.

Finding a suitable doorway, he folded his taut 6ft 2in frame back down to the ground and draped his over-large, moth-eaten and now damp-with-piss coat around himself to continue his vigil, only taking his eyes off his target to take in the commotion and flashing blue lights in the distance when the ambulance arrived for Red.

Just after the clock in a nearby church struck the half hour, something about a solitary figure walking from the direction of The Guildhall caught Branigan's eye.

Unlike the cleaners, security guards and street sweepers who exuded a sense of belonging as they worked in the dead of night - making The City of London safe, tidy and ready for the hordes of workers to return the next day - this man looked out of place.

Wrapped against the cold October air, he was glancing over his shoulder periodically as he walked down the street towards where Branigan sheltered in the doorway. Speaking in hushed tones on his telephone, he threw the unsavoury tramp a barely disguised look of contempt and paused his conversation as he walked by.

Used as he was to the way people responded to him when he played the role of the down-and-out, Branigan was familiar with the look; he was also familiar with the face giving it.

Anatoly Kozlow, a one-time member of the Soviet Intelligence system who, like many of his compatriots following the dawn of capitalism in the Soviet bloc, was now a paid-for hand providing information to the highest bidder. Branigan knew Kozlow's face well from the days when the two were on opposing sides in their respective countries' intelligence services, before Kozlow opted for the richer pickings to be had in the private sector and Branigan was forcibly marched out of the door of the Secret Intelligence Service with his tail between his legs.

Although it was little more than 5 years since they'd been adversaries in Central Asia - that swathe of land between the Caspian Sea and China where people and arms flood across the borders destined for Iraq, Syria and Afghanistan – so much had changed it really did feel like a lifetime separated them.

In stark contrast to Kozlow's rich and privileged life, Branigan's had become much more suburban.

No longer part of the twilight world of undercover intelligence, Branigan had swapped risking his life trying to shape the political map around the world for tracking down errant husbands, thieving staff and computer hackers.

An interesting juxtaposition; former foes coming face-to-face having set off in opposing directions.

Of course, it wasn't entirely coincidence that Branigan had been given this piece of surveillance in the first place. Marty Freeman, his private investigation employer since exiting SIS - the intelligence service most people knew as "MI6" from books and films - had already surmised that this would happen.

'Look, you and I both know if it is Kozlow he's not going to recognise you if you're properly disguised,' Marty explained when offering Branigan the assignment two days before, if, that is, you can call it "offer" when your boss gives you a choice of just one option.

'Besides,' Marty continued, 'I know you'd like to be up against him again for old times' sake.'

He was right.

The three consecutive nights staking out an anonymous office building in The City of London to see who the cleaner was passing copies of oil exploration maps to, were not the most salubrious part of the job, but being in the hunt for someone who dealt at the top table had his adrenalin pumping in a way tracking husbands who were shagging their secretaries behind their wife's back never could.

Annoyingly, Marty was also right that Kozlow was involved.

'Look, it's a slam-dunk,' Marty actually said, before going on to explain, 'The Organisation tell me Kozlow is in town and working for some shady oil baron.'

"The Organisation," the term used by past and serving members of the Intelligence Service to describe MI6.

'We get a knock on the door from an oil company saying sensitive information is marching out of the door - go figure,' he continued, 'We can't fill the street around the building where the information is leaking from with surveillance because we know it happens at night when the streets are deserted.'

In answer to Branigan's obvious question - why the oil company having the information stolen didn't improve their internal security - Marty had an equally obvious answer.

'Because they want to find out who is taking the information so they can then decide what they want to feed them.'

Counter-espionage.

The bread and butter of Branigan's job when he too was working for The Organisation; first you infiltrated somewhere, then you found out what was going on and then you decided how to use the information you obtained from the enemy to get back at them.

That was all well and good back in the days when Marty started working for the Intelligence Service and even when Branigan started his training. Then you knew who the enemy was because they were sitting behind the Iron Curtain.

Geography defined everyone's political roles.

By the time Branigan was thrown out of the Service, he found himself working shoulder-to-shoulder with rivals like Kozlow in one country and against them in another.

As Marty put it, 'I miss the good old days when people were treacherous because of their political ideals; now even their governments are dazzled by the pursuit of money.'

Branigan stayed huddled in his doorway as he focused on Kozlow's retreating back, his training making him stay put, observe and not break cover.

Then, almost imperceptibly, the three nights of waiting were rewarded as Kozlow pocketed his phone and strode steadily past the front of the building.

Another man - who Branigan recognised from studying surveillance footage from inside the oil company - waved goodnight to the security guard sitting slumped behind the front desk and walked in the opposite direction past Kozlow.

No acknowledgement. Just two people passing each other in the street; only the man who exited the building had his phone in his hand as he did so and didn't by the time he'd brushed past Kozlow.

Branigan couldn't help but admire the switch - better than the British relay team ever managed - and if he hadn't seen Kozlow pocket his own phone seconds before, Branigan would have thought nothing of the Russian appearing to continue his call as he hefted the newly acquired phone up to his ear and pretended to talk.

The consummate professional; even at night on a deserted street he maintained the illusion.

Branigan shrugged. He didn't need to see more - which was just as well, as he was momentarily blinded by flashing blue lights on the ambulance taking Red to have his right leg reassembled drove past. He'd confirmed what he needed to let the oil company know - where their secrets were being passed - beyond that his work was done and he could head home to a warm bed.

Attractive as the prospect of bed was, a little bit of Branigan's inquisitive nature would like to carry on with the operation, to follow Kozlow, remain under cover and do something with the intelligence he discovered. But even though his old self missed staying undercover for weeks at a time, the new Branigan resented even the few evenings he'd lost tracking down the man who'd just walked past.

That's what changing your life, having a loving wife and a beautiful daughter did for you. Working in a less intense environment, settling down and becoming a family man changed you. Yes, it might have been the darkest day for Branigan when he was recalled to London and asked to leave The Secret Intelligence Service, but it also opened the door on the happiest of meetings which changed his life forever.

After taking the only option available to him - working in central London with Marty - Branigan had been browsing a bookshop in nearby Charing Cross Road when a woman recognised him.

'Is that you Branigan?' she asked.

An old flame from college. Sally knew him of old and

didn't judge him as harshly as did others. Their reminiscing over a cup of coffee led to a kiss, which took them on a path to marriage and the arrival of Molly in their lives.

The best things in life coming from the worst.

Now he couldn't wait to get home to Sally as he walked the mile and a half back to the offices of Marty Freeman Investigations where, having punched the code into the lock and disabled the alarm, he was able to stuff the rank tramp costume in a plastic bag which he stuffed unceremoniously into his rucksack before taking a shower.

As the hot water ran first grey from the colouring in his hair, then yellow and white from the skin toner, Branigan felt he was washing away the character he'd been playing when Red stumbled across him.

It was part of the indoctrination at The Academy - the training centre he'd gone to after he eventually heeded his tutor's suggestion that he might be suited to a career serving his country.

At first, he had no idea what the phrase meant.

'What, "serve" as in join the army you mean?' he asked incredulously when Edmund Houseman, his tutor at Oxford, first mooted the idea.

'Not exactly,' the small, bookish and rather effete man replied softly, offering Branigan one of the chocolate biscuits he introduced to his tutorials when he wanted either to show his pleasure over something, or encourage a student, 'I was thinking of a role which took advantage of your brawn, language skills and - dare I say in these politically correct times - skin colour.'

Branigan looked from his own deep olive skin to Houseman's pasty white - Houseman's pallor hinting all too accurately at a life spent cloistered in libraries, lecture theatres and his rooms at college; Branigan's to lazy days in Oxford's meadows or on a boat on the River Cherwell when the sun beckoned.

'I don't think I understand,' Branigan said naïvely.

Houseman laughed softly.

'I'll see if I can bring someone along to give you some careers advice,' he replied, before changing the subject and discussing the use of language in a Russian novel by Alexander Pushkin.

His sights still set on the world of commerce, Branigan thought nothing of the conversation until he went to his tutorial one day and found someone else seated in the battered leather chair he usually chose.

'I'd like you to meet Michael Jenkins,' Houseman said by way of introduction, 'he's an alumni of ours and is here to talk about your career opportunities.'

'It's alumnus,' Michael Jenkins gently corrected, before turning his attention on Branigan, 'I studied English when I was up and think Houseman says things like that just to keep me on my toes!'

Almost as tall as Branigan, Michael had a thin face and the willowy grace of an athlete; he turned out to be engaging, erudite and amusing as he described a world of adventure in which the key words were trust, loyalty and opportunity. It was apparent that Branigan's mixed heritage - well, rather his Syrian mother's input than his father's Anglo-Saxon blood - fluency in several key languages and physical fitness, suited him to what the engaging Michael Jenkins described as "Intelligence Operations."

'To put it bluntly old chap,' he explained, pointing his finger at Branigan in an imitation of Lord Kitchener in the First World War recruitment poster, 'your country needs you. You see, we need people who've grown up in the culture of the Middle East, know the language and candidly fit in; our old recruitment model worked fine when we were putting people in behind the Iron Curtain, but the world is a changing place.'

As it turned out his words were both prophetic and beguiling.

The idea of being trained to use his strength, fledgling

dramatic skills and innate language ability was more than appealing - especially when you levelled the opportunity against Branigan's uncertainty over quite what it was he wanted to do in the commercial world.

Had he wanted to turn to his parents for advice, Branigan would have come up short.

His mother, a translator in the British Embassy in Syria, died in a car accident while he was still at school; his father, a junior diplomat who'd met his mother while stationed in Damascus, had a heart attack during Branigan's final year at Oxford. Overall the heart attack was a good thing as it stopped his Dad's terminal lung cancer from running its inevitable course.

'Listen son,' he'd said just days before he died, pausing to draw deeply on his cigarette and sip from a tumbler of neat Bushmills, 'if you take my advice, don't smoke and stay off whisky.'

Do as I say, not as I do.

But by that stage his father knew he was on the way out, so there was little point in asking him to give up the cigarettes and alcohol which had fuelled his earlier expat-life.

His Dad might not have been there to help with Branigan's career decision, but he did leave two lasting legacies - the run-down North London house he and Sally were still trying to renovate and an odour of stale tobacco which randomly leached out of the fabric of the building.

'And not only do we need your language and cultural skills,' Michael Jenkins said, his eyes running up and down him in what Branigan only subsequently realised was a job interview, 'but the Service could do with someone with your physique and looks to brighten the place up.'

At the time he took it as a compliment, although, as he later worked alongside him, Branigan realised that when making the observation Michael was voicing his own sexual preference.

The comments were, however, echoed by the succession

of girls who'd been drawn to him over the years and especially by his own wife.

After trying - and failing - to pronounce Branigan's given name while standing in an immigration queue when honeymooning in Turkey, Sally studied his passport.

'Why does it only have the scar on your rib cage as a distinguishing mark?' she asked.

When he looked quizzical, Sally laughed.

'It doesn't mention anywhere here that you have a chiselled jaw, abs that look like an anatomical drawing and a frankly gorgeous ass,' she replied, flipping through the pages of his passport, 'or that you look like that actor from Dr Zhivago - what was his name?'

'Omar Sharif?' Branigan ventured.

'That's the one,' Sally said, eyeing his impressive physique, 'at least what Omar Sharif could've looked like if he'd worked out more!'

In fact, in subsequent conversation Sally explained that the only reason they'd re-connected all those years after their brief fling in College, was that she'd admired his ass as he bent down in the "A to E" section of the non-fiction aisle.

'I didn't recognise you when I first saw you; I was admiring you from behind and wondering how to strike up a conversation when you turned around and I realised I already knew you!'

'So really,' she joked, 'the only reason we're together is because I liked your backside!'

The thought of climbing into bed alongside Sally carried Branigan back home as he cycled along the mainly deserted streets which were interspersed with little oases of late-night revelry around the clubs - places he and Sally hadn't countenanced visiting since Molly's arrival on the scene.

Like most newly wedded couples, they'd sworn to their friends that parenthood would neither change their habits nor see them going to bed overcome with exhaustion.

Reality had now dawned.

When they said they liked an early night, their childless friends exchanged knowing looks and assumed they were headed for some form of sexual olympics; while their equally drawn and strained friends with children simply nodded, knowing that sex now took second place to a good night's sleep in the marital harmony stakes.

It was a relief for Branigan to know that he'd identified Kozlow, as it put to an end the successive nights of surveillance which had so interrupted his and Sally's routine.

Whilst it wasn't unusual for Branigan to have to work in the evenings, it was generally only the odd occasion and not successive nights into the small hours of the morning as this had been.

In Stoke Newington, Branigan turned off the main road and weaved through a maze of quiet residential streets before arriving home.

Built when Queen Victoria was on the throne, the street where Branigan and Sally lived was typical of many developed during her reign as the rail network expanded and London's green suburbs gave way to neat rows of houses.

Branigan was lucky, the home he'd inherited from his father went up at a time when land was at less of a premium, so his and Sally's bay-windowed house was set back from the road behind a small brick wall and a front garden which now played host to the various unsightly rubbish bins the local council introduced in the name of recycling.

The front gardens helped to set the houses back from the road, created a sense of space not enjoyed by more modern developments and the trees dotted along the pavement created a vista the estate agents liked to call a "leafy suburb."

What the Victorians didn't do when they laid their neatly-tiled footpath to Branigan's red front door was anticipate his arriving home late at night and having to stow his bike.

The shed in his garden - which was home to his bike and sundry building paraphernalia - was only accessible with the bicycle by either taking it through the house and out of the back door from the kitchen, or wheeling it around the whole terrace to the pathway which ran along behind the houses.

As the kitchen was not on Sally's preferred route, Branigan made his way past a dozen more houses before turning left at the end of the long terrace. From there he was able to turn up the brick-paved path along the back of the houses.

Making his way as quietly as possible along the alleyway, Branigan let himself in through the gate and used the torch on his phone to open the combination padlock on the shed.

Pushing the bike inside and catching a whiff of the urine-soaked tramp's outfit, Branigan elected to leave it there until he'd explained the events of the evening to Sally and she was ready for him to put the soiled coat anywhere near their washing machine.

Quietly pulling his boots off on the horns of a metal boot-jack styled a bit like a crawling bug, closing the back door and tiptoeing into the house, Branigan made his way carefully upstairs and pushed open Molly's door to kiss her as she slept.

Finding her bed disturbed but empty, Branigan knew exactly where to look for his little girl. Sure enough, curled into the crook of the sleeping Sally's arm was the tiny blond miniature version of her mother.

During the day Molly would follow Sally round, make pretend cups of tea, wash dishes and even want to wear the same make-up; at night, Branigan recognised with a wry grin, she even mimicked the way her mother slept.

While Sally's left arm was locked around her daughter, Molly's was wrapped around Puppy - her ever-present brown bear.

Gently scooping up Molly and Puppy, Branigan couldn't help recalling a discussion in which he and Sally vowed they would stand firm.

'You're right,' he'd said to Sally when Molly was first able to wander from her room into theirs, 'we mustn't let Molly share our bed; it's the last place in the house which is ours. If we let that go, it's the thin end of the wedge.'

They were both adamant.

It couldn't, after-all, be that difficult for two educated, intelligent and determined adults to resist a young child and keep the sanctity of the marital bed to themselves. Their resolution lasted until Molly had a nightmare three nights later.

Now, having tucked his precious cargo back into her own bed, it was Branigan's turn to occupy the space beside Sally, her warmth and softness a welcome sanctuary after the evening spent in the draughty doorway.

Sally stirred.

'Did you get your man?' she asked, the hand which had been protecting Molly now stroking his abs reassuringly.

'Yes,' he replied, feeling a stir in his loins which dispelled the weariness he'd felt only moments before, 'Marty was right; it was the Russian I told you about.'

Sally's hand slid down from his abs and explored the hardness of his erection.

'You're pleased with yourself then!' she exclaimed as her fingers worked up the length, before wrapping round the solidity of his girth.

'And I suppose my conquering hero would like to do something about this before he goes to sleep?'

It was a rhetorical question, as Branigan was already responding to Sally by gently nuzzling her in the neck. The spot he knew she found most arousing.

Well, almost the most arousing.

Then his hands were exploring her and pulling her close, a familiarity and growing urgency about their movements which came from not just knowing every inch of the other, but also when to steal the opportunity.

Their mutual hunger stemmed from the lateness of the hour, beckoning sleep and the need to be close with the other.

Before Molly was on the scene, they might have deferred sex until the morning when they would be able to wake refreshed and eager - prospects which disappeared once Molly learned how to clamber out of bed and climb into theirs - so they took the chance now for deep, sensual and urgent lovemaking.

Reaching their climax, they silently held each other close before rolling onto their backs to lie side by side.

'I'm so glad you haven't got to go out again tomorrow night,' Sally whispered.

'I know,' Branigan agreed, 'isn't it wonderful, we've got Molly's party and a whole weekend ahead of us?'

'And this man from the past,' Sally asked, 'this Russian you saw tonight, he's not going to drag you into anything unpleasant?'

Of course, Sally knew about Branigan's history. Most of the population of the UK - or at least those who read the tabloid press – knew about his past.

'No,' he reassured her, 'there's nothing that can drag me back into that; not even this Russian.'

But his words fell on deaf ears.

Sally was already asleep.

SATURDAY 23RD OCTOBER

CHAPTER 3

06:47 Stoke Newington, London

Branigan's experience of working under-cover meant that he was wide awake and propped on one arm by the time Molly had their bedroom door half open.

'Here she is!' he called in greeting, as Molly trailed in with Puppy clutched under one arm and a story book held close to her chest.

Behind him Sally let out a muffled expletive.

It's fair to say Sally wasn't a morning person, which meant whenever possible it fell to Daddy to entertain Molly and get her ready for the day.

'Oh look,' Branigan said as he sat up and settled Molly onto his lap, 'you've got your book of scary fairy tales!'

Molly nodded and riffled through the pages, carefully examining the pictures before alighting on one of an evil king with two monstrous snakes growing from his shoulders.

'Mummy will enjoy this!' Branigan said wryly as he too studied the image.

Beside him Sally stifled another expletive.

'Why do children like such horrid stories?' she muttered before burying her head under the pillow as Branigan began to recount the legend of Zahhāk, the king with a serpent head on each shoulder.

Half an hour later, as he closed the book and ushered Molly off his lap, Branigan prompted Sally.

'I hate to remind you,' he said, 'but we have a birthday party to get ready for.'

It was Sally's turn to prop herself up on one arm, her eyes blinking sleepily as she fought against the powerful urge to collapse back onto the bed.

'And may I remind you,' she said, checking the room to make sure Molly wasn't in sight, 'that someone came home in the small hours of the morning and very rudely interrupted my sleep?'

'That's funny, because I don't seem to recall you objecting last night!' Branigan laughed as Sally's eyes focused intently on his face.

'You weren't working undercover as the tramp last night by any chance?' she asked.

'Yes, why?' he replied, perplexed.

'Because you've still got grey hair sprouting from your left ear!'

Another of the lessons from The Academy.

'If you're undercover do the job properly; nothing gives your cover away more quickly than sloppy characterisation.'

Branigan felt his ear and began to tease the hairs out from where he had glued them the afternoon before.

'Yuk!' Sally exclaimed, 'that means I was fucked by an old man who'd been sleeping on the street last night.'

'That's only the half of it,' Branigan said, instinctively covering his bruised left palm and stopping short of saying anything further - now was not the time to explain about either the smelly coat or, even worse, his scrap with Red.

'I much prefer it when you're someone more robust, like a fireman,' she said, sitting up and starting to rise from the bed.

He wanted to say that the tramp had been fairly robust when he broke his attacker's leg, but thought better of it - Sally wasn't a fan of his more brutal antics.

'I particularly liked it when you were that airline pilot,' she said coyly.

Branigan looked perplexed. He'd come home in character a few weeks before when working on a job to find people stealing from the duty-free trolleys at Heathrow Airport.

'You not only had a uniform,' Sally giggled, 'but probably the cheesiest line I've ever heard.'

She mimicked putting a hat on and donning sunglasses before pretending to push the peak of the imaginary cap up and taking her sunglasses off seductively.

'Why, honey, wouldn't you like to see my cockpit and play with the joystick?' she said in a soft American drawl.

Branigan wrinkled his nose and blushed with embarrassment.

'I did say that, didn't I?' he said, 'but, in my defence, the stewardess had just admired the size of my engines!'

Sally padded round the bed to give her husband a hug.

A hug and not a kiss because of Sally's "no kissing in the morning until we've both brushed our teeth" rule.

Better than some of the rules which impacted on Branigan's life, this one had some merit - it might look romantic on the Hollywood screen when the loving couple stirred the next morning and picked up where they left off, but the reality was a little less captivating.

'Come on,' Sally said, snapping away from their embrace, 'this won't do; I've got to get ready for the party.'

She shook her head, 'Why didn't you stop me when I said, "We can hold it at our house; all we have to do is make some space in the lounge, cook some sausages and organise some games?"'

'But it seemed such a good idea at the time!' Branigan laughed, 'I wanted to do it too if you remember.'

He thought about it for a moment.

'Do you think it's one of those right-of-passage things every parent has to go through? I remember how Karen next door's eyebrows shot up when you told her and she said, "Oh, you're having it at home - that's brave of you."'

'Yes,' Sally said as she made her way to the bathroom, 'I picked up on that too. I think she stopped herself from saying "you must be mad" in there somewhere!'

'Still,' she continued, 'at least I know I've got you here today to help - I don't think I could face it without you.'

Once they'd both got ready for the day, breakfasted and explained three times to Molly that it was too early to put on her frothy red princess party dress, Branigan busied himself by moving furniture to make space for the influx of seven children from pre-school, before hanging decorations.

'Why did they invent long thin balloons?' he asked Sally a while later when she was in the kitchen putting sweets into little boxes for the party bags, 'Not only are they practically impossible to blow up, but I'm struggling to put them in any combination which doesn't look suggestive!'

Sally smiled and shook her head.

'You can't get away from your favourite obsession, can you?' she said, teasingly.

'Very funny,' he replied, 'but you haven't just had to explain to Mrs. Rutherford that it was an oversight when I hung what she interpreted as a cock and balls either side of the front door!'

He paused, putting his right hand to his forehead in a gesture of mock disbelief as he pictured the unsmiling old woman from a few doors down, 'I'll swear the old bat tried to cover her poodle's eyes!'

Sally's laugh caught in her throat as Branigan's phone began to ring.

'God, no,' she said in alarm, 'please not today of all days.'

Branigan pulled the phone from his jeans pocket and looked at the caller ID.

'Marty,' he said.

Sally looked heavenwards.

'Make sure he knows about Molly's party...' she said as Branigan answered.

'I can't go into details now,' Marty explained after Branigan had told him about the party, 'and trust me, I'd like to say you can stay and help with Molly's birthday, but this is more pressing. There's a girl in danger right now.'

'But why does it have to be me who drops everything and comes running?' Branigan replied.

'Because her parents have said it's imperative they meet with you,' Marty said.

Sally looked quizzically at the frown on her husband's face.

'What, they asked for me by name?' he said.

'Yes,' Marty replied, 'they gave your name, said they'd explain everything when we met and emphasised the urgency.'

Sally, who was hanging on every word of Branigan's half of the conversation, mouthed "no!" at him as he spoke.

'Come on, Marty,' Branigan said catching Sally's eye and making it clear he was trying his best, 'can't you just meet them and let me know if there's something I can do; it can't be that personal that they need me to drop everything and come running.'

'From what they said, I think it is. At the very least Branigan I believe you need to come and hear what they have to say. If you do that you can be home by midday.'

Branigan clenched his left fist in frustration.

'What did you say the name of the missing girl is?'

'I didn't,' Marty replied, pausing while he checked his notes, 'Travers, Chloe Travers. She's a student at Sheffield University.'

Branigan shook his head.

'That name means nothing to me - why do you think it has to be me they want to see?'

'I'm afraid that's a question we'll only be able to answer once we've met them,' Marty said, emphasising the word "we" as he spoke.

Branigan looked heavenwards in exasperation.

'I don't have a choice, do I?'

'No, Branigan, I'm afraid not.'

'God, sometimes I hate Marty bloody Freeman and his fucking investigation agency!' Sally shouted angrily as Branigan finished his call, slamming down a box of sweets so hard its contents spilled over the work surface.

'Why does it have to be today,' she continued after Branigan explained that he'd been left with no choice but to go, 'everyone's coming in just three and a half hours and I don't want to be left hosting the party on my own!'

'All the more reason for me to get going now,' Branigan said, doing his best to placate Sally, 'because the sooner I meet these damn people, the sooner I'll be back here to help.'

He glanced towards the door and caught Sally's eye.

Molly was standing there with Puppy tucked under her left arm and her right thumb in her mouth - a sure sign she wasn't happy.

'Aww, honey!' Sally said, immediately stopping re-packing the spilled sweets and going to scoop up her girl, 'Don't worry about anything, Mummy is just a bit cross with the man Daddy works for because he wants Daddy to go out for a few minutes.'

'He won't be long,' she continued, jiggling Molly on her hip reassuringly, before adding in a pointed aside to Branigan, 'will you?'

Branigan stepped forward to embrace both of them.

'Mummy's right,' he said, squeezing them both in his strong arms, 'I promise I'll be back in time for your party munchkin, just as soon as I've met another mummy and daddy who want my help.'

Molly took her right thumb out of her mouth and smiled along with her Daddy, while Sally – also wrapped in his arms - couldn't help but melt.

A family hug.

The warmest, cosiest and safest place in the world.

Nuzzling his face in the matching blond locks of his two girls, Branigan said to Molly, 'Will you help Mummy get ready for the party?'

She nodded.

'Good, then for now you go and watch television and Mummy will call you when she needs a hand - is that a deal?'

Molly high-fived her Daddy and said, 'Deal!'

'Thanks, Branigan,' Sally said when the little girl padded back into the living room, 'I've got enough on my plate without having Molly helping me!'

She peered out into the hall.

'You've got rid of all the cables, dangerous tools and paraphernalia you left out there?'

Branigan nodded. He was re-wiring the house in his spare time, so there were usually plentiful rolls of cable, fixtures and tools dotted around the house.

'Yes, everything's now in either the shed, or the cupboard under the stairs.'

He counted off the jobs he'd done in preparation for the afternoon influx on the fingers of his left hand, 'The balloons are up and no longer obscene; the living room is tidy and the furniture pushed back against the wall; and I've wrapped the pass-the-parcel presents and put them on the sideboard.'

He looked around.

'That's most of what I had to do, other than helping you and pouring a glass of wine for any of the mums and dads who want to stay.'

Sally nodded.

'Great, thanks,' she said returning to the party bags, 'then get your sorry ass out of here and promise me you'll be back in time for the party.'

Branigan winked.

'I promise,' he said, 'and just so I have an incentive, should I bring the fireman or the airline pilot uniform home with me?'

Sally placed her left forefinger on her lips and made a show of giving the idea critical appraisal.

'I think the policeman if you don't mind,' she said after careful consideration, 'because I like the idea of someone tall, dark and handsome giving me a stern talking to!'

'Now,' she said, pushing her husband towards the back door, 'go!'

Branigan did just that, kissing first Sally and then Molly.

'I love you,' he shouted over his shoulder as he went out of the back door and retrieved his bicycle.

At the end of the alleyway he had to swerve to avoid running over Mrs. Rutherford's poodle which came flying out of her back gate, snapping angrily at his wheels, then he was out on the road and cycling through the almost stationary London traffic on his way to the offices of Marty Freeman Investigations.

10:31 Marty Freeman Investigations, The Strand

The small brass plate beside the dark blue doors of the anonymous-looking building at the Aldwych end of The Strand announced it to be the home of Marty Freeman Investigations.

Shiny metallic blinds in the old shop windows shielded the interior of the building from the street, as Branigan carefully wheeled his bike into the reception area and threaded it between a high-fronted walnut reception desk and a corporate-grey leather sofa on his way to a store room at the back of the building. A useful short-cut which saved him going around to the back of the building and through the underground car park.

'Morning Anna,' he called to the raven-haired woman in her mid-thirties seated behind the desk, 'another busy Saturday then?'

Anna Shah pulled her earphones out and flashed Branigan a friendly smile.

It was a standing joke between the two of them.

They'd started working for the firm at the same time and on their first day Marty gave them both his vision for the business.

'I like to think of Marty Freeman Investigations as being client-facing and open to all,' he'd said, using a phrase he'd found in a book about managing your own business.

More or less every Saturday since then, Anna had dutifully sat in reception facing a door through which no clients ever walked.

'Nobody ever turns up unannounced at the best of times,' Anna moaned to Branigan when they last spoke about the waste of time, 'but on a Saturday it's completely dead.'

Branigan had sympathised.

'I agree, a business which spends its entire advertising budget on a 6-inch square brass plaque is hardly inviting people to come in their droves, is it?'

But this Saturday was different.

As ever smartly-dressed - today in a white blouse and black cashmere cardigan - Anna smiled triumphantly and dramatically swept back her long locks.

'I'll have you know, Mr Branigan,' she said enjoying the repartee, 'that not only have I got about a hundred employee applications to check for Strankley Security, but my cup runneth over because we have unexpected clients on their way and joy-of-joys Marty has turned up.'

To emphasise her point she hefted a large pile of papers on her desk which, Branigan surmised, had been passed to her by Andy Meadows who vetted staff for clients in the security industry.

'What brings you in on your day off?' she asked.

Branigan's face fell at the mention of the impending visitors.

'The surprise visitors - the same as Marty.'

'That's all I need,' Anna said, picking up on his mood, 'a grouchy Marty and a gloomy Branigan.'

'Marty has only been in 10 minutes,' she continued, 'and he's already been on the phone twice demanding I get him a coffee.'

As if on cue the phone on Anna's desk rang.

'Hello,' Anna said, catching Branigan's eye and breaking into a grin while she listened in silence.

'Yes Marty, I know you want your drink,' she said, winking

conspiratorially, 'but Branigan is on his way up and insisted he's going to make it for you because he can see how hard I'm working down here.'

'Oh good,' Branigan said sardonically when she put the phone down, 'I appear to have swapped a wife telling me what to do for a colleague doing the same - I take it from that call I'm on coffee-making duty for Marty now?'

'That's the one,' Anna replied, taking an application from the stack of papers and keying some details into her computer, 'and am I to assume Sally's been having a go at you too?'

Branigan laughed.

'You could say, I was in the middle of getting ready for Molly's birthday party when Marty called and insisted I come in to meet his surprise visitors.'

'Ouch,' Anna sympathised, 'of course, it's the birthday party today - I imagine you coming in to work hasn't gone down too well with Sally!'

'That's something of an understatement,' Branigan agreed.

'Are you going to make it back in time, only Sally said you'd got a houseful from just after lunch?' Anna asked anxiously, glancing at the clock.

One of the things about working for a small business like Marty's was that all the staff knew what was going on in each other's lives and, although Branigan was the one working in the office from day to day, Sally chatted regularly to Anna and some of the other girls in the firm.

In fact, there were times when it was impossible to distinguish the people standing round the coffee machine at work from those in his kitchen at home - the consequence of having a gregarious wife.

Not that Sally necessarily saw it that way. She complained it was only through talking to the girls at work that she found out what he was up to - especially when he either forgot to warn Sally of his movements, or was stuck doing something undercover.

'I'd better be back,' he grinned sheepishly, the dimple in his chin becoming more pronounced as his deep brown eyes flashed with amusement, 'or Sally is going to have a word with Marty...'

'That's easy then,' Anna said with a laugh, 'Marty is so scared of Sally he'll fall over himself to get you back home if he knows the alternative is incurring her wrath!'

On his way from dropping his bicycle in the storeroom and changing into the casual jacket he wore at work, Anna waved a handwritten note at him.

'This is for you,' she said, 'someone came in looking for you yesterday and wanted you to call them back, but you were out on one of your secret missions!'

Branigan glanced at the note and put it in his jacket pocket.

'Ahh! The romance of working under cover,' he said, recalling his brush with Red as Anna put her earphones back in and waved him away.

Branigan made his way up three flights of narrow stairs to the top floor of the building and stepped out into the narrow, largely open-plan, office on the top floor.

Smaller than the ground floor, there was a door to an office on his left, a small cluster of three desks in front of him and a fourth desk which was home to an impressive array of computers set at the far-end to his right.

There was no one to be seen.

Turning left, Branigan pushed the office door open.

'This better be good,' he said.

Marty's office was spacious - given the size of the building - and home to a modern desk which incorporated a small meeting table on his right, two small brown leather sofas facing each other over a coffee table and shelves along one wall bearing assorted books, files, a few faded photographs of Marty with his golfing buddies and a modest array of cheap-looking golf trophies.

Scapegoat

Marty looked up from behind the desk - grey-haired, in his mid-sixties and with blue eyes which Sally reckoned made him look like Frank Sinatra in his later years.

'Yes, thank you Branigan, I'd love that cup of coffee you promised,' he said.

'Do you have any idea how much trouble I'm in?' Branigan responded.

'Is it Molly's birthday today?'

'No, the party is today, she's actually four on Monday.'

'Gosh, isn't she growing fast? White, no sugar.'

'Are you taking this seriously?'

'Very seriously,' Marty replied, 'in fact, so seriously I've pulled out of the Seniors' Cup at the golf club and I still haven't got my cup of coffee.'

Reluctantly Branigan turned on his heel.

'You may find Sally has taken you off our Christmas card list if I don't get home for the party,' he called over his shoulder as he walked towards the coffee machine to the backdrop of a muttered expletive from Marty's room which ended with the word "coffee".

'Morning Alan,' Branigan said in the general direction of the bank of computer screens.

There was a strangled mewing sound from behind the wall of technology and a man in his early forties with very fair skin, thinning fair hair and a pointed face peered tentatively over the top.

'Hello,' he said, before sinking back down out of sight.

'Coffee?' Branigan asked.

For answer a white mug bearing an image of the Starship Enterprise appeared above the screens.

As he took the proffered mug, Branigan allowed himself a glance in the direction of Alan Armstrong, the firm's computer expert.

The very antitheses of Branigan, he was short, round and sedentary.

He wore a neatly starched white shirt, with a blue and

white spotted bowtie, burgundy corduroy trousers and a mustard-coloured knitted cardigan which buttoned up the front and had bulging pockets on either side.

'He's quite eccentric really,' Branigan said to Sally when he first tried to describe Alan to her, 'absolutely brilliant with computers by all accounts, but he spends all of his time hidden behind his computer screens, rarely - if ever - venturing out and only then to talk to the servers in the basement.'

He went on to describe Alan's extraordinary dress sense and complete ineptitude when faced with social situations, at which point Sally declared, 'It sounds like he's an Aspie!'

When Branigan looked blankly back at her, Sally explained.

'Asperger Syndrome is high-functioning autism - where people don't socialise very well,' she said, recalling her anthropological studies from university, 'struggle to pick up on social cues and - although often brilliant at some things – they struggle to cope with what is going on around them.'

Branigan had to agree that Alan sounded like he fitted Sally's description, something she later confirmed having asked Branigan if she could meet him.

Alan became a regular feature in their kitchen after Branigan invited him when they had a bunch of people from work and several of the neighbours to a barbecue one Sunday afternoon.

Even though he knew all the people from work and everyone made an effort to engage with him, Alan moved his chair away from the group chatting round the tables and barbecue, preferring instead to sit in silence and count the number of bricks in each house he could see.

Clive and Adam who shared the desks either side of Branigan tried talking about work; Andy, whose security checks Anna was doing, discussed ways to improve the computer system; while Anna herself tried tackling the weather and her origins in Persia - all with little success.

Kelly and Hussain from Accounts managed brief conversations about spreadsheets; Adam's girlfriend Marion talked television programmes; and Sally's best friend Jude only succeeded in turning his ears puce and rendering him completely mute when she tried flirting.

Jasper - Anna's partner who did something to do with finance in The City – was the only one to have limited success when he talked about the currency markets and Alan launched into an explanation of the best computer algorithm to use for futures trading. In fact, Jasper Farhad was so successful in engaging Alan, Sally had to step in to the rescue when she found Alan using a wax crayon in one of Molly's drawing books to sketch complex diagrams.

Despite being the hostess and running around organising food and drinks with her husband, Sally managed to spend time coaxing Alan out from his shell by asking him about his interests, being prepared to listen and - unlike Jasper - stop him when he became too focused.

All those who didn't know him, commented on the funny man who insisted on wearing a bowtie and knitted cardigan in the warm summer sunshine - while Alan himself announced the party the best he'd ever been to.

'He's lovely,' Sally declared, 'but he hasn't got a clue how to behave in a situation like that, has he?'

'No,' Branigan agreed, 'if that was the best party he ever went to, can you imagine the worst?'

After that first meeting, Sally took Alan under her wing and - instead of laughing at his ineptitude - spent time patiently teaching him the inner-workings of the world he struggled so much to understand.

Today, however, there was little to be seen of the more relaxed and out-going man he glimpsed when Alan sat in his kitchen talking to Sally and playing with Molly.

'You won't see much change in him at work,' Sally explained when Branigan commented how consistently isolated Alan remained in the office, 'because he's got established routines and barriers around him there.'

Branigan returned the Starship Enterprise coffee mug to Alan, taking care to place it neatly on the coaster bearing Mr. Spock's face.

'Here you are, white, with four sugars,' he said.

'Thank you,' Alan replied, peering suspiciously at the sweet milky contents, 'did you stir it?'

'Yes,' Branigan said patiently as he returned to the coffee machine to collect his and Marty's drinks, 'three times clockwise.'

Alan nodded with satisfaction, his eyes at no time straying any farther than the coffee mug itself and the array of screens in front of him.

'There,' Branigan declared ungraciously as he put Marty's coffee firmly down on the desk, 'one cup of coffee and will you now tell me what the fuck is going on?'

Marty sat back in his chair, took a sip of his drink and smiled.

'I thought you'd never ask,' he said, glancing down at scribbled notes on a piece of paper in front of him.

'This missing girl, Chloe, is 26 years old; what they call a mature student, studying for a degree in journalism; and she was meeting someone yesterday who could give her information about an article she's writing.'

Branigan sipped his coffee, still failing to see why he'd had to drop everything and come in.

'She phoned her parents to say there was some danger associated with the person she was meeting and she asked them to get your help if she didn't get back in touch with them after her meeting and - as you've no doubt guessed - no one has been able to make contact with her since she went off to meet them.'

Branigan frowned.

'And her parents didn't say why it was me she wanted help from?' he asked.

It was Marty's turn to shake his head.

'No, they said they'd go into all of that when we met.'

'And they didn't give you a name for the person she was meeting?' Branigan asked.

'Again no,' Marty replied, peering at his note as if closer scrutiny might reveal some answers, 'they said she hadn't told them that - only that they must contact you for help if she went missing.'

'What about the article she was writing, did they give you anything on that?' Branigan asked, fishing around for an explanation as to why he'd been singled out.

When Marty confessed that again the answer was no, Branigan swore in frustration.

'This is fucking ridiculous,' he said, 'you've got me in because some girl's parents haven't been able to make contact with their daughter for a few hours. Has it occurred to you she may have lost her phone or be shacked up with some bloke somewhere?'

'How old did you say she was, twenty-six,' he continued, answering his own question, 'don't you think she's old enough to be out on her own?'

'Yes, funnily enough I do,' Marty replied, glancing at his watch, 'and you'll be able to form your own opinion in a moment. All I'll say is her mother was so distraught Chloe's dad had to take over the call. The least you can do is give them the time to listen to their concerns because they sounded pretty genuine to me.'

Branigan snorted and shook his head.

'Sally isn't going to believe it when I tell her you dragged me in for this.'

CHAPTER 4

10:37 Apartment, Limehouse E14

I'm taking care to cover my face and keep myself hidden from any cameras, just as I did when I rang the doorbell. Now I've followed one of the neighbours inside and come up to the top floor.

Although the door looks solid, I've tried it with one firm kick before getting out my tools and it has flown open – I can see that it has been shoddily repaired in the past.

Inside I check the living room, the bedroom and then find what I want in the spare room.

A shiny lightweight Apple laptop, a back-up drive and a file of papers and photographs.

It has taken me less than ten minutes to remove every trace of Branigan and Bishkek from the apartment.

10:44 The Strand, London

There was a tap on the door to Marty's office and Anna came into the room.

'Mr and Mrs Travers to see you,' she announced, stepping back and ushering the girl's parents inside.

An unassuming man with a gaunt face and close-cropped grey hair stepped through the door followed by his diminutive wife.

Mr Travers, who brought with him a distinctive scent of wood and musk from his aftershave, reminded Branigan of his history teacher - lean, meek, rather ineffectual and lacking in any authority. He looked around the room and stepped forward, shaking hands with a surprisingly firm grip.

Mrs Travers, thin-lipped and mousey, peered suspiciously through horn-rimmed spectacles at each of them before offering the limpest of handshakes and a stiff and formal introduction.

Having hung Mrs Travers' tweed coat and fur-trimmed hat behind Marty's door, Anna established no one needed drinks and left with an urgency which suggested the journey from the ground floor with the girl's parents hadn't been filled with light banter.

Marty invited the couple to sit and they settled side-by-side on the edge of the sofa facing the door.

'So how can we help Mr and Mrs Travers?' Marty asked as he sat down beside Branigan on the sofa facing them, adding, 'and please call us Marty and Branigan.'

'I've heard your name, obviously,' James Travers said, his blue eyes focused unwaveringly on Branigan, 'but I don't know whether we call you Mr. Branigan or Branigan?'

Branigan was used to the question.

'It's just Branigan. My mother gave me a first name no one can pronounce - so I've just been called Branigan since I was first at school.'

'Can you tell us why you're here?' he continued, keen to move things forward.

'As I explained on the phone,' Kathy Travers said, her bespectacled brown eyes failing to make contact with either Marty or Branigan, 'our daughter Chloe has gone missing and we need your urgent help.'

'You see Chloe is studying for a degree in journalism and is researching a news article. She phoned us on Thursday to say she was interviewing someone on Friday morning who could give her background on the story she's writing.'

Branigan nodded, showing polite interest and thinking how much better his time would be spent at home.

'Chloe also told us that there were some risks in meeting this person and, I know this sounds melodramatic, she wanted us to ask for help if she didn't make contact after her meeting.'

Branigan raised an eyebrow as Mrs Travers fiddled nervously with her thin fair hair as she continued her story.

'Naturally we told her not to go if it was that dangerous, but she insisted. We tried her all through yesterday but there was no reply.'

James Travers continued as his wife lapsed into silence.

'We thought at first she might've just misplaced her phone or something, but by yesterday evening we were getting really worried and have kept trying until this morning when we knew there must be a real problem,' he said, leaning further forward and, unlike his wife, fixing Branigan unwaveringly with his blue eyes, 'so we phoned her halls and were told that she hasn't been seen there since yesterday morning.'

He too fell silent as the weight of what he'd just said sank in.

'Have you contacted the police?' Marty asked.

In response Kathy Travers snorted in disgust.

'Of course we did, first thing this morning, but I'm afraid they were no help at all,' she said, 'you see Chloe's an adult so the police aren't interested until she's been missing for 72 hours - apparently meeting someone dangerous for a student news story doesn't feature high on their list of suspicious circumstances.'

From where he was sitting Branigan was inclined to agree.

'I understand that,' Branigan said, willing their meeting to end so he could go home, 'so what story was she working on that meant she felt so in danger?'

Kathy Travers looked up for the first time and stared directly at him, her joyless brown eyes disconcertingly magnified through her spectacles.

'I thought you knew,' she said softly, 'she was meeting one of the terrorists you sold the arms to when you were sacked by the Intelligence Service.'

It was as well Branigan was sitting down because despite

his prodigious strength there was every chance at that moment his legs would have given way.

His head swam and it felt like his stomach had gone into free-fall.

'I'm sorry,' he said when his body had restored some of its equilibrium, 'what did you say?'

'I said she was meeting one of the terrorists you sold that container of arms to when you were exposed by the press,' Kathy Travers repeated, 'you see, Chloe is re-writing your story.'

His story.

The event which changed his life irrevocably.

One-minute working undercover, hidden and anonymous in a forgotten part of the world, the next plastered over the front page of the tabloid newspapers at home and branded a traitor.

He'd had better days.

Hauled back to London for several meetings the same tabloids would have described as "heated," he found himself being shown the door by SIS. As if the public humiliation wasn't enough, being shunned by his former colleagues and told by David Price, his ultimate boss, that military intelligence needed people who lived up to the name was the icing on the cake.

'We need people who are clever enough to keep their faces off the front page of the newspapers when they're working undercover,' David Price said in his final meeting with Branigan.

David Price emphasised his point by taking a copy of "Field Operations Conduct - Undercover" off his desk; the rule book to which all undercover agents were bound. It's fair to say Branigan never referred to the tome, preferring instead to use intuition and guile when faced with an armed terrorist rather than leafing through the pages of an encyclopedia-sized handbook.

Amongst the agents to whom it was addressed, the manual had two distinct uses.

Firstly, it came in handy when you needed to prop up a wobbly desk and secondly, in the eyes of the undercover agents, its own acronym summed up their leadership's attitude.

FOC-U.

As soon as David Price picked up the manual, Branigan had known there was only one ending possible to their meeting.

'You might like to refresh your memory of Rule 31 in the manual here,' he said, turning to a page marked by a sheet of paper which, it later turned out, was Branigan's summary dismissal.

Branigan read the brief clause.

Rule 31. Remaining Undercover

Do not break cover unless your life or that of another agent is at risk.

If your cover is broken:-

do not admit any involvement with the Military Intelligence Service

the Military Intelligence Service will sever all ties to you

In the event of any unforeseen circumstances refer to your copy of the FOC-U manual for guidance and take appropriate action

Branigan had to concede that getting his face on the front page of a tabloid newspaper did amount to breaking cover and, in case there was any doubt, the sentence pointing out Military Intelligence would sever all ties with him had been highlighted in yellow.

Refocusing his attention back in the room, Branigan exchanged glances with Marty as James Travers picked up the narrative.

'You see Chloe was rewriting that news article,' he explained, 'and somehow she tracked down one of the men you sold the arms to - now she's gone missing. Can you see why she needs your help?'

Branigan hesitated, conscious that now wasn't the time to start debating the nuances of the story.

The trouble was, there had never been a time when he was able to defend himself with anyone other than Marty and Sally.

Marty, who'd just retired from active service with SIS and was starting his new business when Branigan was fired, had not only turned out to be the only employer in the country who'd offer a highly publicised traitor a job, but also listened patiently to Branigan's explanation.

'How many times do I have to tell you,' Marty said the last time the topic had come up over a beer after work, 'life's a bitch - I get you were working undercover and the press misinterpreted the whole thing. Now move on.'

Sally's version was the same but different - if that wasn't a conundrum.

'I don't care what other people think,' she said, 'because I know you didn't betray your country. Besides, if The Herald hadn't run that story you'd never have been fired, we'd never have met and we wouldn't have Molly.'

Game, set and match.

'I'm sorry,' Marty interjected, 'I don't understand what you mean when you say Chloe is re-writing the story about Branigan.'

Kathy Travers leaned back and spoke patiently, like she was explaining the situation to a three-year-old.

'Chloe is studying for a degree in journalism at Sheffield and has been given an assignment to re-write an historic news article putting a different spin on it.'

While she spoke Branigan took a pad off the coffee table and plucked an expensive ballpoint from a small pot brimming with all manner of pens on the corner of Marty's desk. He began making notes while Chloe's mother explained her daughter's living accommodation in Sheffield, her routines and how Chloe unerringly phoned home if she promised to.

Waiting until she finished, Branigan had a list of questions which included how a student in Sheffield had tracked down an arms trader last heard of in Kyrgyzstan, where Chloe had met him and what her angle on the story was if she was putting a different spin on it.

To each question James and Kathy Travers replied with a shrug and a shake of the head. They knew nothing further.

'So, all we have to go on is Chloe's belief that she was walking into something dangerous?' Branigan concluded.

'Yes, but surely that allied to the fact she's missing doesn't leave any doubt,' James Travers replied, 'and as she identified you as the only person to help her, we're relying on you Mr Branigan.'

Although he correctly interpreted the sidelong glance Branigan shot him, Marty stayed silent - he too didn't know how Branigan could attend Molly's party and search for the missing girl.

'Okay,' Branigan said, trying to buy himself time to think, 'what can you tell me about your daughter?'

Chloe's parents became animated as they took it in turns to give him background on their daughter. It transpired she was studying for a degree at twenty-six because she wanted to break away from local newspapers and work for the BBC.

Kathy Travers went on to explain the connection to Branigan's story.

'Chloe worked for a while at The Herald, you see, in the hope she could get into mainstream journalism that way, but sadly it was just an unpaid internship which didn't lead to anything.'

Mr Travers picked up the explanation.

'We think that's where she met the lady who wrote the article exposing you…' he began, pausing while he tried to remember her name.

'Paige Henderson,' Branigan interjected - you tended not to forget the byline of the person who single-handedly wrecked your career and humiliated you on the front page of a national newspaper.

'That's right, Paige Henderson,' Chloe's father continued, 'which is how Chloe came to choose your story to rewrite.'

Branigan saw a glimmer of hope.

'Then, I think what I can do now is make some enquiries, see if we can trace Chloe's phone and speak with Paige to see if she has any idea who Chloe was meeting,' he said, shuddering at the prospect of speaking with Paige, 'then, if Chloe still hasn't turned up, I can go and look for her in Sheffield tomorrow morning.'

Branigan's smug relief at finding a way to address both of his problems was short-lived.

'Do you have children Mr. Branigan?' James Travers asked, his voice sufficiently calm and controlled to wrong-foot Branigan.

'Yes, I do,' Branigan replied, 'a three-year-old daughter.'

James Travers smiled, his blue eyes holding Branigan's unwaveringly.

'Such a lovely age with her whole future ahead of her,' he said, his tone and tempo of delivery calm and calculated, 'and can you imagine for one moment what it would be like to lose her?'

James Travers saw Branigan's shudder of pain at the thought.

'Exactly,' he continued, 'you don't want to lose your little ray of sunshine any more than we want to lose ours Mr. Branigan, but your little girl isn't missing: ours is. We need you to go and look for her now - not in a day or two.'

A bit below the belt, Branigan thought, but near enough to the mark to strike a chord.

He looked across to Marty who seemed suddenly preoccupied with a mark on the sleeve of his red cashmere sweater.

'Do you have a picture of Chloe for me to look at?' Branigan asked.

'Oh yes,' Kathy Travers said, reaching into her handbag, 'I forgot - we brought three with us in case they were any help.'

She pushed the photographs wrapped in a folded sheet of paper across the table.

They showed an attractive girl with an unruly mop of curly fair hair; in the first staring straight at the camera, in what appeared to be a selfie taken on a boat somewhere; at a party, where she had her arms round a girl and a boy about her own age; and the third, of her sitting laughing with her hair tousled at the table of an American diner.

Branigan studied her face carefully as he flipped through each of the photos again, certain that he'd never seen the vivacious-looking girl with emerald green eyes before.

When he got to the third photograph, he recognised the location. She was in Katz's Deli in New York where Meg Ryan famously filmed the scene from "When Harry Met Sally" in which she pretended to orgasm. Branigan reckoned the laughing Chloe - who looked rather like the actress, even down to the ruffled fair hair – had just reprised the role for the benefit of her fellow diners!

The sheet of paper had essential basic information about Chloe on it - address in Sheffield, telephone number, date of birth and the like. Returning to the first photograph Branigan studied it; he definitely hadn't seen Chloe before and yet somewhere in the back of his mind something about the green-eyed girl set off a distant alarm.

His heart sank.

What Chloe's parents were asking wasn't unreasonable given what she was working on when she disappeared, but even if he set off immediately after Molly's party he wouldn't be in Sheffield before 8:00pm.

There was only one decision he could make, but it broke Branigan's heart to picture the look on Molly's face when she discovered that Daddy wasn't coming to her birthday party.

'Okay,' he said, scooping up the photographs and the piece of paper with Chloe's details on, 'I better go now, hadn't I?'

CHAPTER 5

11:22 The Strand, London

'Sheffield!'

Branigan winced and held the phone slightly away from his ear allowing the level and tone of Sally's voice to reverberate throughout the office.

A clattering noise from behind the bank of computer screens suggested Alan had taken cover underneath his desk.

Marty stood in his doorway unsure whether to either hide in his office and pretend to work, or join Branigan so he could help explain to Sally the urgency of the problem.

In the end he did neither.

'I know I promised,' Branigan said, a note of exasperation in his voice, 'but that was before I knew there was a possible link to me and what happened in Bishkek.'

'But you don't even know for sure she's missing,' Sally said, trying to calm the tone in her voice, 'you only have her parents' belief to go on - for all you know her phone battery is dead.'

'I know, but if you put yourself in her parents' shoes and imagine if it were Molly that was missing, you'd want me to do something now and not wait.'

'I suppose, but even if she is in trouble, you don't really know that it's something you can help with,' Sally said, her voice not quite carrying the same conviction as she thought about Molly vanishing.

'No, but if I accept there is a good chance she is missing and that I can help, I'd be irresponsible not to do something.'

'And because you're such a good man, you can't resist running to help the damsel in distress?' Sally interjected, her tone now more level.

'I suppose so, yes,' he said, 'you know I wouldn't be going if this didn't seem to involve me in some way?'

Having calmed herself, Sally was resigned to holding the party without him. She was used to her husband disappearing at odd times and working unpredictable hours and reluctantly accepted the situation.

'I know Branigan, but it doesn't mean I'm happy to be on my own with a house-full of little children; but I'll speak to Jude and see if she can lend me a hand - it'll be all right.'

Branigan was relieved - Jude was one of Sally's closest friends and her daughter Daniella was already coming to the party so he was sure she would be able to help.

'Thanks, and can you give Molly a big hug from me and tell her I'll be back as soon as I can?'

'That went pretty well then?' Marty observed wryly from the safety of his doorway.

'Well, you know, "Hello honey, I'm leaving you on your own with a house full of 4-year olds" has always been one of my stronger chat-up lines!'

'But seriously Marty,' Branigan continued, 'you're going to need to make amends to Sally somehow. It's fair to say she was no happier with you than she was with me.'

There was a warm camaraderie apparent between the two of them which went far deeper than any usual boss/worker relationship - but then Marty and Branigan had known each other since the first day Branigan had arrived at The Academy to start his training with the Intelligence Service.

'Right,' Marty had said by way of introduction to the small class of new recruits, 'I am going to teach you how to hunt, hide, lie, cheat, disguise yourself, fight and - if necessary - kill. Then, once you've learned the basics of how to cope with your personal relationships, I'll teach you how to be a spy.'

In reality he may not have helped with the relationship

side of things, but Marty - one of the senior instructors in the craft of subterfuge - had delivered on his promise.

He'd also maintained a friendship between them which meant when Branigan's career came to a crashing halt Marty was prepared to employ him.

Their brief exchange of humour over, they both fell back on their training.

'What do you need to take with you?' Marty asked.

It sounded like one of the questions he posed in the classroom, but now Branigan treated it with the seriousness every operation deserved.

"You can't prepare for the unexpected - you can for the expected."

One of the tenets of Marty's teaching.

'Well,' Branigan said, 'I'll need transport, communications and an ability to get into her digs if they're locked; beyond that, I don't know.'

Marty nodded, 'You can take my car, that's downstairs in my space and will save you the time of taking something from the pool.'

Their office location whilst central was a curse when it came to parking. The building only had two underground parking spaces which meant the pool of vehicles they used for surveillance and essential travel - ranging from a white builder's van, through black cab to a faux police car - were kept in a more economical location on a run-down industrial estate south of The River.

'Great, then I have my phone and a penknife,' Branigan said wryly, 'maybe not the most spectacular field-kit I've ever gone out with, but I can't think of anything else I'll need.'

Marty went into his office and returned with a key fob that looked more like a mobile phone than the key for a car.

'There is one other thing,' he said, passing the fob to Branigan, 'you may well need some computer support - I know you and things technical, Branigan; you're going to be useless getting into this girl's computer if there is one.'

He paused and let Branigan work through the possibilities.

'I think you should take Alan,' Marty concluded.

From behind the bank of computers there came a muted sound – rather like someone had trodden on a dog's squeaky toy – and a pair of eyes appeared tremulously over the top of the screens.

'I'm damned if I do and damned if I don't,' Branigan said.

'That's about it,' Marty agreed, 'just make sure you don't get into any scrapes. You might be expendable, but I need Alan to maintain our IT infrastructure.'

Branigan eyed the round figure in the knitted mustard cardigan and burgundy corduroy trousers as Alan stepped out from his desk.

'If you have a green bobble hat for him, he could always go undercover as a traffic light,' Branigan observed wryly.

11:38 Aldwych, London

'Nice car,' Alan said as he settled into the passenger seat of Marty's impressive BMW saloon and placed a large aluminium case placed firmly on his lap.

'Why don't you put that on the back seat, it'll be uncomfortable all the way to Sheffield?' Branigan suggested.

For reply Alan shook his head and clutched the case a little tighter.

'What is in there anyway?'

'It's a bit like watching a flower open,' Sally explained to Branigan one time after Alan had been at their house chatting away to her in the kitchen.

'You just need to find the right thing to talk to Alan about and then there's no stopping him. The trouble is finding the things which interest him.'

It was immediately apparent that the contents of his "field-kit" were one of those things.

'I put it together in case anyone needed me to go out on

an assignment with them,' Alan explained, his eyes fixed on the road ahead and his voice betraying no emotion, 'so it has everything I might need.'

'Really,' Branigan asked to make conversation, 'what sort of things do you think you need?'

For reply Alan explained the practical use, operating parameters and durability of his rugged military-grade laptop, external drive, battery back-up, camera, torch, toolkit and various phones, in such detail that they were out of London and on the M1 heading north before he dried up. Interesting though it was to know that the laptop was built with a magnesium alloy backbone, Branigan was relieved when silence fell.

'Makes my penknife look pretty basic,' he said flippantly.

A mistake as it turned out, as it gave Alan a new source of conversation.

'Oh, yes,' he said, 'I have one of those in here too.'

They were well on the way to Watford by the time the use of the various implements on the knife had been explored and explained in detail.

'I know you're busy,' Branigan said over the speakers in the car when Alan was silent long enough for him to speak with Sally, 'but I just wanted to tell you that I'm thinking of you, missing being there and that I love you.'

'That's nice,' Sally said, 'but I really have to go, Jude and Daniella are about to arrive and I'm nowhere near ready; I can't even find where I put the birthday candles.'

'On the left-hand end of the dresser on the second shelf down,' Alan said.

The big BMW swerved a little in the outside lane as Branigan looked across to his passenger.

'Is that you Alan?' Sally asked slightly incredulously.

'He's nodding,' Branigan explained when there was no audible reply to her question.

'Oh, wow, that's interesting,' Sally said hesitantly, 'whose idea was that?'

'Marty thought it would be useful to have Alan along so he can interrogate any computers we might find.'

'Yes, I can imagine - you'll be really good at that Alan.'

She paused, 'Ahh! Yes, the candles are here, tucked behind the present you left for Molly on Thursday Alan!'

Alan smiled contentedly.

'Were you two cozying up while I was freezing my ass off in the backstreets?' Branigan asked, realising Alan must have made one of his regular visits to talk to Sally while he was waiting for Kozlow.

'Aren't you the jealous husband now?' Sally said laughing.

'Look, I have to dash, so you boys look after each other for me, do you hear? I'll be really cross if anything bad happens!'

They travelled on in silence for a while, the big BMW sitting effortlessly in the fast lane of the motorway.

'Have you taken your VW out recently Alan?' Branigan asked as they shot past an old camper van near Rugby.

Alan didn't own a car, preferring instead to drive the family's 1960s red VW camper which he'd inherited when his mother died.

Christened Mabel by his father, Alan's only family holidays had been spent camping in the van which was almost as prized a possession as his collection of Star Trek memorabilia.

'Oh yes,' Alan, said, 'Mabel and I go out into the country at least once a month to make sure she gets a run - but if the weather's bad I keep her wrapped up.'

Asking about the old camper van turned out to be another of those topics on which Alan could talk incessantly without apparently drawing breath.

Branigan stayed silent and let him speak.

'My favourite place in the country is a bridge over the M25 near Kings Langley.'

Even pre-occupied with his thoughts, Branigan couldn't help but do a double take as he wondered how Alan managed to class a bridge over the busiest motorway in Europe as a trip into the country.

'If I set off early on a Sunday morning, I can buy the newspapers and my supplies and have camp set up by 7 o'clock.'

'There's always something to look at once I've read the papers.'

The papers.

Something of a bête noire for Branigan.

'And I cook myself a bacon sandwich for breakfast, have some donuts for my elevenses, heat a Cornish pasty for lunch and then save myself for a cream tea.'

Branigan looked sideways at Alan's portly figure.

'What is there to look at, Alan,' Branigan asked, 'apart from cars?'

'Well, cars and lorries mainly; but also buses and trailers. I like to keep a record of the interesting vehicles I see, so I have a book I can write them all down in. Although the best time was when there was a contra-flow and an accident.'

Branigan raised his eyebrows quizzically, a gesture completely lost on Alan who was focused on the road ahead.

'It was when they were widening the motorway under the bridge and Mabel and I were camped right over the top. Both sets of traffic were using the same carriageway directly beneath us - you know separated by a concrete barrier - and suddenly all the cars coming towards us started banging into each other.'

'I almost missed it,' Alan continued, a look of concern appearing briefly on his face as he stared fixedly ahead, 'because my frying pan caught fire and I was still dealing with that when it happened. I think it was because there was so much to see that I left my bacon on and then the next thing I knew, my smoke alarm went off and I had to throw the flaming frying pan onto the pavement and use the fire extinguisher on it; while I was dealing with that crisis all the cars banged together beneath us; it was very exciting.'

Branigan tried to picture the scene.

'Were the two events connected?' he asked.

'No,' Alan said with the patient tone in his voice a child gets when explaining the obvious, 'the frying pan caught fire because I left it on the gas too long; the cars crashed because they hit each other.'

On the verge of saying something, Branigan held back as he wondered just how distracted the drivers in the contra-flow had been by a garishly dressed man juggling a flaming frying pan and setting off a fire extinguisher.

'Was there much damage?' Branigan asked.

'No, not really, I scratched the frying pan when I threw it on the ground and the CO2 from the fire extinguisher blew the bacon over the bridge onto the motorway, but otherwise everything was okay.'

Branigan counted slowly to ten.

'I actually meant, was their much damage to the cars?' he said patiently.

'Oh, I see,' Alan said, rocking gently back and forth, 'yes, there was quite a lot of damage to the cars and the road was closed for ages while they brought in all the equipment they needed to sort it all out.'

The description of the aftermath was another subject upon which Alan was clearly able to talk at length, as he went on to regale Branigan with not only the make, model and colour of each vehicle involved in the accident, but also their registration numbers.

The journey continued with more long periods of silence interspersed with brief conversations and Branigan's realisation that, fond as he was of Alan, he was not the easiest travel companion.

Alan's repetitive drumming of an erratic beat on the aluminium case eventually ended when Branigan forcibly removed the case and placed it on the back seat - which stopped the irritating rhythm and freed Alan up to explore the controls of the car.

Much as it annoyed him, Branigan couldn't wait until he was back home sharing a glass of wine with Sally so he could explain, 'Then Alan found the seat controls on Marty's car,' he would tell her, 'but Marty's BMW isn't like your average car. The seats not only move every which way electrically, but also massage you as well! Can you imagine how much time he spent going up, down, forward and back whilst he jiggled on the massager?'

The only respite in the journey came when Branigan pulled into a motorway service station and Alan went to explore the shop.

Having refuelled the thirsty BMW, Branigan ordered a coffee to go and was about to pay when he felt a repetitive tap on the shoulder. Turning, he found Alan clutching a plastic tub of caramel crispy bites, a packet of shortbread biscuits and a hot pasty.

He hesitated momentarily before deciding that now was neither the time to start dispensing diet advice nor worrying about Marty's reaction to the unnecessary purchases on the company credit card.

'Would you like a coffee too?' Branigan offered as he passed the treats to the cashier.

Alan looked at him suspiciously and shook his head.

'I can't,' he said, 'I haven't got my mug.'

The rest of the journey passed without incident, although Branigan did decide that the word "share" didn't feature too high up in the autistic vocabulary, as Alan steadily ate his way through all the purchases - the nearest he got to sharing them was when he spilled the caramel crispy bites over the seat.

Only when the satnav showed they were getting near to their destination did Alan focus on the task ahead.

'Can I look at the three pictures and the piece of paper Mrs. Travers gave you?' he asked.

Branigan was taken aback.

He had no problem with Alan seeing the pictures and background information, but he didn't recall telling Alan he had them.

'Of course,' Branigan said, reaching into the pocket in the driver's door, 'can you just remind me when I mentioned them?'

'You didn't,' Alan replied as he studied each picture in turn, 'Mrs. Travers gave them to you after you asked if she had a picture you could see so you could check whether or not you'd met Chloe.'

'But you weren't in the office with us - how did you hear that?'

'The pen you were writing with has a microphone in it,' Alan said simply.

14:34 Sheffield, South Yorkshire

Branigan drew the BMW to a halt in the carpark of the student accommodation the Travers' had given as Chloe's address, the sleek black saloon looking rather incongruous alongside the array of cheap secondhand student cars.

'Apartment 42 is over there,' Branigan said reading the numbers listed on a nearby communal door.

The modern buildings were clustered round the carpark and, as they discovered heading up the two flights of stairs to Chloe's room, purpose-built for students. On each floor there were five numbered rooms with a communal kitchen and bathroom - a far cry from Branigan's cold room in his Oxford college.

For all the promise the building held on the outside, the peeling paint, threadbare nylon carpet, lack of heating and low wattage light bulbs left little doubt that the building was run on a budget. The underlying aroma of unwashed student which pervaded the staircase reminded Branigan of both his own student days and, he guessed, all other forms of student accommodation throughout the land. Chloe's room - indistinguishable from all the others behind a dark blue institutional front door - was in the back left-hand corner of the block.

Branigan knocked firmly before trying the handle.

The door didn't open.

'What are you going to do now,' Alan asked excitedly, 'blow it off its hinges?'

'No, Alan,' Branigan said patiently pulling his penknife out from his pocket and fiddling with the blade near the simple lock, 'I don't need to because I have this knife and a credit card.'

He pushed the credit card into the doorframe, right beside where he also held the penknife - there was a click and the door opened.

'I should introduce the people who run this place to the concept of security,' he said, stepping tentatively through the door, his eyes sweeping the room as he did so.

They'd stepped into a room a bit like a down-market hotel.

There was a small double bed tucked against one wall, a window opening onto the main road beside the complex, a desk which also housed a chest of drawers, a built-in wardrobe and a door which Branigan guessed led to a toilet.

Beside the desk were several shelves which were home to a small TV, a random mess of books and papers, plus a photograph of Chloe standing smiling with an older woman under the Eiffel Tower.

On the floor there were piles of books, newspapers and files there wasn't space for on the shelving.

Enough space to live, study, watch TV and make a cup of coffee.

'Oh, my goodness,' Alan said, setting his aluminium case down and focusing on the wall behind the desk.

Branigan too was staring at the wall.

Virtually every inch of plaster behind the desk was covered with documents, newspaper cuttings and photographs. Pride of place, directly above the computer screen, was the whole front page of a tabloid newspaper - the majority of which was given over to a photograph of Branigan's face under the sensationalist headline "OxyMoron!"

In bold letters underneath, it continued in the same vein with, "Posh Oxford graduate spy caught selling arms to terrorists."

'That's a nice picture of you,' Alan observed as he studied the photograph.

Branigan took a breath and collected himself.

'Right, Alan,' he said, 'I need you to look at this computer and see if you can find any clues as to where Chloe is. Also, anything else that would help tell us who, where and when she was meeting someone yesterday morning.'

Even as he spoke, Branigan was aware that Alan was largely ignoring him.

'It's all part of his being on the autistic spectrum,' Sally once explained when Branigan commented that Alan seemed oblivious of what was going on around him, 'his sensory world is so different from yours, if he's focused on something a bomb could go off and he wouldn't notice.'

In this case, it was Chloe's computer which was the focus of Alan's attention.

He had his aluminium case open to reveal the equipment he had described at such length, neatly stowed in compartments cut out from the giant piece of foam rubber filling the case.

Like a surgeon selecting the correct implement for a tricky procedure, Alan's right hand was poised above the devices on offer while he pondered the best way ahead.

Seemingly oblivious to Branigan's presence, he spoke to himself as he worked through the options.

'I could take a copy first,' he said, 'but then it might be quicker to just search…'

Branigan shook his head and elected to ignore Alan.

Outside of the computer, he was looking for anything which might give a clue to Chloe's whereabouts and potentially lead him to the person she'd gone to meet. He started with the wastepaper basket which was brimming with the general detritus of student life - receipts for food and drink in cheap bars, used teabags, tissues and cotton wool pads - plus a number of screwed up sheets of paper. He carefully emptied the contents onto the bed and began sorting through, opening each receipt and scrap of paper before placing it strategically on the bed.

'Any rubbish bin is a mine of information,' one of the instructors at the Academy had told him.

Not Marty.

Marty stuck to the practical stuff of fighting and staying under cover - this had been Alex Oldroyd he thought.

'People leave a trail behind like the wake of a boat on a calm sea. The things they touch, the way they look, the places they visit, the words and phrases they use all build a picture of an individual; but what they throw away is most telling of all,' Alex had told him.

As he sorted the contents of the bin Branigan could hear Oldroyd's clipped tones, 'receipts tell you when and where people have been; travel tickets their movements; scraps of paper who they've seen, thoughts they've had and who they've spoken to; even a tissue can tell you whether they've been crying or got a cold.'

'Discard nothing and sort everything into an order which tells you what you need to know.'

As Alan busied himself behind him, Branigan moved the rubbish around on the bed until he had the picture he wanted.

Chloe had come back from London by train on Tuesday, bought food and refreshments, seemingly gone out with friends on Thursday and, bought some milk as recently as Friday morning.

Somewhere near the bottom of the bin, most probably from Wednesday, were 3 sheets of neatly typed A4 paper with highlighted notes and amendments.

Judging by the headline - "British Intelligence Officer sacrificed by his own side" - it was a draft of the news story of which Chloe's parents had spoken. Not wanting to divert himself from the task of finding where Chloe had gone, he folded the article and put it in his pocket, aware that Alan was busily snapping away with his camera.

'Aren't you supposed to be looking at the computer?' he asked as he scanned the room to decide where to focus next.

'I am,' Alan said, 'I'm just copying some files across then I can interrogate it without compromising anything.'

Branigan moved over to the shelves beside the desk and began flipping through the books, files and documents there.

Moving quickly, he was on the fourth shelf of lecture notes, background articles and various pieces of written work Chloe had submitted - none of which pointed to where she might have gone to meet his alter-ego - when Alan tapped him on the shoulder.

'I don't suppose you've seen a small key anywhere have you?' he asked.

Branigan turned to find Alan with one half of a pair of handcuffs locked around his left wrist and a riding crop in his right hand.

Branigan raised his eyebrows and looked into the open drawer in front of Alan which was filled with cuffs, straps, ropes and a host of other bondage paraphernalia.

'You just had to try them on, didn't you?'

Alan flushed and looked around in the vain hope that the key was lying on the surface of the desk. As he peered past Branigan to look on the shelves, Alan let out a whimper and hid the crop and cuffs behind him, his eyes wide in silent alarm.

'What the FUCK do you think you are doing?!'

Branigan turned around to find himself face-to-face with an attractive girl with emerald green eyes and a mop of curly blond hair.

CHAPTER 6

14:57 Sheffield, South Yorkshire

Chloe was prettier than Branigan expected from the photographs her mother had given him - not to say she wasn't pretty in those; rather that the photos didn't do her justice. She was wearing tight jeans, brown knee-length boots and a brown leather bomber jacket which showed off her shapely figure. What the camera had failed to capture was the depth of colour in her emerald eyes, her clear complexion even with minimal make-up, slightly turned up nose and her air of vulnerability.

There was no doubting that Chloe was an attractive young woman.

There was equally no doubting that she was an angry young woman.

'I said, what the fuck are you doing here?' she repeated, looking from Branigan to Alan and back again as part of her subconscious took in what she was seeing.

Chloe's eyes darted round Branigan's face, taking in the chiselled jaw, the dimple in his chin and his deep brown eyes.

Her eyes ran up and down his taut torso, flat stomach and – as he stood frozen in profile – nicely rounded rump.

'Branigan?' she asked.

He nodded.

'Chloe Travers?'

It was Chloe's turn to nod.

'Yes,' she replied hesitantly, running the fingers of her right hand through her hair, 'but I don't understand. What the fuck are you doing here?'

'Your parents made me come after you didn't contact them; you know, after your meeting with the terrorist source?'

Chloe looked perplexed.

'I have no idea what you're talking about,' she said, stepping further into the room and pushing the door closed behind her.

Branigan was exasperated.

He was missing Molly's party to help this girl and here she was, safe, sound and seemingly unaware of the furore she'd caused.

Somewhere in the back of his mind an alarm bell started ringing.

'You did phone your parents and warn them you might be heading into trouble, didn't you?'

Chloe shook her head.

'No,' she replied, opening the brown satchel-like bag slung across her shoulder and holding it open for Branigan to see, 'one, because I've lost my fucking phone and two because I don't have parents plural since my Dad pissed off to Australia when I was 14 - unless he's stopped propping up a bar in Perth and miraculously jetted back to be by Mum's side.'

The alarm in Branigan's head changed from a distant ring to a loud klaxon.

"The one thing you can expect is for the unexpected to happen," Alex Oldroyd said when teaching him the art of operating in the field, "what you do next is what matters."

Branigan suspected there was little helpful advice in the trusty FOC-U manual to help him prepare for the current situation other than to follow the sagely advice of a thousand years of British military experience distilled into Rule 31 - react appropriately and don't get yourself killed; if you do get yourself killed don't let the other side know who you are.

If the mewing noise accompanied by the jangle of a set of handcuffs over his right shoulder was anything to go by, Alan didn't have a better version of how to react than Branigan.

'Okay, three questions,' he said to Chloe decisively after an awkward pause, 'have you contacted anyone to tell them to get in touch with me if you go missing?'

'No.'

'When did you lose your phone?'

Branigan pointed to each of the first three fingers on his left hand as he asked the questions, the urgency in his voice shaking Chloe who visibly stiffened as the direction of his thoughts dawned on her.

'I lost it sometime on Thursday.'

'And is that your mother?' he concluded, pointing to the picture of Chloe standing under the Eiffel Tower.

'Yes,' she replied, 'that's me and Mum when we went to Paris this Easter.'

Branigan thought about the timeline he'd established from the waste bin and then he realised what had made him uneasy when he'd first seen the picture of Chloe; parents with blue and brown eyes didn't have green-eyed children.

'No need to panic,' he said, realising the timing fitted with his suspicions and ignoring Alan who was tapping him repeatedly on the shoulder, 'but I think we all need to move on from here, talk things through somewhere less conspicuous and find you somewhere else to stay while I find out what's going on.'

Alan stopped tapping on Branigan's shoulder.

'Do you still want me to open her computer?' he asked.

'No, Alan, I don't,' Branigan said as calmly as possible, catching a flash of understanding in Chloe's eyes as she cast a glance towards the short, round man, 'I'd like you to pack all your stuff up - we're going.'

'Do you want me to update her operating system, only it's three issues out of date?'

'No, Alan, Chloe can do that herself when she's ready.'

'Are you sure I need to find somewhere else to stay,' Chloe interjected before Alan could offer any other helpful computer-related advice, 'isn't that a bit melodramatic?'

'Possibly, but I'd rather be cautious than blasé.'

'It's something to do with my story about you, isn't it?'

'I have no idea at the moment; but it's possible.'

With Branigan's encouragement, Chloe collected a few essentials which she put into a small backpack while Alan neatly re-packed his aluminium case and carefully fastened it closed.

'Right,' Branigan said, moving to the window and studying the road outside at the same time as taking his phone from his pocket, 'Alan, turn your phone off completely.'

'We're going out to the car - the black BMW parked to the left of the door - and we're setting off as quickly as we can. Alan, can you get in the back seat and look out of the back window to see if anyone is following us?'

Alan nodded enthusiastically.

'This is like the movies, isn't it?' he said excitedly.

Once outside, the three of them moved swiftly to the car and in a matter of moments Branigan had the BMW out of the carpark.

'There's a silver Ford just pulled out behind us,' Alan said from the kneeling position he had adopted on the back seat.

'Yes, I've got it, thank you Alan,' Branigan said, fiddling with the controls in the centre console so the satnav map sprung to life, 'you can sit back properly now - and put your seatbelt on.'

He glanced sideways at Chloe, 'Are you all right there?'

'Yes, just a bit shell-shocked really; it still doesn't make a lot of sense that you've arrived here after I wrote an article for my degree course about you.'

'Hold tight,' Branigan said, transferring his attention to the car in the rearview mirror, 'there's one sure way to find out if they're following us.'

Without signalling he suddenly swung the large saloon car to the right, into a minor side road which was signposted "no entry."

The driver of a passing car sounded their horn, but Branigan's prime focus - aside from avoiding the startled old lady driving the tiny Toyota which was coming straight at then - was on the silver Ford two cars back.

It hesitated long enough to watch the back of the receding BMW.

In the Ford the driver made a call.

'I've had to let them go - they knew I was following. There were three, not two; that changes our plan, doesn't it?'

15:28 Sheffield City Centre, South Yorkshire

Branigan, Chloe and Alan were seated in the quietest corner of the coffee shop on the ground floor of the large, anonymous, city centre hotel.

Styled rather like a wine cellar, with a brick-vaulted ceiling, subdued lighting and windows opening onto the quayside - which was deserted but for a straggle of die-hard smokers - Branigan had chosen the location because they were able to lose themselves amongst the guests in the busy hotel and, just as importantly, hide Marty's BMW in the adjacent multi-storey carpark.

'I need to understand what's happened here,' Branigan began, leaning forward so he didn't have to speak too loudly. Reaching into his pocket he pulled out the folded sheets of paper he'd rescued from the bin and flattened them on the table.

'Is this the article you've written?' he asked.

Chloe glanced briefly at the document and nodded hesitantly.

'Did you take that from my wastepaper basket?'

'Yes,' Branigan replied as he began to read, 'do you mind?'

'No,' Chloe said, shaking her head 'this all just seems too surreal. I wrote the article one day and the next its subject has appeared on my doorstep.'

'I know what you mean,' Branigan replied, 'I should be at

my daughter's fourth birthday party right now - instead I've been sent here to search for you.'

'And,' Chloe chipped in, 'in case you hadn't noticed, I'm not missing.'

He smiled briefly.

'It may have taken all my deductive powers, but I had spotted that!'

'Before you read the article,' Chloe said indicating the pages in his hand, 'can you go through what happened that made you came racing up here?'

Branigan put the paper down and outlined the events of the morning, starting with his call from Marty; as he described the meeting in Marty's office with the two people pretending to be her concerned parents, Chloe put her hand to her mouth and shook her head.

'Oh my God,' she murmured, 'why would someone go to such lengths?'

Just as he concluded his account - ending with his and Alan's arrival in Sheffield - the waiter arrived and, realising he hadn't eaten since breakfast, Branigan ordered a selection of cakes and toasted panini they could all share.

'May I read this now and see if it has any bearing on my being sent up here?' Branigan asked when the waiter left.

Chloe nodded and he turned his attention to the article.

It began with the original one-word headline "Oxy-Moron!" and went on to summarise the tabloid story which brought about Branigan's demise.

Using sensationalist and inflammatory phraseology the article described Branigan as an "Oxford educated toff" who had blundered by delivering arms to the wrong side. It went on to describe him as a moron who had managed to take a stolen shipment of arms and explosives and, instead of returning it back to its rightful owners, sold it back to the arms dealer who'd originally stolen it!

It concluded by asking the reader whether they felt comfortable knowing someone like Branigan was at the sharp end of military intelligence.

Branigan looked up before carrying on reading the paper.

'I don't come out of that bit too well, do I?' he observed.

The next part of the document was a brief summary of the view Chloe had taken in re-writing the story and the information to which she'd had access - most particularly the original journalist's personal files including photographs; a copy of the shipping paperwork; and even the false papers Branigan was using.

She went on to explain how she'd taken an opposite view to the original journalist and cast Branigan as the victim rather than the villain.

Branigan looked at Chloe.

'How did you manage to get access to all this information?' he asked, testing whether the version given to him in Marty's office was true.

'I did some unpaid work at The Herald in the summer and worked alongside Paige Henderson who wrote the article,' Chloe explained.

'We got to know each other fairly well over the inevitable drinking sessions which seem to be de rigueur in journalism, so when I got this assignment to re-write an article and turn a story on its head, it seemed to make sense to do it with one of Paige's. I was intrigued by your story, spoke to Paige and she gave me access to her file.'

Branigan nodded.

'Fair enough,' he said, 'interestingly the people pretending to be your parents knew you'd worked at The Herald for a while and yet they didn't know your father has been in Australia for twelve years.'

Branigan made a mental note of the dichotomy.

'Paige Henderson didn't mind you critiquing her work?'

'I don't know that she was happy, but she herself agreed the story had been rushed the first time around because her editor wanted her to work to a deadline; even Paige thinks the re-write is a fair interpretation,' Chloe concluded.

'She's seen this?' Branigan asked, pointing to the document in his hand.

'Oh yes, I went down to London to see her last weekend; what you've got there is a draft I emailed her afterwards which we the discussed on the phone on Thursday,' Chloe said, indicating the annotated paper.

'You sent this to Paige Henderson on Wednesday I'm guessing?' he asked, thinking about where he'd found the document in the waste bin.

When Chloe confirmed the timing, Branigan looked pensive.

'That makes a lot of sense of all of this,' he said contemplatively as he read Chloe's version of the article. Instead of describing him as a moron, this one began with the headline, "British Intelligence Officer sacrificed by his own side!"

The article went on to suggest that Branigan had been hung out to dry; that his intention had been to follow the shipment and identify the intended end user. Intriguingly it then suggested that the reason Branigan was exposed was not because of investigative journalism, but because someone on his own side leaked the story to stop him discovering where the consignment was going.

Near the end of the article there was a quote from Wáng Jìngzé, a fifth century Chinese general who set out many of the principles of warfare used today.

Branigan recognised the quote as one he'd been taught at The Academy. Chloe had quoted the 11th of the 36 Strategies of War attributed to General Wáng - "Sacrifice the plum tree to preserve the peach tree" - surmising that Branigan was sacrificed by his own side as part of a bigger strategy.

At the end of the article, Chloe made a simple statement.

"An anonymous source inside MI6 confirmed that someone had used Branigan as a scapegoat, quoting the Chinese war strategy of "sacrificing the plum tree to preserve the peach tree": the question is, why?"

'Interesting,' Branigan said, staring into space as he folded the document and put it back in his inside pocket.

'Who is your source?'

Chloe flushed, shuffled uneasily and looked back at Branigan coquettishly.

'Don't tell anyone,' she said, 'but I don't have a source; I used a trick I learned at The Herald - if you can't get a comment, make one up!'

'But Paige had a source for all the information she got in the first place?'

'Oh yes, he existed for sure; that was someone called Cressix,' she said, 'who I assume was working for intelligence at the time as he knew so much about you, the consignment and what you were up to.'

Branigan agreed. He'd spent many hours thinking about the architect of his downfall and the inescapable conclusion was that he was set up by his own side.

'I even tried to make contact with this Mr Cressix using a telephone number and email Paige had, but that didn't get me anywhere,' Chloe concluded.

Branigan shook his head.

'I never heard that name inside The Organisation,' he said, looking up as their waiter arrived, 'and you didn't get anywhere in discovering what it might have been that I was stopped from finding out?'

'No,' Chloe said, leaning back as their drinks were placed in the middle of the table, 'that reference to Peach Tree at the end is purely allegorical, I just wanted to pose the question because the only explanation for what happened to you is that someone was prepared to sacrifice you in order to pursue a bigger goal.'

'That might be,' Branigan said, 'but if you didn't find anything out, I fail to see how this article can upset anyone enough to get people sending me racing up here.'

Alan held his right hand up.

'I have a question,' he said, leaning into the table and keeping his voice low and conspiratorial.

Both Chloe and Branigan waited expectantly.

'Does anyone have a key for these, only they're a little tight?'

He pulled his left hand from his cardigan pocket to reveal the handcuff still ratcheted in place. Branigan shook his head wryly and pulled his penknife from his pocket, selecting a thin pointed tool which he inserted into the lock as he carried on his dialogue with Chloe.

'You didn't come across anything else which might have caused someone at SIS to start sending their spooks after us?'

Chloe shook her head, 'Is that who you think is behind this?'

The lock sprung open and Alan - who had up until that moment been recoiling as if he expected the pointed tool to be thrust through his wrist - gave a little cheer.

'I can't think of who else it might be,' Branigan said as he folded his knife and put it back in his pocket, 'if it's your article people are bothered by, then it must be the inference of it being a home-grown operation someone is worried by.'

'Do you think they want to get at the information Paige gave me then?' Chloe asked.

'No, because if they did, they would have done so already. These people are professionals and can go through your place, look at your computer and take what they want,' Branigan said, casting an eye towards Alan who was busily rubbing life back into his wrist, 'and, believe it or not, they can do it without leaving a trace.'

'And they're not worried I might have information which is a threat?' Chloe asked.

'No, probably not,' Branigan said pensively, 'I think it's far more likely the damage for SIS is already in the paper you've written - I'm just not sure where.'

The waiter brought their cakes, raising an eyebrow as he gingerly moved the handcuffs to one side - when he left, Chloe continued with her questions.

'But if the damage is already in the article, why would

they need to go to such lengths to send you here?' she asked.

This question had been uppermost in Branigan's mind from the moment Chloe had burst in on Alan and him.

'There's only one obvious reason I can see,' he replied, 'they want to put us together so they can smear the story - you know, take pictures of us together and claim we colluded on the writing of it, or even that we're romantically involved.'

'They'd do that?' Chloe asked.

'Half my working life was spent collecting information and then using it against people to either undermine their endeavours, or encourage them to feed us secrets.'

'It really is a dirty world you used to work in, isn't it?'

'That's only the half of it. We haven't even begun to scratch the surface of what they call "Black Ops."'

Chloe looked quizzical.

'The people who do the stuff they'd deny if anyone found out,' Branigan explained, helping himself to a panini as the rest of their food arrived.

Between mouthfuls he continued to quiz Chloe.

'Did Paige have anything to add when you started to write your version of the story?'

'Not about what might have been going on, if that's what you mean,' Chloe replied, 'but she did agree that her version looked pretty suspect. The only thing she contributed was the suggestion I add a comment by an anonymous source at the end - she said it gave the article credence and left the reader wanting more.'

'I hope you don't mind me prying,' Branigan said, conscious that he sensed something more between Chloe and the reporter, 'but is there a relationship between you and Paige?'

He was surprised how relaxed Chloe was about the question.

She threw her head back and laughed.

'Sort of. We got to know each other quite well when I

worked at The Herald and discovered a common interest.'

'We're not in a deep and meaningful relationship if that's what you mean, but I've spent some happy hours tied up on Paige's bed,' Chloe said, pointing to the handcuffs.

She looked straight at Branigan.

'We discovered we both like bondage and fucking.'

Alan began to choke on the sip of mint tea he'd just inhaled.

The people on surrounding tables returned to their conversations once Alan had got a normal colour back and stopped gasping like a beached whale.

Branigan smiled, completely unfazed by the news which helped to explain why Paige had been so free with her background information.

'And is she the only person you've sent the story to?' he asked.

'Yes.'

Branigan nodded contemplatively, glancing at his watch - any hope of being home before Molly's bedtime was long gone.

'Alan, do you still have that spare phone in your case?' he asked, recalling the pay-as-you-go phone Alan had described in such detail on the journey up.

'Oh yes!' Alan replied, at once becoming flustered as he was joined back into the conversation, and scrambling to pick up the case which was planted firmly between his legs. Once he'd sprung the locks, he triumphantly produced a robust-looking Nokia phone and charger.

'It's my old one,' he explained to Chloe, 'but it works perfectly well - and I keep £200 credit on it just in case.'

Branigan's eyebrows went up.

'Do you fund all this stuff yourself, Alan, or does Marty give you a budget?'

'I do it all myself,' Alan said proudly, 'Marty didn't seem to think there was much need for me to have my own field-kit when I asked him.'

'And you don't mind lending it to Chloe?' Branigan asked.

Alan's eyes shot briefly to Chloe and then down to the table, the phone and the handcuffs.

'Oh no!' he said, his cheeks burning crimson.

'Thank you, Alan,' Chloe said, reaching across the table to touch his hand in a sign of gratitude and, in the process, rendering Alan mute.

Branigan remembered Sally's words on the subject of Alan.

'Sometimes he gets overloaded with emotion and doesn't know how to handle it - if you just ignore him it gives him time to process things you and I can do in an instant.'

Sally had also gone on to give Branigan a warning.

'Don't for a minute assume that because Alan is slow on handling emotions, he isn't quick on other things.'

Branigan had experienced that first hand when he'd wanted to input his home Wi-Fi code into his new phone. 17 digits of alpha numeric text and Alan - who'd come over to see Sally and had ended up seated on the floor in the kitchen trying to do a 12-piece jigsaw puzzle with Molly - was able to reel it off.

When asked how he knew it, Alan looked blankly back.

'But you gave it to me when I came around to the barbecue,' he'd said defensively, as if remembering a code like that for 3 or 4 years was perfectly normal.

Having established that Chloe would be staying at her friend Kate Upton's flat, Branigan worried that she couldn't phone and check with her friend because Chloe didn't have her number.

'It'll be okay, I know where there's a spare key for Kate's and she won't mind me staying over - we do it all the time.'

Branigan wondered whether Chloe had a similar interest and arrangement with Kate as she did with Paige.

'That's good,' he continued, digging into the side pocket of his jeans, 'so let's just be clear on what's happening.'

'You've got a safe phone, somewhere to stay and all you

need is some cash,' he said, peeling off a bundle of the notes he'd taken from petty cash and holding his hand up to stop her when Chloe tried to protest, 'I don't want you using either your own phone if that turns up, or your credit cards until I say it's okay. I know it sounds like over-kill, but I know from past experience just how easy it is to keep tabs on someone who is using either.'

He reached into his jacket pocket and pulled out a scrap of paper and pen.

'This is my phone number,' he said, writing his initial and the number out neatly, 'and this is Alan's - you'll need to use this for the first hour after we leave you, as I don't think it's safe to turn my phone on until we're well on our way back to London.'

Chloe nodded to indicate she understood.

'Thanks,' she said, 'and how long do you think it will take to sort out what's happening?'

'I wish I knew - I'm hoping Marty, will be able to speak with his ex-colleagues in SIS and they can make the problem go away; with luck it will all blow over by Monday or Tuesday,' he said, ripping the number off the scrap of paper and passing it to Chloe, glancing at the remaining document as he was about to stuff it back in his pocket - it was the message Anna had given him when he'd been walking through reception. It said Paige Henderson had looked for him at the office and wanted him to call her back. It also said she'd left a letter for him which Anna had placed in his in tray.

'Shit!' Branigan said.

CHAPTER 7

17:37 M1 Motorway, Southbound

'What do you mean, set-up?' Marty asked.

Branigan and Alan had dropped Chloe at Kate's apartment in a converted cutlery works on the North side of the city and were well on their way south on the motorway to London.

Driving to Kate's, Branigan had been careful to make several sudden turns to be sure they weren't being followed and only when he was satisfied there was no one on their tail did he allow Chloe to direct them towards their destination.

Fortunately, Kate was home and Chloe and Branigan were able to assuage her concerns at finding her friend and a 6ft 2in stranger inviting themselves in unannounced. Working on the basis that the best lie was the one nearest the truth, Branigan explained to Kate that Chloe had written an article which his newspaper was hoping to publish and she needed sanctuary to avoid being hounded by a rival paper. Not the most inventive cover story, but the best they could conjure up on the short journey through the back streets on their way to Kate's.

More relaxed knowing Branigan wasn't staying, Kate accepted the story and used the opportunity to berate him with her views on tabloid journalism before he was able to leave Chloe safe in the knowledge she was out of harm's way.

'The couple we met in your office this morning are nothing to do with Chloe Travers,' Branigan explained as Marty blustered on the other end of the phone, 'we'd hardly been in her place 5 minutes when Chloe herself arrived home;

less than happy, I might add, to find two men rummaging through her knicker drawer!'

'And you know for sure that the girl who turned up was Chloe Travers and not herself an imposter?' Marty asked.

On the point of saying she looked like the picture of Chloe the people pretending to be her parents had shown, Branigan realised he didn't actually know she was who she said she was! Feeling like he was back at The Academy where Marty was known for his ability to ask questions which put you on the spot, Branigan stayed silent; he'd made a mistake somewhere between a "schoolboy error" and "elementary fuck-up." He'd taken Chloe under his wing without doing anything to check her ID - he didn't even know for sure if she had a key for her apartment because she'd arrived through a door he himself had already opened!

'It was her,' Alan said from the passenger seat of the car, his voice rumbling slightly as the massage seat sent a shudder through his body, 'I checked her passport photograph, driving license and police record on the way up to Sheffield.'

Branigan looked askance at the funny little man holding his aluminium case firmly on his lap as if his life depended on it. He'd assumed Alan was playing on his laptop when he took it out on the journey north and, candidly, was relieved his travelling companion had lapsed into silence because there was only so much of a monologue on prime numbers he wanted to listen to.

By contrast Marty didn't seem surprised Alan had delved so deeply into Chloe's background.

'Thanks Alan - and was there anything on her we should know about?'

'No,' Alan replied, his teeth chattering as the massager hit a particularly energetic part of its cycle, 'apart from a caution for cannabis possession when she was nineteen and three points on her license for speeding last year.'

'Thirty-seven in a 30 mile an hour limit,' he added helpfully.

'If we know that Chloe is for real,' Marty postulated, 'then, you're right, the people we saw this morning wanted you to go to Sheffield.'

'I agree, but there is more to this,' Branigan said, 'I've read the article Chloe wrote about me and can't help feeling whatever this is all about stems from that.'

'Yes, I can see that it could upset a few people,' Marty said.

It was an evening full of surprises for Branigan.

'Are you telling me you've read a copy,' Branigan asked, 'how in God's name did you manage that?'

'I phoned Gregory Brown this morning to see if he knew anything about what was happening.'

Gregory was one of Marty's cronies. Operations Director in the Intelligence Service, he was one of an eclectic group from SIS who met socially to put the world straight. Drawn together by adversity and a taste for good wine, Marty met the other five members of his "gang" regularly for dinner and an occasional round of golf. A useful ally for Marty as it was Gregory who signed off on out-sourced contracts; most notably the one awarded to Marty Freeman Investigations to do background checks for over-stretched Whitehall departments. Naturally Marty strenuously denied there was any cronyism in the deal which had been thrashed out over a round of golf.

'Gregory sent me over a copy of the story and said that Chloe had created a bit of a stir with it.'

'How on earth did he get a copy?' Branigan asked, 'Chloe only sent it to Paige Henderson.'

'Oh, come on, Branigan,' Marty said testily, 'you and I both know it doesn't work like that. There is no such thing as a private email these days; if the system was set to flag emails to and from Paige Henderson with your name in, then my guess is that some analyst in Cheltenham was busy reading the article even before Paige opened her copy.'

Branigan shook his head.

He knew Marty was right.

'The stir Chloe's article created - do you think it's big enough for someone to send me on this wild goose chase?'

'I don't know,' Marty replied, 'I can't really see it, but I probably need to sound out a couple of other people about some of the stuff in the article.'

Sitting at the wheel of the BMW, Branigan stayed silent while he waited for Marty to say more. After a lengthy silence, broken only by the steady rhythm Alan was absent-mindedly tapping on his aluminium case, Marty continued.

'Look, some of the information in Chloe's article is probably nearer the truth than people are comfortable with.'

'Go on,' Branigan prompted.

The pause which followed was so long Branigan had to check the phone was still connected.

'Gregory Brown and I helped dream up Operation Peach Tree,' Marty eventually said.

It was almost as big a shock as having Chloe barrel into the room while they were searching it.

'You've got to be kidding me,' Branigan said.

'I wish I was.'

'But Chloe made the name up,' Branigan protested, 'the code name and her supposed informant were just fiction!'

'I hope you're sure of that,' Marty asked, 'because right now Gregory and some of the rest of the gang are panicking that someone's been speaking out of turn.'

There was another long pause.

'Well, go on then,' Branigan prompted, 'if you helped to dream it up, what the fuck is Operation Peach Tree?'

Marty was quick to reply.

'I can't tell you that, at least not now while you're in the car.'

Branigan looked sideways at Alan who was now lying almost flat in the fully reclined passenger seat.

'I'll explain it to you on Monday: one to one.'

'What do we do in the meantime?' Branigan asked, making

a mental note to point out to Marty the pen with the microphone Alan had used to eavesdrop.

'You do nothing more,' Marty said emphatically, 'I'll talk with Gregory Brown and see if he can talk to the others and brush the whole thing under the carpet.'

'As long as you're sure she just made up the reference to Operation Peach Tree, I think everyone will be happy if she ditches that story and writes about something else,' he concluded, 'then all this will just fade away.'

Branigan was both relieved and disappointed - for a moment he'd hoped the story might be published, believed and his name cleared.

'That's a turn up for the books,' Alan said from his reclined position when the call ended.

They travelled on in silence while Branigan tried to piece together the significance of what Marty had said. Unsuccessfully trying to phone Paige Henderson using the number Anna had given him, Branigan gave up and called Sally.

'You've decided to come home after all!' she said jokingly when she heard her husband's voice.

'Well, you know, it was a tough choice - either come home to the two most beautiful women in the world or run off with Alan!' he replied, turning to wink at his passenger.

'Oh, Alan is still with you, of course!' Sally said delightedly.

'How have you got on Alan - have you been useful?'

Both Branigan and Sally waited while there was a long pause as Alan found the right words to answer.

Eventually he replied.

'Yes.'

Sally let out a short laugh.

'Fabulous! I can't wait to hear all about it.'

'What you need to know, Alan, is that Molly has opened her present a couple of days early – my mistake, I moved it when I got the candles out and it got caught up with the presents everyone brought today - and she loves it!'

'Alan has given Molly a lovely rag doll, Branigan,' Sally explained in an aside, 'and she's already been christened "Agadee" after I told Molly they were sometimes called raggedy dolls. Molly has been trailing Puppy and Agadee everywhere this evening and all three have just gone up to bed. I'm going up now to read them a story.'

'Did Molly enjoy her party?'

Sally laughed.

'Yes, she had a wonderful time. Jude and I have just been talking about that over a glass of wine and came to the conclusion Karen was right to look dubious about having the party at home,' Sally said, 'Don't get me wrong, it was fun, but it was hard work doing the food and trying to entertain and control a house full of four-year olds! I couldn't have done it without Jude and half the mums who stayed. In fact, Jude and Daniella have only just gone, it took us that long to tidy up.'

Having promised to be home as soon as he'd dropped Alan and the car off, Branigan asked Sally to give Molly a big kiss from him.

'Tell her I'll make it up to her tomorrow!' he said.

'I will,' Sally promised, 'but you're going to have to find a way of making it up to me tonight after abandoning me with a children's party!'

'How am I supposed to do that?' Branigan asked.

'I'm sure you'll find a way,' Sally replied coquettishly, 'but it probably involves lots of wine, love and attention: especially attention!'

Alan giggled with embarrassment.

The rest of their journey was uneventful.

In North London they detoured so Branigan could drop Alan off outside his small terraced house and half an hour later he parked the BMW in Marty's space before going up to his desk to collect the envelope from Paige Henderson. After retrieving his bike, Branigan felt a surge of euphoria as he used his muscles to power himself home, his mind taking advantage of the rush of adrenalin to work through the day's events.

Cycling north along Kingsway he began to analyse the day through the eyes of the people who'd sent him on his wild goose chase. Not perhaps the couple pretending to be Chloe's parents; they were most likely hired to play their part just to get him to Sheffield and - to judge by their shallow back story - had not only been hired in a hurry but also lacked any kind of proper briefing.

He laughed inwardly as he turned right off Kingsway.

If he ever needed proof that the day's events were linked back to military intelligence, it came with the analysis he'd just made of Chloe's parents. An operation put together in a hurry with inadequate thought - the hallmark of the British intelligence machine!

Which did make sense. He was certain the people worrying about their daughter's absence had been sent by someone inside the military intelligence community who'd been spooked by the sight of Chloe's story - in Marty's parlance that was a slam dunk. Marty told him Gregory Brown had a copy of the article filched by GCHQ, the government's listening station, so presumably all manner of people had read Chloe's university essay. Something in that made-up article upset the reader enough to send the undercover agents or actors - Branigan wasn't sure which - to scare him into dashing off to Sheffield.

Turning up towards Mount Pleasant, Branigan stood on the pedals and felt the warmth generated by his powerful thighs spreading throughout his body. Treating the steady rise as a challenge, he closed his mind to his surroundings and pushed himself hard, even managing to surprise a cab trawling for a fare by over-taking it on the uphill climb.

As he neared the bright lights of the postal sorting office, Branigan heard the words from his days at The Academy.

'Don't focus on the what, focus on the why!'

Another of the things Marty had drummed into Branigan

and his fellow-recruits.

'Military history shows us battles are lost when people become preoccupied with what the opposition is doing and not why they're doing it!'

Why send him to Sheffield?

The only explanation he could come up with was to undermine the credibility of the story in the event it became public. The mere fact there was a link between him and Chloe - no matter how tenuous - was enough to throw scorn on the whole story.

He braked and swore as a red postal van pulled out in front of him.

But why not just tell the press it wasn't in the national interest and block the story?

Branigan answered his own question; the newspapers sometimes published first and redacted afterwards - his exposure being a case in point.

So that was it.

Someone wanted the story killed, didn't trust the official system for warning newspapers off publishing, so sent him up to Sheffield to discredit Chloe's alternate version of events. Except, of course, their hurried attempt to link him and Chloe largely backfired because they'd have struggled to get a picture of he and Chloe together without including Alan and his enormous aluminium case!

A dishevelled Arsenal fan who'd spilled from one of the pubs stepped into the road without looking, unable to understand through his drunken haze what was wrong with standing in the road and shouting at cars.

Unable to understand.

Like Alan.

Alan.

'Fuck, fuck, fuck!' Branigan swore as he neared Angel tube station.

He'd been so busy thinking about why the other side sent him on the wasted journey to Sheffield, he totally missed the real question. Why didn't the operation go as planned?

Because he turned up with his new-found partner in tow.

All the military strategists in the world could get together and plan an operation to wrong-foot Branigan without ever considering he'd turn up with a companion who looked like a cupcake sprinkled in bits of crispy caramel bite. It was like stepping into the boxing ring to find Mohammed Ali had got his mum with him - it just wasn't what you planned for.

He forked right up the side of Islington Green, a tiny triangular oasis in a desert of concrete and pondered why someone would put together an operation which focused on getting him to Sheffield without the back-story mattering - and why they'd then abort the operation because Alan was with him.

Overhead there was a creeping blackness of cloud which hinted at rain to come - a blackness which mirrored a growing knot in the pit of Branigan's stomach. He'd seen the whole day as a clumsy attempt to get him to Sheffield to undermine the story; he'd even laughed on the phone with Marty at the ineptitude of the couple playing the part of Chloe's parents.

'Shit, Marty,' Branigan said out loud, 'you were wrong!'

Here he was taking Marty's advice and focusing on the why, before he understood either what it was the opposition was planning, or even who were his protagonists.

As the streets narrowed and he cycled away from the more affluent part of London the first spots of rain began to fall.

It was unlikely the people he met were agents employed directly by military intelligence - resources were scarce enough without diverting people onto efforts to kill a news story. Far more likely, whoever was behind this had hired help.

When he'd laughed at their ineptitude Branigan had assumed they'd hired in a couple of actors to get him to Sheffield for an embarrassing photoshoot.

He could see the headline.

"Disgraced former agent colludes with student to re-write history."

The alternative was that they weren't actors but paid-for help of the kind he'd mentioned in passing to Chloe.

Black Ops.

A group of people lurking on the fringes of legitimate military intelligence who weren't constrained by the normal social conventions when it came to getting the job done. Where he'd been bound by the FOC-U rules, they followed their own, simpler, motto.

"Fuck You."

They were paid well to do a job, didn't need to stick to any rules of conduct in the field and the establishment turned a blind eye to what it was they did. The only rule for Black Ops was to keep distance between themselves and their paymasters.

Branigan shook his head.

No, this couldn't be a Black Ops operation.

If it were, they'd have reacted far more swiftly to things not working out as they wanted in Sheffield. Black Ops would've come up with "plan B" even before "plan A" had gone wrong and he'd seen no hint of an alternate strategy.

He turned into Balls Pond Road.

He didn't know whether or not it was true, but Sally once told him the road was named after John Ball, a seventeenth century innkeeper who had a duck pond behind his hostelry. Legend had it you could pay the innkeeper to chuck a stone at his ducks with the promise you could keep the unfortunate bird if your aim was accurate.

Branigan shuddered.

He didn't fancy being a duck on Mr Ball's pond any more than he wanted Black Ops on his tail. Instead he contented himself with the vision of two unemployed actors propping up the bar somewhere and congratulating themselves over their success in sending Branigan on a wasted journey to

Sheffield; not realising the plan they'd been part of had gone the same way as some of Mr Ball's less fortunate ducks.

As he neared his home, Branigan was comfortable in the knowledge he'd shortly be able to sit down with a glass of wine and laugh about it with Sally.

Branigan smiled as he saw the balloons either side of his front door - it seemed such a long time ago he'd been hanging them up and incurring Mrs Rutherford's disapproval for his lewd display.

Best of all, Molly's light was just peeking through her curtains which suggested she was still excited from her party and refusing to go to sleep; not of itself a good thing, because Sally would be frazzled, but it did at least mean he'd get to spend time with Molly before she went to sleep. By arriving now he'd be able to settle Molly before soothing Sally's nerves over a glass of wine while they swapped tales of their day.

The rain started to fall more heavily as Branigan turned into the alleyway behind the houses and he quickened his pace to stow the bicycle before he got drenched, in his hurry tripping over a black plastic rubbish sack just outside the back door.

'Fuck!' he said as he hurriedly stooped to shove the spilled contents back inside before wiping jelly off his right hand with a screwed-up serviette.

Not exactly the grand entrance he'd hoped for.

Music spilled out as he opened the back door, a track from a collection of children's favourite songs he'd downloaded for the party.

A familiar American voice singing "You are my sunshine, my only sunshine…"

Branigan pictured Molly and her friends excitedly ripping the layers of paper as they played pass-the-parcel, then Molly tugging insistently at Sally's leg when everyone had gone demanding the music be put back on.

'Again!' she'd say repeatedly when she heard a track she

really liked, wanting it played over and over until both he and Sally lost the will to live - there were only so many times you wanted to hear Puff the Magic Dragon.

He peered into the kitchen as he passed.

The lights all on, everything tidied away, an opened bottle of red wine on the side and three wine glasses.

Sally's glass with wine still in, Jude's empty after she'd helped tidy up and put the world straight with her friend and an untouched third waiting for Branigan's return.

Branigan shut the door to the hall cupboard as he turned to climb the stairs.

Even though they were unlikely to hear him over the music, Branigan avoided the creaky fourth stair in the hope he could surprise his girls.

The landing was lit by light spilling from his right-hand side through the open door of Molly's room.

He peered inside.

Bed ruffled, lights on and Puppy lying in splendid isolation in the dent of the pillow – he knew exactly where to find his girls!

Crossing the landing he picked up a rag doll with a mass of brown woollen hair, a smiling face and wearing a pink gingham dress.

Agadee.

The doll Alan had given Molly for her birthday.

Holding the doll close he gently opened the door to his and Sally's bedroom.

His two girls were lying together in bed with the covers pulled right up. Sound asleep.

Almost like last night, although then they'd lain side by side whereas now they were face to face inches apart.

They say the sense of smell is a powerful trigger for memories and as Branigan bent to tuck the rag doll in beside Molly he was struck by a sudden image of his meeting in Marty's office and an unassuming man with close-cropped grey hair.

    He held his nose close to the doll's woollen hair and inhaled a distinctive smell of wood and musk.
    He looked past the rag doll and focused on his girls, Sally with her face pressed close to Molly's and turned so he could just see it poking out above the covers.
    Blond hair spilled down across half her face.
    Eyes closed.
    Complexion more flushed than normal.
    Lips slightly parted and blue.
    Not breathing.

CHAPTER 8

20:04 Stoke Newington

Branigan found himself staring at the faces of his two girls uncomprehendingly.

It felt like his heart had stopped beating as he stood momentarily frozen by the unfathomable horror which engulfed him - only when a distant part of his brain engaged did he wrench the penknife from his pocket and desperately cut the cable tie away from Molly's neck where it had been ratcheted so tight it was lost in the folds of her soft and innocent flesh.

As he cut, Branigan sensed the coolness of her skin and was sickeningly certain his baby girl was dead.

Frantically he switched to Sally, digging in behind the cable tie around her neck, the lifeless response from her cool and clammy flesh the same.

Branigan let out an animalistic cry as he raced to cut the rest of the ties. Not because their legs needed freeing, or Sally's hands untying from behind her back, but because he had to do something to change the tableau in front of him. His wife and child dead, one having witnessed the death of the other just before she too succumbed to strangulation.

Even as he freed them from the awful ties, a remote part of Branigan's brain was analysing their death and wondering whether it was the lack of blood flow to the brain which killed them or being starved of oxygen. Falling back on his combat training he knew it took seconds for an opponent to be rendered unconscious if you held them in a choke hold and blocked their carotid artery - but you didn't kill people that way. Instead you started the gradual hypoxic descent of their consciousness which ended in oblivion after a few minutes. No, it was the lack of oxygen which killed them, their airways pinched by the punishingly tight cable ties so their last conscious moments were clouded by their desperate battle to draw breath.

Surveying the tableau - Sally with her hands tied behind her and Molly with her little hands free - Branigan realised with a sickening dread that the last image burned into Sally's brain was the sight of her precious little girl just inches away from her scrabbling ineffectually at the hard plastic buried in her neck. Sally, so close and yet unable to do anything other than watch her child's life ebb away as did her own just moments later.

Sitting on the bed, cradling Molly's and Sally's lifeless bodies, the music from downstairs playing on continuous repeat edged its way into Branigan's consciousness.

Another momentary flash.

He was in Marty's office with a gaunt-faced and unassuming man.

"You don't want to lose your little ray of sunshine any more than we want to lose ours…"

In the distance the music mocked him.

"… please don't take my sunshine away."

He raced downstairs and snatched the music dock off the dresser in the kitchen, ripping the power cable from the back and hurling it to the floor, his flood of anger turning to a torrent of rage.

Heading back upstairs he took in his surroundings, understanding the significance of the hall cupboard door being open when he arrived home, the back door unlocked and there being no sign of a struggle.

Someone who knew what they were doing had come into his home and used the tools at hand to stage a murder.

No break in.

No violent struggle.

Just the innocuous cable ties from the cupboard under the stairs; part of his own rewiring project and covered with his own fingerprints.

A staged murder.

Carried out by a professional.

It wasn't after all a low-key affair using unemployed actors - he was up against Black Ops. This was their "Plan B."

Back upstairs Branigan lay on the bed with his family, hearing in his mind Sally's accusation.

'Where were you when I needed you?'

He couldn't answer that. All he could do was hold them both tighter as tears of remorse coursed down his face.

'Where were you when someone scooped your frightened little girl out of bed and pulled one of your cable ties around her neck?'

'Where were you while I watched our baby die in front of me, scrabbling uselessly at the plastic buried in her neck?'

'Where were you when someone strangled me?'

'I'm sorry, I'm sorry, I'm sorry,' Branigan whispered over and over again as he rocked gently and held them in one last family hug.

20:41 Stoke Newington, London

Branigan had no idea how long he sat holding the lifeless bodies of his two precious girls.

He only awoke from his reverie with the persistent ringing of his phone.

He ignored it the first time. And the second time. The third time he pulled the phone from his pocket and looked at the number.

It was Chloe.

Pressing the button to answer he held the phone to his ear.

'Yes?' he said, his voice as lifeless as the girls he'd just been cuddling.

'Oh, thank God, Branigan,' a tearful Chloe said, 'I don't know what to do. Kate went to my apartment to collect some things and there was a massive explosion.'

'I don't even know if she's alive. The police, fire and ambulance are all over the place but no one seems to know anything. What do I do?' Chloe pleaded.

'Branigan?' she continued when there was no answer.

Over the sound of Chloe's desperate questioning, Branigan heard Sally's voice.

'Come along Branigan, don't let her down as well. She didn't need you earlier but she does now. You can see what's going on here; you know what she should do!'

He snapped out of his reverie and his training kicked in.

'Run,' he yelled down the phone, 'just fucking run!'

SCAPEGOAT

PART TWO

SATURDAY 23RD OCTOBER

CHAPTER 9

20:54 Sheffield, South Yorkshire

The driver of a silver Ford approached the most senior looking officer and flashed a warrant card.

'Anti-Terrorist Unit, we've had a call. I don't want to tread on your toes, but do you have a list of casualties or victims I can look at so we can run some background checks through our system?'

The obliging officer furnished the driver with all the names they had gleaned so far - he even went as far as giving Kate Upton's address which they'd found on her university library card.

20:55 Sheffield, South Yorkshire

'Where shall I go?' Chloe asked with panic in her voice - oblivious to Branigan's own distress.

'It doesn't matter,' he urged, 'just get away from Kate's apartment. It won't take the police long to work out who she is if they're swarming all over your flat and, trust me, the instant the police have worked it out whoever set that bomb is going to know too.'

He looked at the bodies of Sally and Molly lying on the bed.

'These people are serious, Chloe, just get away as fast as you can,' he said, 'grab anything on your way out which will help you disguise yourself but don't waste any time - I mean it, seconds count.'

Chloe didn't wait.

She snatched a text book and a pair of Kate's reading

glasses off the kitchen work surface before heading to the front door. She hesitated as she was about to take her own coat before grabbing Kate's red and black anorak and a head scarf.

As she raced down the stairs and into the courtyard where they parked when he dropped her off, Branigan ended the call by telling her not to use her credit cards, to use her phone sparingly and not to phone him - he would contact her when he was able.

There was no one in sight as Chloe crossed the road outside and began walking as fast as she could towards the station.

Behind her she heard the sound of an engine being revved to near breaking point as a car raced up the road and then braked suddenly as it swerved recklessly into the old cutlery works she'd just left.

Quickening her pace and trying not to look back, Chloe pulled the hood of the anorak up round her ears and focused on reaching the station a brisk ten-minute walk away.

The last part of her walk was downhill along a pedestrianised street with University buildings on either side. Ahead the yellow brick arches of the modernised nineteenth Century station were lit up with coloured lights which, she was sure, were supposed to be warm and inviting but to Chloe were stark and threatening.

As she crossed the main road to reach the station, she was sure she saw a silver Ford pull up and a figure run into the main concourse.

As she peered through the entrance, Chloe was horrified to see the station virtually deserted. In the throes of closing for the night, it was populated only by a few drunken football supporters and a straggle of people heading for local trains.

She thrust Kate's glasses on, pulled the hood and scarf closer to her face and slowed her pace in an effort to blend in; immediately finding Kate's glasses a hinderance as she tried to read the departure board. Peering awkwardly over the top, she discovered that aside from trains to Leeds, Cleethorpes and Goole the only longer distance options were Manchester and Birmingham - a choice made easy by looking at the time.

The Birmingham train not only took her nearer London, Branigan, and the heart of the madness which had engulfed her, but also left shortly. The Manchester train was over an hour away from leaving.

With just 7 minutes until her train left, Chloe went straight to the only open ticket window and thrust a wad of Branigan's cash towards the man chewing on a limp and greasy sausage roll behind the glass.

'You'll have to hurry, love,' he said, putting the half-eaten pastry carefully down and wiping his fingers on a paper napkin, 'that one's over the bridge on platform 6.'

He pointed helpfully to the steps beyond the barriers to her right-hand side before ponderously pressing the keys to produce the ticket.

'If you miss it, you'll have to catch the 21:55,' he said, blowing his cheeks out to show how tiresome that would be, and, in the process, distributing flecks of pastry onto the dark blue body warmer stretched to bursting point across his stomach, 'after that, there isn't another until the 08:54 tomorrow.'

No sense of urgency.

Peeling off three of the notes, Chloe cast nervous glances to either side as the man held each of them up to the light before scribbling on them with an iodine marker pen to test their authenticity.

Was the grey-haired middle-aged man staring at the departure board the person she'd seen getting out of the silver Ford she wondered?

'You'd better run,' the ticket man said, echoing Branigan's words as he finally pushed Chloe's change and the precious ticket across the counter towards her.

Rushing over the bridge, Chloe tried to keep one eye looking over her shoulder to see if she was being followed and almost bowled over one of her fellow passengers in the process.

To her relief no one else arrived on the platform before the train drew noisily alongside.

Hoping she hadn't been followed, Chloe chose the nearest carriage and settled into an empty set of four seats before allowing a wave of calm to wash through her for the first time since Branigan's urgent instruction to run.

Chloe made momentary eye contact with the woman settling in a seat across the aisle.

Thin-lipped and mousey, the woman gave no sign of recognition as she peered back through horn-rimmed spectacles half hidden by her brown fur hat.

21:25 Stoke Newington, London

As Chloe's train pulled out of the station, Branigan was still sitting with the lifeless bodies of Sally and Molly.

In the dark recesses of his mind he heard the large, gruff, and sergeant major-like instructor during a disastrous training exercise at The Academy.

He and three other trainees were driving through a mockup of a town when their car was halted by a truck skewed across the road. Coming under fire, Branigan and his fellow front seat passenger dived for cover amongst the fake shop fronts and prepared to return fire. Their colleagues in the back seat remained trapped inside.

'Mistake number one,' Peter Winstone yelled during the debriefing, the volume of his voice entirely unnecessary given that his face was no more than six inches away from Branigan's, 'no one checked the fucking child locks on the back doors before you set off!'

'Mistake number two,' Peter Winstone continued, his face now close enough for Branigan to feel the warmth of his breath as he shouted, 'you fucking dithered Branigan.'

Peter Winstone then did a pantomime imitation of Branigan returning fire, hesitating while he thought about how to get back to his trapped colleagues, returning more fire and then running for it.

'While you were dancing the fucking cha-cha-cha, your two colleagues in the car were still dead and your surviving team member needed your help.'

'Don't ever be a sentimental twat again Branigan,' Peter Winstone concluded, 'there's time to sort out the funeral arrangements later - deal with the here and now and focus on your counter-attack.'

Branigan wiped the tears from his eyes and let his training guide him as a police siren wailed in the distance. Knowing how the other side worked, he realised that if that siren wasn't headed his way it was only a matter of time before another one did - whoever staged the murders wanted to make sure he was in the frame.

The rationale for their Plan B crystallised in Branigan's mind. They didn't want to discredit Chloe's story, they wanted to discredit the man about whom it was written.

Moving quickly, Branigan focused on his counter-attack.

21:47 Stoke Newington, London

PC Harold Evans sped toward the address in Stoke Newington in response to an anonymous report of a violent domestic dispute. Another case of a husband who'd drunk too much getting into an argument with his wife or girlfriend and taking a swing at her; he was only too familiar with the scenario.

Still, it got him away from dealing with the lippy drunks outside the pubs and allowed him to drive fast under the cloak of the lights and siren, a respite in an otherwise routine Saturday evening.

Accelerating along the A10 and looking for the turning to the reported address, PC Evans slammed his brakes on and came to a screeching halt.

He cursed under his breath as an old tramp, his head half covered by a woollen hat, lurched into the road without warning and looked blankly at him. The tramp then gesticulated drunkenly at him, in the process almost losing his grip on the black bin liner and bottle of cheap cider.

While the tramp stumbled into the darkness, PC Evans easily found the address, aided by the information left by the anonymous caller.

'It's the one with the balloons either side of the front door.'

Although there were lights on inside, the door went unanswered so PC Evans did the sensible thing and worked his way round to the back of the property.

In the light of his torch he made his way past the open garden shed to the back door where there was a pile of rubbish strewn on the ground - like the detritus from a children's party had been emptied out of a bin liner. Picking his way through the wrapping paper, used paper plates and scraps of food, PC Evans tried the back door and found it open; seizing the initiative he called out and went inside, immediately seeing the kitchen in a mess with drawers opened and contents strewn. Convinced he wasn't dealing with a domestic, PC Evans called it in.

'There's no one at the address,' he told the dispatcher, 'but there are signs of a break-in.'

Climbing the creaking stairs, he saw light filling the landing from the open bedroom doors. He went first into a child's bedroom before putting his head round the door of the main bedroom.

Not a normal Saturday night after all.

In fact, an image which would live with PC Evans for the rest of his days.

'Dispatch!' he called urgently into his radio, 'Request urgent assistance. There are the bodies of an IC1 female aged about 30 and an IC1 girl aged about...'

He didn't manage to get Molly's age out.

PC Evans was used to dealing with drunks and domestics, not stumbling across strangled bodies. As he studied Molly's face, thought about her age and saw the marks left by the cable tie around her neck, not even the teddy bear clutched to her chest in her folded arms softened the blow.

He lost the unequal battle with his fish and chip supper, dashed to the bathroom and threw up.

22:12 Aldwych, London

The black cab pulled to a halt outside the Waldorf Hotel on Aldwych and Branigan climbed out, respectably dressed in jeans, suede boots, a smart casual shirt and a leather bomber jacket.

Clutched in his left hand as he paid the cab driver and thanked the Hotel doorman was a brown leather grip bag, now home to the piss-soaked coat and woollen hat he'd worn to make his escape. Given enough time he would have coloured his hair grey and added the touches like the hair sprouting from his ears to which Sally had objected just this morning.

Sally.

Being stared at, photographed and examined in minute detail by dozens of flat-footed police, forensics and pathologists to whom she would be just another victim.

Molly. The same.

Mind you, the policeman he'd stepped in front of looked like he cared. The shock on his face as he brought his car to a screeching halt when Branigan stumbled out, suggested he didn't want to hurt even a drunken old man. At least the first person to find them wouldn't be as dispassionate as the hordes who followed.

The choice of The Waldorf had been deliberate.

Taxi drivers were far less likely to remember a fare they took to a busy hotel on a Saturday night than one going to a deserted office. It was also deliberate that he discretely changed from the tramp's clothing and brought the unpleasantly soiled outfit with him - he didn't want to leave any more clues to help the police follow him than he had to.

As he walked away from the hotel, he was jostled briefly by the excited audience pouring out from a musical at the Novello Theatre, before he crossed the road and cut across to his destination in the relative quiet of The Strand. Entering the deserted office, he ran through the list of things he had to do and the calls he needed to make.

He started at the top of the building with Marty's office and worked his way down floor by floor before sitting at the desk in reception and picking up the phone.

21:33 Near Birmingham, West Midlands

It was scarcely 2 hours since Chloe heard the explosion rip through her apartment.

She'd known with a dreadful sense of foreboding that it was her flat even before she'd raced the 1/2 mile back from Kate's to find the various emergency services running hither and thither, setting up barriers, securing the scene and tending to the injured.

Even from her position behind a line of plastic security tape on the road outside the student accommodation, it was clear that her flat had been the target - the window and part of the wall were blown out and there were flames lapping out through the jagged hole and licking the roof of the building.

With no idea whether Kate was in the building when the explosion went off, Chloe hadn't known what to do; returning to Kate's afraid to admit that she herself was in any danger and only shaken out of her reverie by the urgency in Branigan's voice when he yelled out that she should run.

As the train neared Birmingham, she wished she had her phone with her so she could search the internet for news on the explosion in her flat - the phone Alan had loaned her was perfectly good for making phone calls and sending texts, but otherwise was as featureless as could be. Across the aisle the thin-lipped lady looked up and glanced her way before returning to the newspaper she'd scooped off another seat.

Chloe wished she had the foresight to do that; The History of Textile Design text book she'd snatched off the side in Kate's was hardly riveting and without either her phone or something more readable she was uncomfortable. She'd toyed with the idea of searching the carriage for another paper, but felt vulnerable enough knowing someone might be following her without exposing herself by walking up and down the carriage.

Then the phone borrowed from Alan rang.

"Ring" is perhaps too simple a verb to use in describing the sound it emitted.

The relative quiet of the train was shattered by the theme to Star Trek wailing from the phone at a volume sufficient for everyone in the entire carriage to jump with a start. In fact, Chloe surmised as she scrabbled in her desperation to silence the unfamiliar device, there were probably people in the carriages either side of them looking for the source of the deafening sound.

As she clicked the button to answer the call, Chloe caught a withering glance from the woman on the other side of the aisle and could hear murmurings throughout the carriage.

It was Branigan.

'Where are you?'

She'd hardly finished her response before he spoke urgently over her.

'Listen, I don't have long so I need to tell you what's happening.'

He explained that he was phoning from the office, was about to send her a new phone number and that she should phone Alan if she couldn't get through to him - he did not tell her about Sally and Molly.

'I've looked on line,' he continued, 'and as far as I can see from the early news reports no one was killed in the explosion at your place, but it does talk about an intense fire - did you see that?'

'Yes,' Chloe said as hope that Kate hadn't been badly injured rushed through her, 'there were flames everywhere.'

Branigan paused as he absorbed the significance.

'And you had electric heating and cooking as far as I saw?'

'Yes, that's right - why do you ask?'

'I'll explain later,' he continued, 'but first I need you to answer these next questions in monosyllables.'

'Okay,' Chloe said, catching on.

'Good,' Branigan replied, 'did anyone else get on the train with you?'

'Yes.'

'How many got into the same carriage as you?'

'Two,' Chloe said, glancing at the woman opposite and picturing the fair-haired youth in a surfer top who'd sat down at the far end of the carriage.

'Man or woman?'

'Each.'

'Okay - I doubt you can get photos easily and send them with that phone. Text me a brief description of them both - age, hair, height, eyes, clothing, anything like that.'

Chloe rang off and typed furiously with trembling fingers, nothing about her conversation with Branigan having made her feel that she was yet out of the woods. She described the fair-haired youth of 19 or 20 in trainers, jeans and a surfing top listening to music on his Beats.

Within seconds Branigan texted back 'Sounds OK.'

She typed in the description of the woman opposite.

'Woman, mid-forties, brown eyes, short, thin, thin lips, fur hat, big old-fashioned glasses.'

The Star Trek theme struck up again.

'She's tailing you,' Branigan said succinctly.

Having established that the train was nearing its terminus, Branigan explained to Chloe exactly what she should do when she reached Birmingham.

CHAPTER 10

22:39 Hendon, North London

Alan was sitting in the front room of his house.

He wasn't one for change, so not only was it the same house he'd lived in all of his life, it remained untouched by the passage of time. His friend Sally said he didn't like change because of his Asperger Syndrome or Autistic Spectrum Disorder as she sometimes called it. Although Sally tried to explain why his view of the world was so different from everyone else's, Alan struggled to pay attention long enough to absorb what she was saying. It wasn't that he didn't want to listen, but unless someone was talking about things that interested him, he found it difficult to concentrate.

Numbers and computers interested him because they always behaved the same way and he could understand them. If it wasn't numbers, computers, or Star Trek, he either forgot to listen or became distracted which made people cross with him. The other thing that made them cross with him was that he didn't know what emotion people expected him to show, so sometimes he laughed in the wrong place or got angry over things other people found funny.

The policeman who'd spoken to him about the accident on the motorway on the day his bacon caught fire had got cross with him. He'd talked and talked to Alan while they stood on the bridge over the carnage on the M25 below - using lots of words like "common-sense," "distraction," and "accident" - then he seemed very upset when Alan pointed out that one of the buttons on his uniform was sewn on upside-down. Alan didn't mean to upset him, he just thought the policeman would be interested to know.

It wasn't that he set out to see things differently to other people - he was just born that way. Where most people would remember the face of the policeman who came along to shout at them, Alan couldn't. He could, however, remember the number of buttons on his uniform, picture the crown and the words on the buttons and tell you the identification number on his shoulder.

Tonight, he was unsettled because he'd had a day when unexpected things happened - and unexpected things were almost as bad as change. Mind you, he'd liked travelling to Sheffield in the car and using his field-kit, but he was relieved that things were now back to normal. Rather later than usual, he'd just finished his steak and kidney pie, mashed potato and peas - the same meal he ate every Saturday evening. Star Trek was on the television and he had his computers to talk to - not only that, but he had a question to answer for his friend Branigan.

Although the question was proving difficult.

He'd looked round the internet and the dark web trying to find details of Operation Peach Tree without success. Not in itself a problem because it simply meant he had to keep looking and when he was doing something important like this it didn't matter how long it took.

The only measure of time came from the 65-inch television screen fixed on the wall high above the fireplace in just the right position so he could look up at it over the top of the monitors in front of him if he needed a break.

Even focused as he was in his search for Operation Peach Tree, he was able to keep tabs of his screen hero, Mr. Spock; if he could be anyone for just a day it would be him. In the episode on the screen Spock was having to deal with a computer which had taken over the Star Ship Enterprise; his favourite episode featuring his favourite character battling his favourite thing.

Alan's attention, however, was focused away from the TV on the screens in front of him. Even after he'd been into the depths of the secure servers at SIS and given himself the highest security level as a new user - M. R. Spock - he'd found nothing.

The same applied over at MI5 which was very unusual; he'd normally find something on a search like this - which left him with two possible answers.

The first that Operation Peach Tree didn't exist, the second - and decidedly more problematic - that it only existed in the recesses of a standalone system he couldn't access from the outside. Alan examined the architecture of the Security Service systems to see if he there were any sign of a discreet system hidden behind the main network and jumped as his phone started playing the Star Trek theme.

At first, he thought he'd missed part of the episode on the television because he wasn't used to people phoning him on a Saturday night - not unless someone was working late in the office and had a problem with their computer. Everyone called it a "problem with the computer," but Alan knew better - the problem was never with the computer - it was always with the people using it.

A withheld number.

'Hello, Alan Armstrong speaking, how may I help you?' he said, putting the handset to his ear and answering the same way he always did - the way his mother had taught him.

'Alan, it's me - Branigan.'

'Branigan who?' Alan replied, following the technique he'd learned from his mother.

'How many Branigans do you know – the one who's just travelled to and from Sheffield with you,' Branigan said, the strain in his voice going unnoticed by Alan who smiled, 'I need you to call me back on this number - it's a new one - make a note of it.'

Branigan reeled off the number and Alan hung up when he started to repeat it.

Alan never understood that; why did people need to repeat things when all you had to do was rewind the conversation like you did with an episode of Star Trek and play that bit again?

'Hello, it's Alan Armstrong here, may I speak to Mr. Branigan?' Alan said having dialled the number back from memory.

'Sorry about that,' Branigan said, 'I'm on a new phone from work and it only has a small amount of credit.'

Alan listened and began fiddling with the keyboard of his computer while Branigan explained about Chloe's flat, how she'd left Sheffield and that he was on his way to collect her from Birmingham.

'And Alan,' Branigan continued, 'I need you to put me on speakerphone because I have more to tell you.'

Alan pressed the button on his handset and, now that he no longer needed to hold the handset, instantly became engrossed back in his computer screen. Branigan's voice became more distant and, even though he was trying really hard to listen, Alan stopped hearing every word. He focused on the architecture of the security service system, looking for any standalone computers which still accessed the internet periodically to gather data and update software - like playing a game of hide-and-seek with computers.

In the background Branigan was saying something about the police and then something about them being after someone and then he was talking about Sally and Molly.

Alan smiled.

'Does she like Agadee?' he asked, moving his attention from the search for Operation Peach Tree and looking back at his phone.

'Alan,' Branigan said sharply, 'you haven't been listening. You need to listen now.'

He took a deep intake of breath and his voice caught in his throat, 'Sally and Molly are dead. They've been murdered.'

It happened quite a lot with Alan, particularly when

people were either cross with him or upset him.

Like the time when the school bullies - who normally kicked him or punched him because he was different - tore up his precious book, the one he was writing every prime number down in and threw the pieces in the boys' toilet. When things like that happened, he needed to go and hide.

Alan was very good at hiding.

He could hide from the things around him when people spoke too loudly; when people did nasty things to him; when there was sudden change; or, like now, when he didn't like what someone was saying.

Sally and Molly were his friends. He understood Molly. They made each other laugh.

He ran to his hiding place - down a corridor in his mind filled with doors to hide behind. Today the door was labelled "prime numbers," but another time it could just as easily be the models and serial numbers of different series of VW Caravanette; the names of people in Highgate Cemetery; or something simple like a list of everyone in the office's addresses, telephone numbers, dates of birth and national insurance numbers.

'4663, 4673, 4679, 4691...' rocking, rocking, rocking.

'Alan!' Branigan's voice.

'4703, 4721...' rocking and covering his ears with his hands.

'I need you to help Sally,' Branigan speaking louder.

'4723, 4729, 4733...' rocking.

'I need you to help Molly,' Branigan shouting now.

Molly's face appeared along with the prime numbers.

Holding her new rag doll - like the one Alan had propped up on his bed upstairs.

'4751, 4759...' Alan felt himself stop rocking and he peered tentatively out from behind the door in his mind, blinking rapidly at the light in his front room.

'Sally and Molly are dead?' he asked.

'Yes, they were murdered.'

'By whom?'

'I don't know, that's why I need your help Alan - to find who killed them.'

Alan took the news that they'd been murdered and this time filed it in a box in his mind and very carefully shut the lid. He then consciously went down a different mental corridor, one he didn't like very much with doors whose labels he'd deliberately left off, and sought an old rusty door that looked like it hadn't been used for a long time. Opening it, he threw the box inside - catching a brief glimpse inside the room of his father pointing at him and laughing - and slammed the door shut before turning the key and making sure the door was properly locked.

He felt better. He had a job to do - a new job helping his friend Branigan find someone.

'What do you want me to do?'

'Nothing at the moment,' Branigan replied, 'but when I come back with Chloe we'll need somewhere to stay where people won't find us while we try and find the bad people.'

'You mean you want to use my house to run a secret mission from?'

'That's it Alan, will you be able to do that for us?' Branigan asked, 'I assume you have access to the internet there and a laptop or something - that would be useful.'

Alan looked at the array of screens in front of him and the series of fat data cables snaking up the wall to the spare bedroom which now functioned as his server room.

'Yes,' he said tentatively, 'I think I can find a laptop somewhere.'

'Excellent, Alan, and you're sure you don't mind us coming - we'll need somewhere to eat and sleep as well?'

Alan smiled and looked at the empty plate beside him.

'That's good,' he said, 'do you like steak and kidney pie?'

Branigan was taken aback.

'Do I like what?'

'Steak and kidney pie - I have 30 of them.'

Alan didn't hear Branigan's intake of breath.

'You have thirty steak and kidney pies?'

'Yes.'

'Why?'

'Because I don't want to run out and thirty-one is a prime number.'

Branigan, who couldn't begin to fathom what he was talking about, didn't reply so Alan carried on.

'Oh, yes,' he said, 'I don't know if it will help you find the killers, but I've just added £200 credit to your phone.'

22:46 New Street Station, Birmingham

Having listened intently to Branigan's urgent advice, Chloe used the last few minutes of her journey to prepare herself.

With her eyes half closed she waited until the train shuddered to a halt in Birmingham before getting up and making her way to the nearest door. By waiting until the last moment to leave her seat, Chloe made sure most of the other passengers were on their feet and already queuing for the exit - which left just her and the mousey-looking woman across the aisle.

'Excuse me,' Chloe said to the woman as they both found themselves standing in the aisle, 'I'm sure I know you from somewhere - have we met before?'

Branigan's advice.

'It'll throw the person who's tailing you if you engage with her - speak to her and say something to let her think you've seen her following you - that'll make her drop back.'

The woman looked at her blankly through her horn-rimmed spectacles.

'I don't think so,' she said, before turning away to avoid any further contact.

'I'm sure we've met somewhere,' Chloe persevered, even though she was now speaking to the back of the woman's fur hat, 'because I rarely forget a face; I'm a journalist you see, so we may have met when I was covering a story or something?'

No response.

Just as they reached the front of the queue and stepped down from the train, Chloe turned to the woman one more time.

'You don't know the way to the Holiday Inn, do you?'

Part of Branigan's instructions as he sat in the office in London with a map he'd pulled up on the internet.

'Let her think she knows where you're going. Ask for the Holiday Inn which is nearby and she'll hang back further once she sees you heading in that direction. It won't buy you a lot of time, but seconds count.'

Receiving no response from the woman, Chloe turned and began walking towards the barrier with the others who'd left the train, listening as she did so for a Birmingham accent somewhere nearby.

Identifying a woman in her forties who'd been travelling in the same carriage with her morose teenage son whose headphones had been emitting a thin, repetitive and very annoying beat throughout the entire journey, Chloe spoke to her just after they'd both passed through the barrier.

'Stop and ask someone you think will know the answer,' Branigan had explained, 'but this time just the other side of the barriers - your tail will have to hang back again and be delayed further with the barrier still to negotiate.'

As the woman with the morose son helpfully directed her, Chloe caught a glimpse of her tail pausing behind the barrier while she pretended to search for the ticket she'd bought from the guard on the train.

The guard's surprise that she'd managed to get to the platform without a ticket should have been a warning to Chloe.

Details.

The things that mattered in journalism also mattered when you were on the run.

Making her way outside, Chloe kept her pace with the struggle of people leaving the station down the ramp to the main road. She looked from side to side, took in her surroundings and studied the road signs, again following Branigan's advice to, 'use the opportunity to take note of the geography - it will matter later, so get your bearings while you pretend to be looking for the way to the Holiday Inn.'

Chloe turned right at the main road and walked steadily past the shops, pausing momentarily to turn and look in a couple of shop windows and glance briefly out of the corner of her eye to check that her tail was there.

She was.

As she neared the main junction ahead, Chloe could see the lights for the Holiday Inn and she prepared for her subterfuge.

Gauging the distance between herself and the woman in the fur hat, she waited until she knew the woman tailing her had lost visual contact. It was only for a few seconds, but, if Branigan's plan was correct, it gave her enough time to seem to disappear into the Holiday Inn and instead sprint the extra yards to the Radisson just beyond.

Thank God she was wearing her comfortable boots.

Never a runner at school, Chloe did her best to sprint fifty meters past the Holiday Inn before turning sharply into the hotel next door.

Not the gainliest of dashes maybe, but she hoped enough for the woman behind to assume she'd turned into the Holiday Inn.

'You're in a hurry!' A man about to enter the hotel said, stepping back and holding the door open for her as she raced not only through the open doorway, but also on through the lobby, the restaurant and the kitchen, before emerging out of a door at the back of the hotel where four members of staff were huddled together smoking. Ignoring their protests that the exit was for staff only, Chloe turned into one of the smaller streets behind the hotel and followed the directions Branigan had given her back to the train station and a taxi.

Breathless from running and with her heart pounding, Chloe didn't hear the huddle of smokers expressing their consternation as a gaunt-faced silvery-haired man of about fifty emerged through the door behind her. Had she turned around as she walked briskly to Navigation Street and the sanctuary of a taxi, Chloe would have recognised the man following her as the one who opened the door of the Radisson for her; Branigan would have recognised him as James Travers.

CHAPTER 11

23:07 Surrey Park Golf Club

Marty was in the bar of the golf club when his phone rang.

'Hey Branigan, how are you doing,' he said cheerily after Branigan identified himself, 'did you make it up to Sally yet or are you still in her bad books?'

Having consumed a succession of large malt whiskies as he and his golf club buddies swapped increasingly outlandish golf stories and lewd innuendo, Marty didn't pick up the atmosphere on the end of the phone. Putting Branigan's silence down to sullenness at having been sent on the fruitless trip to Sheffield, he blundered on.

'Listen, if you're phoning to bollock me on Sally's behalf you can put her on and she can do it direct. I'm man enough to take her on any time! Today was just one of those things, it'll blow over,' he continued.

'But that's the problem Marty - it won't,' Branigan said.

'What do you mean?' Marty said, raising the fresh glass of Glenlivet he'd just been passed by one of his laughing mates and silently toasting his benefactor.

'I said,' Branigan repeated carefully and deliberately, 'that what happened today isn't going to blow over.'

Marty sipped the neat whisky and felt the warm glow as the heady flavours of peat, roasted malt and alcohol slid effortlessly down his throat.

'It will, I'll speak to Gregory on Monday and we'll work out what's best to do,' Marty said, pausing as he heard the wail of a siren in the background, 'Are you in the car?'

Branigan watched the flashing blue lights of an ambulance

as it disappeared behind him.

'You don't understand, Marty - they murdered Sally and Molly.'

For a moment Marty hesitated.

He knew he'd misheard so he gave a short laugh which was echoed by the rest of the table as Frank, the buddy who'd bought the latest round, waggled his little finger to indicate that someone had Marty wrapped round it.

'I thought you said they'd been murdered!' he joked as he waved his arm to shush the rest of his cronies.

'I did.'

Two simple words.

'Fuck!' Marty said, the colour draining from his cheeks.

Even his ribald mates sensed the change in him as some primal pack instinct silenced everyone round the table.

Marty stood up and moved away from his pals' inquisitive ears, stationing himself in the corridor outside the Members' Bar.

'What do you mean, murdered?' he asked urgently.

'They were tied up and strangled with cable ties, Marty,' Branigan said in a whisper, 'The house was staged to make it look like I killed them. Now will you tell me this is going to blow over and that someone isn't too bothered about keeping Operation Peach Tree a secret?'

Marty was lost for words.

'What is Operation Peach Tree Marty?' Branigan asked, his tone now forceful and direct.

'Listen, I can't go into detail now,' Marty replied, struggling to comprehend what was happening, 'but I really don't see how anyone can be taking it that seriously: it was just a joke.'

'A joke,' Branigan exclaimed, 'you mean my wife and child have been murdered because of a fucking joke?'

'I'm sorry, Branigan,' Marty said, 'that's not what I meant. In a nutshell, Operation Peach Tree was something the six of us - you know, the little gang that meet at The Club once a month - dreamed up one evening over dinner as a joke, a flight-of-fancy, or whatever you want to call it.'

'Go on,' Branigan said, the menace in his voice palpable.

'We need to meet so I can explain properly, but we were conscious how much more support the American security services got from their government and the public after 9/11…'

Branigan was there already.

'What, so you decided to stage your own atrocity?'

Marty was immediately defensive.

'You've got the whole thing wrong, Branigan, we didn't want to do something that killed that many people - that was the whole thrust of our theoretical discussion. We wanted to get the most public and political support from the lowest number of casualties.'

'So, you followed one of the Strategies,' Branigan said simply, referring to the list of 36 ancient Chinese War Strategies they'd all learned at The Academy. 'How does the 11th Strategy go - Sacrifice the plum tree to preserve the peach tree - you were prepared to stage your own version of 9/11 and sacrifice your own people to make sure the security services got a bit more money?'

'Yes,' Marty reluctantly agreed, 'but you must understand we didn't want those casualties, they were just an unfortunate by-product. The whole plan was about preserving the safety of people in Britain.'

'And it never occurred to you that even one casualty was too many?' Branigan asked.

'We didn't really expect any casualties; the idea was dreamt up by a bunch of people who'd had a drink and thought the idea would be forgotten by the morning. Look Branigan, where do you want to meet so we can talk about this face-to-face?'

'Tomorrow. Euston. 10.00am under the departure boards,' Branigan said succinctly and ended the call.

'Is everything okay,' Frank asked, putting his head round

the door from the bar, 'only it looked like you had some pretty bad news?'

'It's all right, thanks Frank,' Marty replied, hiding his emotions behind a false smile, 'a colleague has had some bad news, that's all - I was just commiserating with him. I've got another call to make and then I'll be back; tell the others I'll stand the next round.'

Reassured, Frank retreated to spread the news.

As Marty dialled there was a distant cheer from his friends as Frank relayed Marty's offer to buy them a round.

The pack mentality.

How quickly it forgets concerns when something better is on offer.

The call was answered.

'Gregory, it's Marty. Sorry to phone so late, but I've just spoken to Branigan and something dreadful has happened...'

23:15 Stoke Newington, London

Detective Chief Inspector Mark Tenant had that rather jowly look of someone who'd lost a lot of weight in a short space of time, an observation supported by his ill-fitting suit and baggy white shirt.

Sadly, being slimmer hadn't made him happier - his long-suffering Detective Sergeant, Harry Drake, could attest to that.

'The old bugger didn't want to stop to get a takeaway for supper,' DS Drake moaned to the others at the Station earlier in the evening after he'd been stuck out on a job with the DCI, 'he's brought what looks like one fucking chicken wing and a piece of lettuce from home.'

By contrast, the stocky - and decidedly hungry - DS Drake wouldn't mind that chicken wing right now.

He'd just received a call from the front desk to say his chips with curry sauce had been delivered, when PC Evans' call came in to report two dead bodies. One of those

'Drop everything and come with me, Detective Sergeant' moments when your head was delighted you were a detective and your stomach less so. Unfortunately, 'Yes Chief Inspector, let me have my chips and I'll be right with you,' wasn't the answer you were expected to give.

Not only was he now stuck at the house with two dead bodies for hours, but also, he knew the gannets in the squad room would have devoured his meal well before the curry sauce congealed. To add insult to injury, he was poking through more cold chicken nuggets, sausages and chips than you could shake a stick at. They were spread all over the paving outside the back door of the house, evidence of some form of row or demonic house-keeping neither he nor the DCI as yet understood.

'Fuck knows how you pronounce this first name,' DCI Tenant said from over his shoulder as the DS crouched examining the detritus from the party, 'but this Branigan chap looks like the prime suspect, don't you think?'

'Yes, sir.'

'What do you think,' DCI Tenant said speculatively, 'children's party of some kind, stressful day, bit too much to drink, an argument and he shuts them both up?'

'Sounds plausible, sir,' DS Drake agreed.

'We'll see what DNA we have to back that theory up, but his not being here seems to make sense of that, don't you think?'

'Yes, sir.'

'The only issue I have,' DCI Tenant said, pointing to two plastic bags, each sealed in an evidence bag, 'are those.'

One was a plastic bag with a rag doll inside, the other a smaller bag with a pinch of human hair in it; both found in the bedroom with the bodies. With them was a note signed by Branigan which said, "I think you'll find the killer's DNA and scent are on the rag doll. There is mine on it too, plus on the bodies, cable ties and nail scissors. The hair in the other bag is from my head and will give you my DNA for comparison."

'I don't know if you agree Detective Sergeant, but I think our Mr. Branigan is a regular Miss Marple who thinks he can outwit the likes of you and me,' DCI Tenant said.

'And do you know something else,' he continued, not waiting for DS Drake to answer, 'one of the crime scene technicians reckons he's that spy chap who was plastered over the papers a few years ago; do you remember, the one who sold those arms to the terrorists?'

22:49 Chobham, 17 miles South of London

No sooner had Gregory Brown put the phone down on his conversation with Marty Freeman, than he dialled David Price at his central London apartment. There was nothing unusual in that - as Director of Operations Gregory Brown needed to keep his boss aware of operational triumphs and disasters on a regular basis - but what caught David Price's attention was his colleague's opening line.

'I think we have a problem.'

Strong, lean and regarded as unflappable by his colleagues, David Price shut the door to his study and settled behind his large mahogany desk, the creases in his face deepening with a frown as he listened to Gregory Brown's account of Branigan's visit to Sheffield, Chloe's article, the murders and the explosion at Chloe's apartment.

'I take it the article is the one I sent you a couple of days ago?' David Price asked when his colleague finished his summary of events.

'Yes, the one which mentions Operation Peach Tree.'

David Price silently contemplated what he'd just heard.

'Do you think Branigan is involved in the murders?' he asked.

'I don't know what to think at this stage, but Branigan told Marty he came back from Sheffield and found them dead - that he's been set up.'

'And we don't know where Branigan is now?'

'No, neither he nor the girl.'

'It doesn't feel right, does it?' David said, his soft well-educated voice betraying no emotion, 'We both know what Branigan is capable of - if he set out to kill his wife and child, he wouldn't make it look so obvious.'

'I agree, unless he just saw red in the heat of the moment.'

'But his seeing red neither explains the explosion, nor him going to Sheffield in the first place, which makes me worry there might be more to this than a simple domestic.'

'That's what I thought when Marty first told me, but if that is the case it suggests there's something happening which is linked to Chloe Travers' story and I can't see that either.'

David Price was in agreement.

'You're probably right,' he said, 'but for now I'd like you to ask GCHQ for any chatter which may relate to Branigan and Chloe Travers and let's keep an eye on what develops.'

'What would you like me to tell the others?' Gregory Brown asked, making reference to Michael Jenkins, Alex Oldroyd and Peter Winstone who were also at the table when the Operation Peach Tree discussion took place.

'Just let them know we're monitoring the situation,' David Price said, 'and tell them not to discuss our conversation that night with anyone.'

'Okay, and if we pick anything up which may help the police track Branigan down, do we feed it to them?'

'No, I don't think that's wise, we don't need to be seen to be involved in this and, besides, Branigan may not be in our team any more, but he's more use to us in the field than he is behind bars.'

SUNDAY 24TH OCTOBER

CHAPTER 12

01:07 Birmingham Airport

Chloe raced out of the departure hall at Birmingham Airport and jumped into the waiting BMW.

'Dear God,' she said, slumping in the passenger seat as they accelerated away, 'am I ever pleased to see you Branigan - that was scary!'

'But the plan we discussed worked?'

'Yes,' she said buckling on her seatbelt and stretching out, 'I thought I'd lost that woman who was following, but after I'd come out of the back of the hotel I walked on a bit, then turned around and there was a man following me!'

Branigan nodded as he listened.

'And you're sure he was tailing you?'

'He must have been,' Chloe said with certainty, 'the fucker not only held the door open for me when I went into the hotel, but also followed me right through and out of the back.'

'What did he look like?'

'I'd say about fifty, quite tall with silvery-grey hair and a thin, almost gaunt face.'

An image flashed into Branigan's mind.

'That's the man I met this morning - the one who pretended to be your Dad - and the woman following you, I'm sure she was the one who posed as your Mum. My guess is they split after I saw them in London and she came up to Sheffield while he stayed behind...' the words Branigan wanted to say - "to do whatever was necessary if their plan for Sheffield went wrong" - caught in his throat.

Branigan cleared his throat and moved the conversation forward.

'Your feint with the cab worked well?' he asked.

'Yes,' Chloe replied, 'like we agreed, I told my cabbie I was being chased by an ex-boyfriend and he pretended to drop me off at a busy rank in Broad Street. The grey-haired man followed me into a pub, but I dumped my coat and glasses and ran back to the taxi which had waited for me outside; even if he saw me leave, he would've been too late - his cab had already left with another fare.'

'And you found hiding in the airport okay?'

'Yes, you were right, although it's open 24/7 most of the concessions were closed, so I hunkered down behind the counter of a car hire booth in arrivals - that's where I've been texting you from.'

02:13 Stoke Newington, London

Satisfied that all the forensic, pathology and crime scene investigation work was properly underway, Detective Chief Inspector Mark Tenant was preparing to leave Branigan's home and head back to the station.

DS Drake glanced at his watch.

With the takeaways that delivered to the police station now closed and the canteen closed, all he had to look forward to was the vending machine.

As he placed the sealed evidence bags containing the hair and the rag doll Branigan had left at the scene inside into the back of the car, Drake worked through the tempting morsels on offer.

He'd narrowed it down to either the steak slice or the ham and cheese wrap - either would do.

'Right, I'm ready to go back to the Station - are you finished Detective Sergeant?' DCI Tenant said as he approached the car.

'Yes sir,' Drake replied.

As they left the murder scene behind them, it was perfectly evident that the DCI was satisfied with his solution to the case.

'It's Branigan who did this,' he said with certainty.

'If we get a DNA match on the cable ties, we'll be home and dry - and forensics seemed quite sure there were partial prints on them as well, which would be the icing on the cake. All we need to do then is piece together his movements and we have a cast iron case.'

DS Drake hesitated before saying what was on his mind.

'Yes, Chief Inspector, but there are three things missing.'

DCI Tenant looked questioningly at his subordinate.

'We don't have a motive; we don't understand why he bagged up the rag doll and left us what appears to be his DNA; and we don't have him,' he said, before adding, 'sir.'

Tenant snorted and shrugged off the objections.

'I don't know those things either, but we do know from his past that this Branigan chap isn't to be trusted; we know eighty percent of all murders are committed by people close to the victim; and we know our prime suspect was on the scene and has since gone missing. My guess is he bagged that doll thing and the hair to try and throw us off the scent; there was nothing in the crime scene that I saw which suggested anyone else was involved. As to catching him, it's just a question of time.'

DS Drake wished he shared his boss's conviction; the way Branigan had left the bodies - with the ligatures around their necks removed, cuddling each other and with the little girl clutching a soft toy - sowed a seed of doubt in his mind. Added to that there were the pillowcases missing from both where his wife and his little girl slept, as well as the empty photograph frames.

02:17 A1 Southbound to London

Chloe had every right to be scared. Having her best friend

caught in the blast as her apartment blew up and herself being pursued from Sheffield to Birmingham by people seemingly intent on causing her harm was the stuff of nightmares. The fact Branigan was taking a long route back to London to avoid running into any of the people looking for them only deepened her fears.

'Do you have any more of an idea who's after us?' she asked.

'Maybe some,' he replied noncommittally, 'but I won't have proper answers until I've met Marty and done some digging.'

'And in the meantime, we have to keep out of sight, is that it?'

'Pretty much, we're going somewhere safe now and then I'm meeting Marty tomorrow morning.'

Branigan looked at the time displayed on the car's dashboard.

'Well, I'm actually seeing him in a little under eight hours,' he corrected himself.

'Until then, we're hiding where?' Chloe asked.

'Alan Armstrong's.'

For a moment Branigan's reply sounded like a non sequitur. Chloe's image of the oddball man she'd met earlier didn't fit with the concept of somewhere safe to hide.

'What, you mean the Alan who got caught in my handcuffs?' she asked incredulously.

'Yes, that Alan,' Branigan replied, hearing the doubt etched into Chloe's voice, 'we don't really have many other choices.'

'But what's wrong with your house or another of your colleagues'?'

Branigan took a deep breath as a wave of blackness ran through him.

'My house has already been compromised,' he said carefully, 'and I'm really not sure who else to trust at the moment. More has happened than I've told you.'

Feeling the knot in her stomach tighten, Chloe waited for

Branigan to go on.

'If you remember, earlier in the day I said I thought someone had sent actors to play the roles of your mum and dad, and that whoever wanted the story quashed intended to do so by discrediting you and me.'

Chloe nodded.

'I think now they wanted to go further than that and the people after us weren't actors but Black Ops agents.'

Even though Branigan had only briefly alluded to the term, the name "Black Ops" felt to Chloe like a portent of evil.

'And that's bad?' she asked.

'Very.'

'What do you think they're trying to do?'

'I think they want to discredit me by making me look like a murderer,' Branigan said, fighting to keep his composure.

There was a moments silence in the car while Chloe thought about this last remark.

'Who do they want to make it look like you killed?' she asked, fearing the answer.

'I think if I'd arrived unaccompanied in Sheffield, they would've made it look like I killed you,' he said, 'but they had to change their plan when Alan came with me.'

Chloe nodded, conscious of the edge creeping into Branigan's voice.

'Instead they blew up your flat to destroy the evidence you'd gathered for the story and turned their attention elsewhere.'

'But if they turned their attention elsewhere, why were they so keen to follow me?' she asked.

'I think they put their Plan B into place and wanted to track you once you started to run in the hope you would lead them to me,' Branigan explained.

'I'm sorry,' Chloe replied, 'I don't understand.'

'Their ultimate goal hasn't changed - they still want to have me arrested for murder - their Plan B was to change the victim whose murder they were framing me for. They changed it from you, to Sally and Molly: my wife and daughter.'

The stunned silence which followed this statement was broken only by the clickety clack of the big car's tyres as it thumped over the road markings on the approach to another junction and the sound of Chloe taking several gulps of air as she tried to control the tidal-wave of emotion which engulfed her.

'You mean...' she whispered hesitantly.

Branigan nodded, pausing as he choked on his next words.

'I found them when I arrived home this evening,' he said eventually, his voice cracked with sorrow, 'they'd been strangled with cable ties. They were in our bed together, Sally with her hands tied behind her back and Molly with her hands free so she'd...'

Chloe glanced across to Branigan as his voice trailed away, his left hand up near his neck, scrabbling in vain as he acted Molly's last moments.

'It was staged to look like I did it,' Branigan said when he recovered his composure, 'but on the landing I found Molly's new rag doll which smelled of the aftershave the man who posed as your father was wearing. I think that's the same man you came across in Birmingham and tried to follow you in the taxi.'

Branigan's eyes were fixed vacantly on the road ahead as he relived the scene

Chloe pictured the horror which Branigan had just described.

'Oh my God,' she said, working out the timing, 'so when I phoned you to tell you about the explosion in my apartment you were still there?'

They travelled on in silence after that, each digesting the events of the day and contemplating the deaths of Sally and Molly.

Branigan pulled from his pocket a photograph he'd taken

from a frame in his living room and handed it to Chloe; he, Sally and Molly laughing together on a beach as the sea lapped around their ankles.

Chloe stared at the photograph of the happy family and burst into tears.

'I'm so sorry...' she said, her voice breaking with every syllable.

02:19 M1 Southbound to London

The thin-lipped woman in the passenger's seat of the anonymous Audi waited while the driver answered his phone, pressing it to his ear using his shoulder.

'Yes?' the grey-haired man said, turning to her and rubbing his thumb and forefinger together to indicate it was the person paying them.

'No, we haven't found Branigan yet,' he said, 'one of our team has been outside his house all evening, saw him come back, but didn't see him leave before the police arrived.'

He waited while the voice on the other end spoke.

'No, they're all over the place and have obviously found the bodies, but we have to assume Branigan escaped somehow.'

In response to a further question, the man grimaced before answering.

'No, we've lost her too. We tracked her to Birmingham, but somehow she managed to give us the slip.'

The woman tried to make out what the person on the end of the phone said next, but all she could hear was a tone which suggested their paymaster was less than pleased.

'I know,' the driver said when the rant on the other end died down, 'but it's just a temporary set-back. It won't take long for the police to arrest him - we'll make sure of that.'

02:43 A1 Southbound to London

'I've just spoken to Alan,' Branigan said.

They'd stopped at a service station where he'd made the call while Chloe fetched two cups of coffee.

'He told me Kate was in the stairwell when the blast happened. Apparently, she was blown down a flight of stairs, has a broken arm, cuts and bruises and temporary loss of hearing - otherwise she's fine.'

'They're keeping her in overnight but she should be out tomorrow,' he concluded.

'That's wonderful news, I was worried,' Chloe admitted as they pulled back onto the main road, 'how did Alan find all that out so quickly?'

Branigan shrugged.

'It's best not to ask - Alan finds it easier to chat to computers than he does people - so I imagine he's been into the hospital system and looked up her records.'

Keen for conversation which would drag him away from his dark thoughts, Branigan broke the silence which followed.

'What made you decide to go into journalism?' he asked.

Relieved to have something to talk about which didn't focus on their predicament, Chloe answered at length.

'I joined the local paper from school. Not because I wanted to go into journalism at that point, but because it was a job,' she said, 'I spent 4 years progressing from making tea, to covering sports day at the local school and realised that, whilst I liked the job, it would be more interesting working for a national paper - so I started applying for jobs. Then I covered a story about a local fishing competition and all my ambition went away for the best part of two years because I had a whirlwind relationship with the runner-up, Kevin Shaw.'

She took a sip of coffee and stared out of the side window at the passing street lamps.

'With hindsight it was a huge mistake, because within weeks of our getting married I realised I didn't want to spend the rest of my life with a man whose main topic of conversation was fish,' she continued, 'Bored with him and alone most weekends while he sat on a riverbank somewhere, I ended up having an affair with the editor's wife.'

Chloe didn't see Branigan's expression change as his eyebrows shot up.

'We had quite an intense and kinky relationship which went wrong when her husband found out, and, with the subsequent fallout, I ended up without either a job or a marriage. I then moved to London and spent some months working at The Herald on what they laughingly call a "voluntary internship," hoping it would lead to a full-time job.'

'Does that mean you worked for them but weren't paid?' Branigan asked.

'Exactly,' Chloe continued, 'which was when I met Paige and we started having our fun together. It was great until it became clear there wasn't any prospect of a job at The Herald and with my meagre funds from the divorce dwindling I had to leave which was when I realised I had to get the right qualification if I wanted a job in mainstream media - hence my going to Sheffield.'

'Where they asked you to put a different slant on an old news story,' Branigan added.

'Yes,' Chloe agreed, 'and as soon as I got that assignment, I thought of you.'

'Why me?' Branigan asked.

'Because yours was the story Paige used to brag about publicly, but privately I know she doubted she ever got to the bottom of it.'

Intrigued, Branigan glanced across at Chloe.

'What makes you say that?'

'For starters because it wasn't the in-depth piece of investigative journalism Paige made it out to be when she bragged about it.'

Branigan frowned.

'How do you mean?' he asked.

'All Paige did was go to Bishkek to write some puff piece

on tourism and someone tracked her down at the hotel and fed the whole story to her.'

Branigan was stunned.

'What,' he exclaimed, 'you mean she didn't do anything to investigate the story?'

'Nothing - the documents were shoved under her hotel room door and she was given the details over the house phone.'

'She didn't even take any of the pictures?' Branigan asked incredulously.

Beside him Chloe shook her head.

This was news to Branigan who'd always thought Paige had done most of the groundwork for herself.

'There was someone staying in the hotel who fed her the story?' he asked, trying to make sense of this new information.

'Not necessarily,' Chloe replied, trying to recall her conversations with Paige, 'although the man spoke to her on the house phone, she said he wasn't in a room - just another part of the hotel. He called himself Cressix and even though Paige tried to, she never got to see him.'

'But he was physically in Bishkek?' Branigan asked as he realised the significance of what Chloe had just said.

'Yes, Paige was sure of that.'

02:59 Stoke Newington, London

'Forensics have confirmed matches on partials they lifted from both the cable ties used to strangle the victims,' DS Drake said as he entered the DCI's room.

DCI Tenant closed the folder he was reading and leaned back with an air of smugness.

'What did I tell you, Drake,' he said with satisfaction, 'Branigan is our man - or do you still have doubts?'

'I still have an open mind, sir,' Drake replied, 'because it would be easy to argue those prints got there when he took the cable ties off the victims.'

Tenant shook his head.

'That's for the jury to decide; besides, we've nearly ticked all the boxes,' he continued holding up three fingers on his right hand and pointing to each in turn 'motive, means and opportunity. Motive - we've already got a neighbour who says his wife wasn't happy with him after he missed his own daughter's birthday - what you and the team need to focus on is where he went, what he did and if there's another woman involved.'

Drake shrugged resignedly and made a note in his book.

'Means - well we've already got that covered with the cable ties, and by the time we have the DNA results back we'll be home and dry on that point,' Tenant said, before moving on to his third finger. 'Opportunity - there's nothing to argue on this Drake, because the idiot left us a bloody note at the scene, and no doubt you've already sent that off for DNA matching and handwriting analysis.'

Drake nodded and made a mental note to do just that.

'Which means there isn't any doubt, is there?' Tenant said, posing his rhetorical question without waiting for Drake to reply.

'Now we need to build our case with witness statements and circumstantial evidence - anything which helps point to his motive - because if ever there was a man who should be behind bars, it's Branigan!'

Tenant punctuated his statement by sliding a press cutting out from the top of the folder he'd just been reading. It was the five-year-old front page from one of the Sunday tabloids. The front page was filled entirely by a picture of Branigan holding a large wad of cash - underneath there was a single word headline.

"Traitor!"

02:59 A1 Southbound to London

'You need to hear my side of the story now,' Branigan said

as he drained the last of his coffee.

'Two weeks before everything went wrong in Kyrgyzstan I was working undercover on a wholly unrelated job in Syria,' he began, his eyes fixed on the road ahead as he cast his mind back, 'when I got called to a meeting across the border in Beirut where I met my then boss, Alex Oldroyd, who told me he needed me to help with a "problem" as he called it in Kazakhstan.'

'Kazakhstan and not Kyrgyzstan?' Chloe queried.

'Yes,' Branigan agreed, 'arms were being smuggled down from Russia through both countries and a colleague I'd known since training - Ed Khan - had been killed whilst following a shipment. It wasn't the most enticing job offer I'd ever received - stepping into the shoes of a man who'd been bound, beaten and left with half his guts hanging out.'

Chloe screwed her face up in disgust.

'How horrible; and they'd killed him because they found out who he was?'

'I guess so.'

Chloe frowned.

'You were working with the Russians and not against them?'

'Believe it or not, these days we work together in some theatres and against them in others - it seemed that someone in their camp was leaking information to the people running the arms and the hope was that if London used its network there wouldn't be a leak; based on what happened to Ed you can imagine how I saw that prospect when I arrived in Orsk.'

'Where?' Chloe asked.

'Orsk, it's a town in Russia just across the border from Kazakhstan,' Branigan explained, 'I met my Russian counterpart there before posing as a freelance driver looking to take a load back home to Kyrgyzstan. The haulage market there is something of a free-for-all and when the consignment we were interested in came up I undercut everyone to offer my services.'

'Weren't people suspicious if you pitched low for the work?' Chloe asked.

'Not really, you see drivers who've already been paid to deliver loads one way will often accept low paid jobs on their journey home to avoid returning empty - everyone just thought I was eager to get back to my family and didn't want to drive all that way empty-handed.'

Chloe nodded her understanding.

'I'm sure it isn't significant, but coincidentally I saw my Russian counterpart from back then in London on Friday evening: Anatoly Kozlow,' Branigan added.

A crease appeared above the bridge of Chloe's nose as she frowned.

'That sounds a bit too much of a coincidence,' she suggested.

'I know, but he no longer works for Russian Intelligence, and it was only a piece of low-level surveillance my boss sent me on because I know what Anatoly looks like - I can't see that it's linked to what's happening now,' Branigan said, brushing aside her concern before continuing with his story, 'So I picked up my container with my beaten-up old Kamaz truck and joined seven others in a convoy. To make sure we weren't ambushed - and probably that we didn't rob the contents of our own loads - we were accompanied by fourteen surly militia who rode in our cabs and in pickup trucks at the front and rear of our convoy.'

'You had an armed guard in with you?' Chloe asked.

'Yes, Vladimir, a retired Russian soldier who sat next to me stony-faced and holding his AK47 at the ready for the whole 2-day trip - the only time he really spoke was when he had a vodka inside him. The first night we stopped in Kazakhstan and the second in Talas, a mountainous area just over the border in Kyrgyzstan. Everyone was more relaxed by then and we bought food and drink from street vendors and I kept buying the home-brew vodka which came in jam jars; it was practically raw alcohol! I plied everyone with it until they were more-or-less passing out, waited for them to fall asleep and then opened up my container.'

Chloe shifted uneasily. She couldn't imagine what it felt like to put yourself in such danger.

'Our intel was right and despite the manifest saying I was carrying metal-working tools and a generator, it was crammed with explosives, small arms, land mines and a couple of field mortars.'

'I took loads of pictures, shut the container back up and had a heart-stopping moment when Vladimir came around the back as I was reattaching the seal.'

Chloe let out a little gasp of fright.

'It turned out he was taking a piss and was still so drunk he thought I was doing the same. When he'd gone back to sleep, I used a satellite phone I had concealed in the cab to send the pictures to London.'

'The next day everyone was nursing hangovers as we drove to Bishkek where I delivered the container to a local freight forwarder - that's where the photograph in the papers came from; it was me being paid for the transport with a bundle of the worthless local currency.'

'I hung around to see who collected the load, but never did find out anything more because Paige's story broke and I was called back to London where, with my cover well and truly blown, SIS invoked Rule 31 and kicked me the fuck out.'

'Rule 31?' Chloe asked.

'Yes, Rule 31 is the Service's get-out clause if something goes wrong - it says if we allow our cover to be blown, they'll disown us and kick us out.'

'Wow,' Chloe exclaimed, 'that's pretty draconian.'

'It's what I signed up to, so I wasn't surprised,' Branigan said with a shrug, 'and I went off into the sunset, got a job with Marty and married Sally.'

His voice caught as he mentioned his wife's name and he

cleared his throat before continuing.

'And, because I'd moved on, I never thought about where Paige got her information - I just became bitter and twisted about what she'd done with it.'

'I'm probably being really thick here,' Chloe said, 'but I can't see the significance of Paige's source in all of this.'

'It's the timing and the fact they were in Bishkek which matters,' Branigan explained.

'Think about it,' he continued, 'someone was in Bishkek to shove papers under Paige's door within 48 hours of my sending the photographs of the contents of the container to London - that person was either in Bishkek already or dropped everything to get there that quickly.'

Chloe nodded contemplatively.

'Yes, but that could have been anyone - it doesn't help us much,' she said.

'On the contrary, it helps us hugely,' Branigan said, realising it was time to tell her about his conversation with Marty, 'you see I think the link between your article and what happened to me in Bishkek is one of the six people who dreamed up Operation Peach Tree.'

Chloe let out a short nervous laugh.

'Yes, but that's fictitious - I made it up for my story,' she said.

'You may have made it up,' Branigan replied, 'but you chose the same name as had already been dreamed up by six drunken spies in some kind of after-dinner game - I think one of those six wanted the container to turn their fantasy into reality.'

CHAPTER 13

03:34 Police Station, North London

'Fucking typical!' DS Drake swore as he stared at the "Out of Order" sign stuck to the vending machine.

'No time to be messing around with that, Detective Sergeant,' DCI Tenant said as he swept down the corridor towards him, 'we've got work to do and a team to brief.'

Reluctantly Drake followed the Chief Inspector back into the briefing room where the specially assembled team they'd called in were preparing to get the hunt for Branigan underway. Stepping to the front of the room DCI Tenant quietened the bleary-eyed crew of 8 detectives to the point where the words "three o'clock" and "fucking ridiculous" became a soft murmur.

'I know you don't appreciate being dragged in,' Tenant began, 'but we have a double murder, a suspect, and - provided we can get our man - the opportunity to bring this one home quickly. I've been working on this overnight with DS Drake and he's going to give you a briefing after on what you'll find is an open and shut case. We've got partials on the murder weapon, can place our suspect at the scene, and - if the lab delivers - DNA to back-up a water-tight case. What I need from you is a concrete motive and to find him.'

He began reeling off the actions needed.

'Friends, neighbours, employers, work colleagues - find out everything you can about him, especially his movements. Phone records, known haunts and any gossip you can get on his relationship at home. I cannot emphasise enough that I want us to get our culprit; let's nail Branigan today.'

03:47 Hendon, North London

'Is Alan's house near here?' Chloe asked hopefully as they turned off the North Circular near Wembley.

'I'm afraid not,' Branigan replied, following the signs to the station car park, 'the police will work out where we are if we park near Alan's - so we're leaving the car at a station and walking the rest of the way.'

Chloe, her eyelids already drooping with the lateness of the hour, was less than happy.

'Walk!' she exclaimed, 'surely if we're at a station we can catch a train?'

'Yes, we can,' Branigan replied patiently, 'and then we'll be photographed on every CCTV camera between here and our destination; what you have to hope for is that we can catch a bus or find a taxi somewhere which will shorten the journey, otherwise we have a 2- or 3-mile hike ahead of us.'

He guided the BMW into the carpark at Wembley Station and found a space in a quiet corner.

'Now we start walking,' he announced, taking the leather grip bag he'd brought from home and a rucksack he'd found at work out of the trunk of the car.

They walked for 20 minutes before catching a night bus which took them nearer their goal and then continued on foot for another 10 or 15 minutes through side streets before Branigan pointed to the amorphous shape of Alan's VW camper van wrapped up in a silvery cover.

'This is it,' he whispered.

'Thank goodness,' Chloe said softly, her voice muffled by the scarf wrapped across her face, 'I'm freezing.'

Opening a small wooden gate, Branigan walked up the short path to the front door and tapped gently.

When there was no reply he tapped again.

When there was still no reply, he dialled a number and spoke softly into the phone and a few moments later Alan swung the door open.

Branigan was used to Alan's strange attire at work - the starched shirts, bowties and brightly coloured cardigans ceased to be that unusual when you saw them every day.

He wasn't prepared for Alan to be wearing a bulgingly-tight version of Mr. Spock's blue and black uniform and to greet them with a wide-fingered Vulcan salute.

'Live long and prosper,' Alan said as he opened the door.

Having never before visited Alan's home, Branigan had no idea what to expect.

His immediate impression was of a traditional Victorian town house with two reception rooms split by folding doors at the front of the building, a kitchen at the back on the ground floor, two main bedrooms, a bathroom and a box room on the first floor.

Two elements of Alan's version of the archetypal home made it stand out.

Firstly, the furniture, decor and fabric of the house were trapped in a 1980s time warp - having a son who didn't like change meant that Alan's parents left everything exactly as it was from his childhood, a tradition Alan was happy to continue after his parents' death.

Secondly, amidst the sofa and chairs with crocheted head rests and wooden arms, Alan had introduced computers.

A lot of computers.

As Alan showed Branigan and Chloe around the house, Branigan was acutely aware that the building seemed to be heated not by its boiler, but rather the comprehensive array of hardware surrounding the enormous desk in the living room.

As he climbed the stairs and took in the garish carpet, Branigan sensed a change in the atmosphere - not only was the ambient temperature warmer, but also there was the low hum of electricity pervading the landing.

Alan proudly swung the door of the spare bedroom open.

'This is my server room,' he explained excitedly.

Branigan and Chloe stared open-mouthed at the three rows of floor to ceiling metal cabinets which occupied the room.

It was clear there wasn't space to explore the room, so Branigan peered through the open door as Alan beamed proudly beside him.

'Those are all computers?' he asked, pointing to the blinking lights on the neatly stacked equipment inside each cabinet.

'No,' Alan said with a puzzled expression, 'of course not - some are patch boards, routers and power supplies.'

'You must have more computing power here than the whole of the office!' Branigan observed, exchanging a wide-eyed glance with Chloe.

'Oh yes,' Alan replied earnestly, his voice betraying no emotion, 'several times more.'

Branigan looked sideways at Alan and wondered why he needed enough computing power in his spare bedroom to give GCHQ a run for its money.

'What do you need it for?' he asked.

'I like to have it just in case,' Alan replied.

Branigan shook his head in wonder.

Like having 30 steak and kidney pies in the larder: just in case.

Chloe and Branigan both declined Alan's offer of one of those pies before they each collapsed into their respective beds.

Alan in the room he'd always had - the small box room at the back of the house; Chloe in the main bedroom at the front of the house - Alan's mother's, untouched in any way since she'd died, other than to be cleaned and have the sheets changed every Monday; and Branigan on the floor of the dining room with a tapestry cushion for his head and a blanket to cover him.

Branigan was the last to fall asleep; by the time he did so the two pillowslips he'd brought from home to remind him of the scent of his two precious girls were wet with silent tears.

09:31 Chobham, Surrey

'Murdered?' Michael Jenkins exclaimed when Gregory Brown told the story for the third time that morning.

'Yes, but there seems to be some doubt as to whether Branigan did it or not - I'm just calling so you're aware and know that David Price and I are monitoring the situation.'

Gregory went on to explain how there was a suggestion that the Operation Peach Tree theory the six of them had expounded over dinner was at the root of the murders and he needed Michael to let him know if he heard anything about either Branigan or Chloe Travers.

'It goes without saying,' Gregory Brown said, 'that if anyone asks, the conversation about Peach Tree never happened.'

'Naturally,' Michael Jenkins agreed, 'I never dreamed when we sent him off to Kazakhstan that he'd cause so much trouble.'

'I don't think anyone believed that mess was down to either you or Alex,' Gregory Brown said in tactful understatement, referring to Alex Oldroyd, Michael Jenkins' deputy who'd been the man dealing with Branigan's failed operation on a day-to-day basis.

'Absolutely, it was that bloody reporter and Branigan himself who allowed her to get close to what was going on,' Michael railed, taking care to promote the Civil Service line on culpability - you claimed successes and blamed others for failures.

Clearly the embarrassing exposé was Branigan's fault.

'Lord knows how anyone can try and link that silly idea of ours to his fuck-up and the murder of his wife and child,' he continued, using the expletive to emphasise just how much the failed mission was Branigan's problem and not his.

'I agree,' Gregory Brown said in a conciliatory tone, 'and Alex said the same thing when I phoned him a few minutes ago.'

10:13 Euston Station

Marty still had a thick head from the night before.

He blamed it on the stress of Branigan's call, but a more astute observer would put it down to the half-tumbler of whisky he drank at home before collapsing into bed.

Aside from his thick head, Marty was tired because he'd had a poor night's sleep and a rude awakening call from Gregory Brown just after 7:00am.

Blearily searching the station for Branigan's familiar physique, he grunted grouchily as a brusque ticket collector barged into him.

Making no apology, the collector bent down, picked a train ticket off the floor and pressed it into Marty's hand.

'You've dropped this,' he said.

Marty glanced at the ticket as he watched the retreating crumpled grey suit, sloppy peaked hat and shambling gait of the unapologetic attendant - it was to Watford Junction and had "Platform 9" written across it. Following the signs to the platform, Marty was beckoned through the line of barriers by the rude ticket inspector who then insisted on leading him towards the front of the train.

Marty trailed past several coaches - each home to a smattering of passengers - before coming to the completely empty carriage indicated by the ticket inspector.

The electronic sign in the window read "Not in Service" in bold yellow letters.

Tentatively Marty climbed aboard.

Immediately there was a soft hiss and the ticket collector fiddled with the manual control panel for the doors as they shut.

'Right,' Branigan said, taking off the crumpled grey jacket

and putting it, the ticket machine and his hat down on the seat beside him, 'what the fuck is Operation Peach Tree all about?'

As he spoke there was a distant whistle, the train shuddered and then slowly moved out of the station.

'Geez Branigan,' Marty began, as bemused as ever by Branigan's ability to morph into the background, 'I didn't realise it was you - I thought you'd sent someone to fetch me.'

'Look,' he continued, 'I can't tell you how sorry I am about Sally and Molly; if there's anything I can do, it goes without saying.'

'You can,' Branigan replied, taking Marty up on the platitude, 'you can make sure their bodies are taken to Hendon Crematorium when the time is right. See that Molly has her bear with her and that Sally is holding a lock of Molly's hair.'

'It's unlikely I'm going to be able to claim their bodies so I need you to do it for me - as soon as possible.'

Marty was rendered speechless by the unexpected request.

'Of course,' he said when he recovered himself.

'Tell me what's happening,' Branigan prompted, keen to gather information.

'The Police have been on to me this morning, I'm due to meet them in about an hour,' Marty began, looking around the carriage unaware where they were heading, 'That's always assuming...'

'Yes, go on,' Branigan prompted.

'They clearly have you in their sights, Branigan - when they called this morning there was no hint of doubt, they simply said that they wanted to speak with me because you'd murdered your family and were on the run.'

Branigan nodded.

'And there's something else,' he continued hesitantly, 'the police in Sheffield have also phoned and want to send someone down to speak with me. It seems a bomb went off in an apartment there last night; do you know anything about that?'

Branigan gave no acknowledgement and waited for Marty to continue.

'They think the bomb was in a plastic biscuit tub you bought on the company credit card.'

Branigan snorted.

'These people are better than I gave them credit for,' he said, realising they'd opened the locked car and taken Alan's discarded crispy caramel bites tub with a view to incriminating him, 'I'm surprised they didn't find a shortbread wrapper and the remnants of a pasty as well.'

'Aside from being wanted for murder and causing an explosion,' Branigan continued, 'what reaction have you had from the others in your little group?'

Marty looked uncomfortable at the reference to his group - or "gang" as he liked to call them - the five others with whom he met regularly for alcohol-fuelled dinners and occasional rounds of golf.

'Marty, I need to know,' Branigan said, 'you can't go closing ranks with them.'

'Yes, well,' Marty said apologetically, 'they're all very sorry, but you're right - no one is going to stand up and admit that they discussed Operation Peach Tree; you're on your own I'm afraid.'

'I never expected anything different,' Branigan said with resignation, 'now, tell me what happened the night you dreamed it up.'

Marty braced himself - he didn't want to have this conversation, but in the circumstances he knew he couldn't deny Branigan.

'You know the six of us who meet once a month for dinner?'

Branigan nodded. It was an open secret that Marty regularly met "his gang" at the Special Forces Club in London's upmarket Knightsbridge. In fact, it was such an open secret, half the pictures in Marty's office were of him with his gang either playing golf or seated at a wine-laden table in The Club.

'Let me just check I have the names right,' Branigan said, recalling the group playing golf pictured in Marty's office and wishing he had Alan's ability to remember things, 'Gregory Brown, Alex Oldroyd, Michael Jenkins, David Price - and one other....'

'Peter Winstone,' Marty interjected as the train pulled into Queens Park station and a few waiting passengers tried to open the carriage door before realising it was out of commission.

'I'm going back maybe 5 or 6 years,' Marty continued, watching a young couple scurry past to the next carriage, 'when we were just shooting the breeze. Someone said something about wishing we had the same public support in the UK as did the Americans and then David Price said, "That's because we're too successful."'

Branigan pictured the man who'd fired him.

Intelligent, educated and outwardly everyone's idea of a favourite uncle, Branigan knew that beneath the easy-going, gentle and humorous exterior there was a calculating and steely interior.

'Of course, everyone jumped on that and said being successful was what we were all about and then David said, "Yes, but the trouble is the public don't respond to a safe pair of hands - they respond to a failure like 9/11."'

'That was how the discussion started,' Marty continued, 'no one could really deny that David was right. We all know the American security services missed lots of chances to stop 9/11, but because they didn't, they've become bigger and better funded. You must understand Branigan, none of us took this seriously, all we did was talk about what sort of terrorist event in the UK would have the same kind of impact on the British public as 9/11 did on the Americans; then we took it a stage further...'

Branigan waited.

'…and discussed how we could arrange it and keep the casualties to a minimum.'

Branigan's anger rose again.

'You've got to be kidding me,' he said, shaking his head, 'after what you all went through you wanted to do the same thing to your own people?'

'It was precisely because of what we went through that we had the conversation,' Marty snapped back, 'we didn't want something as bad to happen on our own soil, so talked about how to bolster support for the Service so we could prevent something like we witnessed that day.'

'In our minds a few casualties were worth the sacrifice,' Marty continued.

Branigan was disbelieving.

'Correct me if I'm wrong, but your "little gang" as you call it only started because you were all in New York for a security meeting in the World Trade Centre when the first plane struck - are you seriously telling me that something like that is worth recreating to help protect this country?'

'Do you want to hear me tell you about this thing or would you rather lecture me about my moral outlook?' Marty continued, now with a sullen edge to his voice.

He paused waiting for Branigan to acknowledge that he should continue.

'We then spent our time giving the idea a name, thinking about the type of event and working out the practicalities. We came up with the name pretty easily because it amused the strategists amongst us to cite General Wáng's 11th strategy - you know, "Sacrifice the plum tree to preserve the peach tree" - and then we spent ages talking about the type of event.'

Branigan shook his head in wonderment.

'What do you want me to say, "We gave the operation a name and then didn't discuss it?"' Marty asked testily, before resuming his recollection, 'There were three criteria as far as I recall, firstly it couldn't be planes and tall buildings because that had been done; secondly, the enduring image of the event mattered in the way we all still have the smoke billowing from the Twin Towers burned on our retina; and finally, we had to get the most impact from the fewest casualties.'

Branigan said nothing.

'Our ideas largely centred on transport because planes, trains and automobiles seemed to offer the best results.'

'We toyed with a number of events like sinking a liner, blowing up a train in the Channel Tunnel and destroying the Forth Road Bridge - most of which failed the test because of either the image or the number of casualties. If you look back at similar events, we all know about the Titanic, but then only because of the huge loss of life; the train in the tunnel doesn't produce an enduring image - just think of the dreadful fire at King's Cross; and while some of us can picture the Tacoma Narrows Bridge collapsing it's hardly an enduring image is it?'

Branigan chose not to dignify the question with a response.

Marty shrugged and carried on with his narrative.

'We were all wracking our brains when Alex Oldroyd suggested the Genbaku Dome as an enduring image.'

Branigan's heart missed a beat.

'You've got to be fucking kidding me,' he exclaimed, recalling the skeleton of the solitary domed building left standing in Hiroshima after the Enola Gay had flown overhead, 'you can't have been serious about nuking a city and killing tens if not hundreds of thousands!'

'Hear me out,' Marty said, 'we all had the same thought as you, but Alex said he wasn't talking about either the casualties or a nuclear bomb. No one, he argued, remembered the number who died in Hiroshima - they remembered the devastation.'

'So, Alex says, "What if you evacuated everyone and then blew the city up to leave a similar image?"'

'He went on to suggest that you could plant small bombs that would frighten people away from the area before you followed it up with big ones which would do the damage.'

'Then people began to come up with images that would really work, you know, like The Houses of Parliament still standing yet everything else around reduced to rubble.'

'Our flight of fancy just ran from there and we focused on wiping out famous landmarks and or leaving the landmark standing with devastation all around.'

'And did you narrow it down to any specific targets?' Branigan asked as the train slowed for the next stop.

'Yes,' Marty continued with all seriousness, 'we dismissed most of the West side of London because we all live and work there, and ended up with Stratford-upon-Avon, Windsor, Cambridge and the City of London on our list.'

'The finest minds in the intelligence community and that's what you come up with?' Branigan said as he thought of more obvious targets.

'What can I say, we were drunk?' Marty said defensively, 'We wanted a place the world would recognise. By the end of the evening the one which appealed to most people was that we evacuate the centre of Cambridge and then blow it up.'

Branigan caught a momentary glimpse of amusement in Marty's blue eyes.

'Presumably everyone round the table went to Oxford?' he asked.

'Three, anyway,' Marty acknowledged, 'the rest of us were red brick universities.'

'And that's it?' Branigan asked.

'Yes, Branigan, that's it,' Marty said with some finality.

'I don't see it,' Branigan said, pointing to the "Not in Service" sign as a woman tried in vain to open the doors at Willesden Junction, 'you'd need hundreds of tons of explosives to make an impact - even assuming you did manage to get everyone evacuated somehow – and let's face it, blowing up Anne Hathaway's Cottage hardly ranks alongside the

World Trade Centre in the scale of international atrocities!'

'I agree Branigan. We knew you couldn't do something like that with just one person, but then the idea of having a team of sleepers standing by with tons of explosives to hand didn't work either, so the whole concept petered out by the time we got to the port and cheese.'

'I don't buy it,' Branigan said, 'The idea that someone wants to stop a story about a bunch of pissed blokes chewing the cud over the dinner table just doesn't wash, I think someone wants to discredit Chloe Travers' story because it touched on a raw nerve with its reference to Operation Peach Tree - which can only mean one thing'

Branigan focused Marty with a steady gaze.

'Someone sitting at the dinner table has taken the idea and run with it,' he concluded.

'That's ridiculous,' Marty said with passion, 'I'd know if one of the guys in the gang was doing something like that.'

'Then how do you account for Black Ops being sent in to ruin the credibility of Chloe's story?'

'Are you sure it's Black Ops who are involved?' Marty countered.

'Who else is going to step into something like this and blow up an apartment,' Branigan said slowly, trying to contain his emotion, 'and set out to frame me for killing Sally and Molly?'

It was Marty's turn to remain silent.

'I can't think of anyone else either,' Branigan said, as the train crawled past the sidings at Stonebridge Park, 'and you know I'm right about the link with Chloe's story; I'm telling you Marty, Operation Peach Tree is up and running.'

As they neared Wembley Central Station, Branigan tossed Marty the key fob for the BMW and told him where he'd find his car, before putting the jacket and peaked cap back on.

'Thanks, Branigan,' Marty said hesitantly, 'so where do I find you if I need to?'

The train came to a stop and Branigan moved over to the

door release mechanism.

'You don't Marty,' he said, ushering his boss off the train, 'I'll find you.'

CHAPTER 14

11:03 Police Station, North London

'You're never going to believe this Drake,' DCI Tenant said, coming out of his office looking like he'd got the winning lottery ticket, 'I've just come off the phone to South Yorkshire Police - our man is only wanted up there too. It seems he planted a bomb in an apartment in Sheffield yesterday.'

Drake nodded, 'I heard about that on the news; what's his link to the explosion up there?'

'South Yorkshire phoned Branigan's boss because CCTV picked his car up near the scene of the explosion and it turns out Branigan used it to dash up to Sheffield on some pretext yesterday to see a girl called Chloe Travers,' Tenant explained.

'And guess whose apartment got blown up?' he continued, pausing for dramatic effect, 'Only Chloe Travers' and - in case that isn't enough for you - she herself has gone missing!'

Drake frowned.

'What are your thoughts - that he's on the run with her or she too is a victim?' he asked, trying to make sense of the information.

'South Yorkshire think the bomb was intended to kill her, but I don't see it - it's more likely that she's on the run with him, don't you agree? Think about it - Branigan has a girl on the side, makes an excuse to go and see her, then his wife finds out and he murders her in a fit of rage,' Tenant ventured, 'With his wife out of the way, he runs off with this Chloe Travers.'

'It still doesn't make sense to me,' Drake replied, shaking

his head bewilderedly, 'I don't see why he would blow up her apartment in the first place, let alone how. If the news had the timing right, the bomb went off when we have him down here killing his wife and child?'

Tenant waved his right hand dismissively.

'Let's not get distracted by details at the moment,' he said, 'I'm sure Mr Freeman will be able to throw some light on it all.'

11:23 Paige Henderson's Apartment, East End London

'Who is this?' Paige Henderson said testily, not recognising the number for the incoming call.

'This is either terribly important,' she continued after Chloe identified herself, 'or you've been doing an awful lot of drunken dialling!'

Paige had gone into the kitchen to make tea for herself and her current beau, Mitch - or "Master Mitch" as he liked to call himself - and found 23 missed calls on her phone; a record even for someone used to having a twitchy editor who panicked if an article didn't arrive on time.

Shamelessly naked, Paige moved around the counter which divided the small kitchen area from the rest of her living space so she could study herself in the mirror.

She ran her fingers through her slightly tousled raven hair and admired her flat stomach, pert ass, 27-year-old breasts and graceful legs which were accentuated by the 5-inch heels she'd "slipped on" to parade from the bedroom in search of the all-important cup of tea.

Had she been on her own, of course, Paige would never have donned her red fuck-me pumps to make the short walk from the bedroom, but she knew she had eyes watching and that he would be appreciative of what he saw.

She peered more closely at the mirror, looking deeply into her own brown eyes and then examining her seemingly perfect, Asian-tinged complexion for signs of any flaws.

'Paige, it's important,' Chloe began.

'Before you get onto your gossip, I have some of my own,' Paige cut in while continuing to study her reflection in the mirror, 'I had a break in yesterday.'

She continued to speak over Chloe's protests, at the same time changing her pose and half-twisting round so she could examine the red blush and inter-linked Master Mitch-shaped hand prints which brought a tingling glow to her buttocks.

'Yes, the bastards smashed through my front door and turned the place upside down. They stole my computer and back-up thingy, but fortunately nothing else. It took me forever to tidy up but I was lucky - any thief worth their salt would have realised the value of some of my designer handbags and gone for those. Can you imagine?'

Chloe managed to cut in while Paige paused for breath and contemplated the catastrophe of her beige Birkin bag being stolen.

'Listen to me,' Chloe implored, 'there's something big happening and your break in may even be linked to it. I'm with Branigan and we're in trouble.'

'What, you need me to join in - I'd enjoy a threesome with him, he looks quite hunky - or did his wife find out?' Paige quipped.

'No, Paige, his wife and daughter have been murdered,' Chloe replied.

For the first time since answering the phone Paige stopped focusing on her reflection in the mirror and switched her attention to Chloe. Kicking off her shoes and sweeping a roll of plastic tape and a blindfold off a kitchen barstool, she perched at the work surface and moved a pad in front of her.

'What's the story?' she asked.

Chloe went on to outline the events of the previous day, while Paige scribbled notes furiously.

'Can I attribute all of this?' she asked when Chloe concluded her narrative with their flight from Birmingham -

missing out telling her where they were staying.

'Christ, no, certainly not at the moment!' Chloe exclaimed, 'I'm not telling you this to give you a story - I'm telling you this so you can be on your guard, because something I've put into my version of your story has upset the establishment. I need your help in finding out what it is and working out who's behind the murders.'

'I guess,' Paige said, putting down her pencil, 'but if we get to the bottom of it, can I then have the exclusive?'

Chloe could picture Paige pouting at the other end of the phone.

'It was my story in the first place, so it seems only fair.'

Chloe didn't dignify Paige's request with an acknowledgement - fighting over the rights to the story was like arguing over the colour of the lifebelts when the ship was sinking.

'So how soon can I come and see you?' Chloe asked.

Paige was examining the rope marks on her wrists.

'Well I've been a little tied up at this end - which, incidentally, is why you and Branigan couldn't get hold of me - and I need to sort out some loose ends,' Paige said, thinking about Master Mitch currently dozing in the bedroom, before casting her eye over the discarded clothes, lengths of rope, cuffs and other bondage paraphernalia scattered around the room, 'shall we say 3 o'clock?'

'Okay,' Chloe said, 'I'll be with you for then.'

'Great,' Paige said, 'and wear something sexy - we might have time to play a little as well!'

'I don't think that's going to happen, Paige,' Chloe said, shaking her head at the irascibility of her friend, 'before I go, can you just do me a favour - can you check that the file about Branigan is still there; you know, the one you let me look through for background?'

'Of course,' Paige said, 'but I'm sure I'd have noticed if anything else was missing.'

Only when she still couldn't find the file five minutes later did Paige begin to believe Chloe's assertion that it too had been stolen.

11:31 Police Station, North London

Marty took the seat opposite the two detectives in the small windowless interview room, relieved at least to be offered a cup of coffee; his headache had, if anything, worsened since sitting on the train with Branigan.

'Did you drive here this morning, Mr. Freeman?' DCI Tenant asked.

Marty nodded.

'And this is the same vehicle Mr Branigan used yesterday?' the DCI asked.

'Yes,' Marty replied, working out the logistics of collecting the car without admitting he had met with Branigan a short while ago, 'Branigan called me earlier and told me it was in the station car park at Wembley and I caught a train to fetch it.'

'That's quite a long journey for you. Did Mr. Branigan tell you why he left the car there?'

'No, he didn't.'

'Did he tell you where he was when he called you?'

'No, sorry,' Marty said.

'And where did he leave the key for the car?'

Befuddled as he felt, Marty was still one step ahead.

'He left it on one of the wheels.'

'The car is here is it?'

'Yes, it's parked outside,' Marty said before giving the make, model and registration.

'Good, and may I have the key please?' DCI Tenant said, holding out his hand.

Marty looked at him quizzically.

'Because we're going to need to impound it and put it through a forensic examination.'

Marty cursed - maybe not one step ahead after all.

'I know it is an inconvenience, but the car has been involved in a bomb-related incident and - aside from the usual forensics - you'd be surprised what we can glean from the satnav and onboard computer these days,' DCI Tenant said, handing the key to Drake, 'To save us time running through the car's version of events, what can you tell me about Branigan's movements since yesterday morning?'

Marty began by explaining about the couple purporting to be Chloe's parents calling and pleading with him to help find their missing daughter.

'And you don't believe these people were her parents?' Tenant asked.

'No,' Marty replied, 'not now - Branigan told me that the girl's father lives in Australia.'

'You think these were accomplices of Branigan's sent to set up a spurious trail?'

'I don't know that. I believe they were sent to encourage Branigan to go to Sheffield - beyond that I don't know.'

DCI Tenant leaned back in his chair confidently.

'And can you think of one person, other than Mr. Branigan himself, who would benefit from his racing off to Sheffield?'

Marty paused.

'No, I can't,' he said.

'And has Branigan ever mentioned this girl Chloe Travers before?'

Marty shook his head. They were barking up the wrong tree, but there was little he could do without telling them of the news article, Operation Peach Tree and Black Ops; to do that would mean breaking the silence to which he'd agreed.

'No, he's a happily married man.'

DCI Tenant snorted.

'Isn't everyone,' he said with such bitterness DS Drake wondered whether all was well at home for his DCI, 'but for a moment let's just assume he is in a relationship with this girl; you're a detective Mr Freeman, can you see a compelling pattern emerging?'

Marty shook his head.

The DCI leaned across the table.

'Branigan wants to be with this girl and he comes up with an "emergency" at work and dashes off to see her,' he said, using his fingers to draw the quotation marks in the air, 'and he not only gets out of attending a kiddies party, but also gives himself an alibi for when he kills his wife and child.'

Marty shook his head vehemently.

'You've got this wrong,' he said.

'Just hear me out,' the DCI replied, 'because from where I'm sitting this makes perfect sense, and everything went according to plan except you messed things up for him by sending Mr Armstrong along with him - I take it that was your idea and not Branigan's?'

Marty had to concede it was.

For Tenant this was further confirmation that their working hypothesis was correct.

'You see?' he said, turning to DS Drake.

The questioning continued for nearly three quarters of an hour, during which time DCI Tenant established to his own satisfaction that Branigan was the perpetrator of all the previous day's events.

'All we need to do is find him now,' he assured Marty.

'I should warn you,' Marty sa

id to the DCI having being pointed in the direction of the train station, 'you're chasing the wrong man if you think Branigan is behind all this - if he set out to do this there wouldn't be a trail.'

11:45 Alan's House, North London

Even before he stepped through the front door of the house, Branigan could see that Alan had been shopping.

The cover was missing from Mabel - his red VW camper van - and as he stepped into the hallway, he was greeted by two enormous cardboard boxes, a pile of polystyrene packaging, a roll of heavy black plastic sheeting and sundry tools including a length of sturdy chain.

'What's happening?' Branigan asked, taken aback by the sight of Alan holding an electric drill and wearing white coveralls with the hood pulled up, protective goggles, latex surgical gloves and a dust mask.

'I'm just putting up televisions, so we can display everything,' he replied, his voice muffled from behind the mask.

Branigan wasn't immediately sure how the televisions would help them with evidence which amounted to nothing more than Chloe's article and a photo of Marty and his buddies playing golf.

'Alan, you can't go spending money on things like these,' he said, looking at the ultra-thin TV's propped against the wall near the kitchen, 'they're ridiculously expensive for what we need.'

Alan looked a little crestfallen.

'But I've got nothing else to buy with my money,' he said, sounding a little like a small boy caught with a pocket bulging with sweets.

'And the plastic and other bits?' Branigan asked.

'Oh, they're for Halloween,' Alan replied without elucidating.

Not wanting to ridicule his efforts, Branigan helped by holding the mounting plates and then the enormous TV's as Alan drilled into the brickwork and screwed everything in place.

'You know we're going to have to be careful, don't you?' Branigan asked.

'Why?' Alan asked in his muffled voice.

'The police are going to want to interview you because you were with me yesterday. If they come here and see a giant electronic incident board on the wall as they come in, they're going to smell a rat.'

'Oh, is that all,' Alan said, 'I've thought of that.'

Branigan waited in vain for Alan to explain.

'Where's Chloe?' he asked when it became apparent that

Alan had nothing more to add.

'She's upstairs getting dressed. She wanted some fresh clothes and, although I offered her some of mother's, she wanted to get some of her own - so we went to the supermarket on the way to the electronics and hardware stores.'

Whilst not happy that Chloe was venturing out, Branigan could see her predicament. The pictures of Alan with his family suggested the genes which influenced his stature and portly build had come from his mother's side. Somehow, he didn't see Chloe as the sort of girl who wanted to wear a voluminous floral print dress with a vaguely musty smell.

As if on cue, Chloe appeared at the top of the stairs looking fresh and ready for the day in a new pair of jeans and a white cotton blouse.

'How did you get on?' she asked.

'Well, I saw Marty,' Branigan replied, waiting for her at the bottom of the stairs before starting to lead the three of them into the living room, spotting the enormity of Alan's desk and turning to lead everyone into the kitchen, 'and have some idea of what we're up against.'

He went on to outline his Marty's assertions that Operation Peach Tree was aimed at mass destruction of property and the idea petered out by the time they were on their first glass of port.

'Assuming you two are still in, we need a plan to identify who is behind this, which means trying to identify which one of Marty and his mates travelled to Bishkek when Paige encountered Cressix.'

Alan nodded enthusiastically.

'And we can track the container to see where it went,' he said.

'Yes, but how do we do that - there are millions of containers all over the world - it's like looking for a needle in a haystack,' Chloe said, feeling Branigan's frustration.

'We use the serial number, which we know ends in Q7975349552,' Alan replied, looking slightly hurt, 'that would narrow the search considerably.'

Branigan broke the stunned silence.

'How do you know the serial number?' he asked.

'Because there was a picture of the container on Chloe's wall yesterday - I can put it up on the screen as soon as I've got it working, or I can print it off now if you prefer, but you'll find that's the part of the serial number showing in the photograph.'

'You've remembered that?' Chloe asked in amazement.

'Yes,' Alan said, puzzled that Chloe should think it remarkable.

Although taken aback, Branigan was piecing together the rest of what Alan had just said.

'You've got pictures of all the stuff that was on Chloe's wall?' he asked, recalling the little man snapping away frenetically.

'Yes, plus of course any others that were on the hard drive.'

Chloe gasped.

'You've got a copy of my hard drive?'

'Just the data files, there wasn't any point in copying your operating system - it was out of date.'

'You've got all my documents, emails and things like that?'

'I just said that, didn't I - what else would I mean by data files?' Alan replied sharply.

'That's brilliant, Alan, well done,' Branigan said, realising the importance of what Alan had said and prioritising his plan.

Strategy; the next thing on the list if he was going to counterattack.

'That decides what we need to do,' Branigan said decisively.

'They bombed your room for a reason,' he began, looking at Chloe, 'so you need to look at everything you had on the wall to see if you can work out what you had there they might want destroyed - after that, Alan can set you up to do the same with your computer files.'

'Alan, I need you to start looking to see what you can find on our six candidates - we need to know the whereabouts of each of our suspects a week before I was fired, and see which one of them might have dashed to Bishkek. Also, and this is a lower priority, can you try and trace the container - it's a long shot, but it might help tell us who is behind this and what they are planning.'

'Aye, Captain,' Alan said in a passable imitation of Scotty, the engineer on the Star Ship Enterprise, 'but I can't change the laws of physics.'

Chloe and Branigan exchanged glances.

'I'll make a start on it now,' Chloe said, 'but I'm going out to see Paige at 3:00 o'clock this afternoon.'

Branigan's eyebrows rose questioningly.

Chloe went on to run through her conversation with Paige - choosing to miss out the references to "Master Mitch" - and explaining that she hoped to compare notes and look for anomalies with her friend.

Immediately Branigan latched onto the break in.

'They took her computer, back-up and file about the story?'

'Yes, that's right. She didn't believe the file was missing at first until I asked her to check.'

'That's interesting, don't you think?'

'What is?' Chloe asked, not understanding Branigan's point.

'They broke in yesterday morning when I was with the two people posing as your parents - which suggests there are more than just the two Black Ops people we know about. I'm surprised they chose the same time to break in to Paige's as the rest of the team were with Marty and me - but perhaps we'll see an explanation when we go to Paige's.'

'We?' Chloe queried.

'Yes, I'm not letting you take any risks without me being there to help.'

Alan held his hand halfway up.

'I have a question.'

'Yes?' Branigan asked.

'I have a roast for Sunday lunch, are you both okay if we eat at one o'clock?'

Branigan nodded his agreement as he exchanged a look with Chloe - neither of the two was sure how Alan proposed to prepare a roast lunch from scratch in fifteen minutes - a conundrum solved a moment later as he opened one of the kitchen cupboards.

'I didn't know you could buy roast beef in tins,' Branigan said, eyeing the neatly stacked tins of roast beef, boiled potatoes and garden peas.

CHAPTER 15

14:58 Apartment, Limehouse E14

Branigan and Chloe made their way cautiously down an alley between two run-down council houses as they neared the cul-de-sac in which Paige lived. Grabbing Chloe's arm before she marched across the road, Branigan held back and studied the line of parked cars to their left and the litter-strewn playground opposite where a group of youths sat on the swings furtively smoking.

'Where does Paige live?' he asked.

'It's that building over there,' Chloe said, indicating a modern 5-storey apartment built in the shadow of a 1950s redbrick tenement, 'on the top floor.'

They waited as a woman wearing an ill-fitting pink tracksuit was dragged past by a Rottweiler which was intent on getting to the small patch of grass by the playground.

'Okay,' Branigan replied, tightening his grip, 'there's a man and a woman watching the front of the building in that grey Audi with chrome wheels.'

It took Chloe a few moments to find the car to which he was referring, and only then because the shiny chrome wheels stood out. The occupants - a man wearing sunglasses in the driver's seat and a woman passenger - were staring fixedly at the apartment building.

'They're not the people I met in Marty's office,' Branigan said in a low voice.

Having struggled to spot them amongst the randomly parked cars, Chloe was awe-struck that Branigan spotted the couple at all.

'We're lucky they're being lazy and staying in the car,' Branigan observed, 'because it makes them stand out.'

'Will there be others?' Chloe asked, nervously looking from the back of the ungainly woman in the tracksuit to the furtive smokers.

'No, it's a waste having even two people on a speculative stakeout,' Branigan explained, 'but they'll be able to call up for reinforcements if they spot us.'

'What do we do now?' Chloe asked.

'We either march up to the front of the building - which is risky even if we're disguised - or see if we can get in at the back. It's too light for us to start clambering over fences to get behind the building, someone's bound to spot us and we'll end up with the police here too,' Branigan said, his eyes continually scanning the scene in front of him, 'so we're going to need some kind of diversion to let us walk up beside the apartment.'

Chloe looked up the street to the driveway between Paige's block and the tenement, and wondered how they could create a diversion which would allow them to cross the road and go in that way without being spotted.

'How on earth do we do that?' she asked.

'We wait,' Branigan replied, leaning casually against the wall of the alley to give himself as wide a view of the street as possible.

The scent from a joint being passed around by the youths in the playground hung in the air as they waited. Branigan stiffened a couple of times as cars drove up, turned in front of them and headed back down the road. They pretend to be lovers holding each other close to appease the suspicious gaze of the pink track-suited lady when she returned with her much less eager Rottweiler. At one point the passenger got out of the Audi and paced up and down while she smoked a cigarette, allowing them both to study her from a distance. Wearing a green waxed jacket, she was younger than the woman Branigan had seen in Marty's office the day before and her slightly crazy blonde curls gave her a distinctive appearance.

Then they got their break.

A supermarket delivery van rounded the corner and made its way up the road towards them, the driver peering at the numbers on the buildings as he crawled along the road and turned around right in front of them.

'This is it,' Branigan cautioned, 'he's turning around and going back down the road towards the Audi. When I say run, get in close behind the truck and move down the road using it as a screen.'

Which is exactly what Chloe did until Branigan shoved her towards the driveway to the side of Paige's building, timing it to perfection so the two of them had disappeared from the view of the car's occupants by the time the delivery van moved on.

'Crikey,' Chloe said breathlessly, 'that gets the adrenalin pumping, doesn't it?'

'If you think that's bad, you should try doing it under hostile fire,' Branigan replied, leading Chloe through the rear gate and up the short path to the back door of the building.

Chloe raced to keep up as he climbed the five flights to Paige's apartment where he showed not the slightest sign of exertion, pausing to examine the damage around the lock before knocking. Throwing her door open, Paige appeared at the threshold like Fräulein Sally Bowles erupting onto the stage in Cabaret. Overly made-up, under-dressed and very dramatic.

As she swept back the fringe of her jet-black hair, Branigan caught a flash of striking blue eyes before being struck by her shapely figure and the ridiculously short black cocktail dress which definitely wasn't meant to be worn with stockings and suspenders. Glancing down at Paige's towering black stilettos, Branigan was sure her expectations for the afternoon were far removed from his and Chloe's - an observation confirmed by the look of disappointment on Paige's face when she saw that Chloe wasn't alone.

'Oh,' she said as if she'd just stepped onto the stage to find the auditorium empty, 'I didn't realise you were bringing a friend.'

Quick to adapt to a changing situation, Paige looked Branigan up and down.

'I suppose he can join in if ...' she continued, her voice trailing away as she realised who Chloe had brought.

Most people coming face-to-face with someone they'd all-but ruined with a few strokes of their pen would have flinched, been embarrassed or even apologised. Not Paige. Realising Chloe had a news story with her, the vamp on the doorstep vanished and was replaced by Paige the solicitous journalist.

'Oh, you poor man,' she said, stepping forward to take Branigan gently by the arm, 'I'm so sorry to hear your news - come in and tell me all about it,'

As she steered both her guests inside, Paige took her notepad off the work surface and waved in the direction of the sofa.

Branigan had other ideas.

'Sorry, Paige,' he said, refusing to sit down and taking the pad from her hand, 'we're not here for a cosy chat.'

Branigan used every ounce of his self-control to keep polite and calm as he manoeuvred Paige to a vacant armchair and passed her a cushion to place on her over-exposed lap.

'This is serious Paige,' he began, as Chloe perched on the edge of the nearby sofa, 'not only have my family been murdered but also our lives are in danger. Chloe's apartment was destroyed by an explosion last night and there are two people watching for us outside here right now.'

Paige studied Branigan closely as he returned to the front door and ran his hand over the inside of the frame. This was the first time she'd met him and, despite the circumstances, her initial impression was favourable.

He was strong, obviously very fit and his chiselled features and olive-coloured skin combined to make him far more attractive in the flesh than he appeared in the few photographs she'd seen. Deeper than that, however, was his quiet air of command - it was a long time since anyone had stopped her dead in her tracks, wrested her notebook from her and made it perfectly clear that she should do as she was told. The penetrating gaze from his deep brown eyes swallowed her when he turned back.

'That frame has been broken before - was that in your time?' he asked.

'No,' Paige replied, eager to please, 'one of the neighbours told me the people who lived here before were drug dealers and had it broken down in a police raid.'

Branigan nodded.

That made perfect sense; whoever had broken in this time had been lucky - the frame was already weak.

'And they took what?' he asked.

'My laptop, back-up drive and a file from the spare room I use as a study.'

Paige stood up and led Branigan to one of the three doors leading off the hallway and swung it open to reveal a small bedroom crammed with a single bed, a desk, wardrobe and chest of drawers.

'It was in there,' she said, bending down to indicate the bottom drawer and pausing a little longer than was strictly necessary, 'they turned everything out and left a terrible mess.'

Inwardly Branigan noted Paige's behaviour and moved on with his probing.

'That's how you found it then,' he asked, 'with the door kicked in and the place turned upside down?'

'Yes,' Paige agreed, 'they'd even emptied all my toys out in the bedroom and just left those strewn around.'

Bothered that the burglary didn't fit with the bigger picture, Branigan shook his head in frustration.

'Okay,' he said decisively, leading Paige back into the living room, 'before you sit down again, can you look out of the window - are there two people in a grey Audi parked across the road facing the front door of this building?'

Paige peered out of the window.

'Yes,' she said, 'are they the ones looking for you?'

'I think so,' Branigan explained, 'it's the first time either of us has seen those two, but I'm sure they're with the people who killed my family.'

'Can't you just call the police and have them arrested?'

Branigan shook his head wryly.

'If only it were that simple, but they've left a trail which makes me look guilty and if I call the police, I'll be the one being arrested.'

For the first time since they'd arrived the look of concern on Paige's face looked genuine.

'Oh my God!' she whispered.

'Which gets me to the main reason we're here,' Branigan said, pulling from his pocket the copy of Chloe's article he'd retrieved from her bin and passing it to Paige, 'something in this version of the story has upset someone enough for them to murder indiscriminately. Start by telling me how you found the story in the first place.'

Paige glanced at the document in her hand and nodded.

'I was staying in The Hyatt in Bishkek, writing a piece for the travel section,' she explained, flattening the article out on the cushion on her lap, 'and I was struggling, trust me, once you've covered the history - which begins and ends with the Mongols, the lovely mountains and their heritage as a former Soviet State - there isn't much else to say.'

'One evening a note was slipped under my door asking me if I was interested in a story about a rogue British spy selling arms to the wrong side.'

Paige gave an unapologetic shrug.

'Naturally I was intrigued, so I contacted the sender and he gave me the story.'

Not the comprehensive explanation Branigan sought.

'How did you contact this person - Mr Cressix was it?' he asked patiently.

'There was a card with the message which gave an email address for Hubert Cressix, but, of course, I knew that wasn't his real name.'

Branigan nodded, making a mental note of the first name.

'Do you still have the note and the card or were they in the folder that was stolen?'

'I might have put the card in my index at work, but I'm sure the original note was in the stolen file.'

'Can you check,' Branigan asked, 'and see if there's anything else?'

Paige gave a short laugh.

'I can look, but I never keep anything worthwhile at work.'

Chloe helped explain.

'It's a cut-throat business and the last thing you want to do is leave any source material lying around for your colleagues to pinch.'

Branigan nodded in understanding.

'You had an email address, but Chloe said you also contacted Cressix on the hotel's house phone?'

'Yes, that's right, after the initial contact he emailed back with instructions and we spoke every time on the house phones in the hotel - he was very exact about that. I had to call from a phone in reception while he was across the hotel in the conference area.'

Branigan frowned.

'The hotel phones are the only way you communicated?'

'Yes, apart from the documents he shoved under my door.'

Branigan waited for Paige to elucidate.

'You know, the photographs of the arms in the container, of you receiving the cash, the shipping paperwork and your fake travel documents,' Paige explained.

Branigan looked to Chloe on the sofa and then back to

Paige.

'So, you published a story entirely fed to you by someone who was in Bishkek and had access to undercover documentation?' he said.

'Yes,' Paige agreed.

Branigan caught Chloe's eye. It was clear they had a lot to discuss.

'That's a huge help, thank you Paige, but I think we really should be going now.'

'When do I get my story in return?' Paige asked with a pout.

'When I've worked out what's going on here, I'll give you everything I can,' Branigan ventured.

'Thank you,' Paige acknowledged, putting the cushion and Chloe's article to one side and flashing Branigan a glimpse of virtually everything that was on offer under her short dress as she stood up.

'And what about you Chloe,' she continued, 'do you need to go now or can you hang around?'

Chloe gave a short laugh - her friend was incorrigible.

'I think I need to be going now too.'

Paige was unruffled.

'Okay, well next Saturday is the last of the month, so it's party night at JJ's - I'm already going with Marta and Hanako, do you fancy coming?'

'I don't know if I'll be able,' Chloe replied, 'it depends whether or not we've sorted this out.'

Branigan felt a dark shadow pass over him. Even though they were fighting the same battle, for Chloe life might still go back to normal at the end - sadly for him no passing cloud was going to clear and let Sally and Molly come back to life.

'I'll give you a call later in the week then and see if we can arrange something,' Paige said.

'Whatever you do, don't try and contact Chloe from your own phone or email address, you have to assume they're compromised,' Branigan replied quickly, 'so we've set up a new email address for you to use.'

He pulled a piece of paper Alan had given him from his pocket and handed it to Paige.

'Uhura4751,' she read.

'Yes,' Chloe said, 'it's something to do with Star Trek and prime numbers - you've also got the password you'll need and the email address to use for me there.'

'You're Dax4759?'

'Yes, same thing - don't ask.'

'Can you look out of the window again and see if that Audi is still there and whether or not it still has two people in it?' Branigan asked, picking up Chloe's article and putting it back in his pocket.

Paige obliged, brushing closely by Chloe as she went to the window.

'Yep, they're both still there,' she said, straining to see in the failing light.

Branigan put on his small backpack and headed to the door, pausing to pick something off the floor beside the armchair in which Paige had been sitting.

'I think these are yours,' he said, passing her a set of cloverleaf nipple clamps on the ends of a length of chrome chain.

Unperturbed, Paige took them.

'If you ever change your mind,' she said.

As he and Chloe made their way down the stairs back to the ground floor, Branigan paused.

'Now pull your hood up to cover as much of your face as you can,' he said, doing the same himself, 'we're going out of the front door.'

'Is that wise?' Chloe asked.

'The couple in the car are looking for one or other of us going in, not both of us coming out. If we walk out looking like a couple off for an evening stroll and turn away from them there's a good chance they won't spot us - we'll look more suspicious if we start using the back door or climbing over fences.'

With their faces suitably covered, Branigan opened the front door, ushered Chloe through and they walked confidently down the flight of four steps. As they turned away from the parked Audi, they came face-to-face with the woman with crazy blond curls in the green waxed-jacket. Thinking he saw a momentary flash of recognition, Branigan squeezed Chloe's hand, urging her to slow down.

'Fuck,' he muttered when they were a few paces further on, 'keep walking steadily and don't look back.'

'I should have thought,' Chloe whispered back, her heart pounding, 'Paige needs glasses to see clearly at a distance.'

Branigan waited a few moments before speaking again.

'What did you see?' he asked.

Fighting every urge to run, Chloe took a deep breath and thought about the woman they'd just passed.

'Early thirties, angular face, dreadful curly hair,' Chloe began, a woman's eye focusing differently from a man's, 'a green waxed jacket and rather frightening blue-green eyes.'

Branigan waited as they continued to walk.

'There was a smell of cigarettes from her, she's got an earpiece in her left ear and has yellowy coloured teeth,' she continued, 'that's about all I got - she's reminds me of the lady who boils the bunny in Fatal Attraction.'

'I can only add that she has a mole on her upper left cheek, directly under the corner of her eye and there was the hint of a tattoo of a name or something just showing on her left wrist,' Branigan added.

'She's definitely not the woman I saw on the train yesterday,' Chloe said.

'No,' Branigan agreed, 'which confirms my worst fear.'

'Which is what?'

'That someone is taking this thing very seriously indeed.'

They came to a wide 'A' road and dodged between the traffic to avoid having to wait for the lights.

As they crossed, Branigan caught a glimpse of the woman about twenty paces behind speaking earnestly into her earpiece. Ahead was Westferry station.

'Why not take a taxi?' Chloe asked as she darted between a black cab and a motorcycle in her effort to keep pace with Branigan's large strides.

'Because they've got a car too,' he replied as he reached the other side and pulled two travel cards from his pocket.

'Take this,' he said, passing her one, 'you'll need it at the other end to get past the barrier without having to jump over it!'

A useful tip Peter Winstone taught him.

"Never, ever, find yourself having to queue for a ticket or scrabble for money when you're in the field. Seconds lost because you haven't got a ticket can be the difference between life and death."

Chloe glanced over her shoulder as they turned into the staircase which spiralled upwards to the westbound platform.

Bunny Boiler was only a few paces behind and directly behind her was the grey Audi speeding off in the direction they were going to travel.

Chloe could hear the footsteps of their pursuer keeping pace as they climbed the stairs and, as she peered nervously over the rail, she caught a glimpse of the waxed green jacket just below them.

Reaching the platform, Branigan led Chloe along it and whispered urgently.

'They're not making a move so they must be planning to lead the police to me. We don't want to shake our tail off yet,' he said, thinking about the route ahead, 'but we'll need as much distance between us when we get to Bank Station as we can - there we'll split up.'

Chloe started to say something and he held his hand up to silence her.

'No argument. If we separate, it's me they'll go after.'

He explained what Chloe should do and pulled a tightly rolled bundle of clothing in a carrier bag from his back pack as a red driverless train clattered to a halt and they boarded in the second of its four carriages. The Docklands Light Railway connected the rejuvenated docks in the east of London with the financial heartland of the City of London. Aside from having no drivers, the modern trains were made up of pairs of carriages which were joined together to make longer trains depending upon demand. The one they boarded was made up from two pairs of carriages joined nose-to-tail, so although you could move between the first and second of the carriages there was no access between the second and third. Conscious of this, Bunny Boiler walked swiftly past where they stood and boarded in the very front carriage.

A Mexican standoff.

Bunny at one end of the thirty-metre-long section of train - Branigan and Chloe studiously avoiding eye contact at the other.

Staring out of the window at the tired and run-down buildings which mixed incongruously with the smart boats in Limehouse Basin and the new high rises springing up all around, Branigan nudged Chloe and looked towards the flashes of the grey Audi visible through gaps in the buildings as it tracked their train. Nearing Shadwell Station Branigan spotted a white Police Volvo which had joined in the chase.

'Reinforcements have arrived,' he said, his voice and manner far too relaxed for Chloe's liking.

When the doors opened Branigan leaned idly against the frame and took a grip on Chloe's hand. Slowly counting down in his head the time the doors were open and measuring the distance to his next goal.

'Now!' he said, suddenly pulling Chloe onto the platform and moving against the flow of people heading to the exit.

Dragged in his wake, Chloe was conscious of movement behind them as Bunny Boiler reacted by leaping onto the platform and running along behind. Just as they reached the third carriage, Branigan hauled Chloe through the doors as they hissed closed, shutting out the sound of children shouting and laughing in the play area just below the elevated platforms. Behind them Bunny was forced to leap back onto the train through the doors nearest her - the ones Chloe and Branigan had left moments before - leaving her separated from her quarry by the windshields where the sections of train joined. Without even a glance over his shoulder, Branigan led Chloe right to the back of the train, putting 30 meters between them and their pursuer who stood straining to see what was happening from behind the barrier of glass.

'Our friend won't be able to see you changing clothes if you keep pressed into the door,' Branigan said as the train ducked down from its elevated track and began to burrow underground.

'When did you get these?' Chloe asked as she pulled on a shapeless blue top and a knitted hat, while Branigan removed his jacket and put on a grey sweat shirt and a blue baseball cap from his rucksack.

'I bought some bits on the way back from seeing Marty and others I've picked up along the way,' he replied, adjusting the Star Trek baseball cap low over his eyes.

'You remember where you're going?' he asked as the train began to slow.

Chloe nodded nervously.

'Just remember, the police will be looking for two of us and will have the wrong description for our outfits - it's Bunny and the others you need to avoid,' he continued.

'But I don't know what the Audi driver looks like!' Chloe replied as the train began to brake.

Branigan shrugged and gave her a brief grin.

'Nor do I - just work on the principle everyone's out to get you and you'll be fine.'

The train came to a stop and the doors opened.

Branigan's planning was good. The carriage they were in came to a rest adjacent to the exit and even before the doors were fully open he was out and turning into the tunnel beyond. Behind him Chloe took a far more measured approach, walking at the same pace as the other passengers and trying not to stand out from the crowd. Avoiding any eye contact, she was aware of a green-jacketed woman elbowing past others to catch-up with Branigan who not only had the benefit of speed but also a thirty metre head start on his side. Chloe allowed herself to glance up as she joined the upward escalator and saw Bunny with her smoker's lungs struggling for breath halfway up the moving stairway and Branigan breaking for freedom at the top.

What Chloe could not see was the two uniformed police officers he leapt straight into from the escalator. No attempt to disguise himself could hide the fact that Branigan was the man they were looking for - in a sea of slow-moving passengers the only person running stood out. Not wanting to stop and chat, Branigan did the only other thing possible; he barged past the police and headed for the escalator which would take him up to the next level and the daylight. Which was where he encountered his next problem in the form of the man he knew as Mr Travers stepping off the down escalator with four more police thundering down behind him.

Choices.

Either to take on the larger number ahead, or turn and run in the opposite direction. He opted to run, but not before he'd used all the venom raging inside him to lay the odious man he'd met in Marty's office flat with a two-footed kick to the solar plexus which sent Mr Travers thudding to the ground. His senses heightened by the adrenalin coursing through him, Branigan retained not only an image of Travers' startled face at the point of impact, but also the faintest scent of aftershave as he turned and ran back the way he'd come. The unmistakable scent he recognised from Agadee.

Heading back the way he'd come, Branigan was met by the two constables he'd already barged past at the top of the first escalator. For reasons best known to them, when faced with the athletic form of Branigan bearing down on them like an Olympic sprinter, one tried to stop him by holding his hand up, the other by reaching for his baton. Ignoring their demands, Branigan barged past them with the determination of a rampaging bull and headed back towards one of the deeper tunnels.

By contrast to Branigan's mad flight, Chloe reached the top of her escalator, walked a short distance and turned right into the tunnel for the Northern Line trains, unaware of any of the activity going on elsewhere. Forking right to the southbound platform, Chloe was relieved to see no sign of any pursuers as she felt the rush of air pushed ahead of a train arriving at the platform, the small tunnel shortly filled with the loud noise and commotion of the red and silver underground train thundering into the confined space.

"Thank you! Thank you! Thank you!" Chloe shouted inwardly as it halted and the graffiti-covered doors which declared Dazzzz to be the greatest slid invitingly open. Stepping onboard Chloe hovered in the shadows, only allowing herself to breathe again and survey the platform as the doors rattled and slid closed.

Crash!

A figure hit the door right in front of her. So close, in fact, that their noses would have been touching had it not been for the sheet of glass which separated them.

An angry, angular face.

Mad blue-green eyes.

Bared yellowed teeth.

Lips snarling as she shouted and banged on the door.

Bunny Boiler thrust her hand into the soft rubber seal of the doors so the very tips of her fingers pushed through the gap into the inside of the carriage, reaching out to almost touch the side of Chloe's head as she tried to prise the door open. The maddened woman almost succeeded.

The door moved an inch or two before Chloe lashed out, striking at the fingers with her balled up right fist until Bunny Boiler pulled her hand back in defeat, unmistakably mouthing the words, 'I'll get you, you cunt!'

Apparently, the teaching at the Black Ops training school

wasn't high on etiquette and decorum. The train gave a short jolt and hesitated for a heart-stopping moment before moving off more slowly. With her gaze locked onto the mad eyes of Bunny Boiler, Chloe became aware of movement over the demonic woman's right shoulder as the train headed along the platform.

Branigan had appeared through the short tunnel leading onto the platform and was running at full tilt as if making every effort to catch up with the train!

Chloe wasn't sure whether Bunny sensed his presence or saw a flicker in her own eyes, but Bunny swung her crazy blond locks around just in time to see Branigan come past her pursued by a group of uniformed policemen, a man she didn't recognise but assumed was the Audi driver and, bringing up the rear and clutching his chest as if having a heart attack, the man who'd chased her from the Birmingham hotel. Desperately wishing she could reach out and grab Branigan, Chloe watched helplessly as he made it past Bunny Boiler with the others racing behind until he appeared momentarily beside the door where Chloe stood. The antithesis of her experience with the wild-eyed woman with the yellowing teeth, she now wished she could reach out and grab where a moment before she only wanted to repel.

'Branigan!' she shouted, her knees physically trembling with fright and their eyes locking momentarily - then the train picked up speed and he was lost from sight.

It took the train just over two minutes to travel under The Thames, climb back up again and draw to a shuddering halt at London Bridge station - the seconds feeling like hours as Chloe pictured Branigan being led away by the hoard of police and the gloating Black Ops team. Their grand plan to find out what was going on had floundered on its very first day.

She stepped off the train feeling sick and helpless.

In their hurried conversation as they were followed from Paige's, Branigan told her to meet him at a coffee shop near the exit to Borough High Street and the market, but there seemed little point now - every moment she waited would give her pursuers more time to catch up with her as well. Unsure what to do, Chloe turned towards the exit.

'The next time you say, "I think I'll drop in on Paige" and I say, "Do you think that's a good idea?" will you listen to me?' Branigan said over her shoulder.

Chloe turned around with a startled gasp.

'How on earth did you manage that?' she said, screaming with relief and throwing her arms around him.

'You know they have two grab handles on the back of underground trains, well now I know what they're there for,' he said with a nonchalance that suggested he always travelled through the underground holding onto the outside of a speeding train by his fingertips.

CHAPTER 16

18:42 Hendon, North London

Chloe and Branigan were grateful for the cover of darkness as they returned to Hendon to be greeted enthusiastically at the door by Alan wearing one of his Star Trek uniforms and a pair of plastic pointed ears. Stepping into the hallway and shutting the door Branigan's sense of relief was short-lived as Alan blocked his progress.

'Is everything all right?' he asked, as Alan shuffled from foot to foot.

'Oh yes,' Alan replied before lapsing back into silence with his arms straight down by his sides and his fists clenching and unclenching repeatedly - according to Sally a sign that he was excited about something.

Sally.

Before he could become enthusiastic about Alan's activities an enormous wave of emotion ran through Branigan, the antithesis of the high he experienced riding to safety holding on to the back of the underground train. Suppressing the overwhelming cloud of blackness and fighting back the tears which threatened to come, Branigan followed Alan's eyes as they glanced expectantly at the two enormous blank televisions hanging from the wall beside him.

'You've got these working, haven't you?' he said, nodding to the screens.

Alan beamed with pride, totally oblivious to the inner turmoil which had just swept through Branigan. By contrast, Chloe had seen every nuance of his pain.

'Yes,' Alan said excitedly, touching the bottom right-hand

corner of the nearest screen and bringing them both to life.

On the left-hand screen there were six faces lifted from one of Marty's photographs, each with a name underneath. On the right were the two news articles; the one written by Chloe and the earlier-version penned by Paige in Bishkek.

'That's brilliant, Alan,' Branigan said, slightly unimpressed as he couldn't see how the application bettered having a pin-board and scraps of paper.

Alan looked a little confused.

'That isn't what I want to show you,' he said, double clicking on the same corner of the screen, 'this is.'

Immediately both screens were filled with every document from Chloe's wall - photographed with absolute clarity - plus some that Branigan didn't recognise. Branigan's eyebrows shot up in surprise and Chloe squealed with delight.

'Oh, my goodness!' she exclaimed, clapping her hands together with excitement.

'You've recovered some of the stuff from my hard drive as well!'

'Not some, all,' Alan said.

'And look,' he continued, using two fingers on the document nearest him, 'you can make each bigger and smaller like this and move them about by keeping your finger on them. If you want to add a note, you just click on this yellow square in the control panel at the bottom and you can write a note using your finger as a pen and clip it to any document.'

Alan demonstrated and both Branigan and Chloe shook their heads in wonder.

'When did you write this?' Chloe asked.

'Three years ago,' Alan said, 'there was a television programme where they faked a system which did something like this and I decided to write something which worked.'

'It's so clever, Alan,' Chloe continued, 'but what happens if the police or someone comes - won't it look odd to have all these documents on display?'

Alan smiled briefly and touched the top right-hand corner. Both screens immediately transformed themselves into fish tanks - in fact, as Chloe realised as she followed the fish around - one continuous tank where the fish swam seamlessly from one screen to the other and back.

Both of them were briefly mesmerised and bent in closer to study the detail on the myriad fish moving around on the screens.

'That's really impressive Alan!' Chloe congratulated at the very moment a great white shark swam straight towards the screen and devoured the entire contents with one huge gulp.

Both Branigan and Chloe leapt back and all that was left in Alan's faux aquarium was a single mangrove plant bent in the middle at right angles. Branigan smiled.

'Molly would have loved that,' he observed.

20:32 Godalming, Surrey

Even though he'd had a dreadful day, Marty was thinking of Branigan and the phone call he'd just received from Gregory Brown as he drank his restorative scotch.

His hangover, early morning call, meeting with the police and impounding of his car were as nothing to the trauma Branigan had suffered with the loss of his family. Marty should know, having lost his wife two years before. Whilst Mel's death from an insidious cancer wasn't as violent as Sally's, he could empathise with the despair Branigan must be feeling. When you added the loss of a child into the equation it must be like having your heart ripped out. As if Branigan's loss wasn't bad enough, Gregory made it sound like a whole heap of other trouble was currently bearing down on his errant employee.

'I've just heard from Alex Oldroyd,' Gregory explained, 'it seems Branigan has teamed up with Chloe Travers - they've been involved in an incident at Bank Station in which the police tried to arrest him and he attacked a member of the public.'

Marty knew his protégé and didn't need to ask whether Branigan had escaped capture. He also knew there would be a valid explanation for the attack on the member of the public.

'Alex is concerned that Branigan wants to publish this story to prove his innocence in some way,' Gregory said, concluding his narrative.

Marty snorted with derision as he took a swig of his scotch; of course Alex didn't want the story to be published - it would hardly help his career if the world discovered he was the architect of a plan to reduce Cambridge to an apocalyptic wasteland.

21:15

Cressix has been in touch.

He says the "Branigan threat has been sorted," and that it is only a matter of time until he is taken out of play; I tell him I am not sure that I agree. Of course he dismisses my skepticism.

On a positive note, he tells me about the explosion and fire which destroyed the girl's apartment in Sheffield. That is good news. That means a loose end from Kyrgyzstan has been tidied up.

22:07 Hendon, North London

'The police called me,' Alan said.

He was standing next to Branigan who was moving things around on the electronic display board, while Chloe was sitting with a laptop at the kitchen table running through the documents Alan had recovered from her own computer. She was transferring any documents she thought relevant to the screens in front of Branigan who was then sorting them into the growing archive.

Branigan paused.

'When did they call?' he asked.

While you were out visiting Chloe's friend, a detective constable called and arranged for the man leading the investigation to come around and talk to me tomorrow morning. Apparently I have information which may be pivotal to the case,' he said, sounding rather sad about the whole thing.

'Is that a problem?' Branigan asked.

'No, but it means I won't be able to go to work at the normal time,' Alan said.

Branigan nodded.

Alan didn't like change.

He liked his routine just so and clearly that had already been more than disturbed by his and Chloe's arrival.

'Chloe and I will make sure we're out of your way first thing tomorrow and that there's no trace of us anywhere; then you'll be helping me, Sally and Molly if you go through everything with the police. Without your help, the police will continue to believe I killed them and they won't look for the real killer.'

Alan seemed to be placated and returned to his bank of computers where he was making an addition to the software for the TV screen noticeboard - adding a "To Do" list so they each knew who was doing what to take their investigation further.

Chloe came out of the kitchen.

'I can't see anything more on there of any relevance,' she said.

'Then I need you to look at this with me and see if there's anything else you think I should add,' Branigan said, pointing to the electronic board where he'd separated the information under four headings:-

Who?
Operation Peach Tree
The container
Hubert Cressix

Underneath the "Who?" he'd put a list of the six names to-

gether with the photograph of each Alan had scanned:-
Gregory Brown
Marty Freeman
Michael Jenkins
Alex Oldroyd
David Price
Peter Winstone

He'd also added a sub heading for the Black Ops team with the four working titles for each:-
James Travers
Kathy Travers
Bunny Boiler
Audi Driver

Underneath all of these he had a new document open.

'What are you going to put there?' Chloe asked, pointing to the single question posed on the otherwise blank sheet - "How to trace?"

'I'm not sure,' Branigan said, 'I know what we're trying to do at the most basic level is find out which of the six was either in the UK or out of the UK when Paige was speaking to her contact in Bishkek; we need to be looking for anything which helps us with that.'

'Like their diaries?' Chloe ventured.

'I can do that,' Alan called from behind his desk in the nearby living room.

Branigan caught Chloe's eye.

'Okay Alan,' he said with a hint of amusement, 'I'll add that to the board.'

Before he could write anything, however, the words "Check diaries - Alan" appeared miraculously on the screen document.

'I've got it,' Alan called.

'Oh, yes and then there are these,' he continued before the sheet filled up with a list of other places to look:-

Expenses
Public information
Travel visas
Airlines
Air Miles
Hotels in Bishkek
Social media.

'That's very useful, thank you Alan,' Branigan said, silently pointing to Alan's name which had been added beside each search, 'but are you going to be able to do all of this?'

'Yes - I've started already,' he called back.

'Okay, as long as you let Chloe and me know if there is anything we can do to help,' Branigan said, shrugging and turning to the next heading.

'Operation Peach Tree; we need to look for any references to it - you never know.'

Even before he could open a new document, one appeared with just three words on it - "Search for - Alan."

'Okay, thank you Alan,' Branigan said, hitting his forehead with the palm of his hand in a gesture of mock-despair.

'Then if we look at the question of the container,' Branigan said, pointing to the next heading and the collection of photographs underneath which included the one with the partial serial number showing, 'we need to find a way of trying to trace it.'

With a certain inevitability Alan's name appeared beside a note to search for the container's whereabouts.

'Excellent, thank you Alan, which moves us on to the mysterious Mr. Cressix,' he continued, pointing to another blank page, 'where we learned a bit more this afternoon.'

Chloe picked up his thread.

'But most of what Paige told us just leads to more questions - there isn't much there we can search for.'

'Even so, they're worth noting down,' Branigan agreed, 'because I think the answers to these are pivotal to what's going on here.'

Chloe nodded and began to write - a strange sensation as she didn't need a pen, simply to place her finger on the screen and trace the words. In the other room she could sense Alan rocking back and forth and purring with delight as his software took her writing and converted it into neatly typed script.

'You're quite right, Cressix didn't go to Bishkek just to feed Paige with information - we must be missing the real reason that he went,' she said as she wrote.

'His other agenda may well have been to secure that consignment of explosives,' Branigan said doubtfully.

'Oh come on,' Chloe chided, 'you can't tell me our man dropped everything to travel to the back-end of beyond just because there were some explosives there - let's face it explosives aren't the most difficult thing to come by.'

'Then we're missing something obvious,' Branigan said contemplatively.

After a pause he stepped closer to the board and wrote a new line on the To Do list.

"Speak to Koslow - Branigan."

'Who's that?' Chloe queried.

'You remember I told you I ran into my Russian counterpart recently?'

Chloe nodded.

'I think I know how to find him and he might be able to throw a different light on what happened in Bishkek.'

'And do you think he'll talk to you?'

'I don't see why not - he's no longer with Russian Intelligence which will make it easier for him.'

'What about what you said at Paige's,' Chloe prompted, 'you asked what document they stole from her and set out to burn in my apartment?'

'Yes, and why,' Branigan nodded in agreement and wrote the question down.

He looked at the screen when he finished writing and saw

the picture of the contents of the container - the one which had been shoved under Paige's door.

'There's also a question which is bugging me,' he continued, 'I took photos of the contents of the container and sent them back to London. These aren't the pictures I took, which leads to three more unanswered questions - who took these pictures; how did Cressix get hold of them; and was it my pictures which spawned Cressix going out to Kyrgyzstan?'

Both Branigan and Chloe waited in anticipation for Alan to add his name to the list.

When he didn't Chloe caught Branigan's eye and called out, 'Is there anything you want to add Alan?'

'Yes, I've found your container.'

Branigan, who was still concentrating on Cressix, almost missed the non-sequitur.

'You've what?' he asked.

'I've found the container - you know, the one you drove from Orsk to Bishkek?'

Branigan waited, but it became evident no more was coming without his prompting. He and Chloe walked into the living room where Alan was sitting at the enormous desk with four brightly lit screens each displaying entirely different images.

The immediate question was "Where?" but Branigan also knew enough about Alan's psychology to ask his second question first. Sally once said, 'Because Alan doesn't pick upon the social queues that you are pleased, sometimes you need to encourage him with positive affirmation, you know, praising him for what he's done - like you would a child.'

'That's absolutely brilliant, Alan,' Branigan said, 'how did you do that?'

Alan brightened immediately.

'Tracking a container is easy,' he began, 'as long as you have the whole container number and it's being shipped by a company that subscribes to Track and Trace - that's the standard tracking system - but we didn't have either of those.'

'Well, we might have had the latter, but the odds were that we didn't because it was being shipped through dodgy shipping agents and consigned to someone hidden in the shadows.'

'After we spoke about it this morning, I wrote a little programme to go off in search of it,' Alan explained, before going into a detailed narrative on his search programme - using alien words like "crawler," "algorithm" and "intuitive justification" - until Branigan and Chloe caught each other's eye, silently acknowledging that they didn't have a clue what he was talking about. Frustratingly Alan's persistent monologue was drowning out an urgent thought which was struggling to fight its way into Branigan's own consciousness; with the thought lost, he waited until Alan drew breath before jumping in with his most pressing question.

'That's so clever Alan,' he said, patting Alan's shoulder for further affirmation, 'where is it?'

'I don't know,' Alan replied.

It was one of those moments when it seemed as if he and Alan came not only from different planets, but also different galaxies.

Branigan paused, took a breath and pressed forward with a different approach.

'Okay,' he said, forcing himself to be calm, 'when you said, "I've found your container," what did you actually mean?'

Alan was equally as patient with his response.

'I meant, they changed the number on the container and brought it into Felixstowe from Rotterdam seven weeks after you last saw it.'

Chloe was taken aback.

'How did you track it if they changed the number?' she asked.

'If you'd listened properly,' Alan said in an exasperated tone, 'you'd know I didn't need to track it, rather like tracing a bullet, you don't need to follow the route to know where it arrives. I knew where it started and then I made the programme look at different destinations until it turned up.'

None the wiser, Branigan persevered.

'What happened to it after Felixstowe?'

'I told you, I don't know. That's what I've been looking at while you've been jabbering away. It cleared Customs and was driven away by a haulage contractor five days later.'

'You haven't been able to trace it through the haulage contractor?'

'No.'

'Have you tried?'

'Yes.'

'Why couldn't you trace it through them then?' Branigan asked patiently.

'Because they went out of business three years ago.'

So close and yet so far.

'Okay,' Branigan said patiently, 'do either of you have any idea how we can trace it given that the carrier is now out of business?'

'The shipping agent is going to have a name for someone who paid the duty and handling charges, plus they should have a consignee name and address,' Chloe said.

'How do you know that?' Branigan asked, impressed at Chloe's knowledge.

'Paige may not have done any background work on your case, but that doesn't mean I didn't.'

'Then could you work with Alan to get the details, then if we can think of a pretext you can call the agents in Felixstowe?'

'That's no problem,' Chloe said, 'I didn't work at The Herald without learning how to make up a story to get hold of information! I can pretend I'm from a firm of accountants following an audit query.'

'Excellent,' Branigan said, still frustrated that he couldn't remember the train of thought Alan had triggered, 'then I think we have a plan for tomorrow - most of which revolves around Alan.'

He studied the finished version of the board:-

Who
Gregory Brown
Marty Freeman
Michael Jenkins
Alex Oldroyd
David Price
Peter Winstone

Plus
James Travers
Kathy Travers
Bunny Boiler
Audi Driver

How to trace
Check diaries - Alan
Expenses - Alan
Public information - Alan
Travel visas - Alan
Airlines - Alan
Air Miles - Alan
Hotels in Bishkek - Alan
Social media - Alan

Operation Peach Tree
Search for - Alan

The container
Search for - Found by Alan
Contact shipping agent - Chloe
Identify contents of container.

Hubert Cressix
Other agenda?

What in container interested him?
Use for explosives?
What do Chloe/Paige have that Cressix wants destroyed?
Paige break in MO vs. Chloe bomb?
Why does he want it destroyed?
Where did pictures given to Paige come from?
Why not use Branigan pictures?

To Do
Speak to Koslow - Branigan

MONDAY 25TH OCTOBER

CHAPTER 17

08:18 Police Station, North London

'For fuck's sake, they let him get away?' DCI Tenant was climbing into the car on the way to interview Alan Armstrong when DS Drake told him the news of Branigan's escape.

'Yes, sir, it seems there were several wooden-tops there,' Drake explained, using police parlance for the humble bobbies who attended, 'plus two or three members of the public who became involved trying to stop him.'

'And how did he miraculously disappear from the underground station?'

'On a train, sir,' Drake replied, immediately regretting the apparent flippancy of his answer.

'What the fuck did the PC's do, hold the doors open for him?' DCI Tenant exploded.

'No sir, he jumped on the back of a moving train.'

For a moment DCI Tenant was flummoxed - even he could see how difficult it would be to stop someone clinging to the back of a moving train.

DCI Tenant shook his head.

'Do we know what happened to him after he escaped?'

'Yes, sir, we've found CCTV footage which shows him getting off at London Bridge with a girl we think is Chloe Travers.'

'If the two of them are together; that lends credibility to our theory and reinforces the motive for Branigan murdering his family,' DCI Tenant said contemplatively.

08:53 Café, Hendon, North London

An hour before the police were due to interview Alan, Branigan and Chloe left the sanctuary of his house and settled themselves in a café a mile away.

They'd each been up early. Alan because his Monday routine meant he got up at 4:45am; Branigan because he couldn't sleep with all the dark thoughts disturbing him; and Chloe because Alan knocked on her door a 5:00am.

'Morning Chloe,' he called through the door to his sleepy visitor.

Alarmed by the early call, Chloe leapt out of bed and pulled on the voluminous dressing gown hanging on the back of the door.

'What's the problem Alan?' she asked anxiously.

'Nothing,' Alan replied, stepping past her into the room, 'only it's Monday.'

'And that's important because?' Chloe asked, failing to see any connection between the early wake-up call and the day of the week.

'I do the laundry on Monday before I go to work.'

'But you're not going to work this morning.'

'I know, but I always wash the sheets at this time on a Monday.'

Chloe could see there was little point in remonstrating. From her brief understanding of him, it was clear Alan wasn't waking her to annoy her - she was simply in the way of a long-established routine which hadn't changed despite his mother dying eight years previously.

Having declined her offer of assistance, Alan bustled round her bed and Chloe had no alternative but to make her way sleepily downstairs where she found Branigan already up and staring at a photograph on the screens in the hallway. He was studying one of the pictures he now knew had been delivered to Paige's hotel room by the mysterious Hubert

Cressix; it showed Branigan at the freight depot in Bishkek holding an enormous bundle of cash.

'The currency in Kyrgyzstan is the Som,' he said conversationally, 'it's one of those currencies where it looks like I'm getting enough cash to buy a house, when it's really about $1,000.'

'I thought everything was paid for in dollars there,' Chloe said.

'Typically it is for Westerners and on the black market, but don't forget I was posing as a local driver, so I got paid like everyone else. I was wondering if I might remember who took the picture.'

Chloe studied the image and pointed to a folded piece of paper he was clutching along with the cash.

'What's that you're holding?'

'That's my copy of the shipping paperwork; I got that as a receipt for the consignment together with payment for having transported it.'

'And that doesn't show anything useful other than the yard you delivered the container to?' Chloe asked, checking that her understanding was correct.

'Yes, that's it,' Branigan agreed, stepping to one side as Alan came bustling down the stairs with his arms full of bed linen.

They set out in search of a café to use as a refuge while Alan met the police and Chloe was fascinated as Branigan dismissed the first four they came to before alighting on one called Shirlee's. Once inside she couldn't help feeling the tired decor, tables heaving under the weight of fried food and overwhelming scent of body odour blended with stale grease made it a strange choice.

'Why here?' she asked, using a paper napkin to wipe congealed food remnants off the table.

Branigan glanced around.

'I take it you're not drawn to the ambience,' he said, glancing briefly at the menu before explaining, 'my thinking is that it's busy, there are clear lines of sight to the front and the back doors, plus it's near a taxi rank.'

Chloe was perplexed.

'Where does the taxi rank come in?'

'Forward planning,' he replied before heading to the counter to place their orders.

Returning with two cups of strong filter coffee he glanced at his watch.

'It's probably worth trying that shipping agent in Felixstowe now - I imagine they start early.'

Chloe nodded and took out Alan's old phone and the note he'd given her with contact details and relevant information of the container. Conscious of the background noise, Chloe dialled and shielded the phone as best she could with her right hand.

'Hello, I wonder if I could speak with someone who might be able to retrieve some old shipping paperwork and check on a payment for me?' she asked.

Put through to Flora in the office, an efficient girl who brusquely demanded the bill of lading reference and established there was a charge for sending out copies, Chloe was ill-prepared for her next question.

'And can I check who you're from?' Flora asked.

'Yes,' Chloe replied, scanning the room for inspiration and alighting on the adjoining table, 'I'm from Brown and Bacon, we're a firm of chartered accountants dealing with the liquidation of the haulage company. I thought I'd dealt with all the paperwork and then HM Revenue and Customs has come back with a list of queries,' Chloe said, becoming all conspiratorial as she joined Flora into her problem, 'my boss is livid with me - if you can help me with this last one, I should be able to get the Revenue and him off my back!'

Whether it was the conspiracy between two put-upon clerks, the spectre of an irate boss, or HMRC breathing down her neck, Branigan wasn't sure - what became apparent was that suddenly Flora couldn't do enough to help Chloe.

'Tell her we'll collect it,' Branigan mouthed.

'Oh, thank you Flora, is it all right if I drop by and pick it up later this morning?' Chloe said, looking questioningly at Branigan.

Ending the call, Chloe waited while Branigan fetched their breakfasts from the counter.

'Brown and Bacon?' he said when he came back.

'Listen,' Chloe said defensively, 'I had a perfectly plausible cover story - I just hadn't thought about a name before she asked that question; I nearly said Ketchup and Tomato! What's more important is how you intend to get us to Felixstowe - isn't that somewhere out on the East coast?'

'Forward planning,' Branigan said, nodding towards a table which was home to three men ranging in age from thirty to sixty who were having a heated debate, 'who do you know who'll argue about politics at this time day other than taxi drivers?'

09:03 The Strand, London

The Strand got its name from the old English word for a riverbank - "strond".

Originally home to some of the finest houses in London with gardens running down to the river, today it was home to a very discombobulated Marty. Not only had he been forced to use public transport to travel to work as the police were currently tearing his prized BMW to shreds, but also, he'd arrived in his office to find all the photos of him and the gang missing. As if that wasn't enough there seemed to be discord throughout the office.

Hussain from Accounts had ventured up from the first floor in search of IT support.

'Has anyone seen Alan,' he called when he discovered the IT desk to be empty, 'only I can't get onto the internet?'

Marty had just finished explaining that Alan was coming in later when Clive, who worked opposite Branigan, complained that someone had riffled through his desk.

'Someone's taken my spare phone and a backpack!' he complained.

Adam, who had the desk nearest Marty's office joined in the general unrest.

'Yes, someone's taken my jacket, I left it on the back of my chair on Friday and Hussain is quite right, the internet is practically non-existent.'

Just when Marty wanted to slam his door and get some peace and quiet Kelly - who worked in accounts alongside Hussain - appeared clutching a slip of paper.

'Sorry to bother you Marty,' she said over the general hubbub, 'but are you aware that Branigan emptied the cash safe over the weekend?'

She passed Marty a handwritten note.

'It's an IOU for the entire £5,314.'

If Marty hoped the level of noise and speculation about all these seemingly unconnected events would subside, he was sadly disappointed.

Before he was able to explain that he knew about the IOU, Alan would be in later and Branigan may have taken the missing items, Anna appeared with a game-changing contribution.

'Jasper has just called,' she announced, referring to her boyfriend who'd bravely tried to speak with Alan about the equity futures market, 'he's heard something on the radio - Branigan's wanted by the police - they say he's murdered Sally and Molly.'

As the shocking news struck home and brought all other conversation to a temporary halt, the ensuing silence was broken by Marty's mobile phone ringing.

He glanced at the number and rejected the call - this wasn't the time to speak with the oil company.

Almost immediately it rang again - this time it was Gregory Brown.

09:18 Café, Hendon, North London

Having finished breakfast, Branigan walked over to the table of three men.

'Excuse me gents, but I wonder if one of you can help me with a cab?'

The argument round the table stopped and the oldest of the men, the sixty-year-old with hardly any hair and a grey moustache, looked at him.

'There are plenty of cabs outside, hail any one, we're on a break.'

'I can see that, but I'm after a bit more than just a half mile ride - my friend and I need to get to Felixstowe and back today - we won't be there long.'

There was a shuffling round the table as each of the three saw the value of his custom.

The youngest declared his hand first. He folded up his newspaper with the news story which had prompted their argument.

'I could do that. As long as we're back by 5 o'clock.'

The third guy was next to declare.

'Yea, I can - I'll just need to square it with my missus.'

Which left grey moustache who suddenly didn't want Branigan going outside and hailing any passing cab and, in fact, their break was over anyway.

'Yes, I can too,' he announced, 'happy to - it would make a nice change to have a day out of London.'

From her nearby vantage point Chloe watched the negotiation with interest, trying to guess which of the drivers Branigan would choose.

In the end he returned with grey moustache.

'This is Jim Hopkins,' he said, introducing their driver to Chloe, 'and Jim has volunteered to take us to Felixstowe and back.'

Chloe wondered why Branigan had chosen the rather formal older driver as she shook his hand.

On the way to the cab they stopped at a print shop and, with Jim out of earshot, he explained his rationale.

'He doesn't have a wife and young family to come back to and has the added bonus of being in the RAF before he retired and became a cabby.'

Chloe still didn't see how this qualified him above the others around the table.

'He was stationed on Ascension Island when I was being plastered all over the papers over here.'

09:58 Hendon, North London

DCI Tenant and DS Drake were walking to their car parked a few doors away from Alan Armstrong's house. Their interview with the strange man had yielded far less information than they'd hoped and done little to either throw light on Branigan's motive, or give them evidence of a relationship with Chloe Travers. In fact, from the moment the pair arrived at Alan's they had the sense they'd entered an altered state of consciousness.

Mr Armstrong began by showing them an aquarium displayed on TV screens in the hall, regaling them with the technical difficulties of getting a shark to swim from one screen to another. He'd then talked interminably about Star Trek and even shown them his collection of memorabilia which included a toy plastic gun which had apparently been used as a prop in the first series.

They fared little better when they got on to the subject of the car journey to Sheffield. Armstrong sat rocking back and forth and excitedly explained about the car, telling them how fast it accelerated before going into excruciating detail about its construction.

When DCI Tenant explained that the car was being taken apart for forensic examination, Armstrong had become particularly excited because he wanted them to retrieve some caramel crispy bites from under the passenger seat.

'I dropped them you see and then couldn't reach them,' he'd explained, 'You'll also find a blue ballpoint pen and a yellow pencil down there too; I dropped the ballpoint trying to retrieve the caramel crispy bites and the pencil trying to retrieve the ballpoint.'

The interview seemed interminable as Armstrong's mind wandered from one topic to another. No, he hadn't seen any bomb-making equipment, but did they know the chemical reaction that caused weed killer to explode? Yes, they had picked Chloe Travers up, taken her to a café in Sheffield and then dropped her off at her friend's apartment which, incidentally, was in an old cutlery works - the first record of cutlery making in Sheffield goes back to 1297. He read that in a leaflet about the museums he picked up in the hotel where they had cake.

No, he hadn't noticed anything odd about the relationship between Branigan and Ms. Travers, but Ms. Travers did have an interesting collection of handcuffs and other forms of restraint equipment. If he could look at the handcuffs the police used, he would be able to tell them whether or not Chloe's were the same and he might be able to show them how Branigan picked the lock. Then, according to Armstrong, she had pictures of Branigan all over her wall and he actually began to recite word-for-bloody-word the whole of a news article which he'd seen pinned to the wall.

As they got back into the car, DCI Tenant gave a huge sigh.

'Fuck,' he said, 'we're doomed if we ever have to put him in the witness box.'

DS Drake nodded - this was one of those rare occasions when he and the DCI wholeheartedly agreed with each other.

'Yes, sir,' he said as he started the car, 'I think the only three useful things we got are that Branigan did go to Sheffield, the registration of a car that followed them and that there are some biscuits matching the container found by South Yorkshire under the passenger seat.'

It was Tenant's turn to shake his head.

'I may be being cynical here, but I fancy the car that was "following" them,' he said, tracing the quotation marks in the air, 'will turn out to be a little old lady doing her shopping. Still, I guess it's worth passing the details to South Yorkshire; you never know.'

11:47 The Strand, London

Marty was on the phone to Alex Oldroyd when he saw Alan's distinctive shape emerge from the staircase and head straight for the cover of his enormous computer screens. Even over Alex's voice, he was aware of a communal sigh across the whole floor as Alan did something and the internet began working again. Twenty people had spent the last three hours shouting at their computers in frustration and within 30 seconds of sitting down Alan had the problem sorted.

Unfortunately, the other problem wasn't so easy to sort.

Branigan.

Alex had phoned to tell Marty about reports he'd picked up from a contact in the Met Police of an altercation at Bank Station which had seen one member of the public get a black eye and four police officers fail to capture a fleeing Branigan.

'They say he just jumped onto the back of a moving tube train and rode it out of there,' Alex concluded, his voice tinged with a mixture of wonder and regret that Branigan hadn't been caught.

Both reactions were easy to explain in Marty's mind. It was difficult not to be impressed by Branigan's strength and athleticism, but also - for a career man like Alex - there was the worry about not being drawn into something which could impact on his next promotion.

12:07 Felixstowe, Essex

Having started the day being off-hand, Jim, it turned

out, was chatty and interested to know all about Branigan, Chloe, and their reasons for heading to Felixstowe. On the basis that the easiest lie was the one closest to the truth, they explained that they were journalists, writing a story about drug smuggling and were pursuing a lead. Satisfied that he was helping expose some of the people behind the dreadful blight on society, Jim went into a long and graphic explanation of what he would do to the smugglers if he had his way. That was before expounding on race, religion and the current government.

Both Chloe and Branigan were relieved when they drew up outside the freight company and got some respite from Jim's political lecture. Inside they met Flora, a bubbly young Scot who was surprised that Chloe and her colleague weren't more smartly dressed.

'We specialise in insolvencies,' Chloe explained, handing over her freshly printed Brown & Bacon business card which bore Marty's office address plus Chloe's temporary email and borrowed mobile phone, 'and we've been stock taking in a tile warehouse in Chelmsford.'

Satisfied with the this, Flora was quick to sympathise with their plight in having to appease HMRC.

'I've dug the file out,' she explained, placing an open file on the enquiries counter, 'but there isn't anything much there. You know, just the usual shipping paperwork.'

They both studied the documentation and as Branigan used his mobile phone to take photographs of each piece of paper his eyes alighted on a name.

'Do you know anything about these people,' he asked, pointing to the relevant line, 'it says that "Cressix Enterprises" is the consignee for the shipment, but then gives the name and address for the haulage company?'

Flora looked where Branigan was pointing with the vacant expression of someone hoping the answer will leap out of the page at them.

'Yes, they're the people who took the shipment away,' she

said, hoping this simple explanation was enough.

'Thanks Flora,' Chloe said, 'that's really useful - and are you able to confirm that the customs and handling charges were paid?'

'Oh, yes, I almost forgot!' Flora exclaimed, returning to her desk and bringing back a printed slip of paper, 'I got this from Accounts, it shows payment was made by bank transfer from Cressix Enterprises.'

12:23 Police Station, North London

DCI Tenant was used to being the man in charge of an investigation and having little more than cursory oversight from his superiors - this case was turning out to be different. At first the press were all over the story as news of double murder and a suspect on the run came their way, but their interest came to an abrupt halt when the Defence and Security Media Advisory Committee issued a notice to the press.

Similar to the "D Notice" system it replaced, DSMA notices were used to prevent any inadvertent disclosure of something which might compromise intelligence operations. This was both a help and a hindrance to DCI Tenant. A help because the DSMA Notice took the press off his back; a hindrance because press coverage was often the best way to get new leads and information on a prime suspect's whereabouts. Plus, as he was discovering, the issuance of a Notice led to an unprecedented amount of interest in the case from everyone above him right up to the Commissioner and, indeed, the Home Secretary.

'That was the Assistant Commissioner,' Tenant said to DS Drake.

'He wants to know how we managed to let Branigan escape when we had him in our sights yesterday - the way he was speaking, anyone would think you and I were at Bank Station ourselves when he got away.'

DS Drake was familiar with the lead balloon of operational responsibility within the force. Similar to the Civil Service line on culpability - where you claimed successes and blamed others for failures - the lead balloon of operational responsibility plummeted through the ranks until it landed at the feet of whoever was standing too close. No doubt, Drake surmised, the Commissioner had asked his deputy how Branigan was allowed to escape when there were four officers and an equal number of willing members of the public on hand to capture him in what can best be described as a concrete tube. The Assistant Commissioner had dropped the lead balloon down to his DCI and Drake knew Tenant was about to do the same to him.

'I told him that I'd asked you to prepare a report on what went wrong and that I'd see he and The Commissioner got a copy as soon as possible.'

Kerplunk!

The lead balloon had landed Drake's feet.

'Yes, sir,' Drake responded, thinking through his options, 'I've already acted on that and asked the sergeant on duty yesterday afternoon to prepare a report for me, if you're okay with that I'll take his report and attach my comments for you to review.'

DCI Tenant recognised the strategy and nodded his approval.

'That'll be fine Drake, just as long as I can have it by the end of the day.'

Excusing himself DS Drake went back to his desk and searched through the previous day's duty roster and made a call. After identifying himself, Drake moved the lead balloon on.

'I've got a request from on high,' he explained to the duty sergeant, 'The Commissioner wants a report right away on how your lads let this chap escape from Bank Station yesterday...'

Satisfied that his name would be seen as part of the solution and not linked to the problem, Drake returned to the Incident Room to see if there had been any developments.

13:14 A12, Southbound near Chelmsford

Eventually Branigan had to close the sliding glass panel between the driver and his passengers to cut out Jim Hopkins' incessant chattering so he could call Alan and update him with details of their find.

'Sorry Jim,' he said as he slid the panel shut, 'I need to speak with the office.'

Jim shrugged and focused more resolutely on maintaining a steady 50 miles per hour along the busy road.

Chloe accepted their choice of a London Black Cab was the most convenient, but she wasn't that sure it necessarily the best. The trouble is, the black cab had changed little since they appeared in the 1950s when they were designed to carry passengers and their luggage on short trips around the metropolis. Chloe and Branigan's trip was neither short, nor involved luggage. Assuming they wanted to choose slow, noisy and uncomfortable transport they'd certainly hit paydirt, but every time a more conventional mini cab came shooting past them a little bit of her was jealous of the ride and relative speed the occupants would be enjoying.

'Hi Alan, how did you get on with the police this morning?'

Chloe had to stifle a giggle as Alan clearly asked Branigan to identify himself before he listened intently for a long time to everything Alan had to say, eventually himself getting a word in and explaining about the consignee being Cressix Enterprises. Having given Alan the relevant bank account numbers, Branigan was in the throes of explaining what he and Chloe were doing next when he stopped mid-sentence and put the phone back in his pocket.

'He hung up,' Branigan explained.

Chloe nodded with understanding.

'And that's the first time I've been asked "Branigan who?";

but, on a positive note, he thinks the meeting with the police went quite well.'

Chloe waited in vain for Branigan to elucidate.

'But he said an awful lot more than that, he was talking for ages.'

'True,' Branigan replied, 'but I paraphrased what he actually said about the meeting down to the core facts - the rest of it was the extraneous stuff, mainly about how interested they were in seeing his Star Trek memorabilia.'

'He didn't have anything else to say?'

'Well, it seems Adam used the wrong mug to make his cup of coffee, otherwise he thinks he's made some progress with the other search stuff but didn't add any more than that.'

'What do we do next?' Chloe asked.

'Aside from making our way back by a circuitous route, I think we wait to see what Alan comes back with; in the meantime, we can do some searching of our own.'

CHAPTER 18

14:54 The Strand, London

Marty's day had improved considerably.

He'd spoken with the oil company and told them his hunch had been correct and they were being spied upon by a Russian. He'd gone on to apologise that his operative who'd verified this was undercover on another operation and wouldn't be able to follow-up for a few days. Unperturbed, the client went away to start work on their counter-strategy.

Hussain from Accounts seemed to be able to work with the slower than usual internet; Clive on the desk opposite Branigan's was assuaged by the offer of a new phone and backpack; Adam by the offer of a new jacket on expenses; and Kelly had been to the bank and replenished the missing petty cash.

Even the open discussion about Branigan had lessened as the articles to which Anna's boyfriend Jasper had drawn everyone's attention were pulled when the DSMA Notice came into effect.

When Marty's phone sprang to life, he glanced at the caller ID before answering - Peter Winstone; the rough diamond in the group of six.

'Hi Peter, how are you doing?'

'Hello Marty,' Peter replied with his distinctly non-public school accent, 'I'm just checking to see if there's any news on Branigan and if we're still meeting on Wednesday?'

'Yes, I spoke to Gregory earlier and I know he and David don't see any reason for us to change our habits because of one maverick.'

'Did you hear about him running amok at Bank Station yesterday?' Peter asked, his east London accent making him sound more like a TV villain than a spy.

'Yes, I did, Gregory told me this morning.'

16:49 Wapping, East London

Paige read the short piece buried in the news on page eleven for a fourth time.

The article stated in just two paragraphs that a man police were hunting for murder had escaped capture the day before at Bank Station. Her curiosity piqued, Paige looked the story up on the office network in search of a name and saw a single-line note stating there was a 'D' Notice attached to the story.

She headed straight over to Ken Briers at the News Editor's desk. A veteran of the newsroom, Ken had the physique of a heavyweight boxer gone to seed and the ability to look like he'd been up all night even at the start of his shift.

'Ken, are you aware of the story about the man running off at Bank Station?' she asked.

'Yes,' Ken replied, hitting Paige with the stale smell of last night's alcohol on his breath, 'and I take it you know who it's about?'

'I assume it's Branigan.'

Ken, whose eyes were yet to make it past Paige's cleavage, ran his fingers through the few remaining wisps of grey hair.

'You're right, but I don't think there's anything in it for you. Even when he's arrested, we won't be able to publish until after a trial.'

'I can see that, but don't you think a 'D' Notice is over the top for what he's alleged to have done - it's five years since he left SIS and there can't be any national security implications in his supposedly killing his wife.'

Ken shrugged.

'You're probably right, but unless you can bring me a story

which doesn't mention him escaping from Bank Station and the deaths of his family my hands are tied.'

For the first time the news editor's weary eyes contacted with Paige's.

'Now, if you know something more about the background to what's going on here, we might be able to work out an angle which gets us round the Notice.'

Paige smiled conspiratorially.

'I don't have anything yet, but I'm working on it,' she said before returning to her desk where she flicked through her Rolodex looking for the business card for Cressix.

When she found it, she put it in her handbag, made a mental note to tell Chloe she'd got the name wrong and filled in the archive retrieval request for her file on the Branigan story.

She then allowed herself to focus back on her social life and dialled a number.

'Hello Hanako,' she said when her friend answered the phone, 'it's Paige - I was just wondering if you're going to the play party at JJ's on Saturday night?'

18:34 Hendon, London

Chloe and Branigan had been back at Alan's for almost two hours by the time Alan came home from the office.

Their day with Jim had ended in silence as they neared the O2 Arena in the rejuvenated docklands part of London's East End. Branigan was silent because he was remembering the events he and Sally had enjoyed at the arena when they were first married and the hopes they had of re-discovering their social vigour as Molly grew and became more independent. The realisation that their plans and dreams had all been squandered by some bastard bent on political points-scoring led him to a dark place where despair mingled with a hollow feeling which he knew would never go away. Searching the overwhelming sadness inside him, Branigan found the only way he could lessen the pain was to suppress his feelings. To do that he had to focus on the thing above all else which mattered to him.

Revenge.

For her part, Chloe was silent as she remembered the times she'd enjoyed both with Paige and working for The Herald in the area through which they were driving. Then the reality of what had happened in the last 30 hours caught up with her and she wondered whether she would ever be able to regain the life and sense of freedom she'd enjoyed before she wrote her stupid news article.

From the O2, Branigan and Chloe took one of the Thames Clipper boats all the way along the river to Embankment and worked their way back to Alan's.

'You seemed very pre-occupied on the river journey,' Chloe observed when they got back to Alan's.

'I'm working on an idea and wanted to study the boats on the Thames,' he replied, 'and ended thinking about Sally and Molly, and things the three of us will never do.'

'I understand,' Chloe said sympathetically, 'I can't believe how you're holding yourself together.'

'I don't know that I am; beneath the surface I'm really just running on autopilot and focusing on my goal.'

'Which is?'

'Even before I lost Sally and Molly it was to solve this whole conundrum of course,' Branigan replied contemplatively, 'but now it goes much deeper; I want to see whoever is behind this getting their just desserts and I'd like the bastard who murdered my family to face justice.'

Chloe thought about Branigan's answer.

'It's justice you're after and not an eye for an eye?'

'Yes,' he said with absolute certainty, leading Chloe into the kitchen and putting the kettle on, 'don't get me wrong, I want my revenge, but I don't intend to do that in a way which blights the rest of my life - if you read spy novels, you'll believe that people like me murder with impunity.

Trust me, it's not like that.'

Branigan offered Chloe a cup of coffee which she declined before preparing one for himself and continuing with his thoughts.

'Either Marty, or one of his mates, decided on Saturday that it was an operationally sound decision to sacrifice Sally and Molly for the greater good. Putting me in prison - and killing a few of his fellow countrymen - is just as easy for whoever Cressix is, because he isn't dealing with any of us face-to-face.'

What Branigan was saying made sense to Chloe. Coming into the past couple of days she'd only really seen the world of spies and military intelligence through the eyes of Hollywood. Now that she was caught up with the political intrigue, she could see the merit in Branigan's approach. Whichever of Marty and his mates was prepared to sacrifice people "for the common good," was no better than the terrorists they wanted to fight - Branigan was right to fight for justice rather than stoop to their murderous level.

Chloe went into the dining room and began looking online for clues as to the whereabouts of any of the six between the key dates five years earlier; meanwhile Branigan prepared a shopping list of the things he would need in order to carry out both the plans he was working on.

A while later, just as Alan's key rattled in the lock, Chloe came into the kitchen clutching her laptop.

'I think you can discount David Price,' she said triumphantly.

Having greeted each other, both Alan and Branigan peered over Chloe's shoulder while she brought up the relevant page.

'Look,' she said, pointing to the dates in her notepad, 'we know Paige spoke to the person calling himself Cressix on the 7th and 9th of May.'

She opened a document in a parliamentary page.

'And I've found David Price addressing a Parliamentary Select Committee at the same time.'

'That looks conclusive to me,' Branigan agreed, 'how on earth did you find that?'

'It's just the journalist in me!' Chloe explained.

'I just did a few random searches and his name popped up.'

Alan wasn't overly impressed.

He'd been using a staggering weight of computer power and complex algorithms in his search, which had so far achieved nothing aside from bringing everyone in the office's access to the internet to a grinding halt and producing a bewildering number of friend requests on social media from people with the surname Brown.

Unaware that her search success had upset Alan's hopes of coming up with every answer to the questions on the display board, Chloe's thoughts turned to their supper.

'Can I get some food organised?' she asked.

'It's Monday,' Alan said, rising quickly to make sure he got to the kitchen cupboards first, 'so it's chicken in white sauce with boil-in-the-bag rice and frozen peas.'

Branigan had hitherto been treated to tinned peas at Alan's.

'That sounds nice, so these are frozen peas and not tinned?' Branigan asked.

Alan looked at him as if he'd just landed from another planet.

'I like some variety in my vegetables,' he said.

Branigan realised in a strange way he'd missed Alan's input since the morning.

After they'd eaten their main course - which was followed by a sticky toffee pudding with a form of cream that looked, tasted and behaved rather like shaving foam - all three of them tidied away.

'South Yorkshire police are coming tomorrow lunchtime to speak to me about the explosion,' Alan said as he padded out to settle back behind his bank of screens in the living room.

'Are they coming here?' Branigan called after him, fearing he and Chloe would be forced to vacate again.

'No, they're going to the office so they can speak with Marty as well,' Alan replied as he disappeared into the living room, 'Oh yes, did I tell you I've got the names of three of the people who were chasing you?'

Branigan shot a wide-eyed glance at Chloe before rushing down the hall.

'What the people who were at Bank Station?'

'Yes, the police who interviewed me had their names written in their notes,' Alan replied without looking up from his screens.

'Wow that's fantastic,' Branigan said, not quite believing the police would hand over the names of witnesses just like that, 'so what made them give you the names?'

'They didn't, the detective sergeant had a file of notes and as he flicked through them I was able to read them upside down.'

He'd not only read them upside down but, as it turned out, also their addresses and passport numbers.

'When the police check the addresses they've given they'll find they're false, but I've looked their passports up and they seem genuine enough even if there isn't much history behind them,' Alan said.

'How do you mean?' Branigan asked.

Alan clicked on his keyboard and the passport photograph of the man who'd posed as Chloe's dad appeared on the righthand screen beside Branigan.

'That's the passport for Greyson Krantz,' he explained, 'it was issued in Berlin five years ago and has been used regularly since then, but if I look back more than five years there's no trace of him.'

'And it's the same for the others?' Branigan asked, studying the image of the killer as the details of the two other passports appeared.

'Yes.'

Chloe joined Branigan.

'Look,' he said, pointing to the images Alan had just added, 'we have names, Clara Hess for the woman who posed as your mum, Connor Jarvis for the man in the Audi and Greyson Krantz for the man who…'

Branigan stopped short of saying "killed Sally and Molly," instead finishing with '…posed as your Dad and joined the chase in Birmingham.'

Having explained how Alan got the information, Branigan searched on the left-hand screen and added a note beside David Price's name, giving him the alibi of being in front of a select committee.

'Alan, how have you got on with the other searches?' he called from the hallway looking at the long list with Alan's name beside each item.

It was a strange phenomenon that he and Chloe had observed on their journey back from Felixstowe during a lull in the diatribe from Jim Hopkins.

'It's easiest speaking to Alan when he's in a different room, isn't it?'

'Yes, you're right,' Chloe agreed, 'do you suppose it is the lack of eye contact which helps?'

'Yes, plus he doesn't have to worry about picking up on social queues, or body language if he isn't sharing the same space.'

Once they'd come to that realisation, they realised the layout in Alan's house was perfect.

With Chloe and Branigan standing at the screens in the hallway and speaking to Alan seated in the adjacent living room they were at their most productive.

'Much of it has been disappointing,' Alan admitted, glancing at the growing list of friend requests he'd received and wondering which he should accept, 'I've got into the back-office for everyone's diaries but everything older than 12 months is wiped. I'm looking for a back-up but haven't found it yet. I have found the expenses files, but those don't show any detail - only the amounts paid to everyone.'

Branigan picked up on this.

'But I used to send in receipts from wherever I was when I was travelling, what happened to those?' he asked.

'They were signed off by the person you sent them to, but redacted when they were input on the accounts system.'

Branigan nodded.

'That makes sense,' he said to Chloe, 'the Organisation wouldn't want anyone but our immediate bosses to know where we all were.'

'What happened to the original receipts?' Branigan asked.

'They were sent off to secure storage in a disused underground station,' Alan said with a note of satisfaction in his voice.

'How do we get them out?'

'You can't because you have to have special authorisation to view them,' Alan said.

'How frustrating!' Branigan said.

'Either that, or have the right credentials.'

Silence.

'Alan, who has the right credentials?' Branigan asked, using every fibre of his being to control his voice and not shout the question.

'Either the person who put them in storage or a member of the National Audit Office.'

'That's great Alan, but it doesn't really help us,' Chloe said, frustrated not to be able to get to the precious records, 'is there no other way?'

'We don't need one,' Alan replied distractedly, 'I've already gone into the NAO system and put a request in. The files will be available on Wednesday - I just need to tell them who's going and produce a fake ID.'

'Brilliant Alan!' Branigan said, frustrated by the process, but delighted at the positive result.

'Am I the best person to go there?' Chloe asked.

'Probably,' Alan replied, 'I'm booked to go into the SIS

building undercover tomorrow and Marty will be suspicious if I keep taking time off.'

Branigan thought briefly about Alan's potential as a spy operating in the heart of SIS.

'What the fuck?!' he exclaimed.

'I can't get all the way round the IT system in SIS, you see,' Alan explained, rocking back and forth in his chair with his arms folded and his hands buried deep in his armpits, 'they've got two core systems there, one which is connected to the internet and the other they keep discreet from the outside world in case someone breaks through their firewalls; but if you look at the design of their systems there's a fundamental flaw.'

To emphasise his point, Alan disentangled himself and put a diagram up on the right-hand screen in the hallway.

Branigan looked at the jumble of what appeared to be electronic spaghetti.

'If you look where I've put the red circle, you can see the basic error they've made,' Alan announced, 'I imagine it's because someone wanted to be economical with their IT spend, but they've created two wholly independent systems using independent infrastructure then plugged them both into the same printer.'

Branigan didn't understand.

'How does a printer help us?'

'Because if I can put my own filter in the wiring for the printer, I'll have a backdoor into that standalone system.'

'Why is this printer the odd one out?' Branigan asked, peering at the diagram and not seeing any others connected in the same way.

'It isn't a printer like you're used to, it's one of those big ones that runs off a large roll of paper - you know, like an architect would use - I think they were just lazy and figured they didn't need two printers like that and plugged both systems into the same one.'

'They have it on a service contract,' Alan explained, 'and

I've booked myself in to give it a maintenance check.'

Branigan thought about what Alan had said.

'Do you know,' Branigan observed contemplatively, 'you may have found the one undercover job for which you're perfectly suited - but then what happens once you have your gizmo installed?'

'I can search all the personal files, internal memos and operational database on the hidden system,' Alan said, referring to the Military Intelligence equivalent of breaking into Fort Knox as if it were an everyday occurrence.

'Wow!' Chloe said, shocked at Alan's plans and surprised by his calmness.

'But aren't you seeing the police from Sheffield tomorrow?' she asked.

'Yes,' Alan replied, 'but they're coming down for midday - I'm booked into service the printer first thing.'

Chloe nodded and glanced at the list of other searches displayed on the left-hand screen, each of which had Alan's name beside it.

'I imagine with all these other things to think about you haven't managed to look at any of the other things on the list?'

Within moments the screen changed.

Alongside each item on the list with Alan's name beside it the words "Work in Progress" appeared beside his name:-

How to trace
Check diaries - Alan, Work in Progress
Expenses - Alan, Work in Progress
Public information - Alan, Work in Progress
Travel visas - Alan, Work in Progress
Airlines - Alan, Work in Progress
Air Miles - Alan, Work in Progress
Hotels in Bishkek - Alan, Work in Progress
Social media - Alan, Work in Progress

Operation Peach Tree
Search for - Alan, Work in Progress

Plus a new heading appeared at the bottom of the list - Cressix Enterprises.

TUESDAY 26TH OCTOBER

CHAPTER 19

09:18 Vauxhall Cross, London

Alan arrived early for his appointment to service the printer at the huge Secret Intelligence Service building at Vauxhall Cross, made famous by being variously attacked, blown up and set on fire in a number of Hollywood blockbusters. A quick check suggested to Alan that the building was not under attack, which meant he had nothing more daunting than three stages of security to pass before gaining full access to the printer.

It was not the most inviting building. Alan stepped through the outer metal gate which was topped with sharp spikes, before crossing a narrow paved strip and coming to a halt in front of another metal fence with a gate set in it not dissimilar to a football turnstile. Here he was greeted by a perfectly pleasant armed policeman who wanted to check what business he had at the building before letting him through. Once the policeman admitted Alan, he stopped on the other side.

'Is that an EOTech 512 holographic sight?' he asked, pointing to the semi-automatic carbine slung round the policeman's neck.

Once he'd admired the gun, studied the sight, asked the policeman about each of the different types of gun used by the police and asked whether he could hold the weapon, the officer carrying the rifle seemed overly keen to usher him into the main building. Next Alan put his large plastic briefcase into the airport-type screening machine where the security guard showed lots of interest in his cheese and ham sandwiches wrapped in several layers of tin foil. Having explained how he brought them from home every day, toasted them at work and discussed the nuances of different types of sandwich toaster, the guard was in a hurry to take him to the security desk where his credentials, ID and security pass were checked by the woman who greeted him there.

Confronted by a woman asking him questions Alan's ears turned bright red and he found it difficult to answer until he started explaining the different security passes he had in his collection.

'Look, I've already got 13 security passes,' Alan said enthusiastically, waving the heavy clump of tags hung round his neck at her, 'can I get one for here to add to my collection?'

11 of the passes were genuine, all of them produced on the machine at work and bearing the name of one of the firm's clients.

'This one is for Strankley Security Services,' he began, starting with the first badge in the pile, 'and although their name sounds similar to yours, they don't do what you do.'

Before he could work his way painstakingly though them all to the fake one for the firm which serviced the printer and his personal favourite - the one which gave him access all areas on the Starship Enterprise - the security lady waved him through.

In Reception they called for Joe Critchley from IT. When he arrived Alan instinctively knew that Joe was a man after his own heart - he was wearing a Spiderman tie.

They swapped "Live long and prosper" greetings and by the time they reached the first-floor print room Alan had agreed to look out for Joe at the London Comic Con - not the easiest task as their inability to maintain eye-contact rendered it unlikely either would recognise the other.

'I didn't expect the print room to have its own security code,' Alan said as Joe tapped a pad beside the door.

'That's so when they print secret reports not everyone

can see them,' Joe said, swinging open the door onto such an Aladdin's cave of printing, sorting and binding equipment that Alan's knees went quite weak. Having stroked the digital press, Alan spotted his machine at the back of the room.

Fed by a wide roll of paper which could be used to print a giant banner if required and, despite being dwarfed by some of the other equipment, the printer was still the size of an upright piano. Alan superficially checked the machine he had identified from the IT schematic and pulled out some paperwork he'd generated at home. Ticking various boxes, he checked the serial number against his records and made hand-written notes about the condition of the machine.

'It's on lease, you see,' he explained as he noted a scratch on the paintwork and recorded the make and number of the eight ink cartridges which served the machine, 'so I have to record the condition and, if I followed the rule-book I should make a note that your Light Cyan cartridge is not a manufacturer's one but a generic copy - technically that voids any warranty.'

He checked around the machine.

'Do you have the service manual here?' Alan asked.

Joe, who had the unenviable task of unblocking the multiple jams that occurred in the equipment that surrounded them, wasn't aware that there should be a service record kept with the machine.

'Sorry, not that I know of,' he replied becoming flustered and wringing his hands nervously, 'let me have a look around.'

While Joe searched the print room, Alan was able to plug his "gizmo" as Branigan had called it into the back of the printer before starting to take various parts off and cleaning them with sprays and oils he'd brought from home.

Joe drew a blank on the service manual.

'Do you think it might be back in the IT office?' Alan asked.

'We've got couple of filing cabinets for the various manuals, I could check there I suppose,' Joe volunteered before heading off in search of the spurious service booklet.

This gave Alan the time to plug his laptop into the back of the printer, access the print server on the dark side of the local infrastructure and install his revised version of the driver software which gave him his backdoor into the system. By the time Joe returned empty-handed Alan was running a programme on his laptop which said "Service Diagnostics" in bold letters along the top of the screen and appeared to be testing different functions.

'Do you know,' Alan said apologetically, 'I've just realised this is a P9000 which stores its own service record electronically!'

Once he'd reassembled the printer, Alan surreptitiously slipped the spring he had left over into his trouser pocket, stuck a dated service sticker on the back of the huge machine and allowed Joe to escort him out of the building.

11.23 Police Station, North London

'Have they gone?' DCI Tenant asked as he stepped into the Incident Room.

'Yes, sir, about ten minutes ago; they're on their way to see Freeman and Armstrong,' Drake replied.

He'd spent the last couple of hours with two detectives who'd come down from Yorkshire as part of the investigation into the explosion in Chloe's university digs.

'Did they have any useful information?' Tenant asked, his tone dubious.

'Well,' Drake said, leafing through his notebook, 'the main thing is that their DI isn't convinced it was Branigan who set the explosives.'

Tenant's eyebrows shot up.

'Who else do they think did it then?' he asked.

'That's the thing, sir,' Drake replied, continuing to study his notebook intently, 'they don't so much have someone else in the frame at the moment as have Branigan pretty much excluded from it.'

'How so?' Tenant asked, visibly disappointed.

'That car registration Mr Armstrong gave us looks like a genuine lead. It belongs to a silver Ford registered to an address in Canterbury, and South Yorkshire's enquiries have established a car with that number plate followed Branigan up the motorway at the same time as the genuine car was clocked on number plate recognition cameras in Kent.'

'But that doesn't prove anything,' DCI Tenant interjected.

'I agree, sir,' Drake replied, 'but they've also got CCTV footage which shows Branigan and Armstrong arriving at the student accommodation and a little while later Miss Travers arriving.'

Tenant shrugged. None of this altered his view on the course of events.

'Then,' DS Drake continued, 'before any of the three inside the building came out, someone sprayed paint over the lens of the two CCTV cameras covering the car park.'

Tenant sat upright in his chair.

'What someone other than Branigan?' he asked.

'Yes sir, most likely the driver of the silver Ford - they have that on CCTV close to the student accommodation a few minutes before the cameras were put out of action.'

'But how do they know the person in the Ford wasn't an accomplice of Branigan's?' Tenant asked.

'They don't,' Drake agreed, 'but the timing of events and footage of Branigan with Ms. Travers and Mr Armstrong later in the hotel bar in the city centre seem to tie in with Mr Armstrong's version of events; they're pretty sure Branigan didn't have the opportunity to go back and plant the bomb at Ms. Travers' apartment.'

Tenant looked disappointed.

'And do you think they're right?'

'Yes, sir, I do.'

DCI Tenant shook his head.

'I'm still going to stick with my instincts on this Drake.

We'll continue with Branigan as our sole focus and if we're no further forward in a couple of days you can then widen the enquiry; in the meantime, you should stay in touch with South Yorkshire and see if they change their mind.'

12.55 Marty Freeman Investigations, The Strand

It hadn't taken Marty long to give the two policemen from Yorkshire his statement. Following their discussions with the Met Police earlier in the morning, DS Morrison and DC Weston already had a good idea of what Marty had to say. They'd followed the sequence of events Marty had already given to the Met, written it down, and Marty had signed the account. Only when they'd finished the formal statement process did Marty find any of their questioning awkward.

'From the charred remains of a news article pinned to the wall of Ms. Travers' digs we've managed to find this,' DS Morrison said, taking out a copy of the "Oxymoron!" front page and placing it front of Marty, 'do you know anything about Ms. Travers trying to write about Branigan and what he did?'

Marty wasn't expecting their interest to extend this far and was momentarily thrown, a hesitation which wasn't lost on the astute DS.

'No, nothing,' Marty said, shaking his head and feigning surprise as DS Morrison explained about the story Chloe had told her friend Kate she was writing.

Once he'd established he couldn't help them further, Marty went to fetch Alan who he found sitting behind his computer screens gazing intently at a giant diagram of a piece of machinery whilst holding up a spring which he was trying to match to the schematic.

Marty was about to ask what he was doing, but then thought better of it.

'The two police officers from Sheffield would like to see you now,' he said.

15.37 Waterloo Bridge, London

Branigan stood on Waterloo Bridge watching the River Thames flowing beneath.

He'd had a frustrating day.

He and Chloe re-examined all the photographs and documents without finding any further clues to either the identity of his nemesis, or the focus of Operation Peach Tree, and then they'd found Alan's phone turned off when they wanted to find out how he'd got on at SIS.

Now he was thinking about his revenge.

16.42 Vauxhall Cross, London

Gregory Brown shut the door to Alex Oldroyd's office as he entered.

'Have you heard anything more from your contact in the Met?' he asked.

Alex nodded as Brown sat down in the chair opposite his desk.

'I spoke to him earlier,' Alex replied, 'they aren't any further forward in tracking Branigan down, although my contact did confirm Branigan is the only man they're looking for.'

'That has to be good news, doesn't it?' Gregory Brown asked.

'How do you mean?' Alex queried.

'I know it isn't good news for Branigan,' Gregory explained, 'but on a purely selfish note, that can only be positive for us - no one will listen to his story about Peach Tree being a conspiracy if he is arrested.'

'I see what you mean,' Alex agreed, 'I suppose they won't, although there is a slight problem there.'

Gregory Brown looked at him quizzically.

'Two officers investigating the explosion in Chloe Travers's flat have come down from Sheffield and they don't seem quite so convinced of Branigan's guilt.'

'Okay,' Gregory Brown said contemplatively, 'I'll mention that to David and see what thoughts he has - in the meantime could you write a note to that effect and post it to a new case-folder we've opened?'

Alex nodded.

'Until this thing dies down, David thought it would be useful for us all to keep each other informed of anything we see or hear,' Gregory Brown continued, 'can you let Michael and Peter know?'

'Of course - what's the file called?'

A smile crossed Alex's face as Gregory Brown told him.

19:37 Hendon, London

'How did you get on with the printer?' Chloe asked Alan over the frozen lasagne and garlic bread which formed Tuesday evening's staple.

'Okay,' Alan replied.

'Did you manage to do everything you needed?' Chloe persevered.

'Yes.'

'Have you tested your access?'

'Yes.'

It was like pulling teeth.

'How did you get on with the South Yorkshire Police?' Branigan asked, trying a different tack to engage Alan.

'Okay,' he replied.

What was it Sally used to say?

"Sometimes he just needs his own space - so rather than try and engage him, you're better off just letting him go off on his own."

'Why don't we just leave you in peace?' Branigan said, 'Chloe and I will tidy.'

The relief in Alan was palpable as he took his frozen New York cheesecake lathered in the strange creamy foam into the front room and shut the door behind him. Within seconds the strains of the Star Trek theme began.

19:57 Surrey Park Golf Club

Marty was sitting in the member's bar at the golf club with Michael Jenkins. Although it wasn't unusual for the two of them to meet at there, their seemingly chance encounter had been arranged when Michael phoned Marty just as he was about to sit down with the two police officers investigating the explosion in Chloe's apartment.

Much taller than Marty, Michael's graceful movements, bookish air and heavy black spectacles, gave him the air of an eccentric academic rather than the man running half the country's counter-intelligence operations.

'What happened today then?' Michael asked, sipping his glass of white burgundy.

'There were two of them, obviously interested in Branigan's movements and his reasons for going up to Sheffield,' Marty began before pausing to drink the top of his pint of cask ale, determined not to progress to whisky this evening, 'I told them about the people posing as Chloe's parents and Branigan heading off in my car to help search for their supposed daughter; beyond that I couldn't be much help. They tried to get more from my IT guy who went up to Sheffield with Branigan, but he's a computer geek and not communicative at the best of times, so I think they drew a blank there.'

Michael nodded sagely.

'Do you believe Branigan's side of things?' Michael asked.

'I do - well most of it anyway,' Marty replied, 'I think his conspiracy theory about the six of us is rubbish, but I do believe he is being set-up in the most horrible way - the trouble is the longer he spends evading the police the more convinced they'll be of his guilt.'

Michael held his wine up to the light before swirling it

round the glass and sniffing the bouquet.

'Yes,' he said, 'but is there any evidence that it isn't Branigan behind all of this? I mean it would be just as easy for him to organise a couple of people to come and tell you their daughter was in peril and he needed to drop everything to dash off to Sheffield - the whole thing could just be an elaborate sham.'

'I hear what you're saying, Michael,' Marty said, plainly disagreeing with his former colleague's suggestion, 'but this thing has all the hallmarks of being staged and, to be honest, if Branigan was staging it he'd do a better job.'

'I suppose you're right,' Michael Jenkins agreed, 'he's more professional than that.'

20:22 Hendon, North London

It was Branigan who suggested Chloe phone Paige.

'I doubt they're able to monitor every call going into the paper through the main switchboard, so if you call her at work the odds are they won't hear what you say,' he suggested.

'Hey Chloe,' Paige said in greeting, after Alan had set up a secure line and Chloe had reached her friend via the switchboard, 'were you part of that fracas at Bank Station on Sunday?'

Paige delighted in filling her friend in on all she could and informing Chloe of the DSMA Notice prohibiting stories which referred to Branigan.

'We sailed fairly close to the wind even publishing the story we did,' Paige explained, 'but if we'd gone any further and referred to him as a "disgraced former spy" or similar, the editor would have been dragged before the Broadcast Advisory Committee and been given a spanking - mind you, if what I hear is correct, he wouldn't particularly mind that!'

Chloe found conversations tended to go the same way with Paige.

'Have you had any joy tracking down the file you think you might have for Bishkek?' she asked, trying to steer her friend back on track.

'Oh, yes,' Paige said enthusiastically, 'I've found that and ordered it; it'll take 2 or 3 days. And I have found the business card, I don't think there's much of any interest – the only thing is the name, I got that wrong - it's Herbert not Hubert. More importantly, do you have any idea yet whether you're coming to JJ's?'

Chloe had to laugh.

'Paige, I'm up to my eyes in political intrigue, being pursued by the police, SIS and those people you saw outside your place on Sunday - I'm hardly likely to slip into my latex bra and knickers and pop out to the local fetish club in the middle of that, am I?'

'I suppose not,' Paige said sounding genuinely sad, 'but if you change your mind, let me know.'

Their call finished, Chloe went to the display screens and told Branigan about the conversation.

Almost absently she erased the name "Hubert" by rubbing her finger back and forth over it rapidly - a new feature Alan had added - and wrote "Herbert" back in.

Branigan stared at the board open-mouthed.

'For fuck's sake!' he exclaimed.

22:23

I wish I shared Cressix's confidence that Branigan will be out of the way shortly and that everything is going to blow over. From what I know of Branigan, he isn't going to be taken down easily.

If this doesn't go away quickly, I need to think carefully about my family, my objectives and the future. I don't think Cressix will like it if that happens.

WEDNESDAY 27TH OCTOBER

CHAPTER 20

08:09 Marty Freeman Investigations, The Strand

'Good morning Alan,' Anna said breezily as he crossed reception on his way upstairs.

Because Anna was in the same room as him, had spoken to him, and it was unwarranted social interaction, Alan took his preferred course of action - he marched straight past without saying a word. Hussain got the same treatment when they met on the stairs and Marty similarly when Alan reached the top floor and bolted from the staircase to the sanctuary of his computer screens.

Having brought his bank of machines to life, he used them first to step through the intense firewall that surrounded SIS's system and then burrow down to the back of the printer he'd serviced, before opening up the backdoor he'd installed into the rarefied world of the standalone system. There were several governments around the world who would pay handsomely to gain the access Alan had achieved within 10 minutes of arriving at work.

He began his search.

09:24 Data Storage, Old Street

Alan was right, the five boxes of expenses records Chloe was looking to see had been stored in various locations across two different deep-storage sites which had been built as air raid shelters in the Second World War. In keeping with Government tradition and eschewing the move to a paperless society, the documents she needed had been gathering dust in deep dark tunnels for years before being brought to the surface and taken to the document company's offices near Old Street.

Acres of deep storage being used to keep old expenses claims safe from enemy attack. If scanned the same documents would fit comfortably on the hard drives in Alan's spare room.

All that remained was for Chloe to view the documents, take the necessary copies and hopefully eliminate a number of their 5 remaining candidates. That plan pre-supposed there were no hiccoughs with the access Alan had arranged.

The offices of the data company were tired, poorly maintained and exuded an air of budget restraint and thin margins. A cut-throat business, Chloe imagined, where government contracts were prized for their volume rather than their profitability. Pushing on the plywood door beside a sign for "Reception," Chloe stepped into a narrow corridor and through a door beyond.

It was difficult to tell whether she was in the corporate offices of a mini-cab firm, a down-market takeaway or, as she believed to be the case, a government-sanctioned storage depot. The linoleum theme carried across the floor of the stark room which was lit by three of the four strip lights overhead - the fourth flickering annoyingly and just failing to fire-up every few seconds. The dark patches on the white-painted walls indicated the presence of notices and signs in days gone by, and the room's only nod to comfort and welcome were two plastic chairs and a grey-and-white laminate table. Chloe crossed the room to a worn wooden counter, pressed the call-button and heard a bell jangle in the distance. After a long wait a dark-haired man wearing a brown warehouseman's coat appeared; he was about forty with heavy-rimmed spectacles and his name badge announced him as Guy Parkiss.

'Hello Mister Parkiss,' Chloe said, 'my name is Debbie Forsyth from the NAO - I believe you have some files for me to inspect?'

The man on the other side of the counter looked her up and down and made no acknowledgment of the introduction she'd just given. He produced a clipboard and a pen from his side of the counter and thrust them across to her.

'Name, department, details of records, contact details and signature, plus I need two forms of ID and a letter of authorisation.'

No eye contact, no please and thank you - he made Alan look like a social butterfly.

Chloe filled out the form and passed him the NAO identity card and driving license Alan had somehow manufactured on the equipment at work, plus a very convincing letter of authority signed in triplicate. Parkiss sniffed and inspected each item in minute detail before drawing himself up to his full 5 foot 5 inches.

'This is no good,' he said, 'I need the original of the authorised requisition form.'

'Isn't that the form my office emailed through to you yesterday?' Chloe said, remembering Alan printing, signing, scanning and emailing the document.

'Yes, but that's only a scanned copy; I need the original in order to release the files to you.'

'Wait,' Chloe said triumphantly, remembering the map and other paperwork Alan had given her before she left, 'is this what you're after?'

She pulled out the signed original of the form Alan had printed and scanned.

Parks examined it as if checking the authenticity of a Dead Sea scroll.

'There should be a second copy of this so I've got one to file with my records and one to send off to Head Office.'

'I'm sorry, Mr. Parkiss,' Chloe said, trying to be as nice as possible to the jobs-worth little man, 'but I don't have another part to give you.'

He sniffed again.

Not because he had a cold or a runny nose, but because it

was another way for him to show his disdain for his visitor.

'I shouldn't you know.'

Chloe waited in silence - not wanting to give him the satisfaction of hearing her beg any more – while he drummed his fingers as he were being faced with a difficult life-or-death decision.

'Okay, you can look at them,' he said.

Five minutes later, pretending through gritted teeth she was grateful, Chloe got her boxes - each dumped ungraciously on the counter with no offer to help carry them to the pitifully small table. If this was what life was like in the NAO, Chloe was glad that she'd chosen a career in journalism.

Checking the reference numbers, the first box she opened was the one containing Peter Winstone's expenses claim. Following the timeline she'd run through with Branigan, the records should tell of any expenses Peter Winstone claimed from the night Branigan sent the pictures of the truck contents to London, to the day he was sent home in disgrace.

Alan had armed her with a small camera with a spare battery and a huge memory card so when she found the right pages all she had to do was clicked away at each of the receipts.

One box down.

The next box contained Michael Jenkins' claims for the same period and she was halfway through the photography process when Parkiss reappeared.

'I need your driving license again,' the officious man demanded, 'the hologram isn't showing properly on my photocopy.'

Chloe clicked as fast as she could before she answered - she knew for sure there was no hologram on the fake driving license Alan created.

'I don't have the equipment, you see,' he'd worried, 'but no one working in a box storage depot is going to study it that closely.'

Chloe finished the records for Michael.

'But you haven't given me back the driving license yet,' she said, bending to pick up the next box.

Gregory Brown.

'Yes, I did,' Parkiss said with certainty, his voice rising at the temerity of this woman to suggest that he, with all his experience, would make a simple mistake like leaving the driving license on the photocopier.

'I'm sorry Mr. Parkiss, but you didn't.'

Chloe clicked away at the first pages she came to with Brown's name on and let the pompous little man build up a head of steam.

'Why don't you go and check, Mister Parkiss,' Chloe said contemptuously before the little man swivelled on one heel and strutted out to the photocopier.

A minute later he came back triumphantly.

'I told you it wasn't th...' he said, before realising that he was addressing an empty room.

14:54 The Club, Knightsbridge

Branigan had only met Chloe briefly upon her return from the storage depot; what she breathlessly described was one of those unforeseen factors you couldn't plan for.

Alex Oldroyd's words in training, *'Expect the unexpected.'*

They'd planned as carefully as they could, produced all the relevant documentation, made sure Chloe was properly prepared; then fate dropped an obnoxious little man like Parkiss into the mix. Still, it seemed as if Chloe's mission had been a limited success and, in a game where the odds seemed stacked against them, he was happy to accept that.

With luck, tonight would be his game-changer.

He was in a second-floor bedroom of the club frequented by members of the Special Forces and Military Intelligence, housed in a sparingly-decorated red brick mansion in up-market Knightsbridge, The Club was notable for two reasons. Firstly, it had no name plate to announce its presence and, secondly, its hallways and staircase were draped with photographs of luminaries from the world of Special Forces and the intelligence community with neatly typed explanations of their heroics under each.

Having seen Chloe change Cressix's first name, he'd finally understood its significance.

Certain now that one of the diners was responsible for the events which led not only to his ignominious exit from The Service, but also the killing of Sally and Molly, he was determined to confront the group and scare his nemesis. He didn't yet know which of the group it was and, unfortunately, Chloe's problematic mission hadn't got them as far forward in revealing the identity as he would like. That said, tonight wasn't about singling one person out and exacting revenge, instead Branigan intended to use another of General Wáng's Military Strategies - the 13th, "*Stomp the grass to scare the snake.*"

Doing something unusual, strange and unexpected to disrupt the enemy's thinking.

In truth it was something else as well. The instinct in Branigan when it came to fight or flight undoubtedly erred in favour of fighting, yet thus far he and Chloe had flown from foes in Sheffield and Birmingham, run from their pursuers at Bank Station and most recently Chloe had run from a jumped-up little man in a data records office. Branigan wanted all that to change - tonight he was going to put himself in front of all the suspects while they were in one place and scare the snake who'd ordered the murder of Sally and Molly.

Chloe hadn't exactly embraced the plan when he first mooted it.

'I hate to say it Branigan,' she said, when he told her where he intended to strike, 'but that has to be the worst plan since Custer said "let's all head off to Little Bighorn."'

'Don't get me wrong,' she continued, 'I'm all in favour of rattling the cage of whoever is behind all this, but think about where you're planning to do it - The Special Forces Club - don't you think there's a remote possibility there'll be some pretty competent agents in there with you?'

'Of course, there are some risks,' Branigan replied calmly, as if their discussion centred on nothing more daunting than choosing his starter in a restaurant, 'but that's what proper planning should minimise.'

'Okay, supposing you get in there, do what you're planning and then get away - what happens then?' Chloe asked.

'I'll have stomped the grass. Their cosy little group won't be able to close ranks as it did before, because five of the six round the table will have that little seed of doubt in the back of their minds. In addition, the bastard who I really want to get to is going to be panicked by being confronted in his own space - suddenly it isn't going to be a game he's used to playing at arm's length, but a proper in-your-face confrontation which he won't like. I think it will make him do something rash - not at the dinner table you understand, but over the coming days.'

'Okay, then do it,' Chloe acquiesced, 'but Branigan, please be careful.'

Planning, preparation and patience.

Having planned carefully and, with Alan's help, prepared meticulously, he had nothing to do but wait patiently in his hiding place for the next five or six hours.

15:34 Stoke Newington, London

It felt funny for PC Harold Evans to be so close to where he'd found the bodies. He hadn't been back to the road since Saturday evening when he thought he was turning out to deal with a domestic violence incident and ended up being the first on the scene of a double murder. Now was a little different. Drafted in to help with door-to-door knocking - one of the more tedious aspects of life in the police force - he and all the others doing the same thing on the same shift knew they were there because the investigation had stalled.

When the murders first happened, he'd been told the culprit was known and would be found by Sunday. Now apparently, the culprit was a little less clear and they had no idea where to look for him. PC Evans knocked on the door of No.34, the home of Ms. Judith Warde - friend of the murdered woman who'd already been interviewed and given her statement.

'We're looking for you to revisit the friends and neighbours we've already spoken to,' DS Drake had said in the briefing, 'we're after any detail they might have remembered, plus anything which points to the state of Branigan's marriage, infidelity on either side, or places he might be hiding.'

An attractive brunette in her early thirties answered the door.

'Hello officer, how can I help you?' she asked, her eyes running up and down the fit uniformed policeman.

'Ms. Warde?' PC Evans asked, 'I know you've already spoken with my colleagues, but I wonder if I could have a few minutes of your time just to see if anything more has come to you?'

'Please, call me Jude,' she replied, ushering PC Evans inside, before giving him a cup of tea and pouring out her version of that night's events.

'The thing I don't understand,' PC Evans said when Jude finished, 'is why the officers you spoke with weren't interested in the man you saw earlier in the evening. You did tell them about him, didn't you?'

'Of course I did,' Jude replied, 'but they seemed so convinced Branigan was their man they didn't want to listen, trust me I've known him and Sally for years, and a happier, more loving couple you couldn't wish to meet - he'd never murder her and what sane father could kill his baby girl?'

By the time he left, PC Evans was convinced that his colleagues on the murder squad should be looking for the person Judith described as a "rather attractive, older, grey-haired man," but what did he know, he was only a humble PC?

21:24 The Club, Knightsbridge

The six people in Marty's group were defined by a moment in time.

In New York for a discrete meeting to discuss surveillance techniques with their American counterparts, the six stepped out of an elevator in the North Tower of the World Trade Centre at 8:44am on 11 September 2001 - one minute before American Airlines flight 11 slammed into the building.

None of them would ever forget either the shockwave which rocked the skyscraper, or the sight of a 30ft long metal girder as it tumbled in flames past the 44th floor window. Having seen intelligence suggesting terrorists had multiple attacks planned, David Price had his team organised to help with the evacuation almost before the flaming girder crashed onto the street below. By the time the second plane hit the South Tower, they themselves were taking it in turns to carry a stranded wheelchair user - Joseph Quale - down the stairwell, emerging to the scene of devastation below just before the building collapsed.

Drawn together by their shared adversity, the six of them vowed they would celebrate their survival with dinner at the Special Forces Club in London - their initial meeting becoming a monthly fixture where they could swap their recollections, enjoy fine wine and relax in a group with a common bond.

Using the photographs he'd taken from Marty's office, Branigan easily identified the group's usual table and installed a directional microphone on the nearby mantelpiece so he was able to listen to their conversation from his hiding place in a second-floor guest bedroom. As the group took their seats David Price - the most senior person at the table - made it clear Branigan was to be the focal point for conversation.

'Perhaps Marty could fill us in on the events of last Saturday,' he suggested, before Marty chronicled events starting with the call he'd received from the people purporting to be Chloe's parents and ending with his meeting Branigan at Euston on Sunday morning. When Marty's narrative turned to Branigan's questioning of the group's original Operation Peach Tree discussion, there was a murmur of disapproval.

Michael Jenkins - the man who had not only recruited Branigan but also, as head of Special Operations, sent him off to Kazakhstan to fill the place of the murdered Ed Khan – broke the ensuing silence.

'On Sunday I got a call from a contact in the Met Police, telling me Branigan had escaped arrest at Bank Station,' he explained, 'and from what we now know he was accompanied there by Chloe Travers, the girl who wrote the news article making reference to Peach Tree.'

At the mention of the operation the six of them had dreamed up, Peter Winstone spoke, his strident voice suggesting he was facing the microphone more directly than the others.

'How much did Branigan know about Peach Tree before you spoke with him, Marty?'

'Not that much, I guess,' Marty replied, 'in fact he didn't seem to have latched onto it at all until I mentioned it when he was driving back from Sheffield.'

'For fuck's sake,' Peter Winstone said, 'you mean he didn't know anything about our fucking conversation before you told him?'

Branigan smiled to himself, Peter was forthright, loud, and the most junior of the group; his state-education and rough edges leading him to a life of undercover work in London's darker quarters rather than a higher-profile desk job. Thick-set, in his fifties and with shaved hair, Peter looked more like a dodgy used car salesman than a member of military intelligence.

'I'll hold my hands up to that one Peter,' Marty replied defensively, 'we were speaking in the middle of all the furore. You know how it works; I couldn't withhold a piece of material information from a trusted colleague just because letting it out might be a bit embarrassing - neither could you.'

No one disagreed with this basic code of military conduct and it fell to David Price to step in.

'None of us would argue with you telling Branigan about our conversation, what I think concerns people round this table is that we aren't dragged into whatever is happening here unnecessarily.'

'I understand that,' Marty replied, 'but I have no idea what Branigan is up to now - all I can tell you is that even with Black Ops on his tail he won't be sitting around doing nothing.'

'Whoa!' A new voice Branigan recognised as Alex Oldroyd jumped in.

Alex was the assistant to Michael Jenkins and the man who'd had day-to-day responsibility for Branigan's failed mission in Kyrgyzstan. Not a great fan, Branigan hadn't enjoyed Alex's pushy style and innate self-belief which made him a difficult boss and someone who always seemed to know better.

'You don't believe he's really got Black Ops onto him, do you,' Alex said forcefully, 'isn't that just an elaborate ruse on his part?'

It was David Price who leapt to defend Marty.

'We don't know whether-or-not that is the case, Alex,' he said calmly, 'but it isn't Branigan's style to try and blame others. We all know him as someone who tackles problems head on.'

'I'm sorry David, but are you telling us that you believe Branigan's version of events?' Alex asked.

'No, I'm just saying things are going on here about which

we do not know, which means we have to do what every person round this table is good at - we keep an open mind, respond to the facts as they emerge and don't leap to any conclusions.'

Branigan's rush of gratitude towards David Price for not dismissing his notion that someone at the table was complicit was immediately countered by the rough tones of Peter Winstone.

'Are we all suspects then David?' he asked.

'I suppose you could say that, yes. I think we should treat this the same way as the police would and not dismiss anyone as having a hand in the explosion and deaths and what may well be a Black Ops operation until we have evidence to the contrary. I'm sorry if that offends some of you,' he continued in response to the murmur of malcontent around the table, 'but you know it's the right line to take.'

Michael Jenkins picked up on the reference to the police.

'On the subject of the police, should we be doing anything to help them catch Branigan?'

'Come on Michael,' David Price replied, 'you know it's not our role to get embroiled in domestic policing.'

Alex carried on with the theme.

'But can we at least feed them anything which may help if we find it - I mean if there really is a Black Ops team working here, we might identify someone in their number and could let the police know.'

A different voice responded to this - Gregory Brown, whose warm dulcet tones carried all the calm authority of his role as David Price's deputy.

'Come on Alex. We spend enough time making sure there's clear water between ourselves and any other agencies; we're hardly going to knock on the door of the Met and say, "Hello chaps, the people you're looking for are agents who we know because they work with us."'

Branigan could sense Alex Oldroyd's embarrassment as Gregory Brown continued.

'I think we're all missing the point here. David's right - we need to keep an open mind on every angle until we know whether Branigan is either staging things himself, or what else we might be dealing with. All we should be doing is keeping schtum on our discussion round this table a few years ago until the real reason for what's happened to Branigan emerges.'

'There's something else you should all know if we're talking about other possible explanations for what's going on,' Marty said.

In his hideaway on the floor above Branigan stiffened and listened intently.

'At the Academy we used to teach agents not to believe in coincidences,' Marty continued, 'well on Friday night Branigan ran into one of the agents working the other side of the operation in Bishkek - while he was working undercover on an industrial espionage case, Branigan came across a former Russian counterpart - Anatoly Kozlow.'

When it became clear from the murmurs round the table not everyone was sure who Kozlow was, Michael Jenkins elucidated.

'Five years ago, the Russians contacted us believing an operation they were running was compromised and asking us to lend an independent hand tracing some heavy armament being smuggled south through Kazakhstan and Kyrgyzstan. We did that and, as most of you know, when we put Ed Khan in he was killed; we all know what happened when we put Branigan in as his replacement.'

'Our direct liaison in the SVR,' he continued, making reference to the Russian Foreign Intelligence Service, 'was Anatoly Kozlow who stopped working for them not long after and is now on the dark side providing his services on a freelance basis.'

'It can't be a coincidence that he ran into Branigan, can it?' Alex asked.

'I know what you mean,' Marty said, 'but to be fair to them

both I'm partially responsible for the two of them meeting - you see, I had a hunch it was Kozlow who was behind a piece of industrial espionage we were asked to investigate so I deliberately bought Branigan into the surveillance.'

'It's brought, not bought,' Michael Jenkins pointed out.

Listening upstairs Branigan smiled wryly at the awkward silence which followed - he too hated it when the English graduate in Michael came out. Hearing the table being cleared and David Price asking for the decanted Fonseca '97 port he'd ordered, Branigan stretched his stiff limbs before heading downstairs to make the group's evening - it was time to act.

'I'll take that,' he said to the waiter on the landing, 'I want to surprise my friends.'

Used to the antics of some of the wilder members of the Club and - overawed by the tall, strong, and patently determined Branigan wearing full evening dress - the waiter passed the decanter over, no doubt encouraged by the two £20 notes Branigan slipped into his top pocket. Branigan stepped confidently into the dining room and quickly took in his target table near the front window and the four other tables of guests dotted around the room. Seventeen people in total by the time he included the other waiter whose look of shocked surprise softened when his colleague passed him one of the two bank notes.

Carefully placing the decanter on David Price's right-hand side, Branigan allowed the man at the head of the table to inspect the bottle and nod his approval before delivering the glasses to each of the guests. With all eyes focused on the port, no one looked up at Branigan as he stepped back and waited while the port was passed round to the left and David Price stood to make the Loyal Toast.

'The Queen!' the whole table chorused.

Following rank, it was Gregory Brown who next rose to his feet.

'To the victims,' he said, Branigan realising his toast was

to those who died the day the six forged their alliance amidst the carnage of 9/11.

It was Branigan's moment.

'Gentlemen,' he said, stepping forward to stand between David Price's right shoulder and Marty seated next to him.

There was an audible gasp from the whole table.

'I'd like to propose another toast, this one to my wife and daughter,' Branigan said, allowing the pause to become uncomfortable before he continued, 'to Sally and Molly.'

Whether it was Branigan's brooding presence, the nature of the toast or some form of collective guilt wasn't clear, but Marty rose to his feet followed wearily by the others. Elsewhere in the room the other diners glanced across at the table unaware that Branigan was an unwelcome guest. Only the two waiters watched with suspicion, conscious that the guest who'd bribed his way in hadn't been met with raucous laughter.

'I thought having you all together would be a great opportunity' he said conversationally as the six of them sat back down, 'for me to ask you some very basic questions.'

'Come on Branigan,' Gregory Brown said, his deep voice calm and resonant, 'isn't this all a bit melodramatic? Just give yourself up and we can help you get things sorted.'

'What,' Branigan said, the angry edge to his voice causing heads to swivel on the nearest tables, 'sorted like you did when you fired me? Sorted like you, or one of your colleagues did with my wife and daughter? Because if that's your kind of sorted I'd rather do it my way if you don't mind.'

There was an uncomfortable pause while all six round the table struggled to look Branigan in the eye.

'First question,' Branigan continued, 'how many of you are there round the table?'

'Six,' Marty said, breaking the awkward silence that followed.

'Very good,' Branigan replied, placing a piece of paper

with the word "six" typed on it in large letters in the middle of the table.

'Second question - what is the name of the road this club is on?'

'Herbert Crescent,' Michael Jenkins said with a hint of boredom in his voice.

Another sheet of paper appeared next to the first on the centre of the table.

'Final question,' Branigan said into the now silent room as the other diners stopped their own conversations, aware that all was not well, 'what is the name of the man who broke my cover for me and gave my story to the press?'

He met with a response like a school teacher asking a classroom of reluctant teenagers a question - if they knew, no one wanted to give the answer.

Branigan waited in the silence.

'No?' he ventured, 'I didn't know the full name until recently either. I'd heard the name Cressix on a couple of occasions but that didn't mean anything to me until I saw it with his Christian name for the first time yesterday.'

He reached down to the table and pushed the two pieces of paper together so the word "six" covered the last letters of the word "Crescent."

It now read "Herbert Cressix".

'Would anyone now care to venture a guess as to the soubriquet used by the man who fed me to the press?'

Marty was the first to voice anything.

'Shit,' he said, as the implications of the choice of name began to dawn.

'That's one word for it, Marty,' Branigan agreed.

He looked in turn at the faces round the table, conscious that one of the people on the nearby table of four had made a surreptitious phone call. In a room full of people associated with the intelligence community the odds were high the caller had recognised his face.

Branigan slipped his hands into his trouser pockets in a

sign of relaxed confidence.

'I'm not here to point an accusing finger at any one in particular, but I know one of you round the table is responsible. You can try and deny it of course - put the name Herbert Cressix down to coincidence, pretend it's coincidence that Chloe came under attack when she wrote about Operation Peach Tree - even though a few moments ago I heard Marty say that he didn't believe in coincidences - but to whichever of you it is, David, Peter, Alex, Gregory, Michael or Marty,' he said, working clockwise round the table and focusing his gaze on each as he said their name, 'I just want you to know that I am after you and I'm going to get you and the person you sent to kill Sally and Molly.'

Branigan could feel people tensing throughout the room and sensed a shuffling on the table in front of him. Now the shock of his appearance had worn off, people were preparing to react.

One man and eighteen people.

An uneven contest unless you had planning and preparation on your side.

Several things happened at once.

A police siren could be heard immediately outside the front of the building and a blue flashing light crept in through the slight gap in the curtains.

Branigan pulled his right hand from his pocket and threw something which looked like confetti high into the air. All eyes in the room followed the hundreds of little pieces of paper as they fluttered down over the table, the guests and the floor. Each 1/2-inch square of paper bearing one of five images.

The face of Sally after she was murdered; the burning twin towers; a picture of a peach tree; the name "Herbert Cressix"; and Molly's dead face.

In his left-hand pocket Branigan pressed the "send" button on his mobile, which in turn relayed a message to a phone wired to the three rape alarms and the pyrotechnic flash he'd earlier concealed in a large vase sitting on a shelf at the far end of the room. The flash was like a small bolt of lightning in the confined space and the attendant puff of white smoke accompanied by the sound of the three rape alarms - their piercing whistles and wails amplified by the vase in which they were contained - filled the room. Maybe not as effective as a military spec thunder flash, but not bad considering he and Alan knocked it up with limited resources.

As all heads turned to see the source of the piercing cacophony, smoke and flash of light, Branigan pulled from behind the curtain a dry powder extinguisher he'd earlier retrieved from near the electrical supply in the basement. Designed to put out a fire by smothering it with a fine inert powder, the extinguisher wasn't the best thing to let off in a confined space unless, like Branigan, you wanted to fill the room with an impenetrable cloud of fine dust.

By the time the police burst through the door it was clear Branigan had used the white cloud as cover to flee to the balcony before vaulting down to the pavement below.

Even as the first of the police officers peered down onto the street below, Branigan was back in the bright lights of Knightsbridge nonchalantly brushing dust from his lapel.

Still seated at the table, David Price surveyed the detritus.

'You have to admit he has some panache, even if he has no idea how to treat a decent port,' he said ruefully, looking at the layer of dust floating on the surface of his glass.

THURSDAY 28TH OCTOBER

CHAPTER 21

08:43 Hendon, North London

Branigan waited for Alan to leave for work before recounting to Chloe the events of the previous night.

'It's not that I don't trust Alan,' he explained, 'but if Marty mentions anything about it at work, it'll be easier for him if he doesn't already know the story.'

On balance Chloe understood the point - if Alan knew a different version of the story he'd be just as likely to argue about it as feign ignorance.

Having discussed the different reactions around the table, the tenor of the evening's conversation and concluded that they were no nearer identifying their culprit they moved on.

'There's no denying you stomped the ground last night,' Chloe concluded as she placed the pictures she'd taken at the document storage depot on the kitchen table, 'and I think I can help us cross two more people off the list.'

She separated the pictures into three different piles.

'I managed to get all of the expenses for Peter Winstone and Michael Jenkins before that horrible little man spotted that the driving license was fake,' she began, moving two of the piles in front of Branigan, 'and I was part way through Gregory Brown's when I had to leg it. I did think about grabbing the rest of the paperwork but realised I couldn't run properly carrying a heavy box.'

'Sensible move,' Branigan said, flicking through the pile nearest him, 'we were always taught to take nothing more than the bare essentials for survival with us - useful as they might be, I don't see a bunch of 5-year-old expense claims as a necessity!'

He held up one of the photographs.

'It looks like Peter Winstone was buying clothes and getting measured for a suit while Cressix was in Bishkek chatting to Paige.'

'That's how I saw it,' Chloe agreed, 'and if you look at Michael Jenkins, he was staying in a hotel in Manchester for much of that time as well. Unfortunately, I wasn't so lucky with the claims for Gregory Brown, although I did get some of his, in my rush I took photographs of a set from a couple of weeks too early.'

Branigan shrugged.

'It doesn't matter, you did brilliantly to go there and get what you did; and if you think about it, you've managed to reduce six suspects down to three - that's progress.'

'You can't honestly believe Marty is the culprit either, can you?' Chloe asked, 'He doesn't have the same axe to grind for the Service now that he's retired and I can't see him being so callous with you.'

'You're probably right,' Branigan agreed, 'but we can't dismiss him until we have some evidence to prove it.'

Chloe walked into the hallway and touched the screens.

'Aside from Marty, that leaves us with Gregory Brown and Alex Oldroyd.'

09:39 Marty Freeman Investigations, The Strand

Alan had found two interesting things.

The first was the bank account for Cressix Enterprises, the second details of a new operation inside the covert section of the SIS computer system.

The bank account was interesting because not only was there a substantial balance on it, but also there were several different types of transaction coming off it. Even more excitingly, there was a whole audit trail that started with the account being funded with £7,499,039 which Alan decided was a nice balance to have because it was a prime number. However, that number didn't last long because £1,500,000 was transferred out to an anonymous account in Panama. The next payment from the account was to cover the handling charges for the container as it came through Felixstowe followed by a regular monthly payment to an estate agent in Guildford.

The only other transaction was a significant payment in the last week, which, Alan assumed, was to pay for the people chasing Branigan.

This prompted him to do two things.

First, he looked in the estate agent's files and found what the payments were for and, secondly, he moved the remaining balance of £5,724,845 to his own savings account.

His rationale for moving the cash was simple.

If the man running Cressix Enterprises had no money, he wouldn't be able to pay the bad people chasing his friend Branigan and they would go away.

Moving the money, of course, was easy.

Alan never understood why the banks gave you an encryption machine, passwords and complex routines to generate an authorisation for a transfer, when all you needed to do was look inside the computer waiting for that code and see what answer it was expecting. Having authorised the transfer to a general clearing account at the London Stock Exchange he was able to move the money to a share broker's client account and from there onto his own account, each time authenticating the payment but removing traces of it from the account-holder's statement.

The upshot was, that his bank manager would wake up the next morning and find that his customer Mr. Alan Armstrong had paid £5.7m into his savings account from the sale of shares approved, confirmed and authenticated by his own bank's broking arm. Any further enquiry would suggest that Mr. Armstrong was very lucky, his father having invested

£50,000 in shares that were issued the year Alan Armstrong was born. The shares were in a fledgling company called Apple which made computers.

Excited by his find from the estate agents, Alan went into Marty's empty office so he could pass on the news in private.

'Branigan, it's me, Alan Armstrong,' Alan said in a whisper which would have carried across the entire floor had he not been in his boss's office with the door shut, 'I've found the bank account for Cressix Enterprises. They've been renting an industrial unit in Farnham since the container arrived.'

'Fuck – is that for real Alan?' Branigan said, feeling a sudden rush of excitement, 'can you send me details so I can have a look at the site?'

'Yes,' Alan said.

'And there's another thing,' he continued after a long pause, 'I can't find anything about Operation Peach Tree on the SIS system, but David Price has opened a new file on the SIS Intranet for any information relevant to you and Chloe.'

'Let me guess,' Branigan said, 'he's called it Operation Plum Tree.'

10:56 Whitechapel, East London

The man who'd posed as Chloe's dad, Greyson Krantz, wasn't happy.

'You tell me where to find the cunt and we'll get him this time,' he said angrily.

Of course he knew when he took it on that this operation was a little different, that it was being run even more deeply off the radar than usual and that its primary focus was getting a man put behind bars rather than "disposed of" as his paymasters liked to put it when describing murder.

Not that murder wasn't on the agenda.

In this instance Greyson's handler - an anonymous face he presumed was somewhere in the depths of Military Intelligence - didn't mind if people on the periphery died. His instruction had been, 'Just make sure you frame Branigan as the killer.'

Fine by Greyson - as long as he was paid, he didn't really care what job he was given although it helped when he could have some fun like he had with Branigan's family. He was still living off the thrill of knowing Sally's dying vision was of her little girl turning purple as she scrabbled futilely at the plastic tie around her throat. His cock twitched with pleasure as he remembered slowly tightening the plastic tie one click at a time.

'I'll tell you anything I hear Greyson,' the man on the end of the phone said - the man he knew only as Mr. Cressix.

'And when we do find him, do you still want him locked up or can we just kill him?'

'Locked up,' Cressix replied succinctly.

'Does that mean the girl is still off limits?' Greyson asked.

Cressix paused for a long time as he thought through the girl's role and how she had become embroiled since Saturday's monumental fuck-up.

'You can dispose of her if you want to,' Cressix said decisively, 'she was, after all, the original target and as long as you add her death to Branigan's tally you can do what you like; just don't get distracted.'

18:39

What I have found out is a game-changer.

The question is, do I tell Cressix, or do I keep my own counsel and solve the problem myself?

Having taken counsel, I have decided to act on the information, not tell Cressix and to act like a lone wolf.

18:43 Hendon, North London

'They're doing a phone trace,' Alan called out having glanced at a message which flashed on his screen in the front room.

In the hallway Branigan glanced at Chloe quizzically.

'Who is doing a phone trace Alan?' he asked.

'SIS is searching for your phone,' Alan replied.

Branigan thought about his movements.

'Could that be a problem?' he asked.

'Yes, because you have the same phone on you now as you did at The Club last night.'

'Fuck!' Branigan said.

'And they are doing the search right,' Alan continued, 'they're looking for phones which pinged masts near the Special Forces Club and London Bridge Station at the times they knew you were in both places.'

Branigan looked at Chloe.

'We're going to need to change our sim cards more frequently and move out of here right now - it won't take them long to link my phone with the two scenes and then trace it here,' he said, inwardly cursing his stupidity, 'I'm sorry, I've made a schoolboy error.'

'Why do you need to move out?' Alan asked.

Branigan raised his eyes heavenwards.

'Because they'll trace the phone number and then be able to track it to here.'

'No, they'll go to the airport.'

Branigan exchanged an exasperated look with Chloe.

'Why are they going to do that Alan?' Chloe asked patiently.

'Because while I was at work Peter Winstone put a note in the Plum Tree folder on the SIS intranet saying he had instigated a search.'

Branigan muttered an expletive under his breath.

'Why didn't you warn us, we could have made our escape long ago?'

Alan responded by rocking back and forth more quickly.

'But I thought you'd think it was a good idea to tag their search result to a phone in departures at Heathrow Airport,' he said, sounding hurt.

Branigan looked perplexed.

'I'm sorry Alan, are you saying you've mis-directed their search?' he asked, peering round the living room door and catching brief glimpses of Alan each time he rocked forward.

'Yes, I took your real number out of the data string for the phone masts they were searching and replaced it with a pay-as-you-go phone number I found in departures at Heathrow.'

Branigan's shoulders visibly relaxed.

'Oh my God, Alan - that's amazing!' he said, turning to catch Chloe's eye, 'But I guess we should get a series of new sim cards so we don't give them the chance to do the same search another time?'

'There's no need,' Alan said.

'Why's that then Alan?'

'I've made some changes in the phone company's search software so it thinks your phone is in a caravan park in Blackpool.'

'Blackpool?'

'Yes, it's where we always went on our family camping holidays in Mabel - I like it there.'

'So, we don't need to change our phone numbers and start being more careful?' Chloe asked, after struggling - and failing - to picture Alan cooped up with his parents in the VW Caravanette on holiday in Blackpool.

'I said I'd changed the phone company's software didn't I,' Alan said petulantly, 'and if you look at your screens, you'll see I've updated things there too.'

Branigan and Chloe moved the documents on the screen until they came to one they didn't recognise. Headed "Cressix Enterprises" it showed the bank account transactions and traced each payment and receipt as far as possible.

'If I read this right,' Branigan said after carefully studying the page, 'Cressix seems to have paid nearly £7.5 million into the bank - do you have any idea where that money came from?'

'I'm still working on the detail,' Alan called back, 'but it came from an account in The Cayman Islands which was funded with cash seized under their money laundering legislation. Somehow Cressix got the money sent to an account he'd set up rather than the UK courts.'

'Is there anything on there that identifies who was involved in the seizure on our side?' Branigan asked hopefully.

'No,' Alan replied, 'there isn't even a record of the case which led to the seizure.'

'If we can't glean anything from where the money came from, what about where it's been paid to from the bank account - what does that tell us?' Branigan asked.

'There are payments for the Customs' charges and shipping of the container and what look like payments to the people chasing you,' Alan said before pausing long enough for Branigan to wonder if he had anything more to say.

'What about these other payments to Watson and Francis Estate Agents?' Chloe asked, looking at the regular monthly payments leaving the account.

For answer a photograph of a run-down industrial unit filled the entire left-hand screen.

'That's the warehouse I told you about,' Alan said triumphantly, 'Cressix Enterprises has been renting that unit in Farnham since just after the container disappeared five years ago.'

Branigan studied the picture – the unit was one of a line of very boxy-looking industrial warehouses with large roller-shutter doors for the main entrance, a secondary door for normal access, corrugated roofing and the sense that it would have looked contemporary in 1930.

'Is that big enough to store a container?' Branigan asked.

'Oh yes,' Alan replied.

'I think Chloe and I will need to go down and have a look to see if either the container or its contents are still there - did you find anything out about the other payments?'

'Not much,' Alan admitted disconsolately as the bank statement reappeared on the left-hand screen, 'the payment last week went to an account in Switzerland which I haven't yet managed to get into - they keep transaction details on a separate system - and the £1.5m payment shortly after you lost your job Branigan went to an account in the name of Z Tazi in a bank in Panama. It looks like they have a manual accounting system there so I've reached a dead end for the time being with that.'

Alan elected not to mention that the mysterious Mr. Cressix was in for a shock when he next tried to withdraw funds - the £0.13p Alan had left in the account wasn't going to pay for many Black Ops people to try and get Branigan locked up.

FRIDAY 29TH OCTOBER

CHAPTER 22

06.39

To describe this as a lock-up is misleading.

Nestled in a line of five similar units set behind an old garage, my lock-up is 60ft deep, 15ft wide and has a large roller-shutter door – just perfect for hiding things away.

Of course, the neighbours don't know what I have here; while they are busy repairing cars, selling packaging materials and making things in steel during the day, I make a point of only coming here at night.

I've almost finished now. Collecting the things I want, loading the van, tidying the place up and making it ready for any visitors. Not exactly a mat that says "Welcome", you understand, but a few bits and pieces from the hardware store which enable me to pit myself against anyone who drops by.

I wrap myself up, lock the unit and climb into the van, pausing only to glance up at the CCTV camera. Just as I'm pulling out of the yard another vehicle pulls in - a pick-up with the name of the steel-fabricators next door written on the side – my neighbour is starting earlier than I expected.

08:24 Vauxhall Cross, London

Alex Oldroyd was shocked when Michael Jenkins told him where the phone their triangulation search had identified as Branigan's turned up.

'Los Angeles - what on earth is he doing there?' he asked.

'Your guess is as good as mine,' Michael Jenkins said, beckoning Alex into his office and indicating he should close the door.

Alex had put his head round Michael's door as he made his way to his own office across the corridor.

Like their characters, their offices were chalk and cheese.

Michael - tall, lank and almost ethereal - had an office with a narrow view across the Thames towards Vauxhall Bridge, while the stockier and feistier ex-military Alex had an office on the so-called "dark side" of the SIS building. Something of a design fault in the monolithic structure on the edge of the Thames was its use of a north-facing courtyard to provide daylight to some of the offices. Whereas Michael had an enviable view which encompassed the flowing river and the big sky over London, across the corridor Alex looked out over the shadowed void in the centre of the building; a view some people joked had been put there deliberately to remind people what Stalinist Russia looked like.

'You'll see the full report when you log on,' Michael continued as Alex drew up a chair, 'but Peter posted a note an hour or so ago saying the phone his search identified had just pinged a mast at LAX.'

'He said he was going to check the passenger lists on flights from Heathrow to Los Angeles, but the chances are slim that Branigan was on any of them because he'd need an ID which would pass the ESTA checks.'

Alex nodded his understanding.

'So how has he got his phone onto the flight if he isn't on it himself?' he asked.

'Peter's checking into that too - there's a remote possibility someone else connected to Branigan is on the flight, but if they aren't it throws out another possibility.'

'Which is what?' Alex asked with a frown.

'That he's one step ahead of us and somehow managed to put a cloned SIM card into his phone.'

'So, the real phone is the one that's turned up in the States,' Alex said, understanding Michael's inference, 'and his cloned version is still here in the UK?'

'Let's wait and see what Peter turns up, but that's my guess for now - you know how good Branigan can be,' Michael said.

'Too true,' Alex said wryly, 'do you remember when I sent him to find out what Hezbollah were doing in Syria and he turned up as part of the delegation meeting with President Assad?'

Michael grimaced.

'Yes, I think more than a few top brass choked on that one when they saw him shaking hands with Assad on the 10 o'clock news!'

'What do you think is really going on here?' Alex asked.

'I wish I knew, I can't believe any of the six of us is caught up in this the way Branigan suggests,' Michael said, 'but that "Herbert Crescent Six" thing did sound quite compelling.'

'Yes, it did the way he presented it,' Alex agreed, 'but the choice of name could just be chance or someone having a joke at our expense - it's not like we were ever secret about our meetings or the number in our group.'

'That's true and I think if there is anything amiss it's only a matter of time before we find out who is behind it.'

'What makes you so sure of that?'

'Well, think about it from David Price's point of view - in Branigan he has one of his best agents in the field with a vested interest in solving the problem. My guess is he's going to want to leave him out there until he solves the problem for us. If you ask me,' Michael continued, gazing sideways out of the window across the Thames, 'he only wants to know where Branigan is so he can bring him in if the police start getting too close.'

11:19 The Strand, London

Having visited the coroner and found out that the bodies of Sally and Molly could be released the following Tuesday, Marty checked with Branigan's choice of crematorium and managed to book the service for Thursday.

'You're lucky,' the funeral director explained, 'they've

had a cancellation so you can get in reasonably quickly - you often have to wait up to 10 days.'

After wondering under what miraculous circumstances people cancelled a funeral, Marty circulated an email invitation round the office before thinking about how best to contact Sally and Branigan's friends to let them know the arrangements. Calling Anna up from reception, he walked out into the general office and slid Branigan's empty chair away from his old desk and dragged it and a visitor's chair over to Alan's fortress of computer screens. Shocked by the unexpected invasion, Alan shrank back behind his screens and deftly turned the screensaver on so the general background noise of the office was accompanied by the gentle bubble of air through the aquarium which had appeared across all four displays.

'I need a hand, Alan,' Marty explained as he waved Anna to the spare seat, 'Sally and Molly's funeral is booked for next Thursday at 11:00 o'clock and I need you both to look through Branigan's contacts and get a list of people to invite.'

'I've got them,' Alan said, his ears a deep red since Anna had arrived.

'Got what?' Marty asked.

'A list of everyone to invite.'

Marty and Anna were visibly shocked as Alan plucked a list of names, addresses and contact details from his desk.

'How did you know to prepare for this?' Marty asked, running his eye appreciatively down the list.

Alan gave a short laugh and rocked slightly in his chair.

'I saw from your diary you were organising the funeral and assumed you'd need it.'

Lying didn't come easily to Alan and he folded his hands under his armpits as he rocked more vigorously; the reality was he'd sat down with Branigan and prepared the list knowing it would be needed.

'Some of these aren't right, Alan,' Marty said as he passed the list across to Anna.

'What do you mean?'

'I don't think Branigan would want DCI Tenant and DS Drake invited to the funeral.'

In reality Branigan addressed this point when he prepared the list with Alan.

'Marty will get all huffy about them being on the list,' he explained, 'but there's no point not telling them - I'd sooner invite them and then I'll know they'll be there.'

'But if they're going to be there anyway, where's the harm in asking them?' Anna suggested.

'There,' Alan said, relieved that Anna was on his side and adding a line he'd rehearsed with Branigan, 'hoping they won't be there isn't a strategy Branigan would adopt.'

'Okay, leave them on the list then,' Marty said with a shrug of acceptance, 'which leaves the music for the service - Anna, you knew Sally pretty well, can you think about what she'd like?'

'Sure,' Anna replied, 'I'll try and think of some of her favourite music, but I'll need help from other people as well.'

Alan plucked another sheet of paper from his desk.

'These are some suggestions - they were all special pieces to Sally and Molly.'

'Okay,' Anna said, impressed and a little relieved to have the task already done.

'Is there anything else you've got tucked away there?' Marty asked, slightly put out that Alan had stolen his thunder.

'Good,' he said when Alan shook his head, 'I just wish there was a way to tell Branigan where and when it is.'

'I'm sure someone on the list will find a way to let him know,' Alan replied, rocking gently back and forth.

12:43 Police Station, North London

DCI Tenant read the statement PC Evans had taken from Judith Warde before throwing it back across the table to his

Detective Sergeant.

'What are your thoughts on that, Drake?' he asked.

'Well, sir,' Drake replied, trying to gauge his boss's view before replying, 'it's certainly a new avenue and might fit in with the line Branigan suggested when he left his DNA and the rag doll sealed in a plastic bag.'

Clearly not a fan of the theory that Branigan might have been trying to help the investigation with the clues he left behind, the DCI grunted, 'Yes, but if we start going down that avenue it cuts across our whole line of enquiry.'

'But it does make some sense of what the Yorkshire boys found, don't you think - that there may be others involved?'

DCI Tenant acknowledged this with a cursory nod - he clearly didn't welcome this new line of enquiry.

'Have you heard anything more from the team in Sheffield?' he asked.

'Yes, they've spoken with Chloe Travers' mother. She's told them that she wasn't the person who went to Marty Freeman's office and reported her daughter missing. She's also told them that she's spoken at length with her daughter.'

At this news the DCI visibly perked up.

'No, she doesn't have a clue where she is,' Drake continued, answering the DCI's unspoken question, 'but she says her daughter is adamant Branigan didn't blow up her place and she says she's with him hiding from the people who are chasing them.'

'Them?' Tenant queried.

'Yes, Chloe Travers seemed to think both she and Branigan are being pursued and that it's something to do with a fake news article she's written.'

'Do we know about this news article?' Tenant asked.

'Not really sir,' Drake replied, 'and without speaking to Ms. Travers I doubt we will; the Sheffield team know she was working on something but the fire destroyed her computer and any papers in her apartment.'

DCI Tenant shook his head.

'If we open up this new line of enquiry, we have nothing more to go on than this sighting by Judith Warde,' he said, pointing to the statement he'd just read, 'which narrows it down to a "tall, grey, menacing, but quite attractive older man."'

'That's about it,' Drake agreed, 'I guess I'd better interview her to see if I can find anything more to go on.'

12:46 Farnham, Surrey

Branigan and Chloe climbed out of the taxi they'd taken from Farnham station and studied the line of five run-down warehouse units. On the way down, they'd discussed how to approach looking inside the building.

'In an ideal world we'd be doing this at night when no one can see,' Branigan explained, 'but if there is a remote possibility the container is in there, I don't think we can afford to delay - which means we'll need to reconnoitre the place and decide whether we can either go in covertly, or instead need to adopt the brazen approach.'

'And if it has to be the brazen approach, how do we do that?' Chloe asked.

'We pose as debt collectors acting on behalf of the High Court,' he said, pulling an official-looking document from his pocket and waving it in the air, 'with Alan's help I've mocked up this court order showing money due for unpaid rent which allows us to force entry to conduct an inventory and seize goods in lieu of payment.'

All the time he was talking, Branigan was scanning the buildings and weighing up options. The yard was covered in loose stones and in front of each unit there was an area of concrete hard-standing. Aside from the main shutter door and the smaller entrance doors there was no other obvious access.

'Let's go around the back,' Branigan said, leading Chloe

round the right-hand edge of the buildings, 'And be careful, there's a camera on the front of the packaging company to our left - we need to avoid that.'

'I think we need to go through the front door waving the court papers,' Branigan said after circumventing the yard and finding the rear of the buildings to be nothing more than a tall featureless brick wall, 'which means we need to act as though we're full of confidence and that the law is on our side.'

They started with the packaging company and worked their way down the row of buildings. The answers from each came back the same; no, they didn't know who had Unit 2; no, they'd never seen anyone there; and, no, they didn't know what the unit was used for. The only different answer came when they'd worked their way right to the far end and were headed back to Unit 2. A pick-up pulled up next to the adjoining steel fabricators and a slight, ginger-haired man in his early thirties climbed out.

'You're like buses,' he said with half a wave, 'you don't see anyone for years and then two come at once.'

Branigan stopped in his tracks.

'Pleased to meet you,' he said, 'my name's Tony Blair - I work with a court enforcement firm - and you are?'

'Regan Whittaker; I work next door,' the ginger-haired man replied.

'You say you saw someone here this morning?'

'Yes, that's right,' Regan said, glancing at the official-looking papers in Branigan's hand, 'and if you're after money it's my guess they'll have taken anything of value.'

'What did you see then, were they loading something?' Branigan asked, his mind racing as he wondered whether it was coincidence that meant someone else had visited the very same day as he and Chloe.

'No, I didn't see them loading anything. There was a van backed up to the shutter door and leaving as I drove in,' Regan replied, 'I just assumed they'd been loading it with something, but I guess they could just as easily have dropped something off - in which case you might be in luck.'

Branigan shook his head.

'I doubt it,' he said with a wry grin, 'we're seldom that lucky in this business; tell me, did you get a look at whoever was driving?'

'No, I'm sorry, they had their headlights pointing straight at me - I couldn't even tell you how many people there were in the cab.'

'What time was that?' Chloe interrupted.

'I guess about 6:45. I didn't think anything of it other than it was unusual to see anyone there.'

'You're sure of that?' she asked.

'Yes, it must've been about then because I heard the seven o'clock news on the radio when I was in work.'

Chloe turned to Branigan, 'I think we should ask the nice people in the packaging company if we could have a look at their CCTV footage.'

Sadly, the camera angle offered nothing more than the truck backing up to the unit and brief glimpses of a person in a shapeless hooded jacket - aside from a deep scratch on the roof of the van, there was nothing distinctive in the grainy images.

'Well, that was a disappointment,' Chloe observed after they'd left Regan to get on with his work and made their way to the small access door of Unit 2.

'At least we now know he was loading the van,' Branigan observed as he examined the solid padlock securing the door.

'How do you make that out - we couldn't see what he was doing from that camera position?'

'The angle of his headlights,' Branigan explained, taking a fabric roll out of the inside of his jacket pocket and pulled out a series of long thin probes which he began to insert into the lock, 'when he drove in, they were much lower than when he drove out - I figure that means he had more weight in the back when he left.'

Chloe felt a little exposed for the three or four minutes he stood hunched over the lock feeling and twisting each shim in turn until it sprang open and they were able to slip through the door into the featureless grey concrete-walled interior.

'Oh, my God,' Chloe said, putting her hand to her mouth.

If you ignored the few pieces of metal-working machinery, pallet truck and sack barrow, there was only one thing of note in the warehouse - a 20ft long steel shipping container; the same one Branigan had last seen in Bishkek.

Silently he walked round the monolithic steel box, rubbing his left hand along it as if in silent worship. By the time he came back to the double doors with their heavy lever locks he knew two things; firstly, that there was just one way into the container and, secondly, that they wouldn't be able to get into it today.

'He's welded it shut,' he said, examining the padlocks and the metal handles on the lock-bolts.

'Why would he do that?' Chloe asked.

'Well, he might just be cautious because he doesn't want anyone who breaks in to stumble across the contents - assuming they're still there - but you'd have thought the lock on the door would be good enough to deter most thieves. The alternative is more worrying.'

'Which is what?' Chloe asked.

'That he knew we were coming and did this for our benefit.'

Chloe thought about the idea.

'But that isn't possible,' she said, 'Alan found out about this place and you, he and I are the only three who knew we were coming.'

'Do you have any other explanation for someone else being here - today of all days - and apparently taking a lot of stuff away and welding the door shut? Look at the rest of the door,' he said, tracing his finger over the rough painted metal, 'this is the first time it's been welded shut; it can't be coincidence that after 5 years of apparent inactivity someone comes along on the very same day as we're due to arrive.'

'What do we do now?' Chloe asked.

'We take pictures of it, lock the place up and come back when we have the right kit to open the container.'

'What do you use to open it?' Chloe asked, resting one hand on the solid door.

'A drill, an angle grinder, a lot of care and a spy hole camera.'

'What do you need the camera for?' Chloe asked.

'Because it's my guess he's booby-trapped the door.'

Chloe removed her hand as if the metal door was suddenly red hot.

'For fuck's sake,' she exclaimed, 'are you telling me I'm leaning on a home-made bomb?'

'I think that's a fair bet, yes.'

'And your response to that is to come along tomorrow and cut a bloody great hole in this tin can with an angle grinder?'

'Yes - which is why I need that spy-hole camera so I don't cut into anything which will make it go off.'

Chloe was relieved when they'd locked the warehouse back up again and were outside waiting for the taxi to take them back to the station.

'Did you find anything in there?' Regan called through the open door of his neighbouring unit.

'Nothing of any value I'm afraid,' Branigan said disappointedly, 'but that hasn't stopped the office wanting us to come back tomorrow and complete an inventory.'

'I don't envy you your job,' Regan replied, 'it must be really dull taking inventories and trying to get people to pay up.'

'Oh, you know,' Chloe interjected, thinking about the booby-trapped container quite possibly with several tons of explosive inside, 'it has its moments.'

14:24 Wapping, East London

It took Paige a few seconds to recognise the file delivered from storage as the one in which Chloe was interested. She put it safely in her desk drawer, determined to flick through it later to see if there was anything which might be relevant to Chloe and Branigan's hunt for the mystery man who she'd spoken to in Bishkek.

Her computer made a faint pinging sound - it was a message from Ken Briers, the news editor, giving her the number for a woman who'd called the paper. She thought she'd put a winning lottery ticket through the wash and wondered if the paper would pay for her story.

'Don't offer any payment, but there's probably a story here even if it's just that she lost out on a payout from the paper as well as the ticket! There's a good photo of her drinking vodka from the bottle on her Facebook page,' Ken went on to explain.

Paige started searching the woman's social media pages and forgot all about the folder.

22:24 City of London

On a scale of 1 to 10 the idea of spending another evening huddled in a doorway in the City of London clutching a half-empty bottle of cider scored a big fat zero with Branigan. He and Chloe talked about the merit of trying to meet up with Kozlow again in hushed whispers on the train back from Farnham, taking pains not to mention any names while they were in a public place, before repeating the whole process when they got back to Hendon where Alan was able to join in.

It was Alan's simple logic which prevailed.

'You've reduced the list of names from six to three. You've found the container and are going back to look at the contents, but you know nothing about the person Cressix went to meet in Bishkek; I thought you said Koslow might be able to help with that,' he observed whilst staring fixedly at his computer screens.

After consideration, Branigan realised there was no other realistic option and Chloe fetched the repulsive coat he'd brought with him after he'd evaded PC Evans' arrival on the murder scene.

'Have you smelled the thing?' she said, gagging on rank odour of Red's week-old piss before putting it straight in the wash.

So it was that Branigan found himself sitting outside the oil company's offices again, hoping that Kozlow would turn out to be a creature of habit and collect his information from the cleaner in the oil company on Fridays - in reality, Branigan didn't hold out much hope of success; this part of their plan relied upon so many things falling into place it was like guessing the right toss of a coin a dozen times in succession.

Kozlow had to turn up, he had to be prepared to talk, and he had to know something.

Even though it had been his idea in the first place, it still took Chloe's perspective to convince him this effort was worthwhile.

'You said yourself he was active in Kyrgyzstan at the time, you know he was working on the same thing as you - identifying the key operatives on that arms smuggling route - and, if there is one scintilla of compassion in the man, he'll tell you something to help you find who is behind the killing of your family,' she reasoned, 'I don't know much about the dark world you used to operate in, but I can't believe he would see the family of a retired spy as "fair game" when it comes to this kind of thing.'

So here he was - wearing the makeup he'd recovered from the office the night he'd driven to collect Chloe from Birmingham and sitting in the exact spot where he'd encountered Red and his merry band.

The sound of his plaster cast striking the pavement alternating with the tinny rattle of his crutches. Branigan rose unsteadily to his feet remembering to keep cover. Rule 31.

Important in this instance because - despite the evidence to the contrary - Baldy, Acne and Scarface were still coming for him with the confidence of youth believing they were about to take revenge on a drunk old man who got lucky the last time they met. Branigan could imagine the discussion which took place the week before as they tried to work out how Red's leg came to be broken. Human nature, especially amongst a group fuelled by testosterone and alcohol, wouldn't allow the concept that Red had been bested by an old man to enter their conversation.

'That was a fluke...'

'He must have had an iron bar under that cardboard...'

'The old cunt pulled one over on you Red - he didn't fight fair...'

Not that the concept of fighting fair seemed to enter the heads of the quartet Branigan now faced.

Four onto one.

Young taking on old.

A baseball bat, knife, crutches and tyre jack borrowed from the Peugeot versus a sheet of cardboard.

Another uneven contest.

Branigan knew the element of defensive surprise wouldn't work a second time as he prioritised his counter-attack.

Baldy's knife was the most dangerous weapon and Scarface the strongest opponent. Acne handled the tyre lever with all the confidence of someone who believed their weapon made them invincible, while Red - bringing up the rear - offered little or no physical threat.

'You hurt my mate, and the City Firm always gets revenge,' Scarface said, leaning back to shift his weight and making reference to a football gang renowned for their aggression.

As Scarface was about to discover, the problem with a

baseball bat is the predictability of its arc and the difficulty the person swinging it has to shift their weight mid-swing. Fortunately, Scarface didn't know he would be better to jab with the bat as he coiled up like a giant spring, giving Branigan time to focus on the knife in Baldy's right hand.

Baldy thrust the weapon forward with all the graceful aplomb of someone who knew the theory but not the practice of knife combat. In response Branigan used the techniques of Krav Maga he'd been taught at The Academy and grabbed Baldy's leading knife hand in his left as he struck a lightning blow with his right to the centre of Baldy's forehead. In a continuing single motion, Branigan twisted as he held the grip on Baldy's knife hand and kicked his opponent firmly between the legs as he went down.

Not necessarily fair, but an essential element of Branigan's hand-to-hand combat training which aimed at first disarming and then incapacitating an opponent - this last part delivered seamlessly as Branigan stamped with all of his body weight on the offending knife hand where it had been twisted flat onto the pavement.

Crack!

The practiced move was over in a fraction of a second, which gave Scarface as he swung the baseball bat with all his strength, enough time to see that things weren't going as planned. Focusing on a blow to Branigan's chest which would, at the very least, break several ribs, Scarface's concern at the changing situation turned to surprise as the bat found nothing but thin air to connect with - Branigan had followed his training and stepped in close to his opponent, his instructor's voice ringing out in his mind as he continued the practiced move on Scarface, "Let your attacker's own momentum work against them - put your hand on the back of their head and push them off balance as they strike thin air."

Scarface twisted and fell chest-first into the unforgiving pavement.

Down but neither disarmed nor incapacitated until Branigan fulfilled the next part of his training brief by stamping on his opponent's right shoulder with such force that the sound of tearing ligaments spoke of months of physiotherapy.

Two down: two to go. Actually, more like two down and one-and-a-half to go.

Uncertain how to attack, Acne dithered between jabbing and swinging the tyre lever; not the recommended strategy in offensive combat, but understandable given that he'd just witnessed two of his comrades receiving crippling injuries.

He decided to jab at Branigan with the tyre lever and then seemingly changed his mind as he realised how that move had back-fired on Baldy. Given that he didn't want to go the same way and simultaneously develop a headache, have his testicles united with his spleen and nurse a broken wrist, Acne changed to a swinging motion. Sadly, Acne's lacklustre swing did nothing other than see him join Scarface in the queue for the physiotherapist.

Three down; his weakest assailant the only one standing.

Click!

"Expect the unexpected!"

Branigan had prioritised his counter-attack based on his perceptions of strength, weakness and danger. He'd seen strength in Scarface, danger in Baldy's knife and weakness in Red's plaster cast and crutches. Unfortunately, he had not seen the Colt .45 tucked into Red's belt - the fact that it was designed in 1911 and the version pointing at him first saw service in the Second World War made it no less deadly.

'Four onto one and you still need a gun?' Branigan said, focusing on Red's wild and slightly demonic eyes.

R-CAT.

The mnemonic Branigan had been taught when faced with a gun - Redirect, Control, Attack and Takeaway the weapon.

'What happens now?' he asked, glancing past Red to focus on a distant spot behind him.

Red turned momentarily to see where his foe was looking, saw nothing and turned back as Branigan pretended to raise both hands in submission. Taking advantage of Red's momentary distraction, Branigan shot out his left hand, grabbed Red's right wrist and redirected the gun away so it pointed harmlessly up the empty street. Taking a firm grip on Red's gun hand, Branigan then stepped in closer and tightened his grip on the gun.

Having neutralised the weapon, Branigan was in no mood to go gently as he focused on putting his final attacker out of commission. Maintaining his grip on Red's right wrist, Branigan used his free right fist from close quarters to repeatedly punch Red's face like a boxer attacking a punch ball - poor Red could neither defend himself against the onslaught, nor steady himself on his crutches. In a matter of moments he began to keel over before Branigan wrested the gun away with one swift and decisive motion.

'If you want to pick on the weak, my friend,' Branigan said venomously as he kicked Red's crutches out of reach, 'you'd better bring a fucking ambulance with you; now you're going to need to dial 999 and explain how four big strong blokes need putting back together after trying to take out a defenceless old man.'

He surveyed Red's three friends writhing on the ground.

'Tell them that he has a fractured wrist,' he said, nodding towards Baldy before indicating the others, 'and those two have broken shoulders...'

Branigan paused and looked down at Red unpityingly.

'...and that you have a broken leg.'

Through his dull-witted and pained haze, Red looked from his plaster cast to his perfectly good left leg and then at Branigan.

The cogs turned.

His left leg didn't need mending and his right, although still broken, was undisturbed in its cast. On a day when victories were hard come by, there was a momentary flash of triumph in Red's eyes - he might have lost the battle, but he still had one over on the old cunt. Then the penny dropped and his look of triumph turned to fear as Branigan's right heel came crashing down.

Fifty yards away Kozlow started to clap.

'Well done Mr. Branigan,' he said in his native Russian.

Branigan swivelled round, his attention no longer on the quartet of wounded thugs.

'You recognised me,' he replied, switching easily into Kozlow's mother tongue.

'Not the other evening, no,' Kozlow replied, 'I saw you and I saw eyes that looked too intelligent for you to be a drunk old man. But your disguise is good, I fell for it - only seeing you take out your assailants now did I recognise who you are.'

'I came looking for you tonight,' Branigan said, removing the magazine from Red's handgun and dropping it through a drain cover.

'But the other evening you were not looking for me, you were observing to see who came to take the information?'

'Yes, that's right,' Branigan agreed, realising that only by being honest with Kozlow would he gain his trust.

'Which means now you need something else from me, is that so?'

'Yes, tonight I need to talk to you. To ask some questions,' Branigan replied, ejecting the remaining cartridge from the gun and tossing it towards the drain.

Kozlow seemed to consider for a moment before replying.

'I will answer your questions if you answer one of mine first.'

Branigan nodded.

'Last week you saw me collect information and, I assume, you have told the oil company that I am the person collecting it.'

'That's correct,' Branigan replied.

'Then to my question,' Kozlow continued, 'did you tell

them what it was that I collected?'

'No,' Branigan replied truthfully, 'I think they assumed it was their latest exploration maps.'

'It is sometimes wrong to assume,' Kozlow said, a brief smile crossing his lips.

'Come now,' he continued, 'it is my time to answer your questions, but we are civilised - you have some clothes somewhere which aren't so…'

He paused while he searched for the right word.

'…Bohemian.'

As Branigan retrieved a package of clothing he'd concealed under a nearby rubbish bin Kozlow walked past Red who was earnestly pleading for a quick response to his call for an ambulance and turned to the unpleasant youth.

'You are lucky you are not in Russia,' he said in accented English, 'in my country people would not be so kind as my friend.'

Red studied the Russian and added him to his hate list.

'This is it,' Kozlow said, leading Branigan to what appeared to be a greasy spoon café were it not for the signs which announced they were open 24 hours a day and always served alcohol, 'we can get a drink here and talk.'

Inside, the place was starkly styled with exposed brick and timber, white tiled walls and black and white checkerboard flooring. The closely-packed wooden tables were home to a dozen or so office workers who fell into two categories; those who were part way through an overnight shift, hungry and on a break; and others who were well-past the end of their working day, whose after-work drinking had brought them to this refuge in search of bacon sandwiches, more alcohol and - Branigan hoped for their sake - a taxi home.

Clearly familiar with the place, Kozlow led the still grey-haired but otherwise more respectably dressed Branigan away from the baying drunks to the relative solitude of a table upstairs.

'So, why do you want to talk, when last week you wanted to observe?' Kozlow asked.

'Last week I was looking to see who was collecting information from that office - today I am here to speak with the man I met in Orsk when we worked together to track the shipment of arms,' Branigan explained.

'I understand that your life has changed since Friday - I am sorry,' Kozlow said with genuine sympathy.

'How did you hear?' Branigan asked as he fought the rush of emotion which threatened to overwhelm him.

'It is a small community we work in and you know how we watch each other. I was told by one of my past colleagues and sensed injustice when I heard. I take it I am right and you are not responsible?'

The waiter arrived with the bottle of vodka Kozlow had ordered.

A whole bottle, two small glasses and a large bill.

Branigan searched Kozlow's square features, flat nose and broad brow before focusing on the depth of his grey eyes. Whilst he was obviously not normally a compassionate man, Branigan sensed the strong and bullish Russian had a soft spot when it came to family.

They stayed silent until the waiter left.

'No, I am not responsible,' Branigan said as Kozlow poured two full measures of neat vodka.

'Then I drink a toast,' Kozlow said, pushing one glass towards Branigan and raising the other where he held it steadily in front of his face, 'to your wife and daughter.'

Branigan raised his glass too.

'And to revenge,' he added before following Kozlow's lead and downing the shot in one.

'Tell me what happened,' Kozlow said, pouring another shot.

As warmth from the vodka spread outwards from his core, Branigan gave a shortened account of events, explaining the revised news story and the murder of his family, but leaving details of Chloe and Alan, and their current whereabouts from the narrative.

Kozlow listened intently and nodded in agreement when Branigan described Chloe's version of the events which took place in Bishkek.

'You think someone on your own side set you up?' Kozlow asked.

'I believe so, yes.'

'But I am sorry, I cannot help you if that is the case,' Kozlow said, 'the intelligence we had at the time was good, but I know nothing of anyone in your agency who might do this to you.'

'That is not why I am here, Anatoly,' Branigan said, using Kozlow's first name now that the formality of the first toast was dispensed with, 'I am here because you know about the shipment I was carrying.'

Kozlow shrugged.

'Then I may still not be of much help. Of course, we identified the shipment and spoke to your agency about it, but we did not know where it was going - if you recall that was the whole reason we worked together on that mission,' the Russian continued, 'and I need not remind you how badly it all ended. We failed in our primary goal to trace where Zack sent the arms'

Branigan pricked his ears up. He hadn't heard the name Zack before.

'A toast back,' Branigan said, lifting his glass in the same salute as Kozlow had used, 'to you Anatoly, for not walking by, for speaking with your enemy and caring about my wife and daughter.'

They drank their shots, slammed their glasses on the table and Branigan leaned forward.

'What can you tell me about Zack?' he probed as Kozlow savoured the fiery bite of the alcohol.

'Only what we discovered from your side,' the big Russian said with a shrug of indifference, pausing long enough to study Branigan, 'but I see from your face that your people did not speak to you about him.'

Kozlow picked up his empty vodka glass, toying with it as he thought about what to say, before slamming it down and reaching for the vodka.

'We had made contact through an intermediary with the man behind the arms shipments,' he began, his eyes focused on the bottle as he steadily poured, 'but he was intent on furthering his political ideals and wanted more money than we were prepared to pay; so we decided to follow the shipments, see where they went and then reclaim the arms. Unfortunately, before we could trace even the first shipment it became clear our side was compromised when two of our undercover team were taken out - so we turned to your comrades in the British SIS who helped us out by putting Ed Khan in to track the first consignment. It seems he had more success than any of us expected in identifying who was behind the shipment and met with the man behind the convoy somewhere on the route through Karaganda.'

Branigan recognised the region of Kazakhstan as being close to where Ed was murdered.

'After the meeting Ed sent a message to London from an internet café in Jezkazgan – a strange thing to do, don't you think?'

Branigan nodded, he'd been discouraged from communicating via email when undercover because the medium was so open to interception.

'It must have been the only way he could get an urgent message through,' he speculated.

'We thought so too,' Kozlow agreed, 'and we also believe it was the last message Ed sent before he was killed.'

'I take it your side intercepted the message and that it mentioned Zack?' Branigan asked.

'Of course we intercepted it,' Kozlow replied, his tone implying that any other notion wasn't worth considering, 'and it was the first time we were able to put a name to the man who was behind this; the message spoke of a man called Zack who was travelling with his son.'

'Do you recall anything more of the message and who it was sent to?'

'It was not long and we studied it carefully, so I remember it word for word,' Kozlow said, taking hold of his shot glass and with his eyes indicating that Branigan should do the same, 'it went to an anonymous address in Vauxhall Cross, was written in English and said "You need to look up Zack. Travelling with small son who you can find in Port Macau; later parents too," and then he gave a telephone number.'

'That's it?' Branigan said, his hope of hearing something of relevance evaporating.

Kozlow shrugged.

'Yes, that is all. We got a name for the man we were after; your side got a telephone number which was dead by the time we came across it; and within hours someone had disemboweled Ed Khan.'

He raised his glass and Branigan did the same.

'To Ed Khan and our fallen comrades.'

Branigan drank, slammed down his glass and went straight in with his next question.

'Why were these shipments so important?'

'I don't know that they mattered much,' Kozlow replied, his eyes failing to make contact with Branigan's, 'we were most interested in finding the person behind them and where they were going – unfortunately we failed on both counts.'

Branigan had a gut feeling that Kozlow was lying as he thought about his discovery in Farnham and the shadowy figure on the CCTV.

'If I could tell you where one of the containers is and identify Zack, would that interest you?'

Kozlow tried not to react, but the momentary stiffening in his body and the intensity of the look as his eyes met Branigan's spoke volumes; beneath the layer of vodka-fuelled bonhomie Kozlow was still keen to trace the shipments.

'Oh, you know,' he replied, shrugging to feign indifference, 'for old times' sake I would like to know and I am sure I could persuade my former employers to pay well for such information – they don't like loose ends.'

'Then if I get close, I shall let you know,' Branigan said disingenuously, 'but in the meantime I have one more question for you.'

The Russian nodded to say he should go on.

'What can you tell me about Gregory Brown, Marty Freemen and Alex Oldroyd,' he continued, reeling off the names of the three remaining suspects, 'as one of them may be involved in the events in Kyrgyzstan?'

'The first two, I cannot say,' Kozlow replied, 'but Alex is not your man.'

He offered no further explanation.

'Can you tell me why you think that?' Branigan prompted.

'No, but let us just say I would know if Alex had been involved in another capacity in Bishkek. A man may have two faces but not three.'

SATURDAY 30TH OCTOBER

CHAPTER 23

02:37 Hendon, North London

When Branigan returned to the house, he was surprised to find the downstairs bathed in light and Alan dressed in a zip-up white overall - looking to all intents and purposes like a polar bear carrying an electric drill.

'What's up Alan?' he asked.

'Oh, hello Branigan,' Alan said, as if doing DIY tasks in the middle of the night was perfectly normal 'I'm just moving things around in the living room.'

Branigan studied the changes afoot and realised Alan was moving things so his screens shielded him from anyone entering the living room. Apparently this rearrangement also meant moving the TV, repositioning power points and re-routing the myriad thick data cables trailing down the wall.

Chloe appeared down the stairs, wrapped in a pink flannelette dressing gown which, to judge by the volume of surplus material folded round her, was designed for Alan's mother and not Chloe's more svelte curves.

'Hello Branigan,' she said sleepily, 'how did you get on?'

He gave a brief resume, missing out the detail of Red and his mates, before asking about the nocturnal activity to which he'd returned.

'Alan's been doing some home improvements,' Chloe explained, her eyes widening to communicate a silent scream to Branigan.

'I hope I didn't disturb you with the hammer drill,' Alan said defensively, 'only I had to move some of the sockets.'

'I don't think the drill disturbed me any more than the

hammer and chisel,' Chloe replied sardonically, 'probably the worst noise was the banging on the walls from the neighbours - fortunately they seemed to give up with exhaustion after an hour.'

'Oh good,' Alan said, without apparently picking up on the irony in Chloe's voice.

Whether it was the alcohol, the after-effects of his fight with Red and his friends, or just the release of emotion, Branigan laughed for the first time since he'd found Sally and Molly. In the event getting Alan to put away his tools and go off to bed was like ushering Molly upstairs - Alan just needed to be told it was too late to be panicking about the privacy of his workspace and to address it in the morning.

11:37 Police Station, North London

Seated behind his desk, DCI Tenant pointed to the statement DS Drake had taken from the neighbour who'd seen a grey-haired man outside Branigan's on the night of the murders.

'You didn't get much more from Judith Warde then?' he asked.

'No, I'm afraid not,' DS Drake replied, the frustration with the lack of progress in tracking down either of their suspects etched on his face, 'she was very cooperative, but aside from confirming that she saw a grey-haired man outside Branigan's on her way home after the birthday party, she doesn't have anything more to offer.'

'I've got something which may be of interest,' Tenant said with a smug expression, pushing across the desk a single sheet of paper bearing details of an incident report filed at Wood Lane police station a few hours earlier.

Drake read the short synopsis of the fight between four local thugs and a man dressed as a tramp and frowned.

'This sounds like Branigan - what in God's name was he doing there?' he asked.

'But it is him, don't you think?'

'Oh yes, proficient in martial arts, disguised as a tramp and speaking in Russian – that's Branigan.'

'And didn't Marty Freeman tell us it was in the City of London he was posing undercover as a tramp?'

DS Drake scanned the summary again.

'Yes, in the very same road! I'll get over to Wood Street straight away and see what I can find.'

12:32 Hendon, North London

The combination of vodka with Kozlow, a late night and the fight with Red's mates left Branigan dead to the world until 11 o'clock when he awoke to find Chloe tiptoeing around so as not to disturb him.

Apparently, Alan was out.

'You were lucky I ran into him,' Chloe explained while Branigan searched the kitchen cupboards for breakfast, 'I got up to use the bathroom early this morning and found Alan on the landing with a crowbar about to lift the floorboards so he could carry on re-routing the data cables.'

'That would've woken me up.'

'Oh yes, but when I explained that to Alan he seemed almost hurt - he stood there looking all forlorn and trying to explain that he had to do it right then and there because otherwise the data cables would be trailing across the floor. When I put my foot down, he shuffled off to work.'

Branigan alighted upon a cupboard containing eleven packets of sugar frosted cornflakes.

'He's still a child really, isn't he?' he observed, noticing that each pack had been neatly cut to remove the coupon for a plastic Star Wars toy.

'It's probably as well I slept in,' he continued as he poured the cereal into a bowl, 'because we really need to prepare before we go back to Farnham - we have to hire a van so we can take some tools when we go back.'

'Why hire a van and not take Mabel?' Chloe asked.

'Firstly, Alan will have kittens about whether or not we're insured to drive and, secondly, we'll look far less conspicuous turning up in a white van than we will arriving like misfits from a Scooby Doo movie,' Branigan said.

Chloe nodded - he had a point.

'Besides, we'll be struggling to get there today by the time Alan is back,' he continued.

'But surely you're not taking Alan down?'

'Goodness, no,' Branigan exclaimed, 'can you imagine the health and safety lecture if he was watching me cut into a container filled with explosives? No, we need him for his credit card when we hire the van; Alan's is the only one which isn't going to alert the other side when we use it. When he's back we'll go and hire a van and make preparations for breaking into the container - in the meantime there's some interesting stuff to add to the board.'

Chloe followed Branigan as he walked into the hallway, tapped on the screens and opened a new document.

Although he'd outlined to Chloe and Alan his meeting with Kozlow the evening before, neither the hour nor the alcohol he'd consumed was conducive to an in-depth discussion; as a result, Chloe was now keen to hear as much of his conversation as possible.

'You've got to be kidding me,' Chloe said when he finished recounting the fight and Kozlow applauding from up the street.

'No, he watched the whole thing and recognised me from the way I fought.'

'But you have to admit, there can't be too many drunk old tramps around who'll put four armed attackers in hospital,' Chloe observed.

'I guess not,' Branigan conceded with a wry grin before recounting his conversation with Kozlow.

When he'd finished, Chloe stood in front of the display board and wrote a heading for Ed Khan.

He'd been silently waiting for Kozlow for less than an hour when a battered old Peugeot pulled to a stop; he didn't recognise the driver but the presence of lots of football stickers and Acne's leering face pressed against the side window told him all he needed to know.

'You've got to be fucking joking!' Branigan muttered to himself. He'd hoped Kozlow was a creature of habit, but never given a second thought as to whether Red might be also.

Assessing the situation as Baldy, Acne and, when he eventually managed to manoeuvre himself with his plaster cast and crutches, Red climbed out of the car, Branigan weighed their relative threats.

'Well, well, well,' Red said, still obviously the spokesman for the little group, 'look who we have here.'

He edged forward, tentatively putting weight on his broken leg at the same time as steadying himself with the crutches.

Clunk! Clink! Clunk! Clink!

Although the crutches were a threat, Branigan reckoned the biggest danger came from their new friend - the driver.

He was big.

Not big in the fat sense, but in the "this man spends a lot of time at the gym" sense.

Branigan watched him unfolding himself from the small car like a newly hatched pupa emerging from its cocoon; although it was rare to see an insect emerge clutching a baseball bat.

The new member of Red's troupe was large, lean and had a scar which ran diagonally from the top of his left cheekbone down to the corner of his mouth. As he advanced, he menacingly thumped the bat into the open palm of his left hand.

'We've been looking for you,' Red said as he came towards the doorway in which Branigan lay.

Clunk! Clink! Clunk! Clink!

'The starting point with Ed is his meeting with Zack,' Branigan suggested, 'we have no idea where or when that took place. Then there's the message he sent by email.'

Chloe wrote on the screen using her forefinger.

'Also, there's the question of who that email went to,' Chloe added, 'and whether it led to his being killed.'

'That's a good point,' Branigan agreed, 'and assuming it was Zack who killed him, I'd love to know what happened between the apparently friendly meeting and his death.'

'It could have been the email itself,' Chloe suggested.

Branigan frowned.

'What do you mean?' he asked.

'Well, think about what happened to you. Our best guess is that someone wanted you out of the way, presumably so they could strike a bargain with Zack. What if the same thing happened to Ed? After he sent his email to London, someone there spoke to Zack and suggested it was better if Ed was out of the way.'

Branigan shuddered at the thought, but indicated that she should add the point to the list on the screen.

'Before we focus on what we know about Zack, can you add two more headings. One for Alex Oldroyd and the other for Alan?' Branigan asked.

Chloe turned to look at him with a puzzled expression.

'You'll need a bigger screen if you introduce Alan as a topic!'

'You're right,' Branigan said with a hint of amusement, 'but I just have one thing to put there for now. He said something when he was telling me about tracking containers which resonated - I then made the mistake of waiting until he stopped talking, by which time I'd forgotten what I wanted to pick up on!'

Next, they turned to Alex Oldroyd and the question of whether they should rely on Kozlow's assertion that he should come off the list and his enigmatic comment about a man having two faces and not three. Then Chloe began to write under the heading for Zack.

'We know the Russians first came across Zack's name when they intercepted Ed's email,' she said, scribbling furiously, 'and that the shipment was for sale for a very high price to help fund Zack's political goals.'

'Correct,' Branigan agreed, 'although we don't know why he thought the contents were so valuable.'

Chloe nodded as she continued to write.

'Do you think he wanted the funds to support IS?' she asked.

'It's a reasonable assumption,' Branigan agreed, 'in which case we can probably take it that the weapons were originally intended for them as well.'

He studied the screen as Chloe wrote.

'It's worth noting the Russians never met him and that he seems to have been travelling with his family.'

Chloe glanced quizzically at Branigan.

'The email mentions his son and talks about "they".'

'Okay,' Chloe replied as she added to the screen, 'and I guess we should mention that the operation appears to have been compromised on both sides and we don't really know what was in the container.'

They both stepped back and studied the list when Chloe finished her furious scribbling.

Zack
Identified name from conversation on our side?
Shipment was for sale
Zack thought contents had high value
Wanted cash for political goals?
Zack support for IS?
Russians never met/identified Zack
Did Zack travel with family?
Operation compromised (on both sides)?
Why was it important to trace the container – what was in it?

Ed Khan
Where/how did he meet Zack?

"You need to look up Zack. Travelling with small son who you can find in Port Macau; later parents too." Unknown telephone number.

Who did he send email to?

Why was he killed? If by Zack, what changed in hours between the "friendly" meeting and his murder?

Was it the message - or someone responding to the message?

Alex Oldroyd
Off list?
Why off list?
Two faces but not three

Alan
What did he say when talking about tracking the container?

'There is one more huge question before we move on to Ed,' Branigan observed.

Chloe studied the list trying to think of what she'd missed.

'Assuming it was Zack who went to Farnham before we did, how the fuck did he find out we were going there when only you, Alan and I knew about it?' Branigan asked.

15:07 Wapping, East London

Paige's latest story was a follow-up on the woman who'd lost her lottery ticket.

The previous day's piece had focused on the woman's avariciousness in demanding payment for her story, whereas today's focused on what she'd hoped to spend the money on had either the lottery or the paper paid out: breast augmentation.

Paige's article may not have been at the cutting edge of journalism, but it did satisfy the needs of all the parties involved.

For the newspaper it filled space and sold copy; the reader got something to bitch about with friends and colleagues; and the woman concerned got what she most craved - attention.

Paige next settled down to prepare a pitch for a new story she wanted to research.

It was a look at the world of espionage in Britain today.

The way Paige saw it, there might be a DSMA Notice out for the story about Branigan, but that didn't mean she couldn't write a story about the types of things happening in the search for him. To add a little spice to her pitch she had her own account of the woman who'd tailed Chloe and Branigan from her apartment, which reminded her to pull the archive file from her desk drawer and leaf through it - it contained a bunch of photographs of the container and some she'd taken in the hotel lobby.

15:43 Hardware Store, North London

It was an afternoon for spending Marty's cash.

After Alan returned from work, they all ran through the updates on the screen and the new information they had from Kozlow - in the process whittling their list of suspects down to just two names if his information was to be believed.

Marty and Gregory Brown.

'I can't believe it's Marty,' Branigan repeated for the third or fourth time, 'and if it is, I've asked the wrong man to organise the funeral.'

'In which case,' Chloe said, 'it must be Gregory Brown.'

'Yes,' Branigan agreed, 'but I can't dismiss Marty until I've asked him straight and seen the whites of his eyes when he replies.'

Next, they turned to the other things which needed to get done, principally hiring a van and going down to Farnham to inspect the container.

They didn't tell Alan that because of his propensity to panic in a crisis and over-engineer the solution if any risk was involved, he wasn't wanted on the trip; instead they said they needed him to run "mission control" in case they had a problem. Alan was excited by this, and Branigan had to cut short his account of Apollo 13's accident which led to the phrase "Houston, we have a problem." Alan became more reticent when it came to using his own credit card to secure a van being driven by Chloe on a forged driving license.

'But that'll void the insurance,' was his actual objection.

In the end they compromised.

Alan loaned Branigan a keyhole camera and light of a type much favoured by surgeons, safe crackers and special forces, while Chloe found a van hire company who would let her leave a sizeable cash deposit as security if she wasn't paying by credit card. Despite his earlier protestations that the insurance wouldn't be valid, Alan seemed perfectly content to help forge some more proof of identity documents to match the spurious driving license.

After that they headed off to a large hardware store where Branigan bought the tools he needed to open the container plus, at Alan's insistence, a pair of safety goggles.

'What are those for Alan?' Chloe asked when she saw the goggles at the checkout.

'In case there's a problem when Branigan defuses the bomb,' Alan replied, occasioning a sideways glance from the cashier.

Chloe looked wide-eyed at Branigan.

'Yes,' he whispered sardonically, 'the small print says they're indestructible but surprisingly makes no mention of being hit by a 20-ton steel container being ripped apart by several thousand kilos of plastic explosive.'

On an impulse Branigan added a selection of the largest

fireworks the store had for 5 November, shrugging when Chloe asked what they were for.

'They're always useful if we need to create a distraction again - like at the Special Forces Club,' he said.

Their purchases made for cash, Alan drove them to collect the van, stopping on the way at a veterinarian surgery which Branigan had found searching the internet.

'Why a vet's?' Chloe asked.

'Because they have the tools I'm going to need,' Branigan replied, leaving Chloe none the wiser even when he emerged carrying a long thin case which looked like it contained a snooker cue.

One look at the van told them the hire company had covered all bases by demanding a £2,000 cash deposit, as the van was probably worth less than half that, but it did at least appear to run properly even if it lacked power and the bodywork relied upon duct tape for structural integrity.

'Looking on the bright side,' Branigan observed as it struggled to maintain pace with Alan driving Mabel, 'if this thing does get blown up tomorrow it won't be a great loss to the automotive industry.'

Having parked a mile away from Alan's to avoid any risk of the van being linked to his house, Alan picked them up for the last part of the journey.

19:03

I'm surprised there has been no mention of Farnham on the news; perhaps I was wrong and Branigan didn't go.

It doesn't really matter I suppose, because the decision was made when I collected what I needed and brought it back to my workshop. Now all I have to do is get everything ready and think about the timing.

There are two people who are likely to influence that.

Cressix is one, of course: Branigan the other.

21:55 Wapping, East London

Paige was in good spirits.

Her article had found its way onto page 5 of the Sunday edition under the headline "Lottery woes turn to tits shows."

She'd managed to fill a quarter of the page with her fictional story and, although the woman concerned hadn't received any payment from The Herald, Paige didn't think she'd be filing any complaints - even before this later article she'd been booked to appear on breakfast TV and there were rumours that she'd been signed up to advertise a range of washing machines.

Even better, Ken Briers on the News Editor's desk had agreed to Paige's suggestion that she could get one more story out of the woman by writing about the rumoured advertising contract under the headline "Lottery wash-out cleans up."

Having ducked an invite for a drink with a group from the Sports Desk, Paige collected her belongings and prepared to head off to JJ's.

At the last moment she remembered the file containing the photographs from Bishkek.

Writing a hurried email to Chloe, she told her of one picture she thought might be of Cressix and suggested meeting up either at JJ's or her place the following day - adding a lurid scenario of what might happen if Chloe chose the latter. Hitting the "Send" button, Paige scooped up her Hermès bag and set off to her dungeon party wholly oblivious to the consequences of her actions.

22:25 York Hall, Bethnal Green, London

Peter Winstone was in the second row ringside when his phone rang.

He couldn't hear it over the baying cries of the crowd

echoing round the vaulted-ceilinged room which had been a popular boxing venue since being opened by its namesake in 1929 - the then Duke of York - a man who never expected to become King George VI, in much the same way as the welterweight in the blue corner never expected his opponent's left hook to be so powerful.

Feeling his phone vibrate in his dinner suit pocket, Peter let it ring out, excused himself and made his way into the foyer at the end of the hall, casting an appreciative glance at the scantily clad young girl who was about to hold up the card declaring the next round to be No.3.

'It's Peter,' he said searching for somewhere quiet enough not to be overheard.

'GCHQ have intercepted an email which looks like it could lead to a meeting this evening between Branigan and Paige Richards,' David Price explained, 'and we have to assume the Black Ops team know about it too.'

Silently Peter cursed - he was going to miss the rest of the evening.

'And you'd like me to go along?'

'Yes, principally as an observer to see who else turns up, but there is one other thing; Paige believes she has with her a picture of the man who posed as Herbert Cressix - you need to recover that if it exists.'

'And Branigan,' Peter asked, 'do I give him any help?'

'I don't want anyone to think we're colluding with him, but, yes, do what you can to help him stay out in the field.'

As Peter Winstone barged through the doors at the front of the building, a huge cheer from the crowd suggested the blue corner's efforts to put some spring back into their man's failing fortunes had just come crashing down.

'Where is the meeting?' Peter asked before raising his eyebrows in surprise as David described the venue.

'That sounds interesting,' he observed, looking down at his dinner suit, black bowtie and cummerbund, and wondering how he'd blend in with the crowd, 'and who else knows about this?'

'By the time I've phoned Marty all six of us will know and I've also asked Michael to alert the police.'

'Michael and Alex were in the office monitoring another operation,' David continued, 'and Michael has volunteered to head over to the meeting as well.'

It was an evening for surprises.

'Okay, I'll speak with him now - and the rationale for letting the police know?' Peter asked.

'You and I both know they'll struggle to catch Branigan, and I figure their presence may hamper the Black Ops team.'

22:32 The Strand, London

'It feels like we're back where we began,' Clara Hess said.

She was sitting in the driver's seat of a silver Ford parked at the top end of The Strand, watching the offices of Marty Freeman Investigations on the off-chance that Branigan would return there. In the passenger seat beside her, Greyson Krantz was cleaning underneath his nails with the tip of a razor-sharp hunting knife.

'No,' he replied, pausing to blow on the nail he'd been working on and check it for cleanliness in the street light, 'we've gone fucking backwards. A week ago we were sitting in the same room as him playing Chloe's mummy and daddy; now - because this cunt Cressix wanted to set Branigan up rather than just finish him off - we haven't a fucking clue where anyone is.'

'Looking on the bright side,' Clara said, scanning hopefully around for the thousandth time since they'd arrived two hours earlier, 'we know he can't stay hidden forever and we're getting paid by the day.'

'True,' Greyson replied, bending closer to start work on the next nail, 'at least I got that bit right when I negotiated our terms, but it doesn't make hanging around waiting for something to happen any better - at least the others had some action this evening.'

He was referring to Connor Jarvis and Roz Tyzack who Branigan and Chloe had first seen parked outside Paige's apartment when Roz had given chase on the DLR train and been christened "Bunny Boiler" by her foes. The pair had been staking out Paige and followed her from work to a fetish club in the East End while all Greyson and Clara had done was stare at the locked front door to some offices.

'Yes, but the club was a dead end.'

'I know, but a fetish club sounds far more interesting than this godforsaken part of town.'

Clara checked her watch. It was true, the place they were staking out was dead at night with all the nightlife over in the adjacent Aldwych and in the streets around Covent Garden.

'Much as you'd like to be staking out the club, even you have to admit Connor and Roz are better to have moved on to Branigan's house.'

Clara was right.

Their efforts to trace Branigan and get him captured were focused on playing the percentage - watching the places he was most likely to visit and discarding those like the fetish club on a Saturday night where only a diehard fan of leather or rubber was likely to put in an appearance.

'At least the gloves are off now when it comes to the girl,' Greyson said, referring to Cressix's instruction that it no longer mattered to keep Chloe Travers alive.

'I hope there's a chance to have some fun with Chloe,' Krantz said, returning to the subject which Clara found most uncomfortable when she spent time with the psychopath seated next to her.

Although Clara didn't have a problem in killing people for money, she preferred to do so quickly, cleanly and with the minimum of fuss. Krantz was an entirely different animal - he enjoyed the pain and suffering he brought to his victims and could spend hours dreaming of new and more inventive ways of achieving his goal.

'You know, I missed a chance with the girl and her mother,' Krantz continued, straight back onto the topic which he'd obsessed about for the past week, 'I didn't think about what I was going to do because it was a last-minute change of plan. I rushed the whole thing.'

Clara shuddered as she saw out of the corner of her eye a twitch from the growing bulge in his trousers as he thought about the killing of Sally and Molly Branigan.

'I should have taken it more slowly, it would have been so much better to watch the mother's reaction if I'd started to dissect her little girl in front of her - where do you think I should have started to get the most impact?'

Even the hardened Clara felt the bile rising as Krantz asked his wholly rhetorical question.

'Scalping would've been a good start,' he continued, holding up his knife and practicing an almost surgical circular movement with the tip, 'because that wouldn't kill but sure as hell would fuck her up.'

There was no hiding his rock-hard penis now and Clara looked away as he continued dreaming.

'I don't know why I didn't think of it at the time - I could have done it in a few seconds,' he continued, still practicing the stroke with his knife but now adding a swift tug upwards with his left hand, 'just slice and rip. A bit like pulling the skin off a chicken.'

He paused as his phone rang.

Outside groups of people were beginning to surge onto the streets from one of the nearby theatres and there was a flurry of activity as black cabs slowed to a crawl looking for fares.

Greyson answered.

'It's me,' Herbert Cressix began by way of scant introduction, 'we've got a lead.'

Greyson said nothing as he bent forward and slipped the knife back into his ankle holster.

22:32 Hendon, North London

After the evening she'd had the night before with Alan's nocturnal DIY, Chloe wanted an early night.

'Listen,' she said to Branigan who was in the dining room testing and examining all the tools they'd bought earlier, while Alan watched another episode of Star Trek on the big screen in the re-arranged living room, 'I'm going to head to bed - I had a bad night last night and we've a busy day tomorrow.'

Before going upstairs Chloe fetched a glass of water from the kitchen and glanced at her laptop on the table.

'I've got an email from Paige,' she called out, 'which says she's been through the papers retrieved from storage and found some photographs.'

'Oh, that's interesting,' she continued, 'Paige thinks one of the pictures may have Herbert Cressix in it - apparently she hung around in the foyer after she spoke to him and took it on the off-chance. She says she'll take it with her tonight when she goes to a party at JJ's or I can pick it up from her place tomorrow if I promise…'

She read the next bit to herself and elected not to share it.

'If you promise what?' Branigan asked coming into the kitchen.

'Oh, nothing,' she said blushing.

'So, the two options Paige has given you are either going to her place or to a party - neither sounds particularly safe,' Branigan said pensively.

'I think we'll have to persuade her to meet somewhere better, but the trouble is I don't see Paige being particularly good at meeting anywhere surreptitiously.'

'Which means we should try and meet her somewhere very public do you think?' Chloe ventured.

'I don't think that's very wise,' Alan called out from the living room.

'What, meeting somewhere public?' Branigan replied, wracking his brains for a meeting place that would work with Paige.

'No,' Alan called back, 'sending that email.'

Branigan waited in vain for Alan to explain.

'Why do you think it's a bad idea Alan?' he asked, trying to keep his voice calm and even.

'They were monitoring Paige's email when Chloe sent her the news article that sparked everything off - it's fair to assume that they're still monitoring it,' Alan replied over a booming conversation between Mr Spock and Captain Kirk.

'Yes, but they don't have the details of the email account you set up for Paige,' Branigan said, glancing at Chloe and raising his eyes heavenwards.

'I set it up and you gave her the details,' Alan said, his voice sounding more distant as he became distracted by the action on his TV screen, 'but she's used the old email address to send her message to Chloe.'

Branigan looked directly at Chloe who glanced down at her screen and re-read the sender's details.

'He's right...' she said hesitantly, her frightened eyes flying back up from the screen to focus on his as the ramifications hit home.

'Fuck,' Branigan exclaimed, 'when did she send the message?'

Chloe looked at her watch and then down at the screen.

'She sent it at 9.56 this evening, so that's the best part of 45 minutes ago,' she exclaimed, 'which means she'll probably be at the party by now.'

Chloe picked up her phone, dialled from memory and then pressed the button so it played on the loudspeaker.

'Hi, this is Paige Henderson I'm sorry, I'm tied up at the moment; leave your number and I'll get back to you.'

Branigan was on his feet before the message ended.

'Where is the party?'

Racing down the hall, Branigan's sudden urgency snapped

Alan away from his TV programme and he pulled a map up onto the screen in the hallway.

'There it is,' Chloe said, tracing the route from Paige's with her right forefinger until she found the exact location.

JJ's wasn't a house, it was an old postal sorting office which had seen life variously as a community centre, scout hall and dance club before being converted into party space by its namesake for those interested in the darker side of sex. Choosing not to ask Alan where he'd found the crystal-clear satellite images he next put on the screen, Branigan studied the area around the building.

JJ's sat in the middle of a modest plot on the edge of an industrial estate, with a driveway to either side and parking for a dozen or so cars at the back. The other side of the rear car park wall was a modern retail park.

'Oh, there's a description of it here,' Alan exclaimed from the other room, his voice sounding an octave higher than usual.

'That's the place,' Chloe agreed as she looked at the webpage which opened on the screen in front of her.

JJ's promised "6,000 sq. ft. of pure indulgence, with comprehensively equipped play zones, including a complete medieval torture chamber, medical area and prison for slaves."

'Interesting,' Branigan observed, 'presumably once we're in there you know your way around?'

'Yes, of course and if you're thinking the same as me, we need to get going?'

Branigan nodded.

'Cressix - or I should probably say Marty or Gregory Brown - will have found out by now that Paige is carrying a picture of him from Bishkek and at the very least will want it destroyed,' Branigan said as he turned to study the images from inside JJ's, 'Do you need to change if we're going there?'

Chloe checked herself; she was wearing a plain black dress she'd bought when she first arrived and, aside from Alan's mother's wardrobe, had little else to choose from.

'I'll do,' she said, watching Branigan pull off his shirt and top as he headed back into the dining room where his modest collection of rescued clothes was stored. Despite the circumstances Chloe couldn't help but admire the washboard stomach, defined abs and toned torso as he did so. She also had to stop herself asking about the jagged 10-inch scar which ran up over the right side of his rib cage.

While Chloe fetched a carrier bag from the kitchen Branigan called to Alan.

'Can I take Mabel to get there - we're in rather a hurry and it'll save me time over collecting the van?'

'Oh no,' Alan called back, 'I'll have to drive you, you're not insured you see.'

Chloe could sense Branigan counting to ten before he replied.

'Okay, Alan,' he said, 'in which case, will you be able to drive us there as quickly as you can?'

Branigan re-emerged from the dining room, dressed now from head to toe in figure-hugging black trousers, matching polo-neck top with long sleeves and with a pouch attached to the front of his belt.

Somewhere between "wholly appropriate for the club" and "man prepared to disappear into the darkness" Chloe decided.

'What's in the pouch?' she asked as the fastest route to their destination appeared for a fraction of a second on the screen beside her.

'My outfit for being stealthy at night,' he explained, 'so black gloves, balaclava and phone.'

Alan made a remarkable contrast as he stepped out from the sanctuary of his front room dressed as a member of Star Fleet Command.

'Okay, let's go,' Branigan urged once he'd checked they all had working phones and his eyebrows had again found their level.

It took repeated prompting from both Branigan and Chloe to persuade Alan that neatly folding the silver car cover, checking Mabel's tyre pressures and going back into the house to search for his driving gloves were not priorities when Paige's life was in danger. Only when they were on their way did Branigan say anything.

'The gold braid on your epaulets, is that the rank of admiral?'

'Yes,' Alan replied, obviously pleased that Branigan liked the Star Fleet uniform, as he brought Mabel to a gentle halt and ushered a group of young revellers cross the road, 'how did you know?'

'Call it a lucky guess, but I figured anyone with a Star Fleet badge and that many stripes had to be pretty important,' Branigan replied, becoming concerned at the leisurely pace, 'Can we go any faster, only we're trying to get to Paige because we're concerned about her welfare?'

'I'm going as fast as I can,' Alan said, 'but there are speed limits you know.'

'Okay,' Branigan replied, fully aware that as much as he wanted Alan to ignore the rules of the road, he was fighting an uphill battle with that one, 'Chloe, let's think about what we face when we get there - can you describe the venue in as much detail as possible?'

'You've seen it's on the edge of an industrial estate, so the odds are the only people around on a party evening and at this time of night are something to do with what is going on there,' Chloe began, 'The building is single storey, but it's quite high-ceilinged and they've used that height to create a mezzanine floor which you walk up to from the front entrance - there are perhaps twelve or fifteen steps up and then you come out on this raised floor where there's a coffee bar and seating where you can look down on what they call "the dungeon" which is where most of the partying takes place. At the opposite end of the mezzanine there's a bar which serves alcohol which won't be open until later in the evening.'

Branigan looked quizzical.

'No one wants a drink until after they've played,' she explained.

Brannigan nodded.

'What about fire escapes from that level?'

Chloe thought for a moment.

'You know when I was there I tended to be with Paige or one of our friends and not overly focused on that sort of thing,' she observed, 'but I think there was one over on the right-hand side of the building which probably means there will be some steps leading down into the carpark from there.'

'Good, and what about the entrance - you've mentioned steps leading up from there - but presumably there's security on the door and someone checking you in?'

'Oh, yes,' Chloe said, realising she'd missed a whole chunk of detail around the entrance, 'there's a lobby you come into with a desk a bit like a shop counter they let you through once you've shown your ID and paid - two big guys are normally manning the desk but I've never seen any trouble beyond the odd drunk being refused entry. Then there are a whole load of lockers - you know small metal ones like you get in a gym - and a couple of changing cubicles for those people who have brought their costumes with them; believe it or not people prefer not to travel on the underground in a latex catsuit which has cutouts for their breasts!'

There was a mewing noise from the driver's seat.

Turning to check he was okay, Branigan realised with a sense of irony that of the three of them Alan - with his bright red jacket and yards of gold braid - was probably the most appropriately dressed.

'Is there any other way in and out of that area that you can think of?' Branigan asked, picturing the layout which, from the way Chloe had described it, stretched beneath the raised coffee bar so presumably backed onto the main "dungeon" area.

'There might be,' Chloe agreed, 'but I can't be sure.'

'Okay, but let's just look at this from Greyson Krantz and Clara Hess's point of view,' Branigan interjected, 'they're looking for a photograph Paige has brought with her from work - presumably that's most likely to be in one of the lockers?'

'Well, yes, she's not going to wander round a play party clutching a bunch of papers from work.'

'Exactly, so that's where they'll target,' Branigan said, 'which brings me to the next question, how would you find out which locker was Paige's?'

Chloe rocked her head from side to side as she concentrated on the set-up at JJ's.

'It was just a free-for-all where you pick your own locker and look after the key. They come with a nasty rubber wristband which some people wear but others try and tuck into their clothing or even conceal somewhere safe in the building.'

'If I wanted to destroy what is in Paige's locker, I'd need to track her down to find out which one she has?' Branigan asked.

'Pretty much,' Chloe agreed.

'You could always blow all the lockers up,' Alan suggested.

Branigan thought about that for a moment. Clara showed no compunction in Sheffield when it came to destroying whatever perceived threat there was in Chloe's apartment. Certainly she hadn't worried about casualties either - it was purely down to luck and not good judgement that Kate wasn't killed.

'That's a possibility,' he agreed, 'but unlikely. I don't know how many lockers there are, but I wouldn't want to do that - you'd need a huge explosion to even attempt to destroy the contents of forty or fifty steel boxes. It would only work if they knew which locker to target, in which case they'd take the easy way out and just jimmy the door of that one.'

Chloe absorbed what he was saying.

'You think they'll start by trying to find Paige so they can identify her locker?'

'Once they've worked out the protocol in JJ's, yes,' Branigan agreed, 'although the very first thing they'll do is simply recce the place. If you think about it, once they're watching the club, they don't need to go inside to recover the picture as they know at some stage Paige will come out with it.'

'The problem for them with doing that,' he continued, 'is that they'll know we're likely to turn up. Which leaves them with a dilemma - on the one hand they want me to arrive and get arrested by the police, on the other they don't want the police swarming all over the place so they can search for the photograph.'

Chloe was quick to respond.

'Their ideal option would be to get in quick, get the picture and wait for you to arrive so they have a double-whammy?'

'That would be my plan, which means we'll have to go in discreetly without standing out from the crowd,' Branigan paused and he glanced sidelong at Alan dressed as a space admiral. 'What about the smokers - where do they hang out?'

'Why didn't I think of that!' Chloe exclaimed, 'Although there's a smoking shelter near the front door, no one likes using it; most people sneak out of a fire door at the back of the building.'

'Then that's how we'll get in,' Branigan said firmly, 'Alan, there was a retail park behind JJ's, are you able to get us there?'

'Yes,' Alan replied, 'I looked at the map, didn't I?'

Chloe marvelled.

He really didn't think it was exceptional that he could study a map for maybe three seconds and have it committed to memory!

Branigan outlined his plan as they neared JJ's.

CHAPTER 24

23:00 Hackney, East London

'It's a good job you hadn't already left,' DCI Tenant said as DS Drake drove with lights flashing and siren blaring as fast as he could to the club in Stratford. That wasn't necessarily the way DS Drake saw it - due to finish his shift at 11 o'clock, he was all but out of the door when the Chief got a tip-off that Branigan was going to a seedy nightclub.

'Do you have any idea who gave you the information sir?' Drake asked.

'No, they were keen not to leave their name,' the DCI replied, 'but it hardly matters, does it?'

'Doesn't it strike you as strange, sir, that a member of the public should just call in like that?'

'No, not really,' Tenant said, shrugging dismissively as Drake negotiated a set of red traffic lights, 'plenty of people want to help in high profile cases like this.'

'Yes, sir, but there's been no news coverage since the blackout was imposed and we haven't even the remotest idea why Branigan would be going to an off-beat place like this.'

Tenant shrugged.

'With any luck you'll be able to ask him that yourself quite soon,' he replied.

23:03 Stratford, East London

Alan manoeuvred Mabel through a complex series of side streets to arrive in an almost deserted DIY store carpark at the back of JJ's. Almost being the operative word, because there was one other car parked close to the shoulder-high wall separating the store from JJ's - a grey Audi with chrome wheels.

'Right Alan, you go back and park at the side entrance by that container of cardboard,' Branigan directed after he'd told Alan to stop, 'and Chloe and I will make our way on foot - the good news is that they've left the Audi exposed because they think we're coming in the front door.'

He led Chloe to the shadows at the edge of the car park.

'You stay here while I take a quick scout around,' he said, pulling on his balaclava and gloves and disappearing into the shadows.

Chloe had to admit he was good; even though she knew he was there and was looking out for him in the darkness, the most she saw of him was a brief flash of movement beside the Audi.

After five- or six-minutes, Chloe was feeling both cold and nervous that Branigan might have been caught when he re-appeared.

'The two who followed us from Paige's are outside,' he said, making her jump with fright when he appeared out of nowhere, 'Connor is at the front near the smoking shelter and Bunny Boiler is loitering in the opposite corner of the car park at the back. He's got the front door and the fire escape from the mezzanine floor covered, while Bunny is doing the same for the rear exit and car park.'

'And we just march in past them?' Chloe asked uncertainly.

'That's the plan,' Branigan agreed, 'just as long as Alan does his job properly.'

They both contemplated this last comment, neither of them wanting to voice to the other their doubts about a plan which relied on Alan for it to be successful.

Leading Chloe to a point where the wall separating the store and JJ's had been knocked over, Branigan crouched down beside her and whispered close to her ear.

'You need to get ready. Bunny is just the other side of the wall,' he said, indicating a point fifteen feet to their right, 'so try not to make any noise. When I give the signal, we run straight to the fire door.'

It sounded so easy. All they had to do was clamber through the gap in the wall and run thirty feet across a concrete yard.

In preparation, Chloe pulled her dress off and put it in the plastic carrier she'd brought, stowed her phone in her bra and waited shivering in her plain black satin bra and panties. Branigan removed his balaclava and gloves and huddled close to Chloe to help preserve body heat while they waited until without warning five revellers came out of the rear door and propped it open with a chair.

They were an unconventional selection, with a dark-haired man in a black leather waistcoat leading a red-head on a collar and leash at the head of the group; they were followed by a stylish blonde wearing an old-fashioned white girdle, stockings and an imposing 1950s style bra; next came a bare-footed man who sported a pair of tight leather shorts and a ball-gag; and at the rear was a brunette wearing a red rubber dress which ruffled from the waist and was sufficiently short to expose the tops of her stockings.

Studying the group as they huddled close in the chilly November air, Branigan understood why Chloe insisted she'd need to take her dress off in order to blend in. As four of the group lit cigarettes – the man with the ball-gag unable to join in - Branigan pressed the "send" button on his phone and inched Chloe closer to the damaged section of wall.

'Remember,' he whispered, 'keep your eyes lowered and run with me when I grab your hand.'

He hadn't expected to use the fireworks so quickly, but, as it turned out, the "Super Thunderstorm 2000" - which promised "24 rockets designed to explode with a clap of thunder and flash of lightening, all in one large box" - was a wise investment.

The man in the leather waistcoat was the first of the smokers to react as a jet of white light shot across the car-park.

'What the fu...' he said as a salvo of rockets joined the first, shooting towards them at a little over head height before exploding with a thunderous crack which set off the alarm on the Audi at the same time as lighting the area with a bright white magnesium flare.

'Our best chance to get in unnoticed,' Branigan had explained to Chloe as they took up position, 'is to get into the club in the few seconds while people are dazzled after the first rockets go off.'

Grabbing Chloe by the hand, Branigan tugged her through the gap in the wall and raced towards the door as the stream of rockets continued in an increasingly haphazard display, ricocheting off the neighbouring building before strafing the sky around the venue. Stunned by the noise and temporarily blinded by the bright lights, the group of revellers by the door were unaware that anyone pushed past them into the Club. In fact, the diversion was so successful the only people to see Branigan and Chloe run inside were a handful of party-goers who'd been drawn to the door by the noise from outside. Brushing past the people crowding towards them in a flurry of leather, rubber and naked flesh, Chloe used her knowledge of the Club's layout to pull Branigan immediately left into the shadows.

Once he'd adjusted to the light, Branigan took in their surroundings.

It felt like they were standing in a small exhibition hall where the stands were themed to different styles of fetish and the partygoers were free to wander from one to another as the mood took them. The themed play areas ran in three lines from front to back of the rectangular space - one up each of the sides and a third down the middle. There were six-foot wide aisles running between each of the sections and an open space across the back by the rear door through which they'd just burst.

'Once we're inside,' Chloe explained on the journey to JJ's, 'we need to look for Paige who could be in any of the various zones catering for different fetishes; towards the back there's a big medieval dungeon with stone-built walls which dominates the centre of the space, but there are a host of others for kinks like medical fetishes and corporal punishment.'

Slightly overwhelmed by the bizarre world into which he'd just stepped, Branigan studied the medieval dungeon which looked like a small stone church had been lowered into the warehouse-like space.

'This is like a theme park for alternative sex,' he observed, taking in the bizarrely-dressed characters filling the aisles, 'I never expected it to be quite so crowded – there must be two or three hundred people here!'

Chloe pointed towards to a metal staircase which led up to a mezzanine floor built over the front of the play space.

'Plus another hundred or so up there,' she said, indicating the partygoers peering over the balcony rail, 'that's the bar area – that's how you get into this part; there's a set of stairs on the other side which lead up from the entrance foyer.'

Branigan nodded, relieved at least that Chloe had been right - the background music wasn't overpowering.

'If the music is too loud it makes it difficult for a sub to keep a connection with his or her Dom,' she'd explained on the way over, 'and, besides, you have to be able to hear a safeword if you're playing sensibly.'

A safe-word, he discovered, was a code between two people playing D/s games which enable the submissive to let their partner know when their limit was reached.

'Part of the fun of this sort of sex is that you aren't in control of it, but you do need the ability to stop things from going too far - you'll find the motto at JJ's and anywhere else run properly is "Safe, Sane and Consensual"' Chloe had explained.

'The lockers are at the foot of the stairs leading down from the bar to the front door,' Branigan said, continuing to look around him, 'and all we have to do now is find Paige - any ideas?'

'No, she could be anywhere,' Chloe replied, waving briefly to a man swinging a leather paddle against the taut bottom of a naked girl stretched over a pommel horse.

Catching the man's eye and receiving a nod which he presumed to be from one dominant male dressed in black to another, Branigan declined the offer - however well-intentioned - of taking a swipe at the girl's upturned backside.

'That's Ross - he's a friend of mine,' Chloe whispered, helping to explain the man's generous gesture, 'let me find out if he's seen Paige.'

Branigan hung back while Chloe spoke briefly to Ross.

'He doesn't know where she is now,' Chloe said when she came back, 'but he did see her earlier with two friends of ours - Marta and Hanako - over on the other side.'

'Hanako,' Branigan queried, 'is she Japanese?'

'Yes, that's going to make it much easier to spot Paige - Hanako is a small Japanese girl and Marta a six-foot brunette. The best thing we can do,' Chloe said, leading Branigan into the aisle and walking deeper into JJ's, 'is cut through the medieval dungeon to the medical play area on the far side - that's in the general area where Ross saw Paige - and with any luck we can find something to cover our faces there.'

Passing a semi-naked girl strapped to a wooden "X"-shaped St Andrews cross on their left-hand side, Chloe turned sharply right into a small stone-flagged vestibule which felt like the porch leading into an old church. Stepping through the heavy wooden door at the far end, Branigan felt he'd been transported back to the dark ages as he found himself in a medieval dungeon whose stone walls were adorned by ropes, chains and pulleys, and whose uneven stone floor was home to torture devices which looked like they'd come straight from the Spanish Inquisition. There was a sturdy wooden chair festooned with leather straps; a set of wooden stocks; even a replica of a rack with ropes and cuffs at either end to stretch anyone caught in its grasp.

Branigan's immediate thought was of going home to tell Sally about the bizarre surroundings, the strange outfits all the people having fun role-playing before the pain of anguish shot through. Beside him Chloe indicated a stark-naked woman who was chained spread-eagled to the wall with clamps fixed to her erect nipples.

'That's Phil and Heather,' she said, nodding toward the bare-chested man advancing towards Heather with two purposeful weights, 'I think she's in subspace at the moment.'

Before Branigan could ask the obvious question, Chloe took his right arm and manoeuvred him round a group of spectators surrounding a girl stretched out on what looked like a heavy wooden rack.

'Subspace is like a happy place you go to when you're in a scene,' she explained leading him out through an archway into the aisle beyond, 'it's Nirvana for a sub.'

Scanning the brightly lit space in front of them - which was defined by white tiles, stainless steel and enough medical equipment to satisfy the needs of the average A&E - Branigan realised there was a lot he didn't know about the world of fetish and role play.

'In case you hadn't guessed, this is the medical play area,' Chloe explained as Branigan watched a white latex uniformed nurse attending to a gagged and blindfolded woman strapped to the gurney in front of her. Chloe spoke with the nurse before returning with two white surgical masks she'd taken from a shelf beside the gurney.

'Put this on,' she said, passing one to Branigan, 'it's better than nothing.'

'I don't see Paige in here,' she continued, scanning the faces around and pulling the square of white fabric over her mouth and nose before hooking the two loops of elastic behind her ears, 'so I guess we just carry on down this side and search methodically?'

'I can't think of another plan,' Branigan said, adjusting his own mask and leading her back into the aisle, 'and we need to keep moving - it won't be long before we have company.'

Turning right they walked further towards the front of the building and the overhead bar area - the medieval dungeon wall on their left giving way to a space dominated by a cage, while on their right the medical area morphed into an area occupied by a dentist's chair. As they studied the faces of everyone around them, Branigan suddenly froze.

'Krantz has just appeared on the upper level,' he said, glancing up to the bar area, 'and you can be sure it won't be long before he has company.'

'He already does,' Chloe replied, tugging on Branigan's arm and pointing with her head towards Bunny Boiler who'd left her hiding place outside at the back and was now no more than twenty paces behind them staring wild-eyed into the medical area.

'We need to find Paige quickly,' Branigan said urgently, pulling Chloe away from Bunny and ducking into the crowd watching a woman strapped in the shape of an "X" to the face of a large wheel, 'they're going to spot us very soon.'

He pulled his phone out and quickly typed a message.

'What are you doing?' Chloe asked, her eyes alternating between the naked girl suspended upside down on the wheel and the aisle behind them where she looked nervously for signs of Bunny.

'I'm asking Alan to call the police and giving him a description of Connor, Bunny and Greyson,' he said, hitting the "send" button, 'which I know sounds crazy, but the confusion they'll cause when they turn up gives us the best chance of escape.'

Although far from convinced that having the police on the scene would help, Chloe nodded and let Branigan lead her into the space underneath the bar where the metal four-poster bed they'd seen on the webpage hove into view. Suddenly Chloe grabbed Branigan's arm and pointed towards a statuesque brunette who was enthusiastically spanking the backside of a girl kneeling bent over a heavy wooden bench. Branigan nodded and studied the kneeling girl who was not only restrained by a leather straitjacket but also had her head encased in a matching hood.

'Is that her?' he asked.

'Yes, that's Paige,' Chloe said as the tall brunette - wearing a black and red corset and matching knickers - beat a steady tattoo on her victim's naked bottom.

'How on earth can you be sure?' Branigan asked incredulously.

Chloe shrugged.

'I just know,' she said, hurrying closer and spying a diminutive Japanese girl in a short red-latex kimono, 'and that's Hanako over to Marta's left near the Prison Section.'

'At least with Paige dressed like that no one is going to recognise her,' Branigan observed as he took in the smooth black leather of the hood which tightly encased her head, 'but if we're going to get her out of here, you'll need to free her arms and remove the blindfold and gag.'

He pointed to her ankles which were cuffed to either end of a metal spreader bar.

'You'll also need to sort those out.'

Chloe nodded her understanding before approaching her friends. After a hurried conversation with Marta and Hanako, she beckoned Branigan over.

Marta nodded a greeting as he drew near.

'From what Chloe tells me you need to get Paige out of here,' she said, 'we'll get a few of the regulars to help distract the other reporters, while you make a break for it.'

Perplexed, Branigan thanked her before pulling Chloe to one side.

'What did you tell them?' he asked.

'Almost the whole truth,' Chloe said, grimacing apologetically, 'I said Paige was working on a story and the person she was writing about had sent some seriously nasty people to take her out and steal the background material she's brought with her.'

'Okay,' Branigan said, reluctant to join in anyone who didn't know the dangers, 'as long as they realise just how bad these people are.'

He turned and bent down beside Paige's head.

'It's Branigan,' he said firmly through the leather, 'I'm with Chloe and we need to get you and the photograph you brought with you out of here - you're in trouble. Now, tell me where I can find the key to your locker.'

Despite the gag strapped across her mouth, Paige was able to make herself enough understood for him to discover she'd left it with one of the people behind the bar. Not a great deal of help, as to get it he'd not only have to walk past Krantz, but also persuade a barman to give a complete stranger the key with which he'd been entrusted.

'Okay,' he continued, his strategy determined, 'what number is your locker?'

'Forty-two,' came the muffled reply.

Conscious that Greyson and Bunny were only yards behind, Branigan thanked Paige before moving swiftly to the emergency exit leading out towards the front door and hitting the crash bar with his hip.

Thirty paces away Bunny - or Roz Tyzack as her colleagues knew her - caught a brief flash of light as the fire exit door under the raised bar area opened and closed. She touched a button on the earpiece of her two-way receiver.

'Greyson, are you on radio?' she asked.

After a long silence Clara replied.

'It's Clara,' she said, her whispered voice barely audible, 'Greyson's not wired, his earpiece stopped working and the spare is in your car.'

Roz swore.

'Okay, copy,' she said, looking around in the vain hope

she'd spot her colleague in the melee of people, 'where are you?'

'Clara has gone around the back to take up your position,' Connor interjected.

'Copy,' Roz said, 'I think something is happening - someone's just opened the fire exit at the front of the building and I'm going to investigate.'

'Roger,' Connor replied.

Unaware of this conversation, Greyson was working towards the back of the building in the first aisle he'd come to, taking his time to studying the faces of the partygoers and absorb the atmosphere and scent of the room. Like a wild animal following the scent of its prey, his nostrils flared as he smelled leather, rubber, sweat and sexual excitement; the aroma which most excited him was, however, missing: that of fear. The life-blood of a thoroughbred sadist. Greyson shook his head, not understanding why these people pretended to control and hurt each other instead of doing it for real.

He studied a girl ahead who was draped over a leather-covered horse while the man behind her beat her ass with a paddle and pictured what he would do with her - the leather cuffs replaced by thin cord pulled so tight it sank into her soft flesh and in his hand a surgeon's scalpel. His cock stiffened as he imagined her begging for mercy as he worked slowly, patiently, one little slice at a time.

At the front of the building DS Drake pulled the unmarked police BMW to a halt and waited for the Honda behind to disgorge its occupants. Drake took in the innocuous building and felt a knot in the pit of his stomach; instinct told him this wasn't going to end well.

Peering from behind the smoking shelter Connor spoke over the earpiece to Roz.

'You've got incoming,' he said, moving from the shadows

to get a better view as Tenant led the way through the front door, 'five new people. The police by the look of them and they're coming in the front door.'

'Copy,' Roz acknowledged, pleased that as long as they could contain Branigan for the next few minutes their target was about to be caught.

Despite SIS being the source of the tip-off, their own men were late on the scene because Michael Jenkins had insisted on picking Peter Winstone up from Bethnal Green.

'The police are here ahead of us,' Peter said ruefully as he climbed out of the car, reinforcing his point that Michael had wasted twenty minutes or more by wanting them to arrive together.

Looking around and seeing signs of neither blue light nor reflective police logos, Michael was quizzical.

'How do you know?' he asked.

'Because the BMW and Honda have extra lights and a display sign in the back window,' Peter said, nodding to the two unmarked cars in front of them before pointing to the group of men crammed in the entrance, 'and you've only got to look at that lot to know they're not here for a party.'

'What do we do now?' Michael Jenkins asked uncertainly, his more desk-bound involvement with operations making itself obvious.

'We go in through the fucking front door of course,' Peter replied dismissively, the same contemptuous feeling welling inside him he'd had when Michael asked a similar question in the stairwell of the South Tower on 9/11. Then, faced with a helpless invalid in his wheelchair and flight after flight of crowded stairs leading down from the 44th floor, Michael dithered as he wondered whether to offer help or just walk past. When Michael asked Peter what he thought they should do, the answer was succinct.

"We pick him up and fucking carry him of course."

Peter, the hardened military foot-soldier; he may not

have known the man in the wheelchair, but in his world you left no one behind.

Branigan was aware of a commotion feet away from him, as he located Paige's locker and pulled out his knife.

'I'm sorry gents, no warrant no entry,' he heard a doorman say to a group by the front desk.

Clearly the police had arrived, but, Branigan reasoned, it was too soon for the local coppers he'd asked Alan to call which meant someone must have tipped off the police who were looking for him. Over the sound of the ensuing argument he worked swiftly, sliding a thin penknife blade into the mechanism, forcing it, and swinging the locker door open to reveal a pile of Paige's neatly folded work clothes and a brown designer handbag. Ignoring the clothes, he grabbed the handbag in his left hand, shoved the still open knife hurriedly into his pocket and turned towards the fire door leading back into the main play space.

The only flaw in his escape plan was the huge black security man who'd emerged from the toilets while he'd been forcing the lock. A full head taller than Branigan and probably 100 pounds heavier, the giant flexed his muscles menacingly as he barred the way.

'What do you think you're doing?' he asked, the question rhetorical as he'd clearly decided Branigan was stealing the bag.

Given that there wasn't time to enter a protracted debate about ownership and the rights and wrongs of opening the lock without a key, Branigan weighed up his two options; fighting past the giant blocking his path, or running out towards the front into the arms of the posse of police officers. Feinting as if to strike, he encouraged the big man to bunch his huge right fist and take a swing at him. Anticipating the fearsome blow, Branigan shielded his head and took advantage of their difference in height by ducking down low and stepping in towards the man's chest.

Confounded when his punch connected with thin air, the huge doorman wasn't able to stop his own momentum as Branigan rolled under his opponent's flailing arm and deftly pulled his feet out from under him.

The bigger they are, the harder they fall.

The giant hit the ground like a tree being felled and Branigan took the few seconds while his victim lay stunned as his cue to dart through the fire door and slam it shut.

By the entrance the doorman arguing with the Met's finest heard the thump as his colleague hit the floor.

'Fuck…' he said, putting his head through the opening behind him and seeing his colleague laid out on the floor and a figure escaping through the fire door.

Seizing upon the expletive as reason to stop messing around, DS Drake and the three other officers ducked under the counter and joined the hitherto obstructive doorman in trying to prise open the fire door.

Pulling the fire door firmly shut, Branigan picked up Paige's discarded spreader bar and jammed it into the door's release mechanism.

'We need to move,' he said urgently, 'they're the other side of the door.'

Paige, her head still hooded - despite the gag and blindfold being removed - hesitated as Chloe set off towards the aisle at the foot of the stairs.

'Where are they then?' she asked, casting around for their pursuers.

Unceremoniously Branigan propelled her down the aisle towards the rear of the building where they'd seen the girl being paddled when they first arrived.

'We haven't got time,' he said.

At the front door, DCI Tenant watched his men desperately trying to follow Branigan and decided to keep an eye on what was happening outside rather than add to the scrum inside. Politely holding the front door open for two men to enter, he stepped onto the pavement and wondered where before he'd seen the man wearing the dinner jacket.

Coming through the door the other way, Peter Winstone thought he saw a momentary flash of recognition in DCI Tenant's eyes.

'Come along,' he said, appraising the melee trying to open the fire door and pulling Michael Jenkins up the stairs while everyone's backs were turned.

Stepping into the crowded bar area and striding forward to the railing so he could take in the bizarre scene below, Peter studied the layout and positioning of the exits.

'If Branigan is here, he'll be down there somewhere,' he said looking at the sea of party-goers on the floor below, 'and his options are to make his way out through the front, the back, or the door up here - if we split you can watch for him heading out towards the front and I can go to the back.'

Michael, who was far less practiced in the field than he cared to admit, had a sheen of sweat on his top lip.

'What do I do if I see him?' he asked uncertainly.

'David Price probably told you the same as he did me,' Peter replied tersely, 'we do nothing except observe and provide low-level assistance if it helps Branigan stay out in the field.'

As they made their way down the steps, Peter Winstone privately hoped Branigan wouldn't need assistance from Michael Jenkins. Short of shaking any pursuers warmly by the hand and engaging them in small talk, he wasn't sure what use Michael would be.

Behind them DS Drake and his colleagues had given up their unequal tussle with the jammed door and were racing up the stairs, while, on the dungeon floor, Roz and Greyson searched separately for their targets.

Finding no sign of Branigan underneath the raised area, Roz went to check the fire door she'd seen opened a short while earlier.

She spoke urgently into her earpiece.

'Connor, he's jammed a metal bar into the mechanism of the escape door at the front of the building - I think he's trying to stop people getting in the front while he heads out the back.'

'I'm on it,' Connor replied, 'I'll join Clara round there.'

Roz turned on her heel and hurried towards the back of the building.

Branigan, Chloe and Paige were pushing past the porch of the medieval dungeon when he glimpsed movement in the stone-flagged lobby leading into the play-space. Although quick to respond, he wasn't quick enough to avoid being barrelled to the ground by a shoulder charge.

Even as he fell, Branigan recognised his assailant from a glimpse of his closely-cropped grey hair and the musky scent of aftershave.

Greyson Krantz stood leering down at him.

'Oh, I'm sorry,' he said disingenuously, his blue eyes alive with malice, 'I didn't see you there.'

Krantz stepped forward and deftly kicked Paige's handbag into the depths of the small porch from which he'd just emerged.

Branigan got warily to his feet, conscious he was facing someone who wouldn't be as easy an opponent as either Red or the doorman he'd brought down a few minutes before; Krantz was wily, trained and - judging by the look in his eye - looking for a fight. Branigan shook his head imperceptibly at Chloe who was standing behind the Black Ops man in case she was thinking about trying to do something to help.

'He's right Chloe,' Krantz said without even looking over his shoulder, 'by all means have a go, but you'll end up like little Molly.'

Meaning his words to shock, Krantz circled his prey, delighting in the shiver of pain which he saw run through Branigan.

A few yards away Marta was talking to Ross when she sensed a ripple of tension in the crowd behind her and turned to see Branigan being confronted by a menacing-looking grey-haired man; undaunted, Marta grabbed a belt from the floor and steered Hanako carefully towards the trouble. Seeing what she was about to do, Branigan manoeuvred himself so that the grey-haired man had his back turned towards the two approaching women.

'She called for you at the end, you know,' Krantz goaded, the smile on his face broadening but not making it to his emotionless eyes, 'of course she was struggling for breath so it wasn't easy to hear.'

He held his right hand up to his own throat and squeezed with thumb and forefinger.

'Daddy, daddy, I want my daddy,' he said in a hoarse gurgling rasp before mimicking pulling tighter on the plastic cable tie around her neck.

'You should have brought Sally here,' Krantz continued almost conversationally as he encouraged Branigan to strike, 'because she obviously got a kick out of being tied up; you should have seen the way she struggled when your little girl started to turn purple!'

He mimicked the sounds deep in his own throat of Molly losing her battle for life. Branigan fought the urge to tear Krantz limb from limb as he guided the Black Ops man into the right position. Caught up with his own rhetoric and riding an almost sexual thrill, Greyson focused more intently on Branigan and practically salivated as he picked up his narrative, deliberately choosing words which were designed to hurt his prey.

'Of course, you weren't there at the end to comfort her, but I like to think I helped Sally to die happy.'

Krantz licked his right forefinger and wiggled it suggestively. Just as he made the disgusting gesture Marta and

Hanako struck, dropping the belt over Krantz and pinioning his arms to his sides as Branigan mercilessly charged at him.

'You're a dead man,' Branigan said, his face pressed close to Krantz's as he helped bundle the odious man into the confines of the stone porch.

'Go,' Marta said urgently as she ratcheted the belt buckle tighter and, with Hanako's help, forced Krantz into a seated position on the floor, 'leave this piece of shit to us - ask Ross for help if you need it.'

Branigan didn't need prompting further. Picking up Paige's handbag he thanked the girls and started to leave.

'Watch him like a hawk,' he said over his shoulder as he stepped back into the aisle and found Paige and Chloe, 'he's dangerous.'

Marta nodded.

Krantz smiled demonically, his bright blue eyes alive with excitement.

'I didn't need to lick my finger you know,' he called after Branigan's retreating back, 'she was wet already.'

As he reached the foot of the stairs Peter began pushing his way past people as he became aware of a disturbance towards the back of the club.

At the top of the stairs DS Drake pushed a well-dressed spectator out of the way and turned to his three colleagues.

'There are four of us,' he said, unaware that it was Michael Jenkins he'd just manhandled, 'take a corner each and work back in to the centre - I'll go this way,' he said indicating the back right-hand corner.

Branigan couldn't see Ross as he guided Chloe and Paige passed the pommel horse and nearly made it to the rear exit; but, as Sergeant Major Brackbury at The Academy drummed into him when he'd failed a tough training exercise, "Nearly isn't fucking good enough, Branigan," he'd barked so close to his face that Branigan could feel a light spray of spittle, "you ask the captain of the fucking Titanic what happened when he nearly didn't hit that fucking iceberg."

A few yards further back Peter Winstone's attention was drawn by a trio of gyrating bodies in the darkness of the stone-built entrance to the Medieval Dungeon. As his eyes adjusted to the darkness, he quickly dismissed the three of them. None was Branigan and he didn't want to dwell on what form of sexual kink they were acting out. He shuddered and turned back outside, his way barred a few steps further on by an enthusiastic party-goer dressed in a pink satin maid's outfit.

By the rear door Branigan, Chloe and Paige's way was barred by a wild-eyed Roz who'd stepped in front of them as they neared the exit.

'I told you I'd get you,' Roz said, aiming her remark at Chloe and recalling their exchange through the door of the underground train.

Branigan didn't hesitate, he dropped his shoulder, ran headlong into Roz and sent her crashing into the rear wall. Scarcely missing a beat, he stepped over the winded Roz and pulled Paige and Chloe into the cold night air.

Not overly versed in the ways of the fetish scene, Peter was ill-prepared to have an eighteen stone truck driver from Glasgow wearing a pink satin French maid's dress grab him by the balls.

'Where are you off to in such a hurry,' Jock - or Jacqui as he preferred to be called when in drag - asked suggestively in his thick accent, 'I'd like to get to know you.'

Jacqui was probably hoping for a reaction other than being felled by Peter's left hook.

Greyson Krantz stepped out from the porch and turned left, following Branigan and not giving a second glance to the man in a pink dress lying prostrate on the floor. Ahead he saw Roz struggling to her feet beside the open rear exit.

He quickened his pace.

Branigan might have hoped he would be home and dry once he was outside, but, as he hurried towards the gap in the wall, he heard a short gasp from Chloe and whirled round to find Connor behind them.

'Keep going,' he said to Chloe and Paige as he prepared to take on the fight.

The next thing that happened came as a complete surprise.

From the midst of the gaggle of smokers, a man dressed all in black broke away and rugby tackled Connor to the ground. Taking the precious seconds bought for them by Ross - the friend of Chloe's they'd encountered when they first stepped inside the Club - Branigan raced after Chloe and Paige who were stepping through the tumble-down section of the wall leading to the superstore car park. Just as he caught up and reached the gap, a new face appeared from the shadows intent on stopping him.

Clara Hess.

Physically no competition for Branigan, Clara was intent only on delaying him as she too blocked their way.

'Run, just fucking run!' he yelled to Chloe and Paige as the wiry Clara grabbed the strap to Paige's bag and wrenched it free. Snatching the bag back, Branigan found himself having a tug-of-war with Clara as she locked her arms through the loop of the strap.

Driving forward with all his power, Branigan dragged Clara through the gap in the wall into the superstore car park, yet, like a terrier with its teeth locked onto a favourite toy, the Black Ops woman simply refused to let go.

Inside the building DS Drake briefly looked into the darkness of the stone porch. Branigan wasn't there and all he could see in the dim light was two women - one lying on the ground and, propped against the wall, a second holding her chest with one arm and making feeble efforts to adjust her black wig with the other.

Branigan feared reinforcements had come to join Clara as another figure stepped through the gap in the wall into the store carpark and was shocked to find himself locking eyes with Peter Winstone. Wordlessly acknowledging each other, Peter grabbed Clara from behind, buying Branigan enough time to wrench the knife from his pocket and slice through the strap of the handbag. As the thin strip of leather slithered through Clara's hands Branigan turned and ran.

At the front of the building there was a splash of blue light as a police van drew up and a squad of 6 officers in protective clothing piled out from the back and ran past DCI Tenant.

Meanwhile Peter Winstone's fortunes had changed for the worse.

Still clutching Clara - who was flailing like a recalcitrant toddler - three new figures were honing in on him. The man who'd been fighting with the party-goer dressed in black; the woman Peter had stepped over by the exit; and a grey-haired man he didn't recognise.

'Shit!' Peter said under his breath as Clara's three accomplices encircled him and the grey-haired men produced a knife. Using Clara as a human shield in a vain attempt to stop them advancing, Peter could see no way out until he caught a flash of blue light reflected in the eyes of the man with the knife.

Seeing the police car racing across the tarmac towards them, Peter loosened his grip enough for Clara to wriggle free and join her colleagues as they fled towards the grey Audi.

Glancing over her shoulder as she ran towards Mabel, Chloe saw their four pursuers climbing into the powerful

Audi and cursed.

'Unless the police stop them, they'll be able to catch us now!' she yelled.

'No, they won't,' Branigan replied, deliberately slowing his pace, 'unless they've got four spare tyres with them.'

Chloe and Paige slowed too.

'Did you really?' Chloe asked.

Branigan nodded.

'When I was scouting round,' he said as they watched the Black Ops team climb out of the stranded Audi and run back through the gap in the wall and away from the clutches of the pursuing police.

'I asked Alan to give the police a description of the car and say it was being used in serious crime,' Branigan observed as they turned the corner to find Alan pacing nervously up and down beside Mabel.

Paige looked from Branigan to Chloe and back to Alan.

'What the fuck is Captain Pugwash doing here,' she asked, taking in the funny little man and all the gold braid on his Star Trek outfit, 'and could someone get me out of this fucking straitjacket?'

As they clambered onboard Mabel, Branigan couldn't help but notice that the air was thick with smoke and the smell of singed hair.

'Did you have any trouble with the rockets?' he asked as Alan started the engine, checked his mirrors and gently pulled away.

'Oh, you know,' Alan replied, manoeuvring round the smouldering remains of the stack of cardboard, 'they were a bit more powerful than I expected, so I got blown about a bit - the first four found their target but after that they got a bit more random.'

Branigan conjured up an image of Alan waving the giant firework wildly as it sent its series of rockets like anti-aircraft flak across the sky.

'A few rockets hit the building you were in, some the store beside me and then it all went a bit wrong,' Alan continued sorrowfully, glancing down at the scorch marks on his magnificent jacket, 'and I set fire to the stack of cardboard.'

23:34 JJ's, Stratford, East London

The arrival of the uniformed police in response to Alan's call galvanised events both inside and outside JJ's.

Having found their hopes of giving chase to Branigan dashed by the Audi's slashed tyres, the Black Ops quartet hurriedly torched the car. In a move they'd prepared for by stashing 2-litre drinks bottles filled with petrol under each of the seats, Krantz stabbed the bottle under the passenger's seat and tossed in a match. The succession of "Whoomph!" sounds behind them as they ran back through the gap in the wall, down the side of the building and into the road at the front, told them any evidence they'd left behind was being destroyed.

With all the uniformed police inside the building, their only obstacle was DCI Tenant at the front - wholly unaware of the events which were taking place elsewhere. Seeing four people come running from behind the building, Tenant held his hand in the air as if to indicate he had a question for them, but, when the quartet ignored him and carried on running, he ended up looking like he was waving to them.

At the back of the building a shaken Peter Winstone helped Ross to his feet and checked he was no more than bruised from his fight with Connor, before heading back into the building to look for Michael Jenkins. Finding the aisle to the left packed with people, Peter changed direction and went down past the Medical Section as he headed towards the front of the building. A girl in a white latex nurse's uniform cradling a dozen or so rolled bandages in her arms bumped into him.

'Sorry, medical emergency,' she said seriously, before

hurrying into the medieval dungeon.

When he finally reached Michael Jenkins, who was still stationed at the foot of the stairs, Peter pointed to the solid mass of people towards the back of the club.

'What the fuck's happening up there?' he asked.

'No idea,' Michael said with a shrug, tucking a scrap of paper with a phone number scribbled on it into his pocket, 'to be honest, apart from the uniformed police arriving nothing much has been going on. Have you seen any sign of Branigan, or has this whole thing been a waste of time?'

23:41 Stratford, East London

'You could've brought my fucking clothes as well,' Paige said.

She was sitting next to Chloe on the bench seat in the back of Mabel using a picnic rug she'd found in one of the cupboards to cover herself now the straitjacket was removed. Chloe was little better off. She'd had no time to collect her dress from beside the broken-down section of wall and was doing her best to use a spare corner from Paige's rug for warmth as much as modesty.

Never in a million years had Alan ever expected to be carrying two almost naked girls in the back of his camper van and, as a consequence, his ears were virtually lighting up Mabel's interior and he was rendered mute as he focused on the road and avoided using his rearview mirror. Branigan tried to tell Paige that in the scheme of things coming out with her life was a bonus and the loss of a few clothes really didn't matter, but from the tone in Paige's voice, it was clear she wasn't in a receptive frame of mind.

'Look,' Branigan said, turning around to pass Paige's handbag back as a peace-offering, 'there's a supermarket coming up, I'll go in and buy you something to tide you over.'

Given the choice between Alan's old rug and something new to wear, Paige calmed down a little and accepted the situation - right up to the point where she examined her handbag.

'What the fuck have you done to my handbag?!' she exploded.

Apparently, you were neither supposed to use designer handbags in tug-of-war games, nor slice through the strap with a penknife.

'This was my favourite,' Paige ranted, holding up the two cut ends, 'and look what you've done to it - who in their right mind cuts through the strap of a fucking Hermès handbag?'

23:41 JJ's, Stratford, East London

DS Drake was still inside the stone porch leading into the medieval dungeon.

When he first looked in, he'd assumed the two women had taken something which had knocked them out. The larger of the two looked like she was passed out on the floor whilst the smaller girl was propped against the wall and seemed far removed from proceedings. Despite his need to search the building, Drake checked the girls were okay by shaking the one lying on the floor.

She didn't move.

When he'd knelt on the hard-stone floor beside her warm blood had soaked through the knees of his trousers and, realising the urgency of the situation, he'd attempted to roll the girl onto her side, twisting her body with one hand and supporting her head and neck with the other. As he did so his left hand disappeared into a warm mess of flesh, muscle, sinew and sticky blood. Fighting back his desire to retch, Drake looked intently at the wound; there was no hope for the victim, her head had more-or-less been severed by one deep slice through the base of her neck. Turning his attention to the girl in the red latex kimono, he realised she was trying to stem the tide of blood spilling from the wounds in her chest which were inexorably filling her lungs with blood.

It was only when he began calling for help that he realised he'd been wrong about her adjusting a wig; the hairpiece she'd been adjusting was her own. Still connected in places to the white fatty membrane over the top of her skull, the girl was trying to put her own scalp back in place after her assailant had all but ripped it from her head after slicing round with the tip of his knife.

Drake stayed with Hanako and held her scalp in place while the man in the leather waistcoat - an A&E doctor in real life - tended to her stab wounds.

23:48 Outside JJ's, Stratford, East London

Outside the front of the building DCI Tenant only became aware of the problems inside when a medical emergency response car arrived and the driver dashed inside. Making his way into the building he was joined by a woman who'd just arrived in an unmarked police car.

'Evening sir, how did you get here so quickly?' she asked.

Tenant turned and looked into the face of DI Amanda Cartwright, an intelligent and feisty officer with whom he'd shared a brief relationship with when they both joined the service; a relationship which didn't end well.

'Hello Amanda,' he said, failing to keep eye contact, 'what's happening?'

Amanda frowned as they started up the stairs.

'But surely you got the same shout as we received?'

Tenant shook his head.

'No, I have a team inside trying to apprehend a suspect and I was stationed outside to stop him escaping that way.'

'You don't know there's been a murder inside, do you?' Amanda asked.

23:50 A11 Bow, East London

'If only I hadn't rushed it; I was so close,' Greyson Krantz said, sounding like a schoolboy bemoaning a missed goal.

No one in the car passed any comment. Even for three hardened mercenaries, Greyson's obvious glee at the culmination of the evening's events defied comprehension. Krantz re-enacted a circular slicing motion with his right hand and a sharp upwards tug with his left.

'I think I tugged when I should have ripped,' he continued, slowing down the movement of his left hand as he repeated the action, 'there was more tissue holding her scalp in place than I expected - next time I'll need to use both hands to peel it back, you know, like taking the skin off an orange.'

Clara involuntarily ran her fingers through her own hair as she caught the eye of Roz seated next to her in the back of the car. They both knew Greyson hid a dark side underneath his seemingly calm exterior, but this cocky, aggressive and wholly irrational person was more unpleasant than even they expected. In fact, Roz, Clara and Connor had each been surprised to find Greyson recruited to the current operation in the first place as, by all accounts, this personality trait had made him persona-non-grata with most of the intelligence services which used Black Ops.

His former position as one of the go-to members of the Black Ops network evaporated after an incident in Germany a few years earlier, since when he'd been shirked by the intelligence community. Clara and Roz only knew the bare facts of what happened to Greyson in Cologne; working for a European intelligence service he'd infiltrated a neo-Nazi cell, become a key member of the group and all had gone well until he walked out of one of their meetings. It wasn't the fact he walked out which upset the intelligence community, it was what he left behind.

All five members of the cell had been butchered in an attack which turned the stomach of even the most hardened German policemen, with one news agency describing the scene as like something from a horror movie.

23:58 Vauxhall Cross, London

David Price took the call from Peter despite the hour.

'Branigan has escaped with Chloe Travers and Paige Henderson, but there's a serious situation unravelling at the club,' Peter began as soon as his call was answered, 'not only were there four Black Ops people there, but also two casualties among members of the public. One of them fatal.'

'Are you still there?' David Price asked, already leaving his apartment to make the short walk to his office on the other side of the Thames.

'Negative,' Peter replied, 'the police who attended the Special Forces Club are on the scene and they know me.'

'Understood,' David said, making his way down the stairs, 'what about Michael?'

Peter Winstone cast a glance at his colleague in the driving seat beside him. Michael had proven himself less than capable in a live situation, an interesting revelation given his occasional role as an instructor at The Academy.

'He's with me - but he doesn't have the operational experience to remain undercover in the situation we've left behind.'

Peter didn't amplify his concerns, but in his view leaving Michael there on his own wasn't an option. Not only was his major success of the evening the swapping of telephone numbers with a transvestite he'd met on the stairs, but also, he almost ended the evening without finding out about the carnage left in Branigan's wake. Understanding the subliminal message Peter Winstone was giving him, David Price called Alex Oldroyd in the Operations Room before he was halfway across Vauxhall Bridge.

'Alex, I need you to go over to the fetish club I talked about earlier - Branigan did show and the whole thing seems to have turned into an unholy mess. One person was murdered and another horribly injured.'

'Okay,' Alex agreed, happy to have something to do other than monitor a hostage situation in Pakistan where, candidly, nothing was happening, 'was Branigan one of those hurt?'

David Price explained events as best he could from the sketchy information he'd received from Peter Winstone and, by the time he'd finished walking across Vauxhall Bridge to his office, Alex was already on his way to see what he could find out at JJ's.

While he waited for Michael and Peter to get back from the club, David called Gregory Brown and Marty to keep them up to speed with the situation.

Gregory, at home in Surrey, asked if he could be joined into a conference call with Michael and Peter when they returned and to be kept up to speed with any further information Alex managed to glean. By contrast, Marty sounded like he'd had one too many at the golf club and David seriously wondered whether he'd even remember their conversation in the morning.

SUNDAY 31ST OCTOBER

CHAPTER 25

00:01 Hotel, Whitechapel Road, East London

The hotel was a concrete monstrosity painted bright blue to advertise the popular budget chain - not for Clara and Connor the fancy prices and round-the-clock service of the posh West End hotels - when you paid for accommodation from your own pocket, you shopped around and stayed cheap. Without a bar to drown their sorrows, Clara was sitting on a lime green stool in Connor's cramped room sipping Glenmorangie from a china mug, her host perched on the bed.

'Not our finest hour,' Connor observed, taking a gulp from his mug and shuddering as the warming liquid hit his stomach.

'No,' Clara agreed, 'not only did Branigan get away again, but also Greyson seems to have become a liability.'

Connor snorted.

'After Cologne it was always on the cards,' he said, 'you hardly do what he did and then become normal again overnight.'

Clara nodded and sipped her drink.

'Yes, but clearly our Mr Cressix isn't bothered by that.'

'And why should he be?' Connor asked, taking another gulp of whisky, 'It's results that matter to him.'

'And we're getting precious few of those in case you hadn't noticed.'

As they contemplated their lack of success, Clara's phone broke the silence.

'What the fuck went on this evening?' Cressix said without introduction.

Clara's heart sank.

'We almost held him for the police to arrest,' she said, glancing at the marks on her forearms where she'd latched herself onto the bag strap, 'but he escaped just before they could catch him.'

'You might not have got Branigan, but you sure as hell left a mess behind - whose idea was it to start killing and maiming civilians along the way?' Cressix asked.

Clara was silent for a moment as she wondered what to say.

'That wasn't the collective will of the team,' she replied, choosing her words carefully, 'Krantz was cornered and possibly over-reacted.'

'Oh, that's what you call murdering one bystander and butchering another,' Cressix yelled so loud Connor didn't need to strain to overhear, 'a bit of a fucking over-reaction?'

Clara was lost for words.

'You do know the whole idea of this operation was to make a minor problem go away,' he continued, so loudly Clara held the phone away from her ear and wondered if he could be heard in the next door room, 'instead you've thrown a fucking spotlight on Branigan, are leaving a trail of the wrong fucking victims behind and Krantz has created a crime scene which is going to have the press crawling all over it! I thought you were supposed to be fucking professionals?'

00:13 Canonbury, North East London

Greyson was still feeling a warm glow following his little skirmish.

He'd managed to overcome the intense anger which coursed through him after the brunette and the Japanese cunt had the audacity to tackle him. What the stupid girls didn't realise was that not everyone bowed courteously and played fair when it came to a fight - especially if they had a hunting knife strapped to their right ankle.

It was the most obvious move in the book, but even Branigan didn't spot that it was Krantz himself who'd elected to sit on the floor; a position of weakness in the eyes of his captors, yet one which changed the whole dynamics of his predicament. His crossed legs had brought the knife within easy grasp, and folding his arms as he sat gave him space to pull his right elbow back and slide his arm out from under the belt the girls had wrapped around him. Being on the floor gave him a strength advantage over his captors who were forced to stoop if they wanted him under control.

He'd waited until the tall one turned her back - too busy checking that Branigan was okay to keep an eye on her prisoner – and struck with two swift stabs into the Japanese girl's upper abdomen; under the ribs, through the diaphragm and into the lungs.

One. Two.

The Japanese girl went down without making a sound, her face a picture of shocked surprise as her lungs filled with fluid and she tried to draw breath through her punctured abdomen. Even then the other girl didn't turn around.

Blissfully unaware that anything was happening behind her, he reached round and plunged his knife deep into her throat, cutting with one ferocious slice low through the base of her neck. People who didn't know what they were doing always went high in the neck. Not Greyson. By cutting deep and low he'd severed the brunette's arteries even before she'd begun to wonder what was happening.

He was about to run when he'd caught the eye of the Japanese girl sitting behind him making funny little gurgling noises. That's when he had recalled his fantasy about Branigan's daughter and grabbed the Japanese girl's hair in his left hand and made one circular slice around her scalp with his right. One cut made with two strokes; exactly what he wanted, right up to the moment he tugged her hair expecting it to come away with a flourish.

But Greyson was disappointed.

Some, but by no means all, of the scalp separated from the fatty membrane underneath and even after a firmer tug he'd only managed to pull seventy percent of the scalp away from her skull. His experiment having failed, Greyson left the two girls and joined the others.

He smiled at Roz beside him in the car.

Ever the gentleman, he'd insisted on dropping Connor and Clara near the hotel in Whitechapel before seeing Roz to her home in Canonbury, fifteen minutes' drive north.

Roz shuddered as Greyson put his left hand on her thigh and slid it suggestively towards her crotch.

00:34 Hendon, North London

Paige was fascinated by Alan's house.

To be more exact, once she'd changed into the jeans and a blouse Branigan had bought her and bitched about the quality, the cut and the fit of the garments, she'd become aware of the welter of information on display in the hallway. So much so that Alan switched the screens so they not only showed the salt water aquarium with a great white shark staring out, but also the shark snapped at Paige's fingers wherever she tried to touch the screens to activate them.

'I am part of this thing you know,' Paige protested, whipping her fingers away as the shark struck, 'you don't have to hide everything from me.'

'We're not hiding it from you,' Branigan explained, 'we're trying to protect you. You've seen the people who are after Chloe and me and the less you know the safer you are.'

'This has nothing to do with me being a journalist?'

'Well, Paige, it has everything to do with that because you started the whole thing off with your original story,' Branigan replied, not being able to miss the jibe at the woman who'd contributed to his downfall, 'but that's not why we want to keep information from you.'

'Can we stop bickering and focus on the picture?' Chloe asked from the kitchen.

'Yes,' Paige agreed, casting an angry glance in the direction of the shark, 'I'm fed up with that thing's eyes following me anyway; I'll go and get it.'

While Paige fetched her bag from Chloe's room, Branigan went into the kitchen.

'You did well tonight,' he said.

'I don't think I did that well,' Chloe said, recalling the fear she'd felt being pursued by the Black Ops team, 'I was so scared. I just did what I had to do to get out of there.'

'It's no different for me,' Branigan replied.

'But you've been trained, so you know what to do.'

Branigan laughed.

'I was given a rule book which told me what I should do to protect my bosses and, in exchange, they set a rule which said they wouldn't back me if I was found - it was hardly comprehensive training for something like this evening.'

Paige came in and put her bag on the table, pointedly examining the cut strap before pulling out a thin manila file.

'I brought the whole folder,' she said, throwing the file down in front of Branigan, 'and don't forget you owe me this story.'

Branigan riffled through the contents of the folder, discarding the photos which showed the inside of the container and him receiving payment for the shipment, pausing when he came across a picture taken inside The Hyatt in Bishkek. The photo showed a typical modern hotel lobby with a reception desk at the back of the shot and a wide expanse of the foyer filling the majority of the central foreground. There were two people walking towards the camera on the left of the photo, four standing huddled in conversation on the right and a woman on the phone in the centre of the picture.

'This is it?' Branigan asked, hiding his disappointment.

'Yes,' Paige said proudly, 'I think Cressix is one of those people.'

Branigan studied the photograph intently before passing it wordlessly to Chloe who did the same.

'Paige,' Chloe said, putting the photo on the table in front of her friend, 'everyone in this photo is Chinese.'

'Yes, of course,' Paige replied defensively, 'there was a Chinese trade show on at the time.'

'But you don't believe the person who fed you the information is from China, do you?'

'No, of course not,' Paige said defensively, 'but look, the girl on the phone is more Western.'

Paige studied the photo more intently, focusing on the dark-haired girl on the lobby phone she herself had used to contact Cressix.

'And there's no reason to believe Cressix is a woman, is there?' Branigan asked.

Paige gave the photograph another quick look.

'Oh, I remember now,' she said, her face brightening as realisation dawned, 'I didn't take that picture because I thought Cressix was in it - I took it because I liked her shoes.'

Branigan took a deep breath and silently counted to ten.

'Can I just get this straight,' he said when he'd got control of himself, 'we all risked our lives tonight to get you out of JJ's because you'd stumbled across a photograph showing a nice pair of shoes?'

'If you want to put it that way,' Paige replied, pushing the photo in front of Chloe, 'but if you look, they are a really funky pair of shoes with a chrome heel and toe.'

Before either Branigan or Chloe could pass comment, Alan called from the living room.

'I think you need to come and look at this,' he said.

By the time the three of them had made it out into the hallway the screens were both displaying a local news report which was clearly coming live from outside JJ's.

Along the bottom of the screen it announced the breaking

news.

"One clubber murdered and another in a critical condition after fight at East London fetish club."

00:34 Vauxhall Cross, London

'Have you told Marty what's going on?' Gregory Brown asked.

He was on the phone from his home in Surrey to David Price, Peter Winstone and Michael Jenkins who were all seated round the conference phone in David's office.

'Yes,' David replied, 'I phoned him and told him - whether or not he remembers is another matter.'

Peter exchanged a glance with Michael and mimed having a drink.

'So where are we up to?' Gregory Brown asked, sounding like he was stifling a yawn.

David went on to explain what Peter and Michael had told him, before going on to outline Alex Oldroyd's current involvement.

'I've taken Alex out from the Ops Room and sent him off to see what he can find out,' David continued, 'he's due to call anytime now if you want to stay on the line?'

Gregory Brown agreed that he would, before posing a question.

'Peter, you're absolutely sure there were four members of a Black Ops team after Branigan?'

Peter bent forward so he was speaking directly into the phone in the middle of the table, 'Yes, one hundred percent, at one point I had hold of one of them and the other three were surrounding me.'

'How did you get out of that,' Gregory asked, his voice tinged with surprise and a hint of amusement, 'did Michael come rushing to your aid?'

'No,' Peter replied, the momentary hesitation in his voice speaking volumes, 'he was busy keeping an eye on things inside the building, I was just lucky the police arrived when they did.'

'You're sure these people were Black Ops?' David Price asked, focusing directly on Peter across the table.

'Yes, they were a well-organised group, clearly prepared to kill to achieve their goal; they have to be Black Ops.'

David Price nodded and said nothing, aware from his hesitancy that Peter wanted to say more.

'There's something else - I think I've come across the man with the knife before.'

David looked up sharply.

'You remember that disastrous operation the Germans had in Cologne a few years back, when the man they sent in undercover ended up wiping out the terrorist cell he was supposed to infiltrate?' Peter continued, 'I think it's the same man.'

'I remember that one,' Michael Jenkins said, 'but I didn't think you were that closely involved.'

'I wasn't, but before it all went wrong three members of the cell came to London for a meeting and the Germans wanted our help with surveillance; I spent a day following them around and that man was one of them, I'm sure.'

'But even if it is him, how do you know he's from Black Ops?' Michael asked.

Peter looked at him askance.

'If you recall, the sole survivor from the cell was the man from Black Ops,' David said tactfully, 'and I suspect Peter has applied some compelling logic.'

'Ahh, okay,' Michael acknowledged, his face reddening as the penny dropped, 'would you like me to speak to the Germans and look into it?'

'No, Peter was the one who saw him, he should speak with Berlin,' David replied just as the call waiting light on his phone began to flash.

It was Alex who explained how he'd used a fake forensics ID to have free access to JJ's.

'It's a bit of a weird place,' he continued, 'and there are lots of half-naked people giving statements, but so far it seems fairly conclusive. The Japanese girl has been taken to The Royal London Hospital and all the accounts suggest that she was attacked by the same man that had the altercation with Branigan and the police believe killed the other girl. The police have plenty of witnesses telling them Branigan escaped with Paige Henderson and Chloe Travers – it seems both girls were regulars here so the identification is reliable, although there is a corollary to that because Paige was wearing a leather hood during the escape.'

David Price turned to Peter Winstone and silently raised one eyebrow.

'There is one other person with them,' Alex added, 'one of the witnesses to their escape swears their getaway vehicle was being driven by someone wearing a military dress uniform with a bright red jacket - like he was in the Coldstream Guards.'

02:09 Stratford, East London

With hindsight Drake wished he had left his shift 5 minutes early. If he'd been on his way home when the tip-off about Branigan came in he wouldn't have been at JJ's, he wouldn't have discovered Marta's body and, most importantly, he wouldn't have thrust his left hand into the gap where her larynx should be.

He was in the toilet feverishly scrubbing his hand. Taking a deep breath, he steeled himself - there were statements to take and a room full of clubbers outside. As he reached the top of the stairs from the toilet and stepped into mezzanine bar area, he was met by Tenant.

'Ah, Drake,' he said, 'could you take a statement from Jock Fraser next?'

He pointed at a burly man with a blackened right eye, who was wearing a pink satin dress; DS Drake sighed - just when you thought things couldn't get worse.

08:39 Hendon, North London

The atmosphere was subdued in Alan's house as the four of them left.

Although they'd all managed to get some sleep, the shock of the events at JJ's ran deep, particularly after Paige phoned the News Desk and discovered the identities of the victims. Only Alan, with his extraordinary ability to file any distressing thoughts away into a little room in his labyrinthine mind, woke up refreshed and raring to meet the new day.

Branigan and Chloe were taking the hire van down to Farnham to inspect the container and Paige had agreed to stay off the radar by going to visit a friend in Brighton. Intent on reclaiming his space, Alan seemed oblivious to everyone else's distress from the night before as he padded round the house in his favourite Spock outfit making cups of tea and coffee.

By the time they were leaving, only Branigan seemed to have fully engaged with the world. He'd checked and re-checked the equipment he was taking and prepared a list of "do's and don'ts" for Paige to help her evade discovery by any of the factions after them. Much as when he'd done the same with Chloe a week before, these covered the basics from phones to emails; credit cards to bank accounts. Alan had somehow produced yet another pay-as-you-go phone for Paige and they'd all swapped the relevant un-compromised contact details; unfortunately, the atmosphere worsened as they prepared to leave.

'I've repaired your handbag,' Alan proudly announced, thrusting the bag with the cut strap awkwardly into Paige's hands.

It's probably fair to say that whatever Paige had anticipated as a repair to her Hermès bag, it didn't involve a 1/4 inch galvanised steel gutter bolt. Mistaking her open-mouthed silence for awed delight, Alan carried on.

'I haven't got a rivet gun, you see,' he said excitedly, his hands opening and closing as he rocked from foot to foot, 'so I drilled through the strap and bolted the ends back together - I used a galvanised bolt so it won't rust.'

After an outburst worthy of a toddler having a tantrum, Paige remained sullenly silent until they dropped her off at Victoria Station.

CHAPTER 26

11:21 Industrial Unit, Farnham, Surrey

Without Alan's risk-averse take on things Branigan drove to Farnham despite not being named on the insurance. Beside him Chloe was very quiet as she contemplated the events of the night before and mourned the horrific outcome.

Respecting her silence and having his own inner-demons to contend with, Branigan analysed the events of the preceding week, thought about the up-coming funeral and plotted his revenge on Greyson Krantz. He also considered the endgame for the nightmare in which he, Chloe - and now probably Paige - were embroiled, realising it could be nearer than he expected if, as he hoped, the weapons and explosives were still in the container. Were that the case, all he needed to do was identify Cressix in order to stop running and hiding - not necessarily that difficult a task given that he only had Gregory Brown and Marty left on his list of suspects.

As they neared Farnham he reached for his phone.

'Marty?' he said when his call was answered.

'Is that you Branigan?' Marty replied.

'Yes, we need to meet.'

'Are you all right, because I had a call from David Price late last night and he said something about another murder?' Marty asked, his voice edged with concern.

'What did he tell you?'

'Jeez, Branigan, I don't really know. I was pretty much asleep when he called and some of what he said didn't register.'

Branigan saw through Marty's excuse and pictured Marty having spent the evening drinking Scotch with his golf club cronies.

'If we can meet, I'll be able to explain.'

'You're not planning anything like the spectacle at our Wednesday night dinner, are you?'

'I promise,' Branigan said, 'no tricks - I just need to talk.'

Agreeing to meet in the bar of a hotel near the office, Marty hung up.

'Is that so you can confront him about whether or not he's Cressix?' Chloe asked, having come out of her reverie as she listened to Branigan's half of the conversation.

'Yes,' Branigan replied, 'I think we're getting close to solving this thing and hope by asking Marty face-to-face I'll know whether or not it's him.'

'And your choice of venue, is that safe?'

'I'm putting my faith in Marty not contacting the police, so, yes, I guess it should be safe. It's near the office so I know it fairly well, plus it has the added advantage of being near where I have to prepare for another meeting.'

Chloe looked at him quizzically.

'Greyson Krantz,' Branigan said, without giving Chloe any clue as to what he was planning.

There was no sign of life in any of the units as Branigan reversed their white van up to the roller-shutter door of Unit 2 and unloaded his tools.

In a move they'd discussed before leaving, Chloe slid across to the driver's seat.

'I'll call you when I'm done,' Branigan said.

She hadn't argued when he'd pointed out there was no point risking them both while he cut into the container – not that that made it any easier for her to drive a safe distance away and leave him to face possible death alone.

For his part Branigan was sanguine. He shut the doors to the unit and set up portable lights so he could see clearly what he was doing and remembered the lessons on bomb disposal he'd received at The Academy.

It was the kind of thing you did your best to remember because, as Sgt Arkwright - his bomb disposal trainer - put it so succinctly, 'People who forget the rules of bomb disposal only do so once!'

The first thing Arkwright told him was to forget about Hollywood.

'I'm sorry to tell you, he'd said, approaching the blackboard, 'there never is a big fucking timer counting down from 1000 to zero, but instead a micro switch which is either on or off.'

'While it's off you are fine,' he'd said, leaving the alternative option to everyone's imagination, 'and for it to remain like that you have to do this...'

He wrote "CRAP YOURSELF" in big chalk letters.

Which was precisely what Branigan now set out to do.

The first part of the mnemonic he'd already done:-

Contain the area
Remove
All
Personnel

With Chloe out of the way and no one working nearby, the area was contained.

Then, as Sgt Arkwright explained, began the tricky process of identifying what set the bomb off.

'In the Second World War it was easy, you dropped a fucking bomb from an airplane and it went off when it hit the ground. What you're going to face is a device which could be set off by movement, heat, time, temperature, pressure, even a fucking cell phone.'

'And just to make your job that much more difficult,' he went on to explain, 'the cunt that made the device will want to fool you when you look at it so you blow yourself up if you try to defuse it.'

Which is where the next part of the mnemonic came in:-
Y
O
U
Reappraise the device constantly
Stop and make sure you're doing the right thing
Execute the disarmament
Live
Fuck off home

Branigan subsequently heard that all this sagely advice stood Sgt Arkwright in great stead, right up to the point he didn't stop and make sure he was doing the right thing while defusing a booby-trapped device in Afghanistan; three months off retirement and he never made it home.

Intending not to make the same mistake, Branigan planned to cut into the container carefully and high enough to avoid the plastic explosives which had been stacked waist high in all the old photographs of the contents.

He chose his spot.

The side-by-side doors on the container were designed so the right-hand door was always first to open, which meant Branigan took to the left side of the container to start drilling.

His reasoning was based on what he'd surmised the instant he saw the welding on the padlocks and not on the doors themselves.

'Why do you suppose he didn't want to weld down the seam?' he asked Alan on their trip to buy the tools with which to break into the container.

'Oh, that's easy,' Alan replied with the frank, guileless innocence of his autism, 'he didn't want to get the doors hot.'

Alan didn't feel the need to explain himself further.

'You think he's set a thermal detector inside?' Branigan asked, looking for confirmation of his initial fear.

'Yes.'

It stood to reason. A motion detector wired to a battery so it would go off as soon as the door was opened. Which is why Branigan elected for the incremental approach with a steady hand, a tiny drill and water to keep things cool. Then he gradually increased the size of the drill until he had a hole big enough to insert Alan's camera and small LED light on a snake-like tube.

'Why on earth did you buy this?' Branigan asked when he'd first stumbled across it in a collection of cameras, concealed microphones and other devices Alan had in a box under his desk.

'I saw one once in a spy film and thought it might be useful.'

'And has it been?' Branigan asked, examining the device which looked like it belonged in a proctologist's clinic.

'Oh yes,' Alan replied excitedly, 'I've found £1.43 in coins under the seat of Mabel using it.'

After drilling a large enough hole, Branigan gently threaded the flexible scope inside the container and, using the pistol-shaped grip on the device to move the camera, surveyed the scene inside using Alan's tablet computer. His heart raced with a mixture of excitement and fear as he focused the image and began to discern what was just the other side of the steel wall - dozens of wooden boxes of plastic explosives stacked waist deep inside with a motion sensor pointing at the door!

Despite the temperature in the cold warehouse, a bead of sweat appeared on Branigan's brow as he tried to work out how the trap was set. It looked simple. There were two black wires leading from the motion sensor into an old tobacco tin and two black wires and one red one leading from the tobacco tin into the bottom-most box of plastic explosives.

Branigan frowned.

Something about what he was seeing didn't make sense.

The person making the bomb had taken the time to set

the detonator in the box at the bottom of a stack of five 25 kg boxes of explosives and he'd carefully sealed the tobacco tin with turn after turn of plastic tape to make it well-nigh impossible to look inside. At the same time, he'd left seemingly colour-coded wires where they could easily be accessed.

Unable to either look inside the sealed metal tin or the box of explosives, Branigan followed Sgt Arkwright's advice. He stopped and re-appraised. The obvious thing to do was cut one of the wires and hope for the best. The red one looked inviting were it not for Sgt Arkwright's warning - 'If he's clever he'll try to fool you.'

Trying to think like his adversary, Branigan recalled the simplest of bomb-making circuits. That would need only two wires and if he cut either of them the bomb would be safe. Five wires and some form of wiring or switch hidden inside a tin and he was able to discard the word "simple."

Five wires suggested a more sophisticated design with a transistor which would pick up the change in voltage when a wire was cut and set the whole thing off.

If he was right it was a lottery. He could cut one of the three wires leading from the circuit and it would be safe - cut either of the other two and it would go off.

While he considered his options, Branigan carefully retracted the camera from the huge metal container and readied himself for cutting one of the wires. He opened the long thin box he'd borrowed from the vets. True, they didn't actually know they'd loaned it to him, but he hoped to return it in one piece before the day was out. It contained a tiny cutter on the end of a pencil-thick rod which could be elongated by adding additional sections. Like they used for keyhole surgery on humans only designed to be used on bigger animals.

Measuring the length of the cutter, Branigan started to drill a new hole in the side of the container in preparation for a game of Russian roulette. Red or black? 'How lucky are you feeling Branigan?' he heard Sergeant Arkwright ask.

His second hole cut, Branigan tested the new device, wandered round the container to calm his nerves and wiped the sweat off his hands using a rag tangled up with a piece of thread he found on the floor near the doors.

He inserted the cutter and edged it towards the three wires, still undecided which to cut.

Drawn to the distinctive red wire, he opened the cutter and began to squeeze the jaws shut around the cable, a reckless part of his psyche almost hoping it was the wrong choice so he would be reunited with Sally and Molly.

The wrong choice.

He heard Sgt Arkwright again.

'He wants you to cut that fucking wire, Branigan, that's why he made it so bleeding obvious.'

Just as he was about to slice clean through the red wire, Branigan understood what he was seeing and snatched the cutter back. A bomb carefully planned using materials its maker had brought with him - even down to a piece of neatly cut rag and a thread so he could cover the motion sensor with the cloth and pull it away just before he closed the doors the last half an inch.

He'd deliberately set out to deceive.

Changing tack, Branigan gently edged the tobacco tin across the cardboard box on which it sat. Nudging it a millimetre at a time until it teetered on the brink of the stack of explosives. As he did so he exposed another black wire coming out from underneath the tin. Hidden from view so anyone attempting to defuse the bomb would blow themselves up - the design such that any of the wires Branigan first saw would trigger the device and only the wire hidden underneath the tin would make it safe.

Now understanding what he was seeing, Branigan reached forward and cut through the wire he'd exposed underneath the tobacco tin.

Bang!

The loud crashing noise of the small metal entrance door being thrown back against the solid block wall made Branigan jump so much his hand jerked and he sent the tobacco tin over the edge, in the process pulling the motion detector with a sudden tug on the wires.

'Hello, is there anybody there?' A voice called.

Branigan looked up to see the ginger-hair of Regan Whittaker from the steel fabricators next door.

'Regan,' he said when he found his voice, 'you remember me, Tony Blair from the Bailiff's?'

Whittaker glanced quizzically at the surgical tools inserted inside through the side of the container.

'Health and safety,' Branigan explained quickly, 'would you believe we're not allowed to open an unknown container without taking pictures and air quality samples first? Too many people have opened them up to find a dozen refugees - or worse - the other side of the door I think.'

Regan grimaced and nodded with understanding.

'That doesn't bear thinking about,' he said, 'I don't envy you having to do that - I just saw the door was ajar and thought there must have been a break-in.'

'I appreciate your concern,' Branigan said, hoping some colour had returned to his cheeks, 'I'll be here for a while and you'll see my colleague turning up later as well.'

Satisfied that all was well, Regan left and Branigan pulled his phone from his pocket.

'Hello Chloe,' he said, 'you can come back now - it's disarmed.'

'Thank God for that, I've been so worried,' she replied, 'did everything go all right?'

'Oh yes,' Branigan said, the tremor in his phone-hand belying his answer, 'as smooth as clockwork.'

13:54 Whitechapel, East London

Greyson was sitting with Clara Hess in a small coffee shop

near Aldgate East underground station while Connor was off stealing a replacement for the burned-out Audi.

Unable to smoke inside, Roz Tyzack was sitting outside at a table in front of the window taking deep drags on her cigarette, shivering - not from the cold, but her recollection of the previous night.

She'd known she was in trouble when Greyson insisted on driving her home. Her fears confirmed when Greyson reached across from the driver's seat and unceremoniously thrust his hand under her skirt and deep between her thighs. Her immediate reaction was to push his invasively scrabbling fingers aside.

'I don't think so,' he'd said, grabbing her right wrist painfully before guiding her hand to his rock-hard erection.

The situation was all too clear.

Roz was being driven home by Greyson's alter-ego, the depraved part of his psyche which was aroused by the blood he'd spilled at the fetish club and, as it turned out, was turned on by rough non-consensual sex.

Taking another deep drag on her cigarette Roz shifted her weight to take the pressure off the bruises and glanced over her shoulder. Her eyes were met by Greyson who leered back lasciviously.

God, how much she wanted this operation to be over so she could be rid of this dreadful man - they needed just one opportunity to lure Branigan into a trap and see him arrested.

She threw her cigarette down on the pavement and ran inside.

'We're missing the obvious,' she said, taking care not to look Krantz in the eye, 'Branigan turned up at that club when an email was sent to Chloe Travers; surely if we pretend to be Cressix suggesting a meeting we can get him to do the same again?'

Clara and Greyson hesitated as they wondered whether it could really be that simple.

'Do you know, that could just work?' Greyson said with enthusiasm, grabbing her right forearm and squeezing it in an apparently congratulatory gesture.

Noticing Roz recoil with pain, Clara put two and two together.

14:22 Industrial Unit, Farnham, Surrey

Branigan and Chloe were taking far longer at the warehouse in Farnham than they'd hoped.

'I know it's a big task,' Branigan said when they'd opened the container and surveyed the boxes of explosives, crates of ammunition, sundry small arms, pieces of machinery and even a wheeled mortar piled inside, 'but I'd like to inventory everything.'

Chloe grimaced as Branigan fetched the sack barrow and pallet jack and they set about hauling everything out of the container and spreading it round the edges of the warehouse, wrenching open packing cases, checking contents and photographing everything they saw.

'This may seem like a daft question,' Chloe said as she wheeled a box of 39 mm cartridges out from the container, 'but why are we doing this?'

Helping her heft the heavy box onto a growing pile, Branigan grunted with exertion.

'Because once we leave here, we won't have a second chance to see what's inside,' he explained, 'and I'm hoping that by knowing what is here we'll discover something about Cressix's plan.'

'He must've seen something special about all this lot,' he continued as he opened the lid of the latest box and checked the contents matched the labelling, 'to have gone to such trouble in such a hurry.'

Chloe nodded her understanding as she set off to collect the next box.

'We're either looking for something which is still here, or

conversely turns out to be missing when we compare our inventory to the photographs.'

'That's it,' Branigan agreed, using the next box to start a separate pile having studied the Cyrillic script on the label.

'Where does this box go then?' Chloe asked.

Branigan glanced at the next box.

'The ones with OZM on them are land mines, so they go over there.'

'This is going to take some time, isn't it?' Chloe said, frustrated at her inability to differentiate the types of weapon.

15:47 Police Station, North London

'Well?' DCI Tenant asked Drake when the Detective Sergeant returned from a briefing with DI Cartwright's team.

'It's still early in their investigation, but the CCTV footage is proving very helpful,' Drake replied, taking a seat opposite Tenant and placing a thin folder on the desk, 'it proves Branigan was there with Chloe Travers; both entering and leaving through the rear exit.'

Tenant nodded triumphantly.

'Does the CCTV show whether or not he did it?'

Drake was aware his DCI still clung to the hope he'd be able to take Marta's murder under his investigation and the two cases would meld into one.

'No, in fact it proves the opposite,' he replied, dashing the glimmer of hope in Tenant's eyes, 'it shows them leaving the building right before the time we think the murder was committed.'

Tenant latched onto the hint of doubt in Drake's voice.

'The time you "think" it was committed; you're not sure?'

'DI Cartwright is ninety-five percent sure by tying in witness statements, but the problem is the Club only has a couple of cameras on the inside - one on the front door and the other up on the bar at the mezzanine level. Something to do with privacy and not wanting to film all the activity in the play area. All they've got is an indistinct shot down towards the rear of the building where the incident took place.'

'But the cameras on the outside give you a better image?'

'Oh yes, there are six of those and by following the timed sequence on those we know Branigan and Chloe entered the building under cover of a firework display.'

DCI Tenant frowned.

'What an organised one?'

'No, this looks like something done for their benefit; it certainly wasn't a professional job judging by the trajectory of the rockets. Whoever set them off sent four or five directly towards the Club, but the rest were distributed all over London.'

'They had an accomplice?'

'It looks like it. More importantly the camera on the front door shows four people entering we can't account for; a grey-haired man and younger woman plus two other men and the cameras at the back show two others who seem to have been stationed outside.'

'For fuck's sake,' Tenant said, all hope of a seamless connection with his case gone, 'how many people has he got working with him?'

'That's the point sir,' Drake replied, 'I don't think they were working with him; if anything, it looks like they were trying to catch Branigan.'

'And they weren't anything to do with us?'

'No, definitely not,' Drake paused and took a deep breath before delivering the next blow to his DCI's pet theory on Branigan's guilt, 'In fact I think we've come across the grey-haired man before.'

He pulled two grainy images from inside the folder and thrust them towards Tenant.

'The one on the left was taken on the CCTV camera in the entrance to JJ's and the other is of the member of the public who tried to apprehend Branigan at Bank Station,' he said, before pulling the remaining piece of paper from the folder and thrusting it towards his DCI, 'and that's the description of the man Branigan's neighbour said she saw on the night his wife and child were murdered.'

Tenant scanned Judith Warde's scant description of "an attractive grey-haired man" and thrust it back towards Drake.

'But that's so vague you can't use it to make a firm link between the two.'

'I agree sir, but neither can you use it to dismiss him from our enquiries; it certainly seems more than circumstantial that the man who appears to have murdered the woman last night was also at Bank Station and could have been at Branigan's house the night the murders took place there.'

Tenant put his head in his hands.

'This isn't going the way I expected,' he said in frustration.

'No sir,' Drake replied, almost feeling sorry for his senior officer, 'and there's another thing you're not going to like; it's on the screen next door, sir, and I should warn you that you're in the relevant footage.'

He led Tenant through to the Incident Room where the raucous hubbub died down the moment those crowded round the screen realised the DCI had entered. Drake hit the play button for the film and studied his superior's face as Tenant watched himself on the screen.

The black and white footage was from a fixed CCTV camera at the front of JJ's looking out over the top of the smoking shelter towards the road. Timed at 23:36 it showed two men and two women running straight past the DCI who attempted to stop them by waving his arms in the air. When the fleeing foursome ignored him, the DCI wandered after them and waved a goodbye with his still raised right arm.

'Fucking bollocks,' Tenant muttered softly to himself as he studied the footage before leading Drake back into his office and shutting the door.

'I'm very disappointed, Drake,' he said, making no mention of his own role in the footage he'd just seen, 'you had three men inside the building and you let this suspect escape.'

Thunk!

Another lead balloon landed at Drake's feet.

17:33 Strand Palace Hotel, London

Branigan was familiar with the layout and ambience of the bar in the Strand Palace Hotel near to the offices of Marty Freeman Investigations - it was a place he and Marty retired to from time to time after work. Soft ambient lighting, a conservative carpet and coloured lights behind the bar tried to create a sophisticated and welcoming air to the space which was largely populated by empty tables at this time on a Sunday afternoon in October.

Branigan cast around to check there were neither lurking police nor Black Ops already in situ. Satisfied, he crossed to the far side of the room where Marty sat nursing an almost empty glass.

'Hello, Marty,' he said noncommittally, trying to decide whether his colleague's pallor was caused by the green lighting from behind the bar or too much whisky the night before.

'Branigan,' Marty said, half rising to give him a stiff and rather formal handshake before beckoning the waiter over.

Their drinks ordered, it was clear neither knew where to start and there was an awkward silence before Marty spoke.

'Are you okay?'

'Yes,' Branigan said with a weary shrug, 'I'd just like this all to be over and for life to go back to normal.'

Something they both knew wasn't possible.

'You do know the funeral is this Thursday at 11 o'clock?' Marty asked.

'Yes,' Branigan said without explaining how.

'Good,' Marty replied, unsure whether or not to go into

greater detail.

'I'm sure you're doing everything you can to make it right for them both,' Branigan said, 'I appreciate it.'

Marty flushed, took the large tumbler of whisky the waiter had brought over and changed the subject.

'What happened last night, I got a message from David saying there'd been another death?'

'I would've expected David to give you more information than that,' Branigan said, surprised that Marty wasn't better informed.

Marty's flush deepened.

'Oh, you know,' he said defensively, 'it was late when he phoned and I was really tired - I'm not sure it all sank in.'

Branigan felt sorry for the man sitting opposite. In the two years since Marty's wife had died, he'd watched his boss become increasingly reliant on alcohol and, he guessed, Marty's poor recollection of the conversation from the night before had little to do with tiredness.

Outlining the events at JJ's, he watched Marty's facial expression as he described each of the four Black Ops people - two of whom Marty had met when they posed as Chloe's parents - before going into detail about Greyson Krantz and his attack on Hanako and Marta.

'You weren't directly involved in that at all?' Marty asked, his expression suggesting everything he was hearing was news to him.

'No, it was the people who are bent on getting me arrested for the murder of Sally and Molly.'

Branigan saw the confusion on Marty's face and decided now was the time to throw in the information he'd thus far withheld.

'Peter was there,' he said.

For a moment Marty frowned as he tried to make sense of what Branigan had just said.

'What, Peter Winstone you mean?'

'Yes, he was there with Michael Jenkins and then - after

it all kicked off - Alex Oldroyd turned up to keep an eye on things,' Branigan said, watching Marty's facial expression intently and stopping short of saying he'd gleaned some of this information from notes Alan had found on SIS's internal computer system.

The look on Marty's face told him everything he'd just covered - from the skirmish with this Black Ops quartet to the involvement of three members of his precious "gang" - was news to him.

'You're not Herbert Cressix, are you?'

Still trying to digest the other information, Marty didn't hesitate in his reply to Branigan.

'Of course not - do you think for a minute I could do this to you?'

With that Branigan knew he was able to unburden himself of what he'd discovered.

Taking care not to mention Alan's name for fear Marty would say something to the wrong person, Branigan told him about the container, the events in Bishkek, Kozlow's involvement, the mysterious Zack and the movement of funds.

He also told Marty precisely where the container was, what he and Chloe had found in it and then he dropped his bombshell.

'We've eliminated five of the six of you Marty.'

'And who does that leave?' Marty asked.

'Gregory Brown.'

Aghast, Marty shook his head in disbelief.

'I don't believe it,' he said vehemently, 'I've known Gregory for most of my adult life - he isn't capable of this level of treachery.'

'Except he doesn't see defending his country as treacherous and the evidence clears everyone else,' Branigan said.

When Branigan had explained how each of the others had been eliminated from their suspect list Marty sat silently for a minute, still remaining to be convinced.

'That's all well and good,' he said eventually, 'but telling me who it isn't hardly makes Gregory guilty.'

Branigan nodded in agreement.

'I know. Which is why I need you to help me expose him when the time comes.'

19:46 Hendon, North London

Passing several groups of children dressed as everything from witches and spiders to skeletons and zombies, Branigan felt a lump in his throat. He'd never have the chance with Molly to emulate the laughing parents as they ushered their offspring from door to door.

As he approached Alan's house Peter Winstone's words in training struck a chord, *'in the field, always look for the slightest discrepancy which differentiates your goal from its surroundings.'*

Whilst Branigan didn't expect to see pumpkins, witches' hats and cobwebs outside Alan's, it did stand out in one way - his was the only house in the entire road without any light whatsoever showing. Barging into the normally free-moving front gate, Branigan's leg crashed against it as it refused to open when he lifted the latch. Finding it chained shut, he had a rush of understanding what the black plastic, rolls of duct tape and padlock Alan bought the weekend before were for.

Stepping over the gate Branigan dialled Alan's number.

'Alan Armstrong speaking, how may I help you?'

'It's Branigan.'

'Branigan, who?'

After patiently establishing that he was the person called Branigan living in Alan's house and right now standing in his front garden, Alan opened the door the tiniest of cracks and suspiciously cast his gaze about to check that there were no Trick or Treaters hiding in the shadows.

'I take it you're not a fan of Halloween?' Branigan said, once he'd fought through the plastic draped behind the front door and the door itself had been shut, locked and bolted.

And then bolted again.

'Not particularly,' Alan said, ushering Branigan down the darkened hall which was noticeably warmer and more humid now the windows had been taped over with the heavy plastic sheeting.

'I did try to embrace it the year after Mother died, but some people were upset by my joke.'

Branigan waited.

'The policeman who came thought it would be better if I used a toy chainsaw to scare the children another time, but rather than that I've just found it better if I pretend to be out,' Alan said gloomily.

Branigan felt a rush of compassion for Alan, who didn't understand the rules by which others operated and couldn't cope when the world brought itself knocking at his door.

Eager for an update Chloe entered the kitchen.

'How have you got on?' she asked, before catching sight of Branigan's bewildered expression.

'Yes, it is an interesting response to Halloween, isn't it,' she continued as Alan joined them at the table, 'but looking at it positively the house is much warmer even if it is a bit airless.'

Alan smiled contentedly as Branigan ran through the salient points from his meeting with Marty.

'I'm certain Marty isn't our man,' he concluded, 'so I told him all about the container and that Gregory Brown is Cressix.'

'What was his reaction to all that?' Chloe asked.

'He's going to alert David Price to the container and let him deal with that, but he isn't 100% sure about Gregory Brown - in fact what he actually said is "an absence of an alibi isn't proof of guilt."'

Chloe looked crestfallen.

'He's not doing anything with the information?' she asked.

'He'll tell David, but thinks we'll need to find more to convince him.'

'Excuse me,' Alan said, when Branigan stopped, 'but have you seen the invite to a meeting you've received from Herbert Cressix?'

Branigan looked to Chloe who nodded.

'He's right,' she said, 'it came in to the email account Paige wrote to last night. It's addressed to you care of me.'

Branigan raised his eyebrows.

'That's a brave move by whoever sent this, they must know the address is compromised - look how many people turned up at JJ's.'

He took the laptop from Chloe and read the message.

'Cressix didn't send this - Black Ops did,' he said decisively.

Chloe frowned in puzzlement.

'It stands to reason,' Branigan explained, 'the only people with anything to gain are the Black Ops quartet. Cressix doesn't want to reveal his identity, the police aren't on the same page and the good guys amongst the six are actually trying to help me.'

Chloe shook her head.

'I don't see what they're doing as helping,' she exclaimed.

'Think about it,' Branigan continued, 'without Peter's intervention at JJ's I would've been caught - you can't tell me Peter, Michael and then Alex turned up like that without a nod from David Price and they wouldn't have stepped in unless he'd told them to.'

'Which only leaves the four from Black Ops who we know are being paid to set me up,' he concluded.

Alan gave a little chuckle at the mention of them being paid and then his ears turned puce and he began to rock back and forward when Chloe and Branigan looked at him quizzically. Branigan shrugged and picked up the thread of the dialogue.

'The only person who won't be there if I accept the invitation is Cressix himself.'

Chloe nodded, seeing Branigan's reasoning.

'I take it you won't be accepting?' she asked.

'On the contrary, it plays right into my hands. Provided you two are prepared to give me some support it means I can bring my own plan forward.'

He went on to outline how they could help him in what he described as "a bit of street theatre."

'Let's send a reply back,' Branigan said, satisfied that Alan and Chloe were onside, 'and tell the sender I'll meet them inside The National Theatre Kitchen Café on the South Bank at 5:00pm tomorrow.'

A place he and Sally visited frequently when they first met - less so after Molly was born; a fitting place to leave his mark on the man who killed them.

'Are you sure you want to do that?' Chloe asked, 'Don't you need more time to prepare?'

'No, I've done that already. Besides, we're so close to having this all wrapped up, I just want it out of the way.'

'I don't think we have much of a role after tomorrow - Marty and his friends can get Gregory Brown locked up and track the person he's lined up to help him with Operation Peach Tree,' Branigan continued, 'all I have to do is put our Black Ops friends out of action and wait for the police to see sense.'

20:40 Unknown Location

Herbert Cressix had just learned Branigan had unearthed the container – thereby ruining any prospect of carrying out the Peach Tree attack. Although deeply distressing after the planning which had gone into it, Cressix was pragmatic; the spate of recent terrorist attacks across Europe had garnered support for funding the Service and it was probably best to now kill the whole strategy and tell Zack to stand down.

That didn't mean Cressix's problems had all gone away:

far from it.

He knew Branigan remained a threat – especially now he'd demonstrated his progress by unearthing the container – which meant he needed to re-double the effort to have him taken out.

Cressix took a pay-as-you-go phone from his pocket and dialled.

'Listen carefully,' he said when Zack answered, 'Branigan has discovered the arms cache in Farnham; we have no choice but to stand down on Operation Peach Tree.'

Cressix paid scant attention to Zack's rant at the injustice of shelving the scheme which was not only of importance to furthering Cressix's cause but also Zack's own goals within the middle east.

'I don't really care about your cause,' Cressix concluded once the rant died down, 'what matters now is that you and I aren't dragged into this - if you want a new cause to go after you should focus on one goal - getting Branigan out of the way.'

Their call over, Cressix moved to his next task - transferring more money to the Black Ops team. Opening the payment system on the desktop, he filled in the details for the transfer and keyed in the authorisation code, whereupon the computer responded with a message to say there were insufficient funds on the account. Cressix cursed at the computer glitch and opened the bank statement to check the balance.

There was just £0.13p left in the account.

The colour drained from Cressix's face. Over £5.7m was missing.

MONDAY 1ST NOVEMBER

CHAPTER 27

05:01 Hendon, North London

If Chloe hoped to be as rested as possible ahead of Branigan's big day, her hopes were dashed by Alan's appearance.

Tap, Tap, Tap.

'Good morning Chloe,' he said brightly, 'I've come for your sheets, it's wash day and our pretend Mr. Cressix has confirmed he'll meet Branigan at 5:00pm.'

08:08 Industrial Unit, Farnham, Surrey

Regan Whittaker was frustrated to find the road cordoned off half a mile from work and traffic throughout the area bumper to bumper.

Turning on the radio he tuned into the local station and didn't have to wait long to find his answer. The announcer was talking excitedly about the day's big story. A bomb disposal team were dealing with hundreds of kilos of explosives discovered in a container in a Farnham warehouse.

09:18 Vauxhall Cross, London

Already seated round the circular table of the small nondescript 3rd floor meeting room were Gregory Brown, Michael Jenkins, Alex Oldroyd and Peter Winstone as David Price entered and shut the door.

'I hope you don't mind meeting here,' he said, sitting down between Alex and Peter, 'but too many people like to watch the comings and goings from my office.'

'If you've had a chance to look at the Operation Plum

Tree file this morning, you'll know that GCHQ intercepted an email exchange purporting to be between Herbert Cressix and Branigan,' he continued, 'and there's the likelihood of a meeting between the two of them at the National Theatre this afternoon.'

He scanned the faces round the table.

'It goes without saying,' he added, 'if one of you is using the soubriquet Herbert Cressix it would save a lot of time and effort if you showed your hand now.'

There was an uncomfortable moment during which no one wanted to catch anyone else's eye.

'In fact, I had a call last night from Marty telling me that Branigan had spoken to him and ventured a name,' David continued, pausing long enough to look at each of his colleagues in turn, 'but I am not taking that information seriously until I have incontrovertible proof; which leaves us with the more pressing question of how should we respond to this afternoon's meeting?'

'It depends,' Alex Oldroyd said, 'what do you see as our primary goal - catching Cressix, keeping Branigan out there, or seeing him arrested?'

'We can dismiss the first,' David replied, 'because if Branigan is right and Cressix is one of us, then we've lost the element of surprise. Candidly I think this is a ploy by the Black Ops team to draw Branigan into the open and have him arrested.'

'Are you still giving credence to the suggestion that Branigan is being set up by Black Ops?' Gregory Brown asked.

David Price answered carefully.

'All of us can see there's more going on here than meets the eye - look how many people turned up at the fetish club the other evening - but I have an open mind on who's behind it. What I'd like to do is monitor what happens this afternoon and, if possible, help Branigan stay in the field without our being seen to be involved.'

'Would you like me to go along and monitor the meeting?'

Peter Winstone asked.

'Yes, I would,' David agreed, 'with as much support as possible.'

'I won't be able to help - 'I've got a meeting in Whitehall I'm afraid,' Gregory Brown said.

'Michael, Alex?' David Price asked, looking from one to the other.

Both agreed that they too could provide support to monitoring proceedings, although Peter's suggestion that Michael might be best placed back in the office didn't go unnoticed by David Price.

'We're agreed then,' David continued, 'Peter will take Alex and Michael with him, provide low-key support to Branigan and report back to us afterwards?'

As everyone got up to leave David Price stopped Peter by the door.

'Did you manage to get photographs of any of the Black Ops people who were at the club on Saturday?'

'Yes C, I did,' Peter replied, using the abbreviated term for "The Chief" used within SIS, 'I was just sorting through footage from the Club before this meeting. It looks like there are good pictures of the two of them on the inside - the images are too grainy from the outside cameras to show much of the others.'

'And do you recognise the two you've got?'

'No, but I'll add their faces to the Plum Tree file so we can all have a look, plus I'm sending the pictures to colleagues in Paris, Berlin and Rome.'

'Good,' David said, 'and I take it you're all up to speed with what's happening with the explosives find down in Farnham?'

There was a murmur of agreement from around the table.

'Box are overseeing what's happening there,' he continued, using the soubriquet for MI5 based on their "PO Box 500" wartime postal address, 'but given that Branigan found the container, the likelihood is the discovery will link back to us.'

10:14

Farnham is in the news, but not in the way I expected.

I thought there would be a big explosion – instead they're reporting bomb disposal people attending the scene and a large cache of weapons; someone has been cleverer than I expected!

Whilst it doesn't really matter, it probably changes the timing of my next move. You see, Cressix has been hiding behind anonymity ever since we first made contact and then using the threat of exposing me to stop us moving ahead with the terror attack we agreed upon back in Bishkek.

At this moment he doesn't realise that I knew Branigan had found out about Farnham and that I got there first. But it can only be a matter of time before he discovers I have taken everything I need for my own attack – one which will put the middle eastern cause back on the map.

Of course, Cressix will think he can still threaten me with exposure - but it's time for me to ignore that threat, side-step Cressix and move things forward.

11:19 Police Station, North London

DCI Tenant came dashing into the Incident Room holding a piece of paper aloft as if he were about to proclaim 'Peace in our Time.'

'Listen up everyone!' he announced as the hubbub in the room quietened, 'We've got another chance to get Branigan. He's going to be at The National Theatre at five o'clock this afternoon - and this time we'll be ready for him.'

'If you don't mind me asking, where's the intel come from?' Drake asked suspiciously.

'The same source as gave us the tip on JJ's.'

Drake's heart sank.

'So presumably there's a chance the same group of people as were at JJ's will also be there; should I feed the tip to DI

Cartwright's team as well?' he asked.

'No, that won't be necessary,' Tenant said, shaking his head adamantly, 'our tip isn't specific on the others so I don't want to waste their time; besides, whoever chose The National doesn't realise the layout of the place. There are only two ways in and out, so even if everyone from JJ's turns up, we'll easily contain the situation.'

DS Drake's eyebrows shot up.

'Just so we're clear, sir, Branigan is the focus of our attention this afternoon?'

'Yes, he's still our prime suspect; of course, if the grey-haired man from JJ's is there, we want to talk to him too.'

'Greyson Krantz,' Drake said.

DCI Tenant looked at him questioningly.

'The man at Bank Station who we also think was at JJ's,' Drake explained, 'gave his name as Greyson Krantz when officers interviewed him after Branigan escaped on the back of the tube train.'

Tenant nodded.

'Well, yes. Then we're primarily after Branigan, but should also make every effort to bring Krantz in for questioning in the unlikely event he too turns up.'

14:42 The Strand, London

Marty barged through the door into Reception and was about to launch a question at Anna when he stopped short. Instead of being in her usual place behind the desk, Anna was standing near the doorway deep in conversation with a client.

As he waited to catch her attention, Marty admired her impeccable dress, from her sharply cut grey suit down to her black and silver shoes - a stark contrast to the shabby jeans and tired trainers worn by her companion.

Anna looked across at Marty and stopped her conversation.

'Can I help you Marty?' she asked.

'No, it's okay, you carry on,' Marty replied before seeing the tan skin, square set jaw, black hair and green eyes of the man she was speaking with.

'Hello Jasper!' Marty exclaimed, recognising her boyfriend, 'I didn't realise it was you.'

Jasper smiled and looked down at his own casual clothing.

'A few days off work,' he explained, 'hence the lack of a smart suit.'

Marty nodded his understanding and spoke directly to Anna.

'I won't disturb you; it's just that I'm looking for Alan - I don't suppose you've seen him anywhere?'

'No. Have you tried the Server Room - that's where he normally goes when he disappears?'

'Alan,' Jasper interrupted, 'isn't that the short chap who cornered me at Branigan's barbecue; the one who ended up counting all the bricks?'

'Yes, that's him,' Anna agreed.

'Then I'm sure he passed me a few minutes ago just around the corner - he was heading out across Waterloo Bridge. He was wearing a duffle coat, bright red trousers and had a satchel round his neck.'

Jasper's description confirmed his sighting.

'That's Alan!' Marty observed wryly.

'Is it anything I can help with?' Anna asked.

'No, it's all right. Just let me know when he reappears. I need him to find some files on the system for me; but there is one other thing, Anna, I don't suppose you could stay late tonight, only Andy has a conference tomorrow and we could do with a hand getting the security passes prepared?'

16:44 National Theatre, The South Bank

Branigan's choice of the café at the front of the National Theatre was deliberate. So too was his timing.

Set at the front of the monolithic grey concrete theatre, the Kitchen Café overlooked and spilled onto the wide strip of paving which ran along the South Bank of the Thames; the paving itself busy with visitors, Londoners going about their business, romantic couples out for a stroll and – today at least - police.

In fact, it was obvious to Branigan as he surveyed the scene that the police were arriving in force, that his Black Ops friends were already at their stations and that three of his erstwhile SIS colleagues had turned up as well. He felt he was witnessing one of the plays for which the venue was famous; only this one was being acted out in and around the café and, candidly, was being performed by a third-rate cast.

Having made his preparations and been in character an hour before the first group arrived, Branigan was able to move around with ease and watch everyone make the same basic mistake - they all thought they were there before him.

He'd watched each of the factions descend on the scene and settle down looking outwards, anticipating his arrival.

The Black Ops quartet arrived first. Roz and Clara sitting at a table inside the café, while Greyson sat with the smokers at one of the heavy wooden tables outside and Connor patrolled the strip of pavement leading to the theatre from Waterloo Bridge.

Next to arrive were the trio from SIS.

Peter Winstone and Alex Oldroyd clearly using their field experience to study the layout as they approached, while Michael Jenkins hung back and read the theatre posters.

Surprised by Michael's inclusion, Branigan watched them split; Peter and Michael taking a table in the café and Alex electing to walk up and down the pavement outside.

Which only left the police, who were not only the last to arrive but also the easiest to spot.

They arrived en bloc. Ten of them, each believing an anorak pulled on at the last moment would be enough of a disguise when going undercover and that no one would notice either their shiny black size 12's or the handcuffs attached to their belts.

Pitched against Branigan and the Black Ops quartet, theirs was a kindergarten performance, compounded by their senior officer directing each of his team as to where they should station themselves. Most eyes in the café were focused on the group as they spread out and dotted themselves at vacant tables with little thought as to how to blend in with the theatregoers.

By contrast to Branigan, DCI Tenant was pleased with his strategy.

His team were in place well ahead of Branigan's anticipated arrival and a quick scan of the tables inside the cafe revealed nothing suspicious about the scene. In fact, even with his trained eye, it was difficult to differentiate his team from the genuine theatre buffs and tourists.

Satisfied he had the inside of the cafe covered, Tenant held the door open for a waiter and two animated Japanese tourists before stepping outside to check on Sergeant Drake propped against the railings beside the Thames.

Drake's choice of a brown anorak over brown serge trousers - themselves with greasy hand marks on the thighs after he'd hastily eaten fish and chips in the squad room - portrayed the air of an East European migrant who just happened to be a fan of contemporary theatre.

'It took me a while to spot you there,' DCI Tenant said after he'd scoured the faces outside in search of his DS, 'are you all set?'

'Yes, Chief Inspector, if he arrives from this direction, I'm ready to alert the team and track him inside,' Drake said, patting the bulge of the radio concealed under his anorak.

Tenant nodded with satisfaction.

'I'm going to wait over there,' he said, nodding his head

past the theatre building to the West, 'and do the same if he comes past me.'

Seated at one of the wooden tables outside the front of the building, Greyson Krantz watched the unfolding tableau with interest.

A confirmed non-smoker, Greyson opened a pack of Marlboro he'd taken from Roz and lit a cigarette before pretending to read the descriptions in a pamphlet detailing the forthcoming productions.

He pulled his woollen Greenbay Packers hat lower down on his face and adjusted his heavy-framed black spectacles, reassuring himself that his disguise was still intact.

Branigan took in the assembled players.

The only person missing was Herbert Cressix.

Without a curtain to rise or a director to shout "Action!" it was down to Branigan to decide when the time was right for today's one-off performance.

'Can you hear me Chloe and Alan?' he said softly into his telephone earpiece.

The confident reply from Chloe and the contorted squeak from Alan told him that his team were in position and ready to play their part.

'Right, Chloe,' he continued looking to the West, 'Connor is in the zipped-up blue weatherproof jacket with black on the pockets and collar, and the senior police officer is the rather jowly man looking up towards the bridge.'

Chloe confirmed she could see them both.

'Let me get into position,' he said, walking towards DS Drake on the eastern flank, 'and when you hear me ask my question you go ahead and create your scene.'

Feeling like a Shakespearian actor who suddenly bursts into centre stage from the audience, Branigan mentally let the curtain go up and approached the figure of DS Drake leaning against the railings above the Thames.

'Excuse me, do you have the time?' Branigan asked.

Such a simple question and a natural reflex for Drake to lift his left wrist to glance at his watch. At the same moment, there was a distant shout from Chloe. Seizing the pre-arranged opportunity, Branigan grabbed Drake's wrist, fixed one half of the set of handcuffs Alan had become so entangled with up in Sheffield to it, and span Drake round so he was facing out across the river.

Branigan's strength and fitness made it the easiest of tasks to thread Drake's arms through the railings and ratchet the cuffs round the other wrist. Stunned by the sudden turn of events, Drake took a breath to yell out, but was thwarted as Branigan first held his hand over the Detective Sergeant's face and then wound a small roll of duct tape round his head three times until the detective's mouth was completely covered.

A fascinating feature of human nature is that no one took any notice.

The three people who walked past while Branigan was winding the tape saw two men grappling in some form of embrace and elected to turn away rather than interpret the scene. By the time Branigan pulled the black balaclava he'd brought with him down over Drake's head and lifted up the hood of the brown anorak, the poor man looked like a drunk down and out struggling to stand up.

Knowing he only had a few moments to enact the next part of his drama, Branigan left Drake to his silent struggle, picked up his remaining props and moved over to the outside tables. In the distance there was a continuing clamour from Chloe's distraction.

Having deliberately worn a short skirt, she'd positioned herself on the pavement towards Waterloo Bridge and in a rehearsed move yelled and struck a stunned Connor Jarvis across the face.

'Help, officer,' she cried directly at the supposedly undercover DCI Tenant, 'this pervert has just put his hand up my skirt!'

Ever the gentleman, Tenant - who didn't question how Chloe knew he was a police officer - stepped forward with an air of flat-footed authority to apprehend the protesting Connor.

The ensuing debacle allowed Chloe to slip away to the adjacent side street where Alan was sitting at the wheel of Mabel as the getaway driver.

Upon hearing the shouting, Alex Oldroyd turned away from the theatre and walked determinedly towards the disturbance.

Seated at his table amongst the smokers, Greyson Krantz focused on what was happening whilst toying with his cigarette and feigning indifference.

'Excuse me sir, your bill,' a waiter said passing a slip of paper on a dish low across the table to Greyson, who reached out to take it with his right hand.

Seizing his moment, Branigan – who was posing as the waiter - brought the serrated blade of a steak knife crashing down through the meaty middle of Greyson's palm, nailing the tip of the blade deep in the wooden table top. Greyson's immediate reaction was to try and pull his hand free, discovering in the process that not only did the knife refuse to budge, but also the movement made the toothed blade saw deeper into the soft flesh on the inside his hand.

As searing pain shot through him, Greyson kept his right hand perfectly still and reached out to extricate the blade with his left - a move Branigan was waiting for with a second steak knife which he brought crashing down, this one slicing through the back of Greyson's left hand, out through the fleshy palm and burying itself even deeper into the tabletop than its predecessor.

Finding himself nailed to the table, Greyson Krantz looked momentarily into the eyes of his assailant.

'This is for killing Molly,' Branigan said softly before unleashing upon Krantz's jaw the same straight-palmed blow which had shattered Red's leg, the impact landing with such devastating force several heads turned at the loud crack of breaking bones.

Fuelled by the rage burning inside him, Branigan bent down and grabbed the two middle fingers of the dazed Krantz's left hand.

'This is for messing with my wife,' he said before bending the fingers back slowly and deliberately until they both folded back flat against the top of Krantz's hand with a popping sound.

'And this is for murdering Sally.'

Branigan delivered a spinning kick with his right leg which landed square on the side of Krantz's head with such force he was out cold before his face fell forward into the ashtray.

Lasting no more than 15 seconds, the attack was over so quickly none of the observers was able to react before Branigan turned and ran across the pavement toward the railings where DS Drake was demonstrating all the attributes of an escapologist whose act had gone horribly wrong.

'I'm sorry about this,' he said, climbing up, 'but you need to know the man I've just attacked is responsible for the murders of my wife and daughter, plus Marta's killing at JJ's - watch him, he'll be armed.'

Drake was the only person to witness Branigan swallow dive into the Thames below.

Preparation.

Branigan might have ruined the waiter's uniform and the phone in his pocket, but the short wetsuit he wore underneath protected him from the shock of hitting the Thames.

His earlier preparations had included checking the tides so he knew where the river would take him as he used the current to take him across the river and downstream under the protective cover of darkness.

17:29 National Theatre, The South Bank

The police were well placed to lend support to Greyson Krantz while they waited for both the paramedics and fire brigade to arrive. Aided by an off-duty nurse, two officers supported the groggy assault victim while others cleared the area, found keys with which to free DS Drake and identified potential witnesses who were directed to sit at tables inside the building to wait for someone to speak to them.

There was a stir around Krantz when the newly-freed DS Drake asked one of the men tending him to check their victim for weapons and they found he was not only wired to a radio but also carrying a concealed knife strapped to his left leg. With the potentially damning evidence collected, the first of the paramedics arrived to take over from the thin-lipped nurse.

Her role completed, Clara Hess wished her patient good luck and scooped up the evidence bag from under the noses of the unsuspecting police officers.

17:38 Blackfriars Pier, London

Unaffected by the police activity on the opposite bank, the Thames Clipper ferry arrived on time and Branigan was able to haul himself aboard and duck into the onboard toilet while the crew were distracted while the boat docked. Once inside he unwrapped the waterproof package he'd concealed under the jetty when he'd visited Marty, and took out the fresh set of clothes, phone, cash and ticket he'd hidden in preparation.

Emerging from the toilet in his dry outfit, he returned to the deck and surreptitiously dropped his discarded clothing and wetsuit into the Thames before making a call.

'Did you get away all right?' he asked Chloe when she answered.

'Yes,' she replied, 'we had to stop just around the corner from The National because Alan had a panic attack, but otherwise it went as smooth as clockwork.'

'Is he okay now?' Branigan asked, surprised by how much concern he felt.

'Yes, he had to spend a few minutes lying on the floor of Mabel breathing into a paper bag which didn't make it the fastest getaway in history, but generally he's good.'

17:43 National Theatre, The South Bank

'For fuck's sake!' Tenant swore as he hurried back to the aftermath of the failed attempt to apprehend Branigan. 'You all just stood by and watched him beat seven barrels of shit out of someone and then let him run off?'

'With respect, sir,' Drake replied, struggling to contain his frustration, 'he was too well prepared and quick for those of us still on the scene; the whole attack was over in a matter of seconds.'

Tenant eased off his anger and nodded to the cluster of medics and firemen working to detach Krantz's hands from the table.

'The man he wounded,' he said, 'do you think he's who Branigan says he is?'

Behind DS Drake flashing blue lights reflected off the water as officers scoured the opposite bank for the fugitive. A little way downstream a Police boat circled mid-stream with a search light focused on the surface of the water.

'It's hard to tell because his face is so swollen, but he's the right age, build and hair colour to be DI Cartwright's suspect; plus, we found a knife strapped to his leg and he was wired which suggest he wasn't here as an innocent bystander.'

'If he was wired, he must have been in contact with others nearby - have you checked all the witnesses you've rounded up to see if any of them has a radio?'

Drake shook his head.

'Good call - I'll go and check.'

Tenant nodded and stared out across the inky waters at one of the scheduled ferries making its way sedately up stream towards Westminster.

'Oh, and Drake,' he called over his shoulder, 'you'd better call DI Cartwright and let her know.'

CHAPTER 28

18:47 Hendon, North London

'You had the easier escape route,' Alan declared, cutting across Branigan's account of diving into and then swimming across the fast-flowing Thames, 'because you didn't have to contend with all the traffic restrictions - I couldn't find anywhere to park and had to wait on double yellow lines.'

Branigan caught Chloe's eye.

The two of them had been excitedly comparing notes on the afternoon and congratulating themselves on all-but completing their mission when Alan - who'd been silently listening in to their narrative - looked up from the kitchen table and joined in the conversation.

'Oh, wow, Alan, so is that what sparked the panic attack?' he asked, hiding any hint of amusement.

'No,' Alan replied earnestly, shaking his head, 'that started when I saw a traffic warden coming up the road.'

'Oh, I see, so it was the stress of seeing the traffic warden?'

Alan looked up at Branigan with a frown.

'No,' he said with a tone which suggested he considered Branigan a complete idiot, 'seeing the traffic warden made me gasp and I inhaled some of the icing sugar from the doughnut I was eating, then the door burst open and Chloe jumped in and yelled, "Drive, drive, drive!"'

Branigan pretended to cough as he suppressed a laugh.

'But Alan did really well,' Chloe interjected, 'he drove three or four hundred metres up the road before he slumped over the wheel gasping.'

They sat in silence for a few moments before Alan left the

table.

'I need to check I didn't get a parking ticket,' he said as he padded back to the living room.

Branigan watched Alan make his way into the sanctuary of his space before grinning across at Chloe.

'I think everyone should have an Alan in their life; it would help them put their own lives into perspective!' he said, pushing his chair back and ushering her towards the hallway, 'Let's go and see what progress we can make with this board; I need a reality check after that!'

As she reached the hall Chloe recoiled with surprise before erupting into laughter as the great white shark on the screensaver sprang towards her.

'I like the hat Alan!' she called out.

Branigan studied the bizarre image of a shark swimming past wearing a tasseled fez and blowing on a party horn.

'Is it celebrating our getting Krantz arrested?' he called.

'No,' Alan replied.

Branigan swiped across the screen and the shark transformed into their main list of actions.

'So, what is he celebrating?' he asked when it became clear Alan had nothing more to add.

'That the Black Ops people have stopped following you.'

'But we don't know that for sure,' Chloe said.

Alan didn't reply as he rocked back and forth and glanced sheepishly to the top corner of his screens where a message from earlier in the day showed an attempted bank transfer to the Black Ops team had failed due to insufficient funds.

Unfazed by Alan's silence, Branigan and Chloe studied the list.

Operation Peach Tree
Search for

Zack
Shipment was for sale

Zack wanted cash, family relocation and political support

Why did Zack think that was possible?

Russians never met/identified Zack

Operation compromised (on both sides)?

Why was it important to trace the container?

Why negotiate if tracing was primary goal?

Zack support for IS

How did Zack know about the warehouse visit?

Payment to Z Tazi - is that Zack?

Ed Khan

Where/how did he meet Zack?

"You need to look up Zack. Travelling with small son who you can find in Port Macau; later parents too." Unknown telephone number.

Who did he send email to?

Why was he killed? If by Zack, what changed in hours between the "friendly" meeting and his murder?

Was it the message - or someone responding to the message?

Alan

What did he say when talking about the container?

'Didn't Alan's name used to be beside "Search for" under Operation Peach Tree?' Chloe whispered.

Brannigan screwed up his face and nodded.

'Yes, but it disappeared when he drew a blank,' he whispered back.

Chloe's eyes darted up and down the list.

'What about everything else on there – presumably most of that falls in SIS' bailiwick now?' she asked.

'I think so; now they know who Cressix is, I'm sure they'll be focusing on tracking Zack down - aside from that, almost everything else is superfluous.'

'Then presumably the same applies to everything on the

list about Ed Khan – it isn't really relevant unless it helps lead us to Zack?' Chloe asked.

'Pretty much. Don't get me wrong, I'm still intrigued to know what was behind his being murdered, but it looks to me like Ed put Cressix – well, Gregory Brown – in direct contact with Zack and – this is only supposition – once that link was established between them Ed became expendable.'

'You think it was as simple as that?'

'Yes, which leaves just the question about Alan on the bottom of the list because I don't think all this Port Macau stuff matters to us today,' Branigan said.

'If you're going to make something Alan said our next focus, we're probably going to need a bigger board!'

'I heard that,' Alan said from the other room.

'Sorry Alan!' Chloe called back.

'Joking aside, that and the question of how Zack knew that we were going to Farnham are the only two things on the board still bothering me,' Branigan said.

'Do you think his going to the warehouse might be a coincidence?' Chloe asked.

'It might be, but when I was training, they had a saying, "Only dead fools believe in coincidence."'

'The people who trained you were a cheery bunch, weren't they?'

'And remember what Regan in the next-door unit said, no one had ever seen activity at that unit - and then both of us turned up on the same day.'

'If it is coincidence, the odds against him choosing the morning of the same day are 41,283 to 1,' Alan added helpfully.

'Thank you, Alan, it would've been useful to have had that kind of input when I was out in the field,' Branigan said, his eyes wide as he looked at Chloe.

Chloe shook her head in bewilderment.

'Let's try and work this through; Alan, you found the container, didn't you?' she said.

'No, you and Branigan found the container - I found out about the industrial unit by tracing the payments from the bank account to the estate agents. I then went into their system, which was really easy to get into because I don't suppose they thought anyone would want to hack into it. I had a look through their files, you know they've got some quite nice houses for sale, although I think there are some that are over-priced. I compared the price per square metre for the ones which hadn't sold, you see, with those which had.'

Branigan cut across him.

'Great, Alan - and Chloe's question about the industrial unit?' he prompted.

'I was getting to that,' Alan said, failing to pick up on Branigan's frustration, 'I went into their database which, incidentally, was really badly put together and did a bit of re-engineering. Their B tree was searching from leaf downwards so I changed it so it now searches from root to leaf allowing them concurrent access.'

Branigan looked at Chloe and mouthed, 'What the fuck?'

'And then I found out about the unit, phoned you and told you I'd found the bank account for Cressix Enterprises and they'd been renting an industrial unit in Farnham,' Alan concluded.

'Did you mention it or the possibility of the container to anyone?' Branigan asked.

'No.'

'And neither you nor I have mentioned it to anyone?' he continued, glancing toward Chloe, already certain that they hadn't.

'No,' Chloe agreed, 'but what about Paige, might she have seen something on the screens when she was here?'

Branigan shook his head.

'We'd already found the container by the time she was here,' he said.

'Then could someone be hacking into our system here?' Chloe ventured.

Alan was quick to respond.

'That couldn't happen,' he said tetchily.

Branigan jumped in.

'Why not Alan, after all you're able to wander round other people's systems with impunity.'

'Yes, but I know what I'm doing.'

'What if the other side do too?' Branigan asked.

'They still couldn't help but leave tracks if they came into my system,' Alan replied, 'it's like asking someone to walk across newly fallen snow - they couldn't avoid leaving footprints.'

Chloe looked at Branigan who shook his head in bewilderment before continuing.

'Okay, so let's assume no one hacked into your computer, could they have overheard you when you called to tell me about Farnham?'

A flicker of realisation passed across Chloe's face. Anyone who'd heard Alan speak on the phone would recognise the vulnerability - he was seemingly unaware of those around him when he spoke in his loud monotone.

'But I went into Marty's office and shut the door,' Alan protested.

Chloe frowned in concentration as she thought through recent events.

'You didn't mention it to Kozlow when you saw him?' she asked, looking directly up at Branigan.

'No, we didn't talk about anything current.'

All three of them were silent for a few moments. Branigan and Chloe in the hallway staring at the screens and Alan in the living room hidden behind his bank of monitors. Within moments Alan began tunelessly humming the Star Trek theme and pictures began appearing on the right-hand screen beside where Chloe stood.

'He's found something else to do then,' Branigan whispered.

'Alan, are those the pictures from Paige?' Chloe called out.

'Yes, she emailed them through to the right address this time,' Alan replied as the card for Herbert Cressix flashed on the screen before being covered by another picture of the contents of the container.

'Some of those look like the pictures I took in Talas when I got all the guards drunk.'

'How can you tell?' Chloe asked.

'Most are taken in daylight but there are some familiar-looking ones taken with the door closed - let's face it, no one else is likely to go into the container and shut the door,' Branigan explained, 'Which gives us another job to do - comparing the inventory we took yesterday to the pictures to see what's missing.'

No sooner had he spoken these words than a line appeared on their "to do" list. It read:-

<u>Container</u>

Compare original contents with current inventory - Alan

As Branigan nudged Chloe and pointed to the new line, the photographs disappeared one by one until only the card for Herbert Cressix remained.

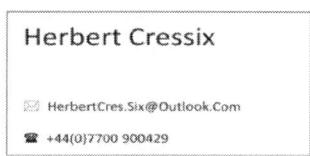

Branigan glanced briefly at the image before staring back at the remaining list of questions and action points.

'While Alan compares the inventories, let's bring it right back to basics with Zack,' he said, 'We know he was unsuccessful when he tried to peddle his consignment to the Russians and that Gregory Brown - posing as Cressix - made contact with him after I sent those photographs.'

'But how would he have known how to get hold of Zack?'

'That's where Ed Khan's communication comes into it. Don't forget Ed sent a telephone number to London, so I'd assume Gregory Brown had already established contact and my photographs confirmed to him that the consignment I was driving was one which interested him.'

'Okay,' Chloe said, picking up the narrative, 'and then Brown paid him lots of money and helped he and his family to come over here. Then, based on Marty's account of Operation Peach Tree, Brown's aim was to keep Zack here as a sleeper and get him to blow up Cambridge or wherever as a way of garnering public support for SIS's activities.'

'That's about it,' Branigan agreed, 'only since then there's been so much terrorist activity in the UK and across Europe, he hasn't needed to enact the plan, which means Zack is probably laying low somewhere feeling particularly frustrated.'

Chloe looked puzzled.

'So how does Gregory Brown keep him undercover - what's to stop Zack just disappearing with his cash if that's the case?'

Branigan snorted and shook his head.

'Spying isn't like in the movies – it's a dirty business where you coerce people to remain undercover by making sure they know you have enough dirt on them and their family to land them in really big trouble if they ever break cover. Your job as handler is to keep your distance; it's quite probable Zack has no idea who it is that's controlling him.'

'Which means Zack might be trapped in limbo?' Chloe surmised.

Branigan nodded his agreement.

'But the danger is that everything we've done has shone a light on what he and Cressix are up to, so that equilibrium may change.'

Branigan stayed staring at the screens.

'I know we should focus on how he found out about our trip to Farnham,' he said after a few moments silence, 'but I'd like also to speak to Marty to see if he has any thoughts.'

Chloe frowned as Branigan pulled his phone from his pocket.

'He knows Gregory Brown far better than I do; it's quite possible he'll have some thoughts on where he might plant a sleeper,' he explained as he dialled from memory.

'Hello, Marty.'

'Is that you Branigan?' Marty asked.

'Yes, I need to ask you a question.'

'Sure, I'm just working late with Andy and Anna doing a run of security cards for a conference at the Excel Centre tomorrow - let me find somewhere quiet.'

Branigan waited, picturing Marty leaving the familiar scene of the reception area piled with plastic ID cards bearing photographs and bar codes for the security people the firm had approved to run an event.

'Okay,' Marty continued when he'd moved away, 'tell me.'

'Now that we've identified Gregory Brown as Cressix,' Branigan began, 'I'd like any input you have as to what he might have done with a sleeper if he brought him into this country.'

'I need to stop you there,' Marty replied, 'I spoke to David Price about your theory and it would be an understatement to say he was unimpressed; he needs more evidence.'

Branigan's shoulders slumped.

'That may be easier said than done; I'm not the one with hundreds of agents at my disposal!' he said, shooing away Alan who'd emerged into the hallway and, seemingly oblivious to the fact he was on the phone, was tapping him on the shoulder.

'I understand Branigan, but I have some sympathy for David's point of view – I'm not convinced either.'

'At least humour me for a moment – if Gregory brought Zack into the UK, he needed to place him somewhere. Can you think of anywhere he might look to integrate him?' Branigan said, walking down the hallway to the kitchen in an attempt to avoid Alan who was following behind.

'I can't Branigan,' Marty said, 'I'm sorry, but I can't.'

There was a long pause before he continued, during which Alan stepped forward again and tapped Branigan repeatedly on the shoulder.

'Of course, there is one possibility, but that doesn't make any sense.'

'What's that then Marty?' Branigan asked, pushing Alan away.

'Leave it with me,' Marty replied distractedly, 'and I'll do some digging. It's such a silly idea I don't want to dignify it until I've looked into it more deeply – call me tomorrow morning and I'll have had some time to think it through.'

'Yes, what is it?' Branigan snapped at Alan who was now standing with his right arm raised.

'I have a question.'

There was a long pause.

'Yes, Alan, what did you want to ask?' Branigan prompted, using every ounce of his considerable patience to keep his calm.

'Did you see the portable generator when you visited the container?'

'I'm sorry?' Branigan asked, perplexed.

'There's a generator showing in one of the pictures,' Alan explained, touching the screen and pulling up a photograph taken inside the container when it was in Bishkek. The photo showed boxes of explosives and part of what Branigan assumed Alan was talking about.

'What, this?' Branigan said disinterestedly, pointing to the waist-high metal frame and cooling fins just showing on the left-hand edge of the picture.

'Yes, I just wondered if you knew where it went,' Alan persevered.

Branigan shrugged.

'No. Is it important?'

'Oh, you know,' Alan said noncommittally as Chloe,

standing in the background, mimed banging her forehead with her hand, 'it would probably be good to know because it's an RTG.'

Branigan looked blank.

'A what?' he asked.

'A radioisotope thermoelectric generator,' Alan explained, touching the screen so a picture of an industrial-looking portable generator with lots of cooling fins surrounding the motor appeared.

Branigan compared the two images.

'Yes, that looks like the same model of generator,' he agreed, still not seeing Alan's point, 'and I seem to remember there was one itemised on the paperwork, but it definitely wasn't there when we emptied it in Farnham - we'd remember having to move something that big.'

'Oh,' Alan said, disappointedly, 'that's a shame.'

Branigan glanced over Alan's shoulder at Chloe who was looking puzzled.

'I think I'm missing something here,' Branigan said as Alan silently stared at the floor, 'help me out – why is this generator significant?'

Alan stared at the floor and rocked from foot to foot as he explained.

'An RTG is a generator they use when in far flung places where there is no easy power source - for things like radio beacons, lighthouses and satellites - it doesn't generate a huge amount of power but that isn't the problem,' he said.

'So the problem with this is?' Branigan asked, an uneasy feeling in the pit of his stomach ever since Alan mentioned the word "satellite."

'Well, I've looked up the model in the picture,' Alan explained, 'and it carries 2.6 kilos of plutonium 238.'

Branigan felt as if the ground had opened under his feet.

Chloe looked blank.

'Sorry Alan, what is plutonium 238?' she asked.

'It's a radioactive isotope they use to power the generator

instead of conventional fuel,' Alan explained.

'Okay Alan,' Branigan said slowly, 'I don't know too much about this stuff, so can you tell me, is it dangerous?'

Alan gave a nervous smile.

'Not compared to some isotopes, it has a short half-life of 87.7 years, you see, so obviously produces a fair amount of power for its mass, but that power is in the form of alpha decays, so needs much less shielding than other beta decay isotopes.'

Branigan wasn't any the wiser.

'If it doesn't need much shielding,' he said, latching on to the alpha decay comment, 'presumably it isn't that dangerous?'

Alan giggled.

'It won't kill you instantly, if that's what you mean, but it's not very good for you,' he said, 'but I just found a quote online by Ralph Nader - an American environmentalist – who once said a pound of plutonium could kill every human being on Earth; the generator contains nearly six times that.'

Chloe gasped.

'Of course, he's not accurate there because you'd need to give an even dose to everyone and that wouldn't happen,' Alan added helpfully, 'so there's probably only enough to kill ten or twelve million people inside that thing and even then it would take a long time because they wouldn't be killed by radiation poisoning, you see, but the cancer caused by ingesting the radioactive material.'

Branigan felt sick.

'How would you disseminate the plutonium?' he asked.

'Well, it comes in the form of ceramic beads, so they're quite tough to break back into their core components,' Alan ventured, 'but if you look, there's also a field mortar missing from the container.'

'What's that?' Chloe asked, doing her best to keep up with the conversation.

Alan sighed disparagingly, marched to the screen and

swiped rapidly through several pages before revealing what looked like the kind of large field gun the army tows behind its vehicles.

'It's a tube you point up in the air towards the enemy, drop a shell into and then it lobs a mortar at them,' he explained, speaking slowly as if to a three-year-old.

Unruffled, Chloe shook her head.

'I still don't see the significance - is the idea to fire the plutonium out of it?'

It was Branigan this time who responded.

'Not exactly,' he replied, 'the idea will be to seal the beads of plutonium inside the mortar with some explosive and vaporise them.'

Alan nodded with satisfaction - at least one of his audience was keeping up.

'Mind you, that would make a bit of a mess of the mortar,' he observed.

Branigan glanced at the board.

'Now it makes sense why Gregory Brown was willing to pay so much for that particular container,' he said with a sickening dread, 'he saw the nuclear material and the means to disseminate it and suddenly Operation Peach Tree was a reality - he didn't have any need to lay waste to Cambridge with hundreds of kilos of explosives when he could make it a no-go zone for a hundred years with a few radioactive beads in a dirty bomb!'

'And the icing on the cake was the person trying to sell the container,' Chloe added as the pieces of the jigsaw fell into place, 'Zack was not only after money but also a home in the West for his family; Brown was able to buy him and keep him undercover until the time was right to set off the dirty bomb.'

19:22 St Thomas' Hospital, Lambeth, London

Having spent time at the scene of the attack on Krantz,

interviewed witnesses and spoken to DS Drake, DI Amanda Cartwright elected to walk the ten minutes along the embankment past the London Eye to St Thomas' Hospital.

'What's happening?' she asked when she tracked down her two DC's in the grandly-titled "surgical admissions lounge" which meant, in fact, they were perched on two plastic chairs in the corridor.

Hardly the most glamorous feature of life as a detective.

Putting down her well-thumbed magazine, DC Helen Owen stood up hurriedly.

'Evening, ma'am,' she said, smoothing her grey woollen skirt and checking her white blouse was tucked in, 'he's in theatre now.'

'The surgical registrar has filled us in on the procedures he's going through,' she continued, while behind her DC Phil Simpson - who wasn't the greatest advocate of female equality - stayed seated and largely ignored his Detective Inspector, 'there's nothing life-threatening - he's got a severed tendon in his right hand, his jaw needs putting back together and the fingers on his left-hand need setting.'

DC Owen flipped through her note book.

'He'll be out of theatre in an hour or so and then pretty groggy from the general anaesthetic until tomorrow morning,' she continued, 'and he'll be in one of the critical care units until the morning when he'll be transferred to a lower-dependency ward. The doctor thought we'd be best to wait until he's been transferred there before we tried to interview him.'

19:22 The Strand, London

Marty was helping Andy and Anna pack the neatly stacked plastic photo passes into cardboard boxes when Branigan called again.

'What now?' he asked testily as he once again made his way into the hallway.

'This is a lot worse than I thought,' Branigan said, before explaining about the plutonium and the missing mortar.

'Jeez, Branigan,' Marty said, 'I know this is serious, but I hope you have some concrete evidence I can give to David - only your last revelation has left me with rather shaky credibility.'

'I've identified the generator from a section of it showing in one of the original photographs,' Branigan explained, being careful to keep Alan's involvement to himself, 'I can send that across to you - the manifest just lists it as a "portable generator."'

Marty thought for a moment before acquiescing.

'I know he's having dinner at The Club this evening; it'll look better if I deliver the news in person with some physical evidence.'

'I'll email it straightaway.'

20:20 Hotel, Whitechapel Road, East London

'Anything?' Roz asked hopefully.

'No,' Clara said, shaking her head and putting her phone down, 'there's still no money in the account and he's not answering his phone.'

Perched on the foot of the bed in the small hotel room, Connor sat pressing buttons on the TV remote, switching channels as he searched randomly for news of the debacle they'd left behind.

'What do we do now?' Roz asked.

'Candidly, nothing,' Clara replied, 'I'll try Cressix again in the morning, but with no money in the account and him not answering his phone, I don't hold out much hope.'

'And Greyson?' Connor asked.

'You know the rules, Connor,' Clara said, taking her small suitcase out from the wardrobe and putting it on the bed beside him, 'we help a colleague, but we don't jeopardise our own position.'

Connor nodded, his focus still on the TV.

'I think my removing the knife was the best we could do,' Clara continued, tossing Greyson's hunting knife which she'd spirited away from the National Theatre into her case, 'so I have every intention of packing my things and going home in the morning. I suggest you both do the same.'

TUESDAY 2ND NOVEMBER

CHAPTER 29

04:55

It's a relief now that Cressix believes Operation Peach Tree is over.

He's become all focused on saving his own skin and was ranting to me last night that we need to drop everything to do with Peach Tree and focus our efforts on getting Branigan out of the way.

Of course, he's right with that: Branigan is a threat. If I hadn't had a stroke of luck and found out about him going to Farnham, he might have ruined everything.

It can only be a matter of time before Cressix discovers that I took the essential components out of the container before Branigan got there. I'm sure he isn't going to feel comfortable when he realises I have a different agenda, but even he must be able to see that there is no time left to wait before making the strike. Branigan is proving both resilient and persistent and Cressix must be able to sense that the whole pretence is crashing down.

If I don't strike for our cause now, then the opportunity may be lost forever, which is why I'm out so early; just walking the streets, seemingly about my normal business.

08:11 The Strand, London

The first sign Anna had that this wasn't going to be a normal day at work, was the police car and ambulance drawn onto the pavement at the front of Marty Freeman Investigations.

The second, was finding Kelly sitting at the reception desk crying hysterically and being comforted by Clive.

'Oh my God, what's happened?' Anna exclaimed, running

around behind the desk to comfort Kelly and tripping over Alan who was stretched out on the floor having his pulse checked by a paramedic.

'What's wrong with Alan?' Anna asked as she took in the confusing scene.

'Nothing,' Clive explained, 'He fainted when Kelly told him what's happened; you see Kelly brought her bike in through the downstairs garage and halfway up the stairs she came across Marty's body - he's been murdered.'

09:18 Stoke Newington, London

Branigan wished he hadn't allowed natural curiosity to take him past the front of his house on his way to visit Jude, the neighbour who'd shared a glass of wine with Sally just before she was murdered.

The deflated balloons flapping in the breeze either side of his front door and the fluttering lengths of police barrier tape were stark reminders of what had happened. His mood didn't lift when he arrived at Jude's a few doors down the road either; the identical layout and homely feel of her house served as another reminder that his home was now reduced to a hollow shell.

After leading him down the hallway to the kitchen at the back of the house, Jude sat Branigan at the kitchen table overlooking the small garden.

'How are you getting on?' she asked, placing a sympathetic hand on his arm and leaving it there while he gave a much-abbreviated resume of his life since Molly's party.

'Lovely as it is to see you,' Branigan explained, 'what I'm really here for is to ask a massive favour.'

'Ask away,' she said.

Branigan went on to explain how Jude could help.

09:21 Hendon, North London

Chloe felt she should let Paige know what was happening.

'Listen, Paige,' she said, phoning her on the mobile Alan had supplied, 'I'm not saying it's a hundred percent safe to come back, but you should know Branigan put a pretty big dent in the team which was behind the events at JJ's.'

'Does that mean they've got someone for Marta's murder?' Paige asked.

'Not exactly, I think it's probably best that you run the details of that one past Branigan when you next see him, but it's fair to say the man we think did it is in hospital and hopefully will be in custody soon.'

'Which hospital did you say he's in,' Paige asked, fishing for information, 'and what can you tell me about him, age, colour, occupation and background?'

'Paige,' Chloe said, exasperated, 'you're supposed to be lying low, not fishing for a story - I only phoned to let you know things were a little safer and that you can probably come back to London soon.'

'That's just as well,' Paige replied, 'because I arrived back yesterday; I'm at work now writing up my eyewitness account of the events at JJ's - that's why anything you can give me on the man in hospital would be useful'

Chloe did a double-take.

'But Paige,' she said, 'you didn't see anything; you were wearing a straitjacket and a leather hood while all that was going on.'

'Exactly,' Paige said, her eyes falling on the news-feed running along the bottom of her computer screen, 'so I was there – you can't tell me that my being blindfolded stops me giving a first-hand account.'

About to remonstrate with her friend, Chloe was cut off before she could say anything.

'The place where Branigan works,' Paige said urgently, 'that's Marty Freeman Investigations isn't it?'

'Yes,' Chloe replied, puzzled by the non sequitur.

'The newsfeed has just reported that Marty Freeman has been stabbed to death.'

11:20

Cressix has just phoned again.

At first I thought he'd found out about the things missing from the container, but instead he was panicking about being caught; he says Branigan has mentioned his name to a colleague. He also said that he doesn't have the money to keep paying the people he'd recruited to - as he put it - 'make Branigan go away,' so he suggested we should join forces in disposing of him.

Of course I said I'd help – now he's explained his plan it plays right into my hands.

11:33 Hendon, North London

Branigan arrived back at Alan's to find Chloe desperate with worry.

'Thank God you're here,' she said the instant he walked through the door, 'have you heard the news?'

From his blank expression it was clear that Branigan had not.

'Marty has been murdered.'

Visibly rocked, Branigan absorbed the information.

'Do you know what happened?' he asked.

'Only what I heard from Paige - she saw it on a news feed - he was stabbed probably sometime last night. They found him on the stairway down to the car park at work.'

'That's all you have?' Branigan said, his mind racing.

'Yes.'

'Last night, you say?'

Chloe nodded.

'That's what the report Paige found said.'

'Have you tried speaking with Alan?'

'No, I figured he's got enough on his plate without me hassling him for information,' Chloe said, 'so I've just been quietly panicking especially since I couldn't get hold of you.'

Branigan reached for his phone.

'I'm trying to think why someone would want to kill him,' he said, staring at the front of his phone and flicking a switch on the side before dialling, 'Sorry, I had it turned to silent.'

'Alan?' he said when it was answered, 'It's me, Branigan.'

He listened to the voice on the other end and raised his eyebrows in exasperation before continuing.

'The Branigan who is living in your house at the moment.'

When he'd finished the call, Branigan gave Chloe a resume of what Alan told him.

'Alan doesn't have much more information than you do, to be honest,' he began, 'he says he's been "a bit withdrawn" from what's going on, which is Alan-speak for hiding behind his computer screens and rocking.'

'What he did say was that Kelly - she works in Accounts - went to bring her bike through the garage this morning and found Marty on the stairs down to the carpark. He'd been stabbed. The police believe he'd been there some time, so my guess is it happened last night when he was leaving work.'

Chloe latched onto this.

'Does that mean he didn't go over and see David Price at The Club?'

'I'd assume so.'

'Then you, Alan and I are still the only people who know about the nuclear threat!' Chloe exclaimed.

'I think so,' Branigan agreed, 'and based on what Alan has just told me, it sounds like our friend Zack killed him; the same man as killed Ed Khan.'

Chloe looked blank.

'He was killed by a single stab wound to the upper abdomen which pulled his insides out as the knife was withdrawn - he was eviscerated,' Branigan explained.

Chloe felt the same nausea she had when Branigan told her the first time.

'Oh, that's horrible,' she said, screwing her face up in disgust, 'what sort of knife does that?'

'One with two parallel blades designed to splay on their way in, lock and then drag your insides back out.'

14:32 St Thomas' Hospital, Lambeth, London

In a room off the nurse's station, DI Amanda Cartwright spoke earnestly with the Registrar.

'In the normal course of events I could discharge Mr Krantz now,' the Registrar explained, 'provided, of course, that there was support at home for him given the damage to his hands.'

'Just how incapable is he?' Amanda asked, frustrated at not yet being able to question the malingering Krantz.

'He'll struggle with some basic things, like feeding himself, washing, dressing and going to the toilet,' the Registrar explained with the weary patience of someone who'd seen it all before, 'but otherwise there's nothing to stop him answering your questions.'

Amanda Cartwright thought for a moment.

'Then if I transfer him somewhere where we have a custody nurse, we can hold him in a cell and question him properly?'

The Registrar shrugged.

'I don't see why not.'

'Would you be able to write a report, detailing for me the level of support he'd need in custody, any limitations on diet and if there is any medication and on-going care he needs?' Amanda asked, angered that the Human Rights Act extended to people like Krantz.

'I can't do all of that,' the Registrar replied, shaking his head noncommittally, 'but if I get Occupational Therapy, his oral surgeon and Dentistry involved we'll be able to pull something together for you.'

'That's good,' Amanda replied, looking at her watch hopefully, 'how soon do you think you can get that done.'

Used to working at the pace of the health service, the

Registrar didn't need to look at his watch.

'Assuming I can get everyone to treat it as urgent,' he said, glancing briefly at the calendar, 'I should be able to write the report and pass him over to you by the end of the day tomorrow, at worst Thursday.'

16:05 Hendon, North London

Branigan looked up sharply from the laptop at the sound of a key turning in the front door lock.

'Is that Alan back?' he asked.

'It must be,' Chloe replied, her voice tinged with concern, 'should I go and see how he is?'

Branigan shook his head.

'Sally used to leave him alone when he was particularly stressed – I think we're better to let him settle back into his home routine before we start questioning him.'

Chloe nodded, while in the background the strains of the Star Trek theme gave way to an annoying half-heard chatter from Alan's room as the programme got underway.

Branigan managed to heed his own advice for a full ten minutes before the distant murmur of Captain Kirk's voice got to him.

'On the other hand,' he said, shutting his laptop and standing up from the table, 'there's only so much Star Trek I can have rumbling away down the hall.'

Alan didn't look up from the shelter of his computer screens as Branigan came into his room, turned the television down a few notches and positioned himself carefully on the floor near the door where Alan could hear him but not directly see him.

Sally's advice – "When he's stressed, you're best not to break too many of the barriers he's built around himself."

'Not a good day then?' Branigan asked softly.

'Oh, you know, I've had better.'

'What happened?'

'Marty got stabbed to death and they're talking about the business having to close.'

'I expect there were lots of police there?'

'Yes.'

'Did they interview you?'

'Yes.'

'Did you speak to anyone about the stabbing?'

'Yes.'

'What did they say?'

'I spoke to one of the forensic people who was wearing a white suit like I wear when I'm doing DIY - I think I should put one in with my forensic computer kit don't you, you know, the kit that I took with me to Sheffield when we went on our mission to rescue Chloe?'

Branigan glanced out into the hallway and caught Chloe's eye.

'I wanted to show him my kit,' Alan continued, his sudden stream of verbiage showing no sign of a let-up, 'but he said he was too busy and he said Marty died last night – apparently they'd worked that out from the temperature of his body and the way the blood he'd spilled had congealed. He'd been killed by one stab wound which had ripped most of his intestines out although it wasn't those that killed him but blood loss from what the forensics man called traumatic aortic rupture.'

'Did the forensics man tell you anything else?' Branigan probed.

'I don't know,' Alan replied.

Branigan was perplexed.

'Why don't you know?'

'Because I felt a bit queasy about what he'd told me and had to go and lie down in Accounts; it was quite a different feeling to this morning when I fainted in Reception when Kelly told me Marty had been murdered.'

Branigan sensed Alan was about to launch into another rambling story.

'Did you speak to anyone else?' he asked.

'Oh yes, Anna said that Marty had been fine when she left work last night and that Andy was the last person to see him alive. Also, I spoke to Hussain and Jasper who were both worried about whether the business would have to close without Marty.'

'Jasper was there?' Branigan asked.

'He was out on the pavement behind some barrier tape the Police had put up; he'd come to see if Anna was okay but the Police wouldn't allow him into the building; they made him wait outside on the pavement with Hussain and all the "non-essential" people.'

'Apparently I'm non-essential too,' Alan continued mournfully, 'or at least I was just as soon as they'd taken a statement from me - that's when they made me go and wait outside on the pavement.'

Branigan shot a knowing glance at Chloe who was listening from the hallway.

'What happens now?' Branigan asked.

'I don't know, they said the office would probably be closed tomorrow but I'm going to go in anyway. They'll need me to show them how the computers and the CCTV system work.'

'That's a good point,' Branigan interjected, 'do you think there might be CCTV footage which shows what happened?'

'No,' Alan said with a tone in his voice which implied Branigan must be mentally challenged, 'the cameras are all focused on Reception and the front of the building; whoever attacked Marty came in the back way.'

'What did you see on the footage from Reception?'

'Andy, Marty and Anna packing passes for the security people at the conference, Marty leaving a couple of times to take calls in the hallway, Anna going home and then some time later Andy leaving.'

'And both Anna and Andy went out of the front?'

'Yes.'

'The Police have seen this footage too?'

Branigan noticed that Alan was rocking back and forth in the silence which followed.

'I doubt it,' Alan said eventually, 'because I encrypted access to it when they said they were professionals and didn't need me to show them how to use a CCTV system.'

Branigan glanced at the giant TV screen where Mr Spock and Captain Kirk were busy fighting aliens of some kind.

'Can you help me do something Alan?' he asked.

'Yes,' Alan replied distractedly, clearly now caught up with the action on the screen.

'I need to tell the people at SIS about the nuclear generator and the things missing from the container.'

19:21 Apartment, Limehouse E14

Paige collected her mail and flipped through it while she waited for the lift up to her apartment. Amidst the jumble of bills, junk mail and fast food advertisements, the crisp, white, hand-addressed envelope stood out - not only because of the linen paper but also the addressee: Branigan c/o Ms. Paige Henderson.

After a moment of hesitation Paige crudely ripped the envelope open and pulled out the letter and business card from within.

She was already dialling the number Chloe had given her by the time she inserted the key into her newly-replaced door.

'Chloe, does the name Harris mean anything to you in connection with Branigan?' she asked when her friend replied, 'Only I have a message from Cressix with a business card and everything, it says, "Branigan, we need to meet so we can sort things out. Just you and me, 10:00am tomorrow where Harris was followed by 20 others," and then he gives a telephone number for a reply and says if Branigan sends back a number he'll text the precise location to meet tomorrow.'

There was an expectant pause before Paige continued.

'What the fuck does all that mean?' she demanded.

19.29 Hendon, North London

When Branigan read the message, Paige had photographed and sent to Chloe he smiled wryly; he knew precisely where Cressix was expecting to meet.

'He wants you to go to Hampton Court Maze,' Alan called out a moment after he'd posted it on the screen before reciting, '"Harris said he should judge there must have been twenty people following him in all." It's from Three Men in a Boat.'

'How do you remember all this stuff Alan?' Chloe marvelled.

'I don't,' Alan replied without guile, 'I looked it up on a search engine.'

'I remember it from school,' Branigan said, 'it's by Jerome K Jerome and Harris is an incorrigible buffoon who leads everyone round the maze for hours before finally stumbling across the middle whilst looking for the way out.'

'Do you know,' Alan said, 'most mazes are either right or left-handed which means if you were to keep your hand touching the left or the right-hand wall it will lead you to the centre. Of course, that doesn't mean it will get you there directly and there are some exceptions to the rule. Technically Hampton Court is a right-handed maze, although you can use the left.'

'Thank you, Alan,' Branigan interrupted before Alan could launch into a more detailed explanation of the theory and handing of mazes.

Alan didn't reply, instead a few moments later a plan of the maze appeared on the screen and Alan came bustling out of his room to explain the nuances of left and right-handed mazes to Chloe. The fact that he was wearing a grey and black Klingon uniform complete with a moulded headpiece which gave him a crenelated bald cranium and shoulder-length black hair occasioned only the briefest of raised-eyebrow glances between Chloe and Branigan.

21:07

Cressix has called again.

He says Branigan has managed to post a message on the SIS internal system telling everyone about the nuclear-powered generator and the threat it poses.

He was ranting about the generator going missing and saying he'd been double-crossed by me until I asked him how on earth I would know Branigan was going to Farnham - he calmed down a little when I said that and by the end he was agreeing with me that the most likely explanation was that Branigan himself had taken it and the rest of the things that are missing.

'It sounds to me like he's hidden them somewhere so he has something to barter with if he's caught,' I suggested.

Cressix seemed to buy that, because he went on to talk step-by-step through the plan for the following day; apparently Branigan has confirmed that he'll be at the meeting.

I didn't mention that I'm going to change the plan slightly and bring along my friend Betty.

WEDNESDAY 3RD NOVEMBER

CHAPTER 30

08:30 Hampton Court

Branigan crossed the bridge over the river at Hampton Court and glanced at the deep red-coloured brick façade of Hampton Court Palace through gates to his right. Famous for being the home of Henry VIII, The Palace is in an enviable position on the of the banks of the River Thames 10 miles outside London.

His destination was not the historic building, but a triangular half-acre yew hedge maze set in the formal gardens immediately behind The Palace. Normally accessed through the main park gate – two 20ft high columns of Portland stone topped by giant stone lions - Branigan chose a more modest entrance, taking a path which threaded between the maze on his left and a café set on the edge of the old jousting grounds on his right, before arriving at the kitchen gardens behind the Palace. Ignoring the signs making it clear members of the public were not welcomed, he went into the sheds used by the gardeners and emerged a few minutes later wearing a tunic emblazoned with the Park logo and pushing a squeaky wheelbarrow,

Adjusting low over his eyes a beaten old leather bush hat he'd found, Branigan began sweeping the pathway along the long edge of the maze which ran parallel to the road outside. Making the slow progress of someone who wasn't in a hurry, he swept the path and studied the people he saw. None was his target and the only person who acknowledged him was a middle-aged woman whose dog tried to launch itself at him as he studied a yellow marking on the ground which, he presumed, indicated a section of the yew hedge singled out for repair.

He doffed his hat to the woman and the angry terrier straining on its lead before continuing to sweep the path.

08:49 St Thomas' Hospital, Lambeth, London

Greyson Krantz knew he wouldn't have another day to himself.

Moved down to a room off a general ward the day before, he'd had some woman Detective Inspector come bustling in, caution him and arrest him for carrying a concealed weapon.

Knowing the rules well enough he'd recognised this move as a ploy to detain him so they could make further investigations, presumably into the death at the fetish club. Krantz also knew the rules well enough, to immediately tell his nurse that he felt too ill to see the police and by the time the doctors became involved he'd bought himself a day of peace and quiet.

Sadly, it hadn't bought him a day of freedom as two police officers were stationed outside his room and they'd cuffed his right wrist to the frame of the bed after declaring him a flight risk.

He looked at his hands.

His right hand was next to useless. Apparently the doctors needed to join two ends of a severed tendon together and as the little posse of medics who'd visited him explained, they'd had to put a splint round his entire right hand to stop him flexing it.

His left was a different story.

His middle two fingers were useless. Dislocated and broken, they had been put back into their respective joints, had splints secured along them and then been taped together. Whilst not fully operational, Krantz was surprised how much he could do with his thumb, forefinger and little finger; at the same time feigning incapacity whenever the police looked in on him. Secretly, he'd used his day of peace and quiet to practice holding, gripping and manipulating with his left hand.

09:43

I'm sure Branigan and Cressix will come through the main gates, so I've stationed myself across the road where I can wait inconspicuously.

I did make one brief trip in to look at the maze and make sure everything was still in place and aside from a woman walking a terrier, a couple walking hand-in-hand and a gardener sweeping the paths, there was no sign of either of them.

Cressix told me last night that he'd be here just after 10.00 o'clock and that Branigan would arrive first - he was very clear with his instructions. He told me he'd already been and marked out the exact spot where I am to stand and then all I have to do is wait until I hear Branigan calling his name and I can open fire.

I have to admire Cressix for devising this scenario.

He's actually found a location where he can lure Branigan into a trap, give me the opportunity of disposing of our common enemy and yet remain completely unseen by me. It is win-win for Cressix. He gets rid of Branigan without having to find the money for his hired hands and he manages to retain his anonymity.

He's clearly clever, precise and inventive when it comes to strategy; do you know, he's even put an arrow on the ground showing me exactly the direction I should fire? The biggest flaw in his plan is that he hasn't asked how I feel about him cancelling Operation Peach Tree.

09:57 Hampton Court

Branigan was frustrated.

Having studied the surroundings of the maze, swept everywhere clean and watched each of the faces of people coming into the Park in to keep control of his meeting with

Gregory Brown, he'd just received a text telling him to head towards the café he'd passed earlier.

He hated it when someone gained the strategic upper hand; but then he knew Gregory to be shrewd, astute and a careful planner.

Any element of surprise now gone, he abandoned the hat and tunic with the wheelbarrow and headed to the café where a flurry of staff activity suggested they were about to open. His hopes of sitting down with a cup of coffee and discussing things face-to-face with Gregory Brown were dashed when a new message arrived - this one sent him back to the inside of the maze with an instruction Alan would have been excited about, "Follow the left-hand hedge. Call me when you get to the white cross."

Briefly smiling at the thought of Alan, Branigan made his way to the wooden hut which served as a ticket office for the maze.

'One please,' he said to the girl behind the counter, 'and I don't suppose you've seen my friend come in yet?'

She shook her head disinterestedly.

'You're the first person in today; you've got it all to yourself,' she observed, shoving his change and a plan of the maze back at him.

As he turned to go through the gap in the hedge, he caught the briefest sight of movement out of the back door of the ticket office - as if someone had just made their way into the maze using the exit. Pausing briefly before electing to take the more conventional route, he turned left and continued into the maze, following the hedge on his left.

Alan would have been proud.

The proscribed path took him up the left-hand outer wall of the maze, before he doubled back and then turned up a dead end on the long outer edge, running parallel to the pathway he'd been on when the yapping terrier had come at him. Following the hedged passageway to the end, he came upon a cross marked with white paint on the ground.

Branigan checked around – there was no one in sight.

'Cressix,' he called out, 'are you there?'

'Branigan – is that you?'

He immediately recognised the deep warm voice coming from a distance away beyond the thicket of hedge forming the dead end of his alleyway.

'Gregory?' Branigan ventured.

'You're in a different section to me,' Brown replied, 'wait a moment and I'll come as close as I can.'

As he pictured Gregory Brown moving along the section of the maze the other side of the hedge, Branigan heard a vague whirring sound followed by a click and the jangle of something small and metallic bouncing along the pavement he'd not long before been sweeping.

The pavement where he'd met the terrier whilst he was studying the yellow marking on the ground.

His mind went into overdrive as he associated the yellow mark on the path outside with the sound of a furled-up steel wire being unwound and the click of a metal pin being tugged from its housing.

'Gregory,' he yelled, 'get out of there – it's a trap!'

10:03

I just saw Branigan going into the maze, so now it's time for me to take up my position by the yellow mark on the footpath Cressix so helpfully placed there for me.

I wait silently until I hear Branigan call out, "Cressix, are you there?"

That's my signal to pick up the end of the coil of wire I placed under the hedge last night when I came along with Betty. I walk away towards Lion Gate as fast as I can. When I'm five metres away I feel the satisfying tug on the end of the wire followed by the jangle of the pin as it bounces along the pathway behind me.

I keep moving fast towards the gate, putting as much distance between me and Betty as possible – you see she's a good-time girl and doesn't really mind who she plays with. She originally came from Germany I think, but before long was adopted by the Russians which is where my Betty came from - stowed in the container I shipped for Mr Cressix.

It's quite ironic really that Betty should come out to play for Branigan and Cressix; one the man that brought her to freedom in the back of a truck, the other the man that bought her.

Betty's proper name is OZM-3, although she is colloquially known as Bouncing Betty, not, you understand, because she has big tits but because she's a fragmentation mine that bounces 4ft out of the ground before saying "hello" by sending deadly shrapnel shooting out in every direction.

Last night I brought her along to the spot Cressix had marked for the meeting and buried her under the hedge. Cressix is now making his way to the rendezvous believing that I am about to open fire in the direction of the arrow and kill Branigan for him.

What he doesn't realise is that I'm electing to kill two birds with one stone and rid myself of he and Branigan at the same time. The "3" in Betty's proper name is the kill radius for this type of fragmentation mine. Anyone within three metres of Betty is assured of death, outside that distance you have a chance; unfortunately for Cressix, I placed the tripwire less than a metre away.

I am passing through Lion Gate when I hear the "boom!"

10:04 Hampton Court

It had taken Branigan a fraction of a second to join the dots.

The mark on the ground on the opposite side of the maze from where he was standing; the whir of the cable being unwound; the click of the metal pin being removed and then jangling along the ground; and finally, a box of mines amongst the ordnance he and Chloe moved in Farnham.

He was already bent low, turning and running as he yelled out his warning to Gregory Brown.

He covered the 8 metres to the next turning and then was

faced with a dilemma – whether to go back out the way he'd come and stay close to the mine or put as much distance between he and the deadly shrapnel as possible - he elected to run for deeper into the maze.

Then he heard the "pop" as Betty was triggered, sending her deadly cargo bouncing into the air, a fraction before he was sent sprawling by the "boom" and warm blast of air of the main explosion as the mine exploded and peppered his back with tiny fragments of metal and bits of hedge.

Dazed by the blast and momentarily deafened by the tsunami of rushing air, Branigan took a few moments to gather his senses before working his way back the way he'd just run. As he neared the epicentre of the blast, it was clear the cushioning effect of the thick hedges had saved him from the worst of the blast and that Gregory Brown had not been so lucky. Where moments before he'd been running down a narrow avenue bordered by yew hedge, there was a 10ft diameter hole in the walls of the maze leaving it open to the pathway outside; a jumble of twisted and broken branches signalling where the missing hedge had been.

Bewildered onlookers peered back at him through the opening as he made his way to the motionless form of Gregory Brown. He studied the tripwire and the mine's housing and realised the force of the blast had blown its victim backwards seven or eight feet. Any doubts that Gregory was dead were dispelled when Branigan bent down to examine his body. He was lying on his back with his shredded woollen coat ripped away from his chest exposing a mess of torn and broken flesh – if Branigan had not heard his dulcet tones a few moments before, he would now have struggled to recognise the mangled remains as those of Gregory Brown.

'Is he dead?' One of the spectators on the outside pathway asked, the man Branigan had seen earlier strolling hand-in-hand with his partner.

'Yes,' he replied, 'and I need you to do something for me. When the police arrive, I need you to ask them to contact someone for me.'

Having ensured that SIS would know that Gregory Brown was the victim and that he had escaped the ambush, Branigan turned and left - by the time the first of the police arrived he was a quarter of a mile away and when his message was relayed to SIS he was sitting on a bus in Hounslow.

10:32 St Thomas' Hospital, Lambeth, London

DC Phil Simpson was back on duty outside Krantz's room when the occupational therapist arrived wheeling a trolley that looked as if it would be more at home on an airplane.

Taking his feet off the side table and a putting down one of the collection of car magazines he'd gathered around him, Simpson looked the shapely black woman up and down, his eyes failing at any point to meet with hers.

'What do you want with him?' Simpson asked, displaying all the charm you'd expect from a forty-five-year-old constable whose love of beer, fast food and inactivity had earned him the nickname "Homer" from his peers. Having established her role was to report on Krantz's ability to look after himself, the married Simpson hid the silver and gold of his wedding band in his left trouser pocket and asked the girl - who was at least ten years his junior - if she fancied a drink after work.

Before Sabrina Kidane could rebut the older, balding and pear-shaped detective by pointing out she not only had a boyfriend, but also favoured men who asked your name before they invited you out, Simpson's colleague arrived. Putting down the coffees she'd been fetching, Helen Owen introduced herself and led the shapely OT in to see Krantz.

'This is your occupational therapist,' Simpson called to Krantz over the top of the two ladies, while eyeing Sabrina's generous curves from behind and jangling the change in his trouser pocket, 'she's going to teach you how to wipe your arse.'

Helen Owen, felt the intensity of Krantz's bright blue eyes as he studied first her and then Sabrina. She also saw the unmistakable malevolence in his eyes as Simpson pushed his way to the front.

'Sabrina Kidane,' the OT said, positioning the trolley between herself and DC Simpson, 'I'm here to work out what you can and can't do in your current condition and see how I can help.'

'I've got lots of different aids here to help you eat, exercise and so on,' she continued, pointing to the trolley, 'but in order to do that I'm going to need your handcuff removed.'

Sabrina turned and looked from DC Owen to DC Simpson.

Reluctantly Simpson stepped forward and released the cuff from part-way up Krantz's right forearm where it was pushed by the all-encompassing splint which covered his hand down to his wrist.

'With your right hand in this thing,' Simpson said, indicating the rigid splint, 'you might need to ask her for some lessons in how to wank with your left.'

Krantz raised a smile which didn't extend as far as his eyes.

'Oh, I don't know, constable,' he said softly, the wires around his damaged jaw making him sound like a softly spoken ventriloquist, 'I think you might need the lessons more than I do.'

Simpson laughed.

'Not me,' he said taking his left hand out of his pocket and squeezing his own crotch suggestively, 'you see, I'm left-handed already.'

Sabrina Kidane grimaced and shared a look with Helen Owen.

'I think we'd better leave Ms. Kidane to do her job, Phil,' Helen said, guiding her colleague towards the door.

10:44 Vauxhall Cross, London

Michael Jenkins and Alex Oldroyd had both been drafted in the evening before to oversee the burgeoning incident.

David Price's immediate reaction had been one of bemusement that Branigan was able to post on the wall of the ICR, but his mood changed dramatically as he read details of the threat.

'This is a clear and present danger on a scale we haven't yet seen in this country,' he said when he'd absorbed the information, 'Michael, I need you and Alex to jointly take over the running of the search for the nuclear material.'

When Michael queried having two of them in charge, David explained, 'I realise its unusual – but these are unusual circumstances. With a cloud of suspicion over each of our group, I can't afford to have just one person running things; conversely, I can't afford to put someone in charge who doesn't already understand the dynamics of the Branigan, Cressix, Zack and Peach Tree conundrum.'

Michael and Alex stayed on duty overnight as people were drafted in and the ICR brought to life to manage a major incident, their only respite being alternate two-hour breaks; now the ICR was alive with people, the loud hubbub of urgent conversations and the sense that this was the heart of a significant event. On the enormous screens were summaries of the known victims, locations and details of the different events – at the centre of which were pictures of the plutonium-powered generator, a screen grab of CCTV showing the van at Farnham and pictures from inside the container.

Seated at the back of the room, Alex received a call on his mobile and listened intently whilst making hurried notes - he then leapt out of his chair and shouted above the background noise of the ICR.

'Listen everyone!' he yelled, 'I've just received a report of a live incident at Hampton Court – this has come in via the Met. There is at least one fatality, and, according to a message relayed via a member of the public, Branigan was there and said the perpetrator was called Zack. You all need to get onto this now!'

Alex then ran across to Michael, grabbed him by the arm and hauled him out of the ICR.

'No time,' he apologised, 'that's only part of the message – we need to give the rest of it to David Price now before it goes public.'

Without explaining further, Alex led the way as he jogged up three flights of stairs to David Price's office, breaking his stride only to call across to Gregory Brown's secretary, 'Is he in?'

'No, he's at The Foreign Office,' she replied.

'Can you call and check that he really is there?' Alex asked.

'What's going on Alex?' Michael Jenkins queried.

'No time to explain, I need to tell David this right away.'

Approaching David Price's office Alex ignored the questioning looks as he ran the gauntlet of support staff before reaching the more formidable and imposing barrier of his principal secretary. With the look of a school teacher about to admonish a recalcitrant child, Moira Markham looked over her spectacles as Alex marched towards her.

'You don't have an appointment,' she stated.

'No time,' alex replied.

Sensing the urgency in Alex's voice Moira made to alert her boss of the impending visit, but was thwarted as Alex marched straight past her and wrenched open David Price's door without knocking. Startled by the sudden intrusion, David ended the phone call he was making.

'I'll have to call you back,' he said, replacing the receiver, 'now, gentlemen, I assume there are developments?'

'David,' Alex said as he firmly closed the door, 'I've just come off the phone to the Met. There's been an incident at Hampton Court - an explosion in the maze of all places – with one fatality and a message relayed back to us through a member of the public by Branigan.'

Alex held his hand up to stop David Price asking him questions.

'He says the victim is Gregory Brown and the perpetrator, he believes, is this Zack character Cressix brought back with the weapons.'

'But Gregory is at The Foreign Office,' David Price protested, 'I spoke with him first thing as he was heading out.'

'I've asked them outside to check that he went there,' Alex replied.

David picked up one of the three phones on his desk and had a brief exchange with Gregory Brown's secretary.

'He isn't at the Foreign Office and didn't have a meeting there,' he said succinctly before speaking directly to Alex, 'Can you speak with the Met and get a photograph of the victim so we can ID him, then, assuming it is him, I'll need to go down to Chobham and tell Fran before anything leaks out.'

'There is one other part to the message,' Alex added, 'Branigan said he'd gone to Hampton Court to meet Cressix.'

The enormity of what he was hearing suddenly struck home and the usually calm head of MI6 slammed his fist down on the desk.

'Shit,' he exclaimed, 'I didn't want to believe it of him! How could he betray The Service like this?'

Despite the multiple wounds to his face and torso, when the photographic evidence arrived it confirmed the victim was Gregory Brown.

Before being driven to Chobham for the thankless task of telling Fran, Gregory's wife, that not only was her husband dead there was also a probability that he was a traitor, David authorised searches of his office and home.

'Make sure the search in Chobham is delayed until I've told Fran,' he said, 'and Michael – you'd better come with me to oversee the search; it's bad enough for Fran finding all this out – she at least deserves a friendly face heading the team rummaging through her home.'

11:11 Police Station, North London

'That was the Deputy Commissioner,' DCI Tenant said, putting the phone down, 'there's been an incident at Hampton Court and it has Branigan's name all over it.'

'Apparently one person is dead,' he continued, his face betraying a hint of smug satisfaction at the news of Branigan's involvement, 'and the security services are all over it like a rash – for whatever reason they think the incident is terror related.'

'Does that mean they think Branigan is a terrorist?' Drake asked, taken aback at the new turn of events.

Tenant shrugged.

'He didn't say; only that we need to open our investigation to MI5 and MI6 and put every effort into tracking Branigan down.'

'In which case, sir, shouldn't we all be focusing our attention on the funeral tomorrow?'

Tenant looked blank for a moment before understanding Drake's train of thought.

'You're right,' he exclaimed, 'Branigan is bound to be close by for his wife and child's funeral!'

11:24 St Thomas' Hospital, Lambeth, London

Krantz hadn't enjoyed the visit from the Occupational Therapist.

Her efforts to test his abilities on handling cutlery, dressing and using the toilet had highlighted the extent of his incapacity while he waited for his wounds to heal. At one point his frustration had boiled over and he'd swept all the specially adapted pieces of cutlery Sabrina Kidane had been testing him with onto the floor in frustration.

'I know how difficult this is Mr Krantz,' she said sympathetically as she picked them all up, 'but it will get easier, I promise.'

In the end she'd written some notes on his chart before leaving him with a spoon designed for people crippled by arthritis, a set of exercises, and the promise that she would write her report by the end of the day. As a parting gesture, Sabrina gave him a business card which she tucked into the top pocket of his pyjamas.

'Just in case you need anything,' she said.

After the OT left, DC Simpson re-affixed Krantz's handcuff before reading the notes with relish.

'Looks like you're going to be drinking an awful lot of soup, but otherwise you'll be fine,' he said with a grin, 'and where you're going there'll be plenty of people willing to wipe your arse for a price.'

13:11 Hendon, North London

Branigan arrived back at Alan's house having taken a tortuous route from Hampton Court involving two buses, two taxis and a lot of walking to make tracing him as difficult as possible. Letting himself in through the front door his attention was drawn by the familiar soundtrack to Star Trek.

'Hello Alan,' he said, peering into the front room, 'I thought you went into work this morning?'

'I did,' Alan replied without looking up.

'And?' Branigan prompted.

'And the police said I couldn't come in because I wasn't essential; they only wanted me to give them the access code for the CCTV system,' Alan said dolefully, 'which seems very unfair because they'd allowed Anna in all day so she can answer the door and deal with phone calls. They asked if I can go back in on Friday to help with the computer system.'

Hearing the voices Chloe came out of the kitchen.

'Jesus, Branigan,' she exclaimed when she saw the front of him, 'what the hell happened to you?'

Branigan looked down at his torn jeans, shabby gardener's tunic and bloodstained hands.

'To be fair,' he replied sheepishly, 'the blood on my hands isn't mine and it's my back which is the worst.'

He turned and removed the tunic he'd hastily snatched from the wheelbarrow before leaving Hampton Court and his jacket.

'Oh my God!' Chloe exclaimed when she saw the myriad tears and blood stains on the back of his shirt. Unable to resist coming to have a look, Alan padded round his desk and appeared in the doorway to the front room before having to hurriedly sit down because his head was swimming.

'It looks like you were caught in the blast from an explosion,' he observed perceptively when he'd recovered some of his composure.

Branigan agreed and, lying face down on the kitchen floor, went on to explain in detail all that had happened while Chloe busied herself finding tweezers, a bowl of warm salty water and dressings, before beginning to remove the little pieces of metal and hedge which had managed to bury themselves in his skin.

'You were lucky none of these pieces was much bigger,' she said as she tweezed a piece of bent metal the size of a small coin out of his right shoulder, 'because you'd be needing surgery and stitches.'

'I was,' he agreed, 'it was pure chance I managed to get far enough away to avoid any permanent damage.'

'I might be permanently damaged from the firework burns,' Alan observed sadly from the other room, harking back to his experience at JJ's four days before, 'where my eyebrows were singed is still pretty sore.'

'Just so I can understand all this,' Chloe said, ignoring Alan's comment – both she and Branigan were aware that Alan's most minor ailment had a habit of growing to mammoth proportions, 'you're convinced that Gregory Brown was Cressix and that he lured you to Hampton Court to kill you?'

'Yes, it's all falling into place now. We know Gregory Brown is the only member of the six not to have an alibi for when Cressix was in Bishkek and can assume that he maintained his anonymity with Zack so he could control him with the threat of exposure; that's right out of SIS's handbook on how to coerce operatives.'

'He lost the Black Ops team when Krantz was removed and needed to find a way to use his one remaining asset, Zack,' he continued, 'without losing his anonymity. Luring me there and then hiding himself behind a hedge was the perfect way to do that.'

'Whilst I understand that,' Chloe said, 'I don't see why he thought Zack would only go for you.'

'That was the bit that confounded me on the journey back, but then it struck me; Brown probably didn't know Zack had liberated the plutonium from the container – remember, we've only just worked that out ourselves. If you think about it, Gregory was labouring under the misapprehension that both he and Zack thought the whole Peach Tree dream was over and he and Zack had a common goal in stopping me exposing them.'

Chloe nodded her understanding.

'From Zack's point of view, you were the lesser of his threats – his focus was on Gregory Brown who would most likely shop him as soon as he realised his asset had gone rogue,' she said.

'Precisely. We mustn't forget Zack might have been motivated by money when it came to selling his shipments, but his underlying fight is entirely different; Cressix wanted Peach Tree to help fund SIS, but Zack wanted it to further his cause.'

'With the whole Peach Tree operation falling apart, Zack has seized the opportunity to strike a blow for the Islamic State and wipe out the person in the best position to stop him?'

'I think so, yes,' Branigan agreed.

'So, what do we do now?' Chloe asked.

Branigan glanced at the kitchen clock.

'I need to make my preparations for the funeral tomorrow,' he said, 'but you and Alan could look in on the SIS system and try and surreptitiously fill in any missing bits of information.'

'How do we do that?'

'He means I should update their files with any information they're missing,' Alan interjected from the other room.

Branigan nodded in agreement.

'Yes, you know, the files we found under Plum Tree - that way we're quietly feeding the information to the right group of people. Give them all the help you can and I'll see you tomorrow at the funeral.'

Chloe nodded her understanding.

'I'm sure the Police are still after you - aren't you just going to be walking into a trap if you try to attend tomorrow?'

Branigan shrugged.

'I assume so,' he replied.

13:13 Police Station, North London

DCI Tenant poured over the large-scale map of the 42-acre Hendon Cemetery.

'If he comes in by road there is only one main entrance,' he observed, studying the L-shaped site which was bordered by roads on three sides and Hendon Golf Club on the other, 'and if he comes in by foot, he's either going to come through the main entrance or across the golf course.'

'If we have a group of under-cover officers in with the mourners and officers stationed around the whole site but principally focused here and here,' he continued, pointing first to the entrance gate and then the flank bordering the golf course, 'he's not going to be able to get away.'

'Isn't there a danger we scare him away if we have that heavy a presence?' Drake queried.

Tenant thought about this for a moment.

'Yes, you're probably right; why don't we focus our resources in the crematorium itself at the start of the service and only deploy the team around the perimeter when the service begins?' he suggested.

'That probably makes the most sense, sir, in which case we should probably speak with the Golf Club and the Council and see if we're able to keep the perimeter team out of sight until you give the go-ahead.'

'An excellent idea, Drake,' Tenant commended, 'so if I can leave you with the logistics for that part of the operation, can we now look at the vehicles we'll have available?'

By the time they'd finished, Branigan was facing an uphill struggle to escape this time. Inside the Crematorium he would find a posse of eight plain-clothed officers in the congregation with another six immediately outside the building posing as mourners from a different funeral. In addition to those fourteen officers there were a further twenty - including six trained firearms officers – designated with guarding the periphery with additional support from two dog units. As if that wasn't enough manpower, the Assistant Commissioner had also authorised four unmarked cars, two motorcycle units and the helicopter to provide air support.

'Can you see how he can get away?' Tenant asked.

Drake shook his head.

'No sir, I can't.'

13:27 Police Station, Stratford, London

DI Cartwright was frustrated.

Not only was she as yet unable to interview her prime suspect in the murder at JJ's, but also the hospital had left her on hold for fifteen minutes while they tried to track down the registrar to find out if he was on schedule to release Krantz at the end of the day.

On top of that she'd just been told that a critical piece of evidence was missing - the knife all of DCI Tenant's team could remember seeing at the National Theatre had vanished. She'd spoken earlier with DS Drake who'd confirmed it hadn't been entered into his team's Evidence Log and a check by DI Cartwright with her own team showed the same. Cartwright didn't fancy having to explain to her boss that she currently had a suspect she couldn't interview, couldn't take into custody and she'd arrested on a charge for which there was no evidence.

'Sod it!' she said, slamming the phone down and getting her coat.

She could either spend the rest of the day hanging on the telephone, or head over to the hospital and try to chivy things along.

13:46 St Thomas' Hospital, Lambeth, London

DC Simpson read the piece of paper the orderly thrust into his hand.

'You are popular today,' he said to Krantz, 'this gentleman wants to take you down to see a Mr Tyrone in Dental Care who's going to look at your teeth; if you're lucky he'll give you a set of dentures and you'll be able to progress to solids.'

Krantz made no comment. He'd found the best way to deal with Simpson's incessant jibes was to ignore them. He remained calm, quiet and docile as the orderly transferred him to a wheelchair, wrapped him in a blanket which covered his cuffed wrists and wheeled him towards the lifts.

13:46 Vauxhall Cross, London

The first person Michael Jenkins met on his way back into the Incident Control room was Peter Winstone.

'You're back earlier than I expected,' Peter said.

'Yes, after David broke the news about her husband, Fran Brown called her daughter who came and took her away – so I didn't need to stay and supervise the search,' Michael replied.

'How did she take it?'

'Not good. They've been married for 40 years, so you can

imagine; what made it worse for her, was the discovery that he's quite possibly a fifth columnist.'

'Poor woman,' Peter replied, turning to go, 'I can't stop – I'm in a hurry, Alex will explain.'

Intrigued, Michael sought out Alex in the ICR.

'Where was Peter going in such a hurry?' he asked.

'He heard back from the Germans about Krantz,' Alex explained, 'and they've confirmed he's the same man who wreaked so much havoc in that Cologne operation of theirs. Given his history and the likelihood that he's killed three or four more people in the last few days, Peter said he'd go and lend support while I speak with the Met and get a heavier guard put on him. He's only five minutes away in St Thomas', so with any luck Peter will be back soon.'

Michael nodded his understanding.

'Have you made any progress with Hampton Court and tracing either Branigan or Zack?' he asked.

'All of our efforts are on that at the moment,' Alex replied, 'Bomb Disposal has looked at the remnants of the mine used to kill Gregory Brown and have confirmed it is a Russian OZM-3 fragmentation mine from the same batch discovered in the container – which gives us a direct link with whoever took the nuclear generator.'

He pointed to the CCTV picture of Zack loading the van in Farnham, 'Unfortunately CCTV from this latest incident doesn't help us much as he wore a crash helmet and escaped on a motorcycle with the plates covered up.'

'And you've not managed to trace the route he took leaving the scene?'

'We've tried,' Alex said with a shake of his head, 'but he obviously knew what he was doing and avoided the main roads; we lost him less than a mile away.'

'What about Branigan?'

Alex gave Michael a knowing look.

'We know he caught a bus heading to Hounslow – at the moment we don't even know where he got off because he managed to disable the bus's own camera.'

13:55 St Thomas' Hospital, Lambeth, London

Krantz took a keen interest in his surroundings as the hospital porter wheeled him into Daniel Tyrone's surgery.

A cross between a normal dentist's treatment room and a workshop, it enabled Tyrone to work on a patient stretched out on the chair at the same time as using the tools, workbench and vice to adapt and mould any fittings he was installing. Of course, it was too early for Krantz to have that kind of treatment, but the room also provided a space in which Tyrone could measure, photograph and x-ray Krantz's jaw and teeth for his report.

After introducing himself, the dentist used his best bedside-manner to explain to Krantz what to expect.

'In a moment I'll ask you to stretch out on the chair,' Tyrone said, brushing his greasy black hair away from his face, 'and then I'm going to take pictures, moulds and x-rays of your teeth.'

As the dentist spoke, Krantz focused on the equipment surrounding him and tried to ignore Tyrone's breath which he attributed to the empty onion, garlic and chicken sandwich wrapper on the side.

'Then I'll have everything I need to write a report for the police,' Tyrone said, nodding towards the two officers, 'which will tell them what still needs to be done to your teeth as your jaw mends.'

'Now,' Tyrone said, choosing one of the pale blue linen coats off the back of the door and beginning to prepare himself for the procedures, 'perhaps you'd hop onto the chair and this gentleman and lady can leave us.'

Behind him Simpson glanced at DC Owen.

'We can't do that,' Simpson said, 'one of us will have to stay with him.'

Krantz looked with interest from Tyrone to Simpson and

back again as Tyrone bent down and pulled a paper cap and face-mask similar to that Branigan had worn at JJ's from a low shelf beside him.

Helen Owen - who was vaguely repulsed by the undercurrent of garlic and onion, the dentist's worn and shiny trousers and his greasy hair - was quick to volunteer.

'I'll wait outside then,' she said, without giving Phil Simpson a choice.

Krantz broke the silence which followed Helen's departure.

'I didn't realise you used so many different glues,' he said softly, nodding towards a line of bottles, tubes and tubs along the back of the workbench.

'Oh yes,' Tyrone said enthusiastically as he waved his hand and invited Krantz to stretch out on the light blue vinyl-upholstered chair, 'it's surprising how many different types the scientists have come up with now.'

'You'd think superglue would be enough,' Krantz replied, continuing to survey the adhesives and the shiny stainless-steel tools hanging from hooks on the wall behind them.

Tyrone laughed softly.

'Yes, a lot of people think that,' he said, leaning in and adjusting the headrest for Krantz who recoiled slightly as he caught a waft of the dentist's breath, 'we do have it - ours is called Universal Adhesive - but we only use it as a sealant and primer.'

Krantz climbed onto the chair, stretched out with his cuffed wrists on his lap and studied the suction pipe and spit bowl beside him.

'I have some trouble swallowing,' he said softly, looking up into Tyrone's eyes, 'am I able to use that?'

'Of course,' Tyrone said, bending down to switch the machine on before using his foot to press on the switch which made the chair recline.

'I'm sorry,' Krantz said, holding up his damaged hands and cuffed wrists when he was fully reclined, 'there are no arms to support my elbows - these are dragging on my splint.'

He clearly had a point.

The weight of his arms was being supported by the cuffs which, in turn, were pulling awkwardly on the cast-like splint on his right hand.

Daniel Tyrone looked to DC Simpson who examined the clean lines of the armless chair, the hefty suction machine and the overhead lighting gantry, realising there was nothing obvious to attach him to.

Seeing his dilemma, Krantz spoke.

'I just need the pressure off my wrists,' he said, looking at Simpson, 'why don't you lock yourself onto my left wrist?'

There was a pause while the cogs turned in the DC's brain. It made sense even though it wasn't strictly in the rule book.

'Okay,' Simpson said, 'but I'll attach myself to your right wrist.'

He smiled inwardly as he showed Krantz who had the upper-hand.

Wheeling over the office chair from the workbench, Simpson settled down beside Krantz, released the cuffs and fixed them around Krantz's right wrist which was now resting more comfortably on the vinyl padding of the dental chair. Catching Krantz's glance as he went to pocket the key having fixed the other cuff to his own left wrist, Simpson had another idea.

'Could you take this to my colleague outside and tell her I'm cuffed to Krantz?' he said, holding out the key to the dentist.

While Daniel Tyrone was out of the room, Krantz continued to study his surroundings intently.

'Is that where you cook your lunch?' he asked the dentist when he returned, nodding towards a box that looked rather like a microwave.

Krantz laughed.

'I'm not sure how well that would work,' he said, 'it's an autoclave for sterilising equipment - it's like a pressure cooker that steams everything inside at 130°C, so I suppose it might work!'

Tyrone pulled up his face mask and bent low over Krantz's face.

'Right, shall we begin?' he asked.

14:00

Betty clearly did a good job and has got herself all over the news – the only frustration is that they're only reporting one dead. That has to be Cressix because I placed the trip wire on his side of the hedge, which means Branigan has escaped again. It's ridiculous that he's proving so difficult to dispose of now when I could have done it so easily on so many occasions in the past.

It's good that Cressix has gone. He was the biggest threat because he'd stopped seeing the need for Operation Peach Tree and knew where to point the finger when it went ahead without him. That was a huge failing on his part. Hiding his identity for all these years and then relaxing his guard because he thought we were on the same side!

On the TV they're speculating that the attack might be an Islamic State terrorist attack – that's because The West seems to think there is only one struggle happening in the world, but once Operation Peach Tree has happened everyone will know about our cause. Unlike those other terrorists, I have no intention of becoming a martyr, which is why I need to speak with the rest of my family.

We need to work out how to get rid of Branigan. If he'd only gone to Sheffield and been locked up for murdering that journalist girl like Cressix intended, none of this would have happened. But, oh no, not Mr Branigan. He's stuck in there and is the most likely person to identify me - not only because he is persistent, but also because he doesn't realise what he has in his possession.

14:03 St Thomas' Hospital, Lambeth, London

Comfortably settled in the waiting area a short distance

down the corridor, Helen Owen was engrossed in a magazine filled with outlandish stories and ridiculous domestic tips.

Shutting out the screeching of drills coming from the various rooms nearby, Helen scarcely looked up as Krantz's dentist swept past bearing a tray covered with a white cloth.

He was on his way to the lab and would be back in a few minutes, he explained, without stopping, as a particularly shrill rasping sound from one of the rooms made Helen's toes curl; it was a sound worse than fingernails on the blackboard she decided.

Watching the shiny trousers and greasy black hair peeking out from under his hat as the dentist walked up the corridor, Helen briefly wondered whether there was a Mrs Tyrone to tell him about his hair, breath and personal hygiene before she returned to her salacious story.

It was about a bus driver who shagged one of his passengers on the top deck while the bus was on a turnaround and focused on the driver's unfortunate discovery by a ticket inspector. The headline, "Ticket nicker nicks knicker ripper" was worthy of Paige.

Meanwhile, Amanda Cartwright was scanning the signs in the foyer of the hospital searching for the South Wing where Krantz was currently having his jaw and teeth looked at according to DC Owen.

Frustrating though it was to have to wait for each of the reports to be collated so she could take the man into custody, Amanda was relieved to know the hospital was at least making progress.

As Amanda walked along the long corridor, Peter Winstone was making his way down in the lift from the 10th floor ward in the North Wing, after being told Krantz's whereabouts by a helpful nurse.

'Is it the nice man the police are protecting you're looking for?' The nurse asked when she found him peering at an empty bed in Krantz's allotted room.

Stopping short of pointing out "nice" wasn't an adjective

he'd use for Krantz, Peter let the nurse direct him towards the Dental Centre on the ground floor.

Amanda smiled wryly as she passed a vending machine in the corridor. You had to wonder at the location for a machine selling sugary drinks, chocolate bars and crisps just outside the section devoted to the care of people with damaged teeth.

She found Helen Owen sitting alone in the waiting area.

'Where's Homer?' Cartwright asked, using DC Simpson's nick-name.

'In with Krantz and Mr Tyrone who's writing the report on his jaw and teeth,' she said, pointing to a door a short distance to her left, 'although we're just waiting for Mr Tyrone to come back from the lab.'

Amanda Cartwright nodded and took a seat next to Helen.

Confused by the layout of the giant hospital, Peter Winstone made his way to the main entrance, before realising he had to back-track along the winding corridors to find the dental area where Krantz was being treated. He tried to hurry his pace, but the corridors were busy with patients and staff and he had to keep breaking his stride to avoid barging into either the slow-moving patients or the trolleys and wheelchairs which seemed to make up the bulk of the traffic.

Seeing the sign to Dental Care his attempt to hurry his pace were thwarted, first by a porter pushing an empty wheelchair who came jangling past without leaving him room to pass without stepping out of the way and again to swerve round a large mother and equally large child who were oblivious to the obstruction they were causing as they dithered over what to buy from a vending machine.

Inside the dental area, Amanda Cartwright glanced at her watch.

'How long has he been?' she asked.

Before Helen Owen could reply a high-pitched alarm

began to wail from behind one of the nearby doors.

'That's going right through me,' Amanda said, recoiling from the strident alarm at the same time as looking for the source.

Standing up, Helen walked a few paces to her left.

'It's coming from in here,' she said, pointing to the door behind which Krantz was being examined.

Joining her, DI Cartwright pushed the door open.

As Peter Winstone made his way into the dental area directly ahead, he could see two women entering one of the rooms. They didn't look like medical staff and, guessing they were the police officers he was looking for, he quickened his pace.

Before he could reach them there was a scream from the corridor behind him.

Hearing the cry of distress, Peter didn't hesitate to turn and run back to find the mother and daughter holding each other and cowering against the wall opposite the vending machine.

Perplexed Peter ran to them.

The child was too hysterical to say anything, but her mother used her left hand to point to the dispensing flap at the bottom of the machine.

'In there,' she said.

Unsure what to expect, Peter gingerly pushed the flap, half expecting to find the machine had dispensed a Diet Coke instead of a Cornish pasty.

Seeing what lay within, Peter turned and ran towards the room he'd watched the two women entering a few moments before.

'Mother and daughter up there need help,' he yelled to a nurse coming up the corridor towards him, 'don't open the flap on the vending machine.'

14:10 Vauxhall Cross, London

David Price hurried into the ICR following an intense morning, during which he'd visited Chobham to break to Gregory's wife the news of her husband's death and potential treachery and been bounced between the Foreign Office and Downing Street trying to explain the developing situation.

He registered surprise when he saw Michael studying the matrix of large screens on the end wall.

'You're back sooner than I expected - is the search finished?' he asked.

Michael turned sharply.

'No, Mrs Brown was whisked away to stay with her daughter so I was just getting in the way of the search team; I left them to it and came back here.'

Alex Oldroyd came across to join them.

'How did his wife take it?' he asked.

David grimaced.

'Not well, but the worst part was having to tell her we fear he's been plotting a terrorist attack on his own country; she was heartbroken to think the man she'd been married to for forty years was capable of something like that.'

'I'm afraid the search of his office here has confirmed his involvement,' Alex said, 'they found entries in his diary, some bank statements as well as a stack of Cressix business cards; the report is on your desk C.'

'Shit,' David cursed softly, 'so where are we up to here; are you making any progress?'

'We still haven't traced either Zack or Branigan, but we are developing some leads on this Zack's activities - aside from today, we have him linked to Marty Freeman's death and a break-in in Limehouse,' Alex said.

'How did we link the break-in?' David asked.

'If I'm honest, I'm not sure,' Alex replied, 'the break-in was at Paige Henderson's – she's that journalist - and she's a common thread to Branigan, was used by Gregory out in Bishkek to expose the arms shipment and was at the club when Krantz murdered that girl; we're trying to find out what was taken to see if that helps explain her involvement.'

'But something must have made you look at it,' David observed perceptively.

It was Alex's turn to grimace.

'*We* didn't make the connection,' he said, pointing to the matrix of screens where the events appeared in chronological order and were joined by arrows which linked back to the name Zack, 'all of that appears to have been added by someone on the outside including a note which says the break-in happened whilst the key members of the Black Ops team were either in Marty Freeman's office with Branigan, or in Sheffield.'

'Is it possible for someone on the outside to access the screens,' David Price said with a frown, 'I thought this system was for internal access only?'

'So did the IT Department,' Alex replied sardonically.

David Price shook his head.

'And I take it the shark swimming along the bottom of the screen is nothing to do with us?' he asked after studying the screen.

Alex shook his head.

'Who is speaking to Ms. Henderson?' David continued, his eyes still following the shark across the screen.

'Peter is, just as soon as he's back from St Thomas's – he's gone there to keep an eye on Krantz; the Germans have positively ID him as the man behind the deaths in Cologne,' Alex said.

David raised his eyes heavenwards.

'This is a situation which just keeps giving, doesn't it?' he said, 'Keep me posted and get Peter over there as soon as you can.'

14:11 St Thomas' Hospital, Lambeth, London

What Peter Winstone found in the dentist's room would live with him for the rest of his life.

The two women he'd assumed to be police officers were standing transfixed as he burst through the door. There was a lifeless form on the floor and a man sitting motionless at the workbench with blood sprayed around him and pooled at his feet.

Peter Winstone surveyed the scene with horror before turning to the younger woman on his left.

'Go and get help,' he yelled over the wailing alarm.

One look at the man beside him told Peter that the only help he needed now would come from the mortician.

He was lying perfectly still, stretched on the floor by the blue vinyl dental chair, his trousers and shoes removed so he lay ingloriously in his day-old Y-fronts.

Protruding from his right eye was the nozzle from the suction pump.

The nozzle had been punched through the dentist's right orbit so hard it had shattered the sphenoid bone at the back of his eye socket and plunged deep into the soft pulpy grey-matter of his right frontal lobe.

Struggling to do the job for which it was designed, the pump had become clogged as it sucked the blood, bone fragments and soft grey tissue from inside Daniel Tyrone's head through its 1/2-inch diameter tube.

As if that weren't injury enough, his hair was missing too.

A neat incision had been cut around his head and the scalp he'd handled moments before when he thrust his hand into the dispensing slot on the vending machine had been peeled off to reveal the white fleshy membrane underneath.

Peter looked away as he took in the spectacle and realised what the grey pulp was clogged inside the transparent tube leading from the nozzle to the pump at the base of the suction unit. Leaning across he flicked off the mains switch for the machine and immediately the straining pump became still and the alarm stopped; Peter also hoped it would stop the smell of warm flesh seeping through the atmosphere.

The woman police officer stepped forward hesitantly to

the other man sitting by the workbench at the back of the room.

'Phil,' Amanda Cartwright said mechanically, trying to work out how best to lend support to her colleague.

Simpson was seated on a wheeled office chair with his left arm leaning through the jaws of the vice bolted to the top of the workbench. He was trying to speak, but he had the large-handled knife designed for an arthritis sufferer - which Krantz had taken from his therapist - rammed into his larynx.

Peter followed Simpson's arm down through the tightened jaws of the vice to where he held his right hand tightly over the stump of his left forearm.

The stainless-steel bone saw lying on the workbench told the first part of the story - Krantz had sawn through the officer's wrist to remove the cuffs.

The second part was told by the empty bottle of "Universal Adhesive" lying amidst the blood sprayed over the worktop. He'd glued Simpson's right hand over the open stump.

'Fuck,' Peter said under his breath as Simpson caught his eye and then looked meaningfully across the room.

Peter followed his gaze to the glowing red light on the autoclave.

Crossing the room and studying the display which told him it was at 121°C and pressurised, Peter glanced back at Simpson who nodded weakly. Switching the sterilising machine off, he pulled on the handle and waited while the machine billowed out steam which was heavy with the sickly scent of boiled pork. On the tray inside sat a part-cooked hand wearing a distinctive silver and gold wedding ring and clutching a decomposing business card. Krantz's parting gesture made little sense to Peter.

'Here,' he'd whispered, producing Sabrina Kidane's card out of his top pocket and placing it between the fingers of the hand on the autoclave, 'you might need to give this lady a call - she'll be able to teach you how to wank with your right hand.'

14:18 Taxi, Birdcage Walk, London

Greyson Krantz was in good spirits; there was nothing better than the rush of a plan coming together - especially one where he'd had to improvise so much.

It had almost gone wrong, he knew that. The handcuff dangling off his right wrist was jangling against the wheelchair he was pushing away from the scene, when a man he thought he recognised from JJ's walked past. He was unsure how the man fitted into the scheme of things, but assumed he was from SIS. Anyway, whoever he was, he was too focused on his destination to recognise Krantz as they passed each other.

After that he was home and dry. The large hospital afforded plenty of scope to lose yourself and within a few minutes Krantz was outside and in a taxi wearing the unfortunate Daniel Tyrone's shiny trousers, scuffed black shoes and an anorak he'd taken from a nurses' station.

In his pocket he had Tyrone's wallet with enough cash for his fare and DC Simpson's warrant card. He doubted Simpson would need it any more.

'How's your day been, sir?' The driver of his black cab asked.

Greyson leaned back into the seat for a moment and relived his escape from the hospital.

The policeman had been the first. When the dentist had his back turned the stupid cunt just gawked as Krantz pulled out the knife he'd stolen from the OT girl and taped to his side. That's why he'd wanted the policeman on his right; so he could swing with his left and haul him in like a fish on a line using the cuffs joining them.

The most Simpson had managed was a garbled cry before the knife punctured his larynx and Greyson followed it up with repeated open-palm punches to his forehead.

Disturbed by the commotion, the dentist turned around just in time to see the nozzle as it pierced his eye.

Greyson wasn't sure if that blow killed him, but by the time he'd waggled the nozzle around inside Tyrone's head it was pretty clear most of his consciousness had been hoovered up by the machine and he was dead.

Then came the fun part.

Getting his own back on Simpson.

He'd sawn slowly, relishing every rasping cut as he severed the man's hand and freed himself. He doubted, even if the key had been available, he would've used it - it was so much more pleasurable cutting-off the hand.

Next, he'd used the glue the dentist had identified and liberally wetted the semi-conscious man's right hand. He'd only had to offer it up to the open stump for Simpson to clamp one on top of the other without realising the consequence of his actions.

Then he'd popped Simpson's dismembered hand into the autoclave and set it to the steam sterilisation setting before taking a scalpel to the dentist's hair. Even though he only had one hand, it worked much better this time because he was prepared and rolled it back steadily - a bit like he was lifting up a fitted carpet.

Wearing the dentist's hair under the hat had felt pretty odd - rather like he'd put on a warm yarmulke - still, it seemed to fool the police woman waiting outside the dentist's room.

'Yes,' Greyson replied to the cab driver, as he reached into the pocket of his anorak and pulled out Simpson's phone, 'I've had a really good day, thank you.'

He dialled the number he'd committed to memory and waited before an answerphone cut in.

'Hello Sabrina,' he said, feeling his cock twitch with pleasure, 'I wonder if I could make an appointment for you to visit a friend of mine who's a patient in your hospital. His name is DC Homer Simpson and he needs your help with quite a delicate personal matter.'

He looked out of the window as the taxi passed Buckingham Palace.

'He may struggle to tell you this himself,' he continued, 'but poor Homer needs you to teach him how to resurrect his sex life using his right hand.'

THURSDAY 4TH NOVEMBER

CHAPTER 31

08:49 Stoke Newington, London

There were so many people crammed into the briefing room that someone had found a stack of bright orange plastic chairs which were interspersed with the more robust blue fabric ones. Standing to the side of the crowded room, Drake took in the cheap flooring, broken vertical blinds, shabby paintwork and authoritarian figure standing at the front and realised it was only when it came to the subject matter pinned to the wall that this vista differed from school.

Behind the somber-looking figure of Tenant were the large map of the cemetery; pictures of the broken bodies of Sally, Molly, Marta and Gregory Brown; an image of Krantz nailed to the table; plus, a large photograph of Branigan.

'I need to be clear,' Tenant intoned, 'Branigan may not have committed all of these acts, but this is the carnage he's left behind and we need to stop him.'

He pointed vaguely at the gallery behind him.

'He's wanted as either a witness or a suspect in five different investigations,' he continued, his flat delivery failing to capture his audience, 'which are each either terror or murder related. At the same time, we need to recognise that today's operation is a delicate one - we're attending the funeral of his wife and daughter so must be respectful and tactful. We believe he will find a way of attending and our paramount aim is to contain Branigan and arrest him without disrupting the other mourners.'

'We've had some debate over whether we should allow

him to remain for the duration of the service,' Tenant said, his glance in Drake's direction speaking volumes, 'and I have to accept it is a basic right that he be allowed to stay in close custody.'

The murmurs that accompanied this statement suggested the room was split on this decision.

'Now,' Tenant said, raising his voice to quell the mutterings, 'the eyes of the whole force are on us - the Assistant Commissioner himself is taking a keen interest and has, I believe, been asked to report on our success to the Home Secretary – and the scope of Branigan's actions has brought some colleagues from outside into today's operation.'

He nodded to a small posse from the Counter-Terrorism Unit.

'Today's operation is simple; by the end of the service we'll have two armed officers on the door to the chapel, eight plain-clothed officers inside mixed with the congregation and the rest of you on foot – that's the uniformed, armed, CTU, plus dog handlers – will form our own version of the Maginot Line around the perimeter of the cemetery.'

Drake fought the urge to point out that the Maginot Line failed when the Germans flew over the top and waged the blitzkrieg on the French.

'Now, just in case our first and second forms of containment are not sufficient, we also have three unmarked cars, two motorcycles and a helicopter to take up the pursuit.'

Tenant then handed over to Drake who focused on the timings, mechanics and standing orders for their operation.

'I need to emphasis how important it is that we orchestrate the timescale to ensure we achieve our primary goal,' he explained, 'We want Branigan on the inside when the perimeter is secured. The worst thing we can do is secure the periphery before the service and prevent him from entering. With this in mind, only the plain-clothed officers will go in at the start.'

He pointed to himself, Tenant and half a dozen others

wearing dark suits and black ties.

'The rest of you will wait in unmarked vans until the service is underway. Is that clear?'

10:32 Hendon Cemetery & Crematorium, North London

The November sky was grey, overcast, and it felt like there might be rain in the air as the old man came out of the chapel, pausing in his slow progress to steady himself on his walking frame and exchange pleasantries with the vicar. The last of the congregation to leave, he walked slowly and deliberately to look at the floral tributes under the sign stating "10:00 – Brenda Carter," scooped up a simple bunch of lilies and then made his way slowly to the empty space reserved for the floral tributes of the next service.

Here a spindly plant in a pot was all that was on display. Perching the lilies on his frame, he bent to pick up the message, read it and wrote something on the back of the card before replacing it.

The sign under which the plant was stationed read "11:00 – Sally and Molly Branigan" and the label on the plant named it as a Prunus Persica: a peach tree.

The old man made his way slowly towards the graves, glancing briefly at the red VW camper as it came to a stop before gingerly inching over the shallow speed bump.

Onboard the VW, Alan concentrated on the task ahead as he navigated the narrow road which threaded through the cemetery and led to the chapel. Beside him Chloe surveyed the gravestones interspersed with trees and grass.

'It's strange having a crematorium in the middle of a graveyard,' she observed, her heart feeling heavy as she spotted a well-tended grave with a teddy etched into the headstone.

'It was a cemetery first,' Alan said, 'but I suppose they had to move with the times. Mother was cremated here.'

They drove carefully around the flint-walled chapel.

'Are they all here for our service?' Chloe asked as they saw a swathe of people milling round the busy carpark.

'No, they're from the service ahead of ours,' Alan replied as he manoeuvred Mabel into one of the few spaces, 'It was like this when I arrived for Mother's funeral; then everyone went and only four cars were left.'

He pulled a handkerchief from the side pocket of his jacket and dabbed under his right eye.

'I'm not very good at funerals, I'm afraid,' he said.

Chloe touched his arm sympathetically.

'I understand,' she said, 'I'm just as bad, so you'll probably set me off.'

It took them two trips to carry the metal-framed stand, pictures, various packages and service cards Alan had in the back of Mabel round to the main door of the chapel.

They were the first to arrive and stood for several minutes shivering in the grey November air until they were joined by a fair-haired man in his thirties whose overly tight dark suit was buttoned all the way up the front. The iPad and clipboard he was holding gave him the air of an estate agent more than a fellow-mourner.

'Hello,' he said, introducing himself, 'Derek Brett, celebrant for the er, Braningham service.'

'You mean Branigan?' Chloe asked.

'Yes, that's right,' he said correcting himself and casting a glance in Alan's direction before looking at his clipboard, 'I didn't know we were having live music.'

Seeing exactly what he meant, Chloe let out a short laugh.

Aside from the collection of music-like metal stands and unusually shaped packages which looked like they might contain various woodwind instruments, Alan's choice of funeral attire did make him stand out. The dark suit was fine, but the black and white patent leather shoes and sparkling diamanté bowtie tipped him over the edge from funeral mourner to New Orleans band leader.

'But Molly would like it,' Alan said emphatically when

Chloe queried his choice of tie, 'it would make her laugh.'

She had to admit he was probably right.

'No,' Chloe explained to Derek Brett, 'there's no band, we're just here to put a picture up.'

They were saved from further conversation as a stocky middle-aged woman opened the chapel door.

'Are you for the Branigan service?' she asked before inviting them inside to set up.

After the grandiose exterior, the inside of the chapel was something of a disappointment. Under a white barrel-vaulted ceiling, the plain magnolia walls, leaded light windows and neat rows of basic wooden chairs gave Chloe the feeling they were setting up in a school hall.

Positioning the display with care, the pair assembled the four huge poster-sized images into a single tall rectangular picture showing a laughing Molly perched on Branigan's shoulders as she threw a ball to Sally. Stepping back to admire their handiwork, Chloe's eyes filled with tears - she would never know the joyous family in the picture. Beside her Alan - who was similarly overcome - began blowing his nose noisily into a giant white handkerchief. Any chance of a moment of reflection was lost for Chloe when Derek Brett blew into the microphone and practiced his eulogy.

'I never had the privilege of meeting Sally and erm...' he began before finding the name, '...Molly, err, Braningham, but I can safely say if I had...'

'There's nothing like the personal touch at a funeral, is there?' Chloe said wryly, as much to herself as Alan who was by now busy working out where to place the "Reserved" seating notices.

Their work done, the pair left Derek to stumble over his not-so-personal references to Sally and Molly and went back outside where the first arrivals were beginning to gather in that awkward way people do at a funeral.

Alan introduced Chloe to a knot of people from work.

'Chloe is a friend of the family,' he said as Adam and his

girlfriend Marion, Clive, Andy, Hussain and his wife Nadiya each introduced themselves.

After a brief social chit chat during which Clive reminisced about barbecues at Branigan's house and Kelly spoke of Sally's warmth and generosity, Hussain asked the question everyone else was skirting round.

'Do you think Branigan is coming,' he asked, 'only there was a squad car parking by the entrance when we arrived?'

Chloe feigned indifference.

'I have no idea,' she said with a shrug, wondering whether the police had learned anything from the National Theatre incident.

It didn't take long for the group from Marty Freeman Investigations to turn their attention to Marty's murder and the potential consequences for their employment.

'Do you think the business will close now?' Nadiya asked Clive.

'No one seems to know,' he said, 'none of us really knows the finances of the firm or who inherits Marty's shares, but it can't be good for the company's image to still have the police there.'

'The police have asked me to go in tomorrow; their technicians are struggling with the computer system,' Alan announced proudly.

'You'll find it's a bit busier than normal on the top floor,' Andy said, 'because I've had to move my security pass machine up there and Anna's moved up from reception.'

Chloe noticed Alan's ears turning bright red as he stood opening and closing his hands.

'Why haven't I been allowed back in?' he eventually asked, clearly deflated by the news.

'I think you'll find computing comes under the heading of "non-essential" activities as far as the police are concerned,' Hussain said.

Beside him Kelly nodded.

'Yes, they've been letting us in to do invoice runs and the

bank reconciliation,' she said, 'and otherwise they've only allowed people in who've got essential things to do.'

Clearly Alan wanted to say something but was struggling to find the right words.

He looked around the group, his mouth opening and closing soundlessly before he eventually spoke.

'Is a receptionist's role essential?' he asked.

'I'm afraid so, Alan,' Andy Meadows said, 'not only does Anna answer the door, but also she makes endless cups of tea for the police.'

Alan absorbed this further information.

'Do you know there's been a cemetery here since 1899, but the crematorium wasn't added until 1922?' he said, repeating more of what he'd read up about the place.

When no one showed any interest in his historical knowledge - instead turning to debate the police activity inside the firm - Alan took himself off to search for prime numbers amongst the gravestones.

Chloe turned to a well-dressed raven-haired girl beside her who introduced herself and her boyfriend.

'Anna Shah,' she said, flashing a smile, 'and this is my fiancé, Jasper Farhad - I work with Branigan.'

Chloe remembered Branigan talking about the bubbly receptionist.

'Chloe Travers,' she said, realising she hadn't prepared an explanation for her presence, 'friend of the family.'

Anna looked searchingly at Chloe.

'I know your name from somewhere,' she said contemplatively, 'I suppose either Sally or Branigan spoke of you.'

Keen to change the subject, Chloe turned to Jasper.

'And what do you do?' she asked, searching the face of Anna's handsome, if slightly weary-looking, boyfriend.

'I work in the City,' the thirty-something Jasper replied, looking Chloe up and down appreciatively, 'you know, buying and selling things.'

'And you,' he continued, touching Chloe on the arm in a

gesture she might have taken for flirting had they not been at a funeral with his girl-friend standing beside him, 'what do you do other than brighten the place up?'

'Oh, I'm a student at the moment,' Chloe said, blushing slightly and looking away as she wondered whether that was still the case. She hadn't spoken to anyone at the university since having her accommodation blown up, disappearing without trace and being wanted by the police - so it was entirely possible she no longer had a place at Sheffield.

As the engaging Jasper asked what she was studying, Chloe realised she should've prepared a better cover-story - she knew Branigan would. Just as she was on the cusp of blurting out the first subject which came into her head, she was saved by Anna.

'I'm sure that's Paige Henderson,' she said, nodding to someone over Chloe's left shoulder, 'the woman with the black hair standing beside the man taking photographs.'

Anna turned to Jasper.

'She's the reporter who wrote the article exposing Branigan a few years ago,' she explained, 'and accusing him of selling arms to terrorists.'

Chloe's heart sank. She'd wrongly assumed Paige wouldn't come. The presence of a photographer by her side suggested the promise of a good story outweighed any social awkwardness she might feel about having vilified Branigan in the past.

For her part Paige had discussed the question with her editor. In the end they'd decided that despite the 'D' Notice on the murders, there was nothing to stop the Herald publishing a story which focused on the people at the funeral.

Encouraged by the opportunity to keep her name in the byline for a story which mentioned Branigan, Paige was now casting around the mourners looking for the "angle" which would give her a story.

If Chloe wanted to be low-key about her involvement in Branigan's life, her chance to do so disappeared when Paige caught her eye.

'Chloe, darling!' Paige called loudly, causing many of the mourners to turn and stare.

'Oh, I know who you are now,' Anna exclaimed, 'you're the girl who wrote the recent article about Branigan!'

Before Chloe could pass comment on this observation Paige stepped in.

'I'm sorry, I need to take Chloe away from you,' she said to Anna and Jasper before guiding Chloe to one side and whipping out her notebook, 'So tell me - who are all these people and where's Branigan?'

In the carpark DCI Tenant called his officers around him in what looked like an American Football team's huddle just before an important play.

'Here we go then,' he began, 'Drake, you know to signal the rest of the team either when Branigan appears or the service starts?'

Drake nodded and held up his pager.

'And if anyone asks,' Tenant continued, 'we're colleagues from work.'

It was DS Drake who voiced everyone else's concerns at this ruse.

'I'm sorry sir,' he said, 'but won't the rest of his workmates be here too?'

Tenant looked heavenwards.

'Exactly,' he said.

Leading his team from the carpark Tenant marched past an old man with a walking frame who was checking underneath a floral tribute.

On the other side of the chapel a black Range Rover pulled to a halt.

After glancing out of the side window, David Price turned

to Michael Jenkins seated beside him.

'I see the police are here in force,' he said, nodding towards DCI Tenant as he led his contingent towards the other mourners.

'Can you see Branigan anywhere?' Michael asked.

'No, but I imagine he'll leave things to the last minute – there's little point in showing his hand too early,' David Price said, before nodding towards two women on the edge of proceedings, 'Is that pretty girl with the curly fair hair Chloe Travers?'

'I think so,' Michael agreed, remembering the picture he'd seen on the matrix, 'and that black-haired girl she's speaking to looks like Paige Henderson.'

'Oh yes, it must be,' David Price said as he studied them both, 'who else would be at a funeral scribbling away in a reporter's notebook with a photographer beside them?'

Looking down the narrow road leading to the chapel, Branigan saw the top-hatted funeral director walking ahead of the hearse carrying Sally and Molly.

Alan would have told him the practice of walking in front of the cortege was called "paging away" and dated back to the time when the funeral director had to slow the horses. As it was, Alan's attention was so focused on counting the flints in the wall of the chapel he hadn't even noticed the approaching hearse.

Charles Whittle set a steady slow pace at the head of the cortege, beating his path with a shiny ebony stick which had been his father's before him and his father's before that - although he doubted either of his forebears had ever had a start to their day like his.

Charles Whittle - third generation principal of Whittle and Hawley, funeral directors - had the shock of his life when he'd opened up the office at 07:15 this morning. After unlocking the front door, he'd gone inside, turned off the alarm, rolled up the metal shutters and put the kettle on to make a cup of tea.

Only when he was checking the day's schedule did he become aware of the soft murmuring coming from the Prep Room.

There are some businesses where an unexplained voice coming from the store room might be acceptable, but, on your own, in a funeral parlour, on a dark morning, is not one of them. Armed with the very paging-stick he was now carrying, Charles Whittle had pushed the door of the Prep Room open to find a man sitting perched on a stool between two whicker coffins - one large and the other tiny - reading aloud in the soft light from under the cupboards above the workbench.

As Charles entered, the man held his finger up for silence.

'You see Molly's always been afraid of the dark,' he'd explained softly, as if not wanting to wake them, 'and I couldn't leave her alone for her last night - so I've brought her favourite books along and have been reading them to her.'

Charles realised the man must be the father of the little girl and husband of the woman he was sitting with. Used as he was to the need of the bereaved to see the deceased - even occasionally sit with them in the chapel of rest - he'd never had one let themselves in so he could read to them. Perhaps he should've been outraged that someone had managed to break in without even setting off the alarm, but it was difficult not to feel compassion for the bereaved husband and father.

'I just need to finish this story,' Branigan explained, 'I read it to her on the morning she died.'

Wordlessly Whittle pulled up a stool and listened as Branigan read the tale of Zahhāk, a mythical king with serpent heads growing from each shoulder.

As the man leading the hearse drew near, Chloe felt someone move in next to her. Half-expecting it to be Branigan, she turned and came face-to-face with someone she knew from the screen at Alan's. Seeing the flash of recognition, he nodded and introduced himself.

'David Price,' he said, 'and I believe you are Chloe Travers?'

'Yes, that's right,' a slightly stunned Chloe replied.

'I just wanted to say how proud you and Branigan should be of what you've achieved,' he said.

Lost for words, Chloe nodded her thanks.

'I'm sure we'll have a chance to speak another time,' he continued, his gaze turning away from her to focus on the photographer Paige had brought with her, 'but you'll have to excuse me, I need to stop this intrusion.'

Chloe watched in fascination as the quietly authoritative man spoke with the photographer, somehow persuading him to relinquish the memory card from his camera before leaving. Outraged by what she was seeing, Paige briefly engaged with David herself, before she too capitulated and gave him her notebook.

While she wondered what he'd said to the pair, Chloe's eyes were drawn to the two coffins in the back of the hearse which had drawn to a halt.

The pall bearers climbed out, opened the rear door and took their positions to carry in Sally, on top of whose coffin was a single hand-tied bunch of freesias with a note attached in Branigan's hand. Molly's coffin, a tiny version of her Mummy's, was adorned with a single sunflower - her favourite since she'd grown one at pre-school - and a rag-doll.

As the pall bearers picked up Sally's coffin and prepared to take her into the chapel, there was an audible gasp from the mourners.

Branigan had cast off his disguise, stepped away from the walking frame and moved into place to carry his little girl inside.

As he effortlessly lifted the tiny whicker casket, the voice of DCI Tenant rang out.

'There he is, arrest him!' he called, rushing forward and placing his hand on Branigan's shoulder.

His team all hesitated, unprepared to intercede in a father's grief.

Branigan summed up the feeling of the mourners.

'Why don't you just fuck off,' he said, drawing himself up to his full height and turning to follow Sally into the Chapel with Molly's coffin held on his forearms, 'while I carry my baby girl's body into her funeral?'

Clearly unsure what to do, Tenant stood with his mouth open while Jasper, Anna's boyfriend, stepped forward and spoke to the policeman.

'This isn't the time for that - you need to let him take Molly into her funeral,' Jasper said.

David Price joined him in confronting the policeman.

'I suggest you sit with him and arrest him after the service; that's what any decent man would do,' he said softly.

Acquiescing, Tenant stepped a short distance away, allowing Branigan to carry his precious cargo through the door and, as if God were sending a message, at that instant the low winter sun broke through the clouds for the first time that day.

'Look at all the lights,' he whispered to Molly as the sun's rays caught Alan's diamante bowtie and the shoes of one of the mourners, sending little twinkles of sunlight dancing over the ceiling of the entrance.

Following close behind him, Tenant turned his focus to the rag doll perched on top of Molly's coffin.

'Where did that come from,' he asked Drake, 'I thought we had that in our evidence locker?'

Drake shrugged.

Branigan would have told him it was a different rag doll, the one on top of the coffin was Alan's own childhood version. On Wednesday morning Alan had appeared carrying two items; the rag-doll and the faded and worn child's woollen blanket Branigan had seen carefully folded on his bed when he'd first been shown round Alan's house.

'I want you to give these to Molly,' Alan said, his eyes downcast as he thrust them both out for Branigan and rocked gently forwards and backwards.

'I can't take them,' Branigan replied, both touched and painfully aware how much they meant to Alan.

Alan shook his head firmly.

'No, I want Molly to have them.'

In the end Branigan compromised. He arranged with Charles Whittle for the rag-doll to sit on the coffin and stay with Molly right to the end. While inside the coffin, Molly had her head snuggled against "Blankie," Alan's comforter since he was a baby.

'I need you to promise you'll get the rag doll back,' Branigan explained to the funeral director as he gave him Alan's address, 'only there's a child living there who won't be able to sleep without it.'

Tenant would have been more animated had he realised that something from his precious evidence locker was in with Molly; she was cuddling Puppy, the teddy she trailed everywhere with her and had seen her through all the ups and downs of her young life. The night before, Branigan had disguised himself as a cleaner and rescued Puppy from the police station so she would be with Molly for the biggest journey of her life. The Detective Chief Inspector didn't realise it, but he'd not only brushed past Branigan on the way from the car park, but also asked him to empty his bin.

'Now we know he's here, you can call in the cordon,' Tenant said to Drake, 'then we'll sit either side of him and cuff him for the service.'

Unfortunately, he spoke loudly enough for people nearby to hear and earned himself an accidental jab in the ribs from Judith Warde's yellow and black sports umbrella.

Entering to the sound of Cat Stevens singing "How can

I tell you that I love you..." the pall bearers placed Sally's coffin on the dais to their right and Branigan did the same so Molly was snuggled next to her Mummy.

Tenant scanned the chapel before directing his men to guard the main entrance and the fire exit at the back and stepping forward during the dying strains of the music to arrest Branigan who resignedly let his hands be cuffed behind his back. Branigan then seated himself between Tenant and Drake in seats in the front row Alan had marked as reserved.

Chloe and Alan, keen not to alert the police to their involvement with Branigan, positioned themselves right at the back next to Adam and Marion, while David Price and Michael Jenkins seated themselves on the far side near the big family picture.

Keen to stay close to the action, Paige elected to sit in one of the reserved seats in the second row near Judith Warde and the friends Sally and Branigan held most dear.

The start of the service was uneventful.

Derek Brett played his part with the unconvincing passion of a man who was reading from a script, becoming even more distracted when a soft swooshing sound began to echo round the rear of the chapel.

'What's that noise?' Chloe asked Alan in a whisper.

'It's the sound of the bridge doors opening on the Star Ship Enterprise,' Alan explained, oblivious to the heads around them and making no effort to stop the sound emanating from his phone, 'it means I've got a message.'

'I think you should turn your phone off Alan,' Chloe whispered patiently as the phone swooshed repeatedly, 'people are staring.'

Derek Brett continued to stumble his way through the service until the time came for him to say a few words about the deceased; then Branigan caught his minders by surprise by standing up and walking to the front. DS Drake reached across and put a restraining hand on his DCI, while Branigan turned to the flustered celebrant.

'This is my job, not yours,' he explained before surveying the room calmly and beginning to speak.

'Many of you will have heard that I killed Sally and Molly in a fit of rage,' he began, 'and now you see me standing here handcuffed and surrounded by police; those of you who know me will know I'm not capable of that.'

A murmur of agreement rose throughout the chapel.

'You may also hear that I've been involved in events as diverse as the explosion yesterday at Hampton Court and an atrocity at a night club in Stratford; I can tell you that I was there on each occasion, but that was the extent of my involvement.'

'Let's now turn to these two beautiful girls,' he continued, nodding towards the picture against the side wall, 'who were on a beach in Devon this summer when that picture was taken. We built sandcastles, paddled, went rock-pooling and above all laughed - I would like you remember us that way - it's certainly how I will remember Sally and Molly, but, unfortunately, what brought us together has also torn us apart.'

'We were brought together by two people. One who wrote a story in the press about me and another who reacted to it; they are both here now,' he continued, his eyes flitting briefly from Paige to David Price, 'and I'd like to thank them, because without their actions Sally and I would never have met, we wouldn't have experienced the joy we shared in each other, we wouldn't have had Molly in our lives. My only regret is that we had too short a time together, but, nevertheless, I feel privileged to have spent the time I did with both these wonderful girls.'

He went on to describe the laughter and tears of his little family. He told how Sally was the rock in his life who gave him the focus and stability he needed, whereas Molly brought innocence and light into their home.

'Until I became a daddy,' he explained, 'I didn't realise the wonder of watching a caterpillar eat a leaf, or the joy of trying to catch raindrops. No one could tell me how it would feel to hear Molly say, "Daddy, look what I can do!" and then to watch in wonder as nothing out of the ordinary happened!'

'But of course,' he continued over the muted laughter of the congregation, 'something was happening; the little girl Sally and I created was learning about the world and I was privileged enough to be witness to her triumphs and disasters along the way.'

'Of course, I had to pick her up when she fell, it was my job as her daddy,' he said with tears welling up in his eyes, 'and it will live with me for the rest of my days that I wasn't there for both of my girls when they needed me most.'

Branigan paused to collect his thoughts.

Several heads turned as Alan blew his nose loudly before taking a fresh tissue from Chloe and dabbing at his tears.

'No parent should be standing here and talking about a child they've lost. Life had just begun for Molly and it should have been she who eventually said goodbye to Sally and me: not the other way around. As for Sally, no husband wants to stand where I am now and say goodbye to the woman they've chosen to spend their life with; the woman they want to see first thing in the morning and last thing at night.'

After going on to explain about life in their household and his fondest memories of his two girls, Branigan finished by wishing them a safe onward journey, comforted in the knowledge that they were together.

'When I next look at the night stars,' he concluded, 'I'll know the brightest two will be yours.'

The silence which followed was broken by Alan whispering to Chloe in a voice which carried throughout the chapel.

'Technically the brightest star in the sky is The Sun and you couldn't see that at night,' he said, 'so really he'd be looking at Sirius and Canopus - do you think I should tell him?'

There then followed prayers during which Branigan and many in the congregation leaned forward in silent contemplation while a few, like Judith in the row behind, knelt in supplication.

The remainder of the service was uneventful although Chloe - who kept an eye on Branigan whenever she wasn't handing Alan tissues - did notice his head shoot up part way through Psalm 23.

"Even though I walk through the valley of the shadow of death..."

It was when the service ended to the strains of Age to Age by Hillsong that events took an unexpected turn.

Branigan stood up with his hands cuffed behind his back and moved towards the entrance door so that he could pay his last respects – in keeping with the discussion he'd had that morning with Charles Whittle at the funeral directors.

'I hate it when the curtains draw round the coffin at a funeral and we all leave pretending it's not there,' he explained to the understanding man, 'so I want them to remain open so I can say my final farewell.'

He'd then given the funeral director two heart-shaped brown paper envelopes and a wash-bag along with Puppy and Blankie. Each of his girls were also joined by an envelope containing locks of hair, so Molly had her Mummy and Daddy's with her and Sally had Branigan and Molly's - he was determined they would each have a piece of the other until the very end.

'I know it sounds silly,' Branigan said as he handed over a wash-bag containing a toothbrush, 'but even though she'll be in her coffin for our final kiss, could you see that Sally's teeth are clean?'

Having gently kissed each coffin, Branigan turned to DCI Tenant who was hovering just behind him.

'Okay, I think we're ready now,' he volunteered.

'Just one moment,' David Price called, pushing through a throng of Branigan's friends, 'could I have a very brief word with Branigan?'

Michael Jenkins spoke softly to the startled DCI – presumably explaining who David Price was and why, as the chief of MI6, he should be allowed a brief conversation with their prisoner.

'We don't have much time,' David said softly to Branigan, 'so first off – I presume you have a plan?'

Branigan nodded.

'Good. Then we need to meet as soon as possible.'

'Tomorrow – first thing near London Bridge there's a café on the approach to the station. I'll be there at 07:30,' Branigan whispered.

David nodded.

'I'll find it,' he said, 'and I'll come alone - there's a lot to discuss.'

Branigan began to turn back towards DCI Tenant.

'And Branigan,' David added, 'I'm truly sorry for everything I've put you through.'

'Just one moment for me to say goodbye to my friends,' Branigan said, nodding to the dozen or so people who'd been sitting in the reserved seats in the second row and were now standing near the big picture, 'and then you can take me away.'

Scanning the room and satisfied that he had all exits covered, Tenant watched Branigan like a hawk as he was enveloped by the throng which including Judith Warde.

As Judith marshalled her group around Branigan, David Price waited for Michael before heading out of the chapel.

'Did you see the woman behind him unlocked his cuffs during the prayers?' David said conversationally.

'No, I didn't,' Michael replied, clearly taken aback.

'Yes,' David said, 'but I don't think we need mention that to the officer-in-charge, do you?'

He glanced over his shoulder at Branigan in the midst of the throng of friends and caught a glimpse of him putting on a black jacket Judith had taken from her copious bag before he grabbed a crash helmet offered to him by another.

On the far side of the chapel Chloe too saw him slide behind the giant picture and turned to Alan.

'I wonder how long it will take them to realise there's another door over there?' she asked.

Alan didn't say anything - he was too busy scrolling rapidly through messages on his phone.

Over by the main entrance, DS Drake was the first of the officers to clock what was happening. He started to rush towards the throng of people as his senior officer scoured the faces around for Branigan.

Even Jasper, Anna's boyfriend who was in the midst of the team from work making their way to the front door, spotted the ruse before Tenant.

'I think Branigan has just left,' he said, turning to Adam and Marion who were walking out beside him, 'I saw him get surrounded by those people over there and now he's disappeared.'

For his part, Branigan, had ducked low before making his way outside through the exit door concealed by the giant picture. Stepping into the narrow alleyway between the North and south chapels, he leapt onto the waiting off-road motorbike and raced out across the grounds.

Inside the chapel there was a degree of chaos.

Realising something was amiss with the group of mourners into which Branigan had disappeared, DCI Tenant had unceremoniously barged past the gaggle of friends, cutting a swathe through the middle until a swipe from Judith's umbrella took out his feet and he came crashing to the ground.

From his place on the ground Tenant's voice struck up.

'Quick, after him men. He's getting away.'

CHAPTER 32

11:42 Hendon Cemetery & Crematorium, North London

Branigan's use of the motorbike caught the officers stationed around the perimeter of the Cemetery by surprise. Safe in the knowledge their man was in handcuffs and accompanied by eight of their colleagues, the six officers and one dog guarding the western perimeter were relaxed and unprepared for two hundred and fifty pounds of metal to come racing straight towards them at 30 miles an hour. Scattering to avoid the speeding bike, there was no time for any effort to thwart Branigan's escape – all they could do was recover themselves and watch his retreating back as he guided the powerful machine through a gap in the hedge and onto the golf course beyond.

Turning south on a narrow footpath which led to neighbouring housing, Branigan was able to join the main road within three minutes of his escape.

'I think it's time we left,' David Price said as he watched the ensuing aftermath.

'You're right,' Michael Jenkins concurred, stepping back momentarily to allow one of the police officers to come running past.

Over by the group of friends and neighbours Paige was scrabbling in her handbag for her spare notebook. Drawn by Tenant's plaintive cry she couldn't help but seize the opportunity to make notes for what she knew was a captivating story.

'Oh, I'm sorry,' a fresh-faced brunette said as she accidentally jabbed Paige with her yellow and black umbrella.

Looking up sharply as she felt the point jib at her thigh, Paige acknowledged the woman, realising that she'd seen her sitting directly behind Branigan during the service.

'Excuse me,' Paige said, 'I couldn't help but notice where you were seated - I wonder if you overheard any of the conversation between Branigan and the police?'

Judith Warde studied Paige suspiciously.

'Aren't you the woman Branigan referred to in his address,' she said, 'the reporter who broke the story that he was a spy?'

Used to the reference to the crowning story of her journalistic career - the one which brought her runner-up in the Tabloid Journalist of the Year Awards - Paige feigned being flattered.

'Well, yes,' she said, looking briefly to the ground, 'I am as a matter of fact.'

Making their way up the aisle nearest the entrance, Chloe watched as a brunette woman used a yellow and black umbrella to jab Paige towards the exit.

'Who's that over there?' she asked Alan who was hunched over his phone by her side.

'I don't know,' he said distractedly.

'It wasn't a typical funeral, was it?' Clive mused to the rest of his colleagues as they shuffled towards the door. Beside him Kelly, whose eyes were puffy from crying during Branigan's address, shook her head.

'No,' she said, 'I can't remember the last time I saw the bereaved in cuffs and so many police running around.'

'Did you see the look on their faces when they realised he'd gone?' Anna asked.

'Yes, but I worry how far he's going to get – did you hear the officer who arrested him tell his colleague to alert the helicopter?' Jasper added.

Andy laughed softly.

'If I know Branigan he'll give them a good run for their money!'

Hussain, who was walking slowly beside them holding Nadiya's hand nodded his agreement and paused to allow Paige and Judith Warde past.

'I do hope so - I can't help feeling the wake will be a bit of a letdown after this,' he said, watching Paige struggle towards the exit in her pencil skirt as Judith resolutely jabbed at her.

Confident his pursuers weren't going to catch him, Branigan kept an eye on his mirrors as he rode the motorcycle steadily along the North Circular in the direction of Alan's house - all the while putting distance between himself and the funeral.

As he turned off the main road, he thought about the service and how pleased he was with the way it went.

The turnout was good, the sun shone at the right time and Alan's bowtie sparkled - the specks of light dancing round his little girl as he carried her into the chapel would have made Molly laugh.

Back in the chapel, all but a handful had left and the atmosphere was tense.

'How the fuck did that happen?' DCI Tenant said, oblivious to anyone else nearby, 'On top of Krantz's escape we're going to be a laughing stock!'

'Yes, sir,' Drake said, his ear pressed to the radio, 'but at least the chopper has him in its sights; they're guiding the cars and the motorcycles are gaining ground rapidly.'

Tenant perked up.

'Let's get back to our car – we may still be in time for an arrest after all.'

Over by the picture she was dismantling, Chloe started at the news of Krantz's escape while Alan seemed not to hear, his focus instead on the soft swooshing noises coming from his phone.

Worried by the news of the helicopter, Chloe turned to Alan.

'Is there some way we can warn Branigan?' she whispered.

'I think I may have a problem,' Alan said in reply as he continued to scroll through his phone.

On the motorbike Branigan was pleased with his purchase.

The bike had not only taken him effortlessly away from the chapel, but also the two deliberately large rearview mirrors he'd fitted were giving him all the information he needed. The one on his left told him there were no police cars immediately behind him, whereas the convex mirror on his right - laid almost flat so it gave him a panorama of the sky - told him all he needed to know from overhead.

The reflection from above didn't enable him to identify the model of helicopter, but it did tell him he was being followed from the air. Turning into the access road running beside the giant shopping centre at Brent Cross, he gave a brief wave to the helicopter before driving into the multi-storey carpark - the chopper might be able to pursue him out in the open, but, indoors, in a busy shopping centre, it would have more difficulty.

11:42

The funeral was interesting.

I'd managed to arrive really early and leave the peach tree for Branigan. Just as well, as it turned out, because he escaped again. Of course, I'm not surprised – it's what he does.

No one seemed to see me collecting the card on which he wrote his number.

Incidentally, that was a good disguise; if I hadn't been watching for him, I'd never have recognised him.

Now I'm going to be able to arrange our meeting tomorrow so we're able to have a meaningful discussion – tomorrow's going to be a busy day!

13:55 Vauxhall Cross, London

'Have you heard about the funeral this morning?'

David Price was addressing Alex and Peter who, along with Michael, had just arrived in his office.

'Pretty much, I think C,' Alex replied, seating himself at the conference table, 'Michael filled us in on the way up here; it sounds like more classic Branigan.'

'Good,' David said as he seated himself and clicked on a mouse bringing the agenda up on a screen at the end of the table, 'you'll see he's on our list to talk about, so we can address that later.'

The agenda had just four names on it, with minimal points listed under each.

Gregory Brown
  Results of searches
  Any leads to Zack
  Proof of involvement
Zack/Plutonium
  Progress tracing
Krantz
  Link to Gregory Brown
  Tracing
Branigan
  Leads to Zack
  Information re plutonium
  Evidential support

'Clearly all our effort needs to go into tracing the plutonium, but I've put that second on the list, in the hope the searches around Gregory Brown have thrown some light on Zack and his whereabouts,' David explained.

'Sadly not,' Alex said, glancing at the notes he'd brought with him, 'we found evidence of his involvement both from his office here and study at home. Here we found copies of bank statements for Cressix Enterprises – the vehicle he used to pay for the consignment, rental of the warehouse and the Black Ops team – business cards for Cressix, evidence on his computer that he'd accessed the bank account and telephone numbers written in his desk diary for Krantz and Zack.'

'I don't know whether it is relevant, but he had a different spelling for the name – it was in his diary as Zahhāk. I've asked the question of linguistics to see if they can see any significance,' he continued, 'but otherwise at Chobham we've found only bank account details and an access password on a scrap of paper hidden in his study and a phone which was used to contact Krantz and, we assume, Zack.'

'Have you been able to prove that he used the phone?' Michael asked.

'Yes, it has his fingerprints on it, but none of this has actually moved us any nearer to finding Zack.'

'What about the historical checks,' David asked, 'have you managed to prove Gregory's involvement in Bishkek?'

'This isn't a top priority, but we are going over the ground Branigan spoke to Marty about,' Alex said, 'but we haven't made much progress. The company holding the expenses records says we've filled the wrong requisition forms in and we haven't managed to get the documents released yet.'

David turned to Peter Winstone.

'Can you go and give them a kick?' he asked.

Peter nodded his agreement and David glanced back at the screen.

'Which moves us to our priority: Zack. Are we making any progress?'

They went on to discuss in detail the efforts being made by all the security services to trace Zack, none of which had yet yielded a breakthrough.

'Correct me if I'm wrong,' David said in frustration, 'but the combined resources of all the security services - including GCHQ - have yet to yield anything more than Branigan and Chloe Travers have whilst they've been running for their lives?'

Michael and Alex exchanged uneasy glances.

'I'm afraid C, that that's the long and the short of it,' Michael agreed.

'What about you, Peter,' David Price said, 'did you get anywhere with Paige Henderson this morning?'

'Not really,' Peter said, scanning the sparse set of notes he'd brought into the meeting, 'she's pretty vague and it seems Gregory played her for a fool when he went out to Bishkek. She didn't see him, only saw the pictures and documents he fed her and printed exactly what he wanted her to.'

David Price nodded.

'I had the pleasure of meeting her this morning - I can believe that,' he said.

'If you look at the timing of the break in, it came right after the article Chloe Travers wrote went into circulation,' Peter added, 'which suggests it drew Zack's attention to something she had that he wanted.'

'Peter's right,' Michael said, 'Alex and I have looked at this as well, we all think the line in the article that says Ms. Travers had access to "...photographs, a copy of the shipping paperwork and even the false papers Branigan was using," must be relevant.'

'That's a positive lead, at least – put as much effort into that as you can.'

David looked back at the agenda.

'Which moves us on to trying to find Krantz to see if he can lead us the Zack; now, Peter, I gather you were at the hospital when Krantz escaped – what can you tell us?'

Unusually for Peter Winstone, he became uncomfortable and his face flushed.

'I went to the hospital yesterday to provide support to the local police as soon as we had confirmation of his ID. I arrived seconds too late and must have passed the bastard in the corridor as he was making his escape,' he said, 'He's one seriously messed up person. You've probably seen the reports, but whatever you've read, it was far worse in real life.'

'Suffice to say,' he continued, taking a deep breath, 'I doubt I shall be able to visit the dentist again, let alone eat belly pork.'

There was an uneasy movement around the table as everyone pictured the scene.

David Price broke the silence.

'Any leads on his whereabouts?' he asked.

'No, we're trying to trace the other three in his cell and, of course, work out his link with Gregory Brown – but, as yet, we have nothing.'

David shook his head.

'And finally, Branigan,' he said, 'I can cover this off by saying that I'm hoping to meet with him so we can open a dialogue; I'm sure we'd all find it useful to be able to have his input.'

There was a murmur of agreement.

15:13 Police Station, North London

Tenant looked less than pleased when he put the phone down.

'The Assistant Commissioner,' he said succinctly.

'Not happy?' Drake asked.

'You could say; in short, "How the fuck did you lose him when you had thirty-two officers, three cars, two motorbikes and a helicopter!"'

Drake nodded.

'And two dogs,' he added.

'Thank you, Drake,' Tenant said sarcastically, 'I'll just pick the phone up to him and point out we had more resource at our fingertips than he allowed for in the bollocking I've already received, shall I?'

The pair sat in silence for a whole minute.

'Mind you,' Tenant said, 'we've got off more lightly than DI Cartwright - she's been suspended while the IOPC conducts an investigation.'

Drake flinched. The Independent Office for Police Conduct weren't noted for their bonhomie.

'Who's taking over the Krantz case?' he asked.

'Believe it or not, we are,' Tenant said, 'Apparently the overlap between her case and ours means we're a shoo-in to take it on, but, as the AC has just pointed out, if we fuck this one up as well, we'll both be busted back to the beat.'

'The AC had heard about the kid as well,' Tenant continued once Drake had absorbed the prospect of being back in uniform.

'But you've got to hand it to Branigan, it was a pretty smart move,' Drake said, referring to Branigan's ploy when he drove into the covered shopping centre parking area out of sight of the hovering helicopter. He'd placed his crash helmet, gloves and coat on the bike and abandoned it with the engine running close to an area popular with groups of youths - the subsequent pursuit meant the police lost Branigan while all their vehicles were busily chasing a fifteen-year-old motorbike thief.

'What do you think we best do now to try and trace Branigan?' Drake asked.

'I've been thinking about that and I realise we did get something from the funeral after all.'

Drake waited for his boss to explain.

'Who packed up the picture of the Branigan family, the one he used to hide his escape?' Tenant asked.

'A pretty girl with fair curly hair...' Drake began before the penny then dropped, '... and that computer geek we interviewed – the one with all the Star Trek memorabilia!'

'Precisely!' Tenant said, clearly pleased with himself.

'What was his name,' Drake said, flipping through his notebook, 'that's it: Alan Armstrong.'

'Who we now know is in some way in collusion with Branigan.'

Drake nodded.

'At the very least we could have him for aiding and abetting,' Drake said excitedly, 'and based on our interview he'd crumble in no time flat – but realistically we should try and use him to lead us to Branigan.'

'That's precisely my thinking,' Tenant agreed, 'After the conversation I've just had, we need to be seen to be jumping on the Krantz case right away, but first thing tomorrow we'll put a comprehensive tail on Mr Armstrong and see if he doesn't lead us directly to Branigan.'

15:28 St Thomas' Hospital, Lambeth, London

By a strange coincidence the room DC "Homer" Simpson had been given was the same one Krantz occupied right up until the morning he'd launched his vicious attack.

Sitting in with him while he dozed, Amanda Cartwright sat staring into space, her eyes flitting occasionally across to the detective constable's bandaged right hand, bandaged left stump and supporting neck brace which prevented him from putting any stress on the repair work to his larynx.

Sitting with a man she didn't like whilst suspended and under investigation. Hardly the best time of her life - but still better than Phil Simpson. She'd never be able to forget what she saw and doubted she'd be able to walk past a hotdog stand for the rest of her life without gagging as she was reminded of the smell coming from the autoclave when the man from MI6 opened it.

'There might be some scarring, but the skin on his right hand will heal,' the doctor explained when she spoke with him, 'and he'll get some use of his voice back. He'll probably always have some breathing issues and he won't be able to eat as he used to, but, clearly his missing hand is the biggest thing for him to come to terms with.'

When he awoke, she'd tell Phil Simpson that a lady called

Sabrina Kidane had dropped by and that she'd been sent by to help him get used to doing things with his right hand: that should cheer him up.

16:16 Hendon, North London

Chloe was relieved to be back at Alan's.

The funeral had gone as well as could be expected, but a combination of Alan's subsequent behaviour, worries about Branigan since she'd heard about the helicopter and the stress of having to explain her connection to Branigan to everyone she met at the wake had been a strain.

No doubt when Marty organised the event and put details on the invitation he expected to be there himself; as it was, the perfectly lovely people at the golf club put on a nice spread for a group of mourners who had no one there to support. Instead of putting an arm round Branigan they talked about the funeral, their version of events leading up to the funeral, Marty's death and - in the case of Branigan's colleagues - whether or not they'd have a job for much longer. Chloe had nothing to contribute.

To make matters worse, as soon as they arrived Alan disappeared - so she'd been forced to flit from one group to another, only settling down when she was able to get some of the girls from Marty's office onto the subject of clothes and shoes.

'I enjoyed the wake,' he announced before ducking into the front room to be with his beloved computers and Star Trek videos.

Shaking her head in wonderment, Chloe made her way to the kitchen and went to flick on the light.

'How was it for you?' A voice said from the dark.

She physically jumped and let out a short involuntary scream - Branigan was seated at the table nursing a mug of coffee.

'Jesus, Branigan,' she cried out, 'you made me jump - what

the fuck are you doing there?'

'If you remember, I live here too,' he said with a hint amusement, 'and the usual greeting is "My day was fine, how about yours?"'

'I'm sorry,' she said, running around the table and hugging him tightly, 'but I wasn't expecting you to be there and I've been so worried about you.'

Eventually pushing away, Chloe wiped tears of relief from her eyes.

'How on earth did you escape, the last thing I heard was that they'd got a helicopter following you?' she asked.

While Chloe re-heated the kettle and made herself tea, Branigan recounted his flight from the funeral and how he lost everyone in the covered carpark

'Once I'd abandoned the bike I went into the mall and blended in with the crowd by doing some unhurried shopping,' he concluded, 'and then I walked the long way home - by then the police were swarming all over the place but they were looking for a fugitive, not someone casually shopping.'

'That almost sounds preferable to the afternoon I've had,' Chloe observed as she sat down and sipped her tea.

Branigan raised his eyebrows questioningly and nodded towards Alan's room.

'Yep,' Chloe said, 'at the wake he went missing while he reprogrammed the golf shop's stock control system; then he spoke to no one while he hoovered up an entire plate of sausage rolls; finally, he was thrown out of the Club Secretary's Office where he'd hijacked the computer and settled himself down to, in his words, "Deal with some correspondence."'

'And that's different from normal how?' Branigan asked.

'You're right,' Chloe agreed, 'but he's even more distracted than usual somehow - I don't know whether it's the funeral or all that bloody swooshing that was going on, but there's something up.'

'Yes, I heard that and knew it was coming from Alan; he's the only person who'd lend the sound of the Star Ship Enterprises lift opening and closing to a eulogy.'

'He was oblivious to everyone staring,' she said in wide-eyed wonder before focusing on Branigan with concern, 'and here we are banging on about Alan when we haven't spoken about you, how you're feeling and where you've been since yesterday.'

'Oh, that's easy,' he replied, 'I went and got the motorbike, looked in on home and then made preparations at the cemetery before looking in at the police station, eventually ending up at the funeral directors.'

Chloe said nothing.

'I left my two girls alone once before and I couldn't do it for a second time - so I moved their two coffins out into the light and settled down with them. I gave Molly back Puppy - her favourite teddy - which I'd retrieved from the evidence store at the police station and tucked her in with the blanket Alan had given me.'

Chloe started.

'He gave you Blankie, but isn't she one of his most precious things?' she said, her voice choking.

'Yes, he came to me yesterday and insisted she should have Blankie and Scruffy; in the end I compromised and Molly had her head snuggled into Blankie inside the coffin with Scruffy perched on top.'

Branigan wiped a tear from under his right eye before going on to explain how he'd chatted to Sally and Molly about everything that was going on before reading to Molly every one of her favourite stories.

'She was always afraid of the dark, so I needed to make her safe and let her to know her Daddy was with her on her last night,' he concluded.

By the time he'd finished Chloe had tears streaming down her face.

'What else did I miss?' Branigan asked in an effort to change her mood.

'You missed the excitement with your friend Jude,' she

said, visibly brightening, 'she's quite formidable, isn't she?

Branigan smiled.

'She made full use of that umbrella she was carrying and tripped Tenant with it when he was chasing after you and then used the pointed end to prod Paige out of the chapel when she found out who she was!' Chloe said, smiling at the image in her head before gasping, 'I almost forgot - I heard Tenant say that Krantz has escaped!'

Branigan didn't react with the horror she expected.

'I can't say I'm surprised,' he said, 'I might have hurt him, but he's a professional and I doubt the police had any idea of the measures they needed to contain him; don't worry, when this is all over, I'll find him again - he and I have unfinished business.'

'Wasn't that David Price I saw you speaking with before the service?' she asked, changing the subject having glimpsed the raw hatred of Krantz running inside Branigan.

'Yes, he pulled me to one side and asked if we could meet - just he and I.'

'And are you going to?'

'Yes, it would be churlish not to; he was actually apologetic about everything I've been through.'

'But that didn't stop you having a pop at him during the service?'

'I know, but I wasn't exactly harsh with him, was I?' he said defensively, 'And if I was, he'll be able to tell me over breakfast tomorrow; we're meeting at 7:30 a.m.'

'That's an early start!'

'Yes, but there's a reason for that - did you look at the flowers?'

Chloe shook her head.

'Too busy inside the chapel.'

Branigan shrugged.

'No worries, but see if you can guess what type of sapling someone left.'

Chloe frowned.

'A sapling; what, like a small tree you mean?'

'Yes - exactly that.'

'But why would someone leave a small tr...' Chloe said, breaking off in mid-sentence, '...fuck, no - not a peach tree?'

'You've got it in one,' he said.

'But with Cressix dead who would leave that and why?'

'The card with it was signed "Z" and invited me to meet him on London Bridge tomorrow at 9:00.'

'That's quite a morning you have planned, the head of MI6 and the country's most wanted terrorist inside two hours - I take it you are meeting Zack?'

'Of course.'

18:17 Canonbury, North East London

Roz has been out of town for 24 hours.

With their Black Ops plans in tatters, the three remaining members of the team had abandoned ship and headed to their various homes - Roz returning to hers in Canonbury before realising she needed to act quickly. With Greyson was under arrest, Cressix dead and presumably the security services all over the finance trail, Roz knew she'd have to move swiftly if she wanted to take the money paid to her by Cressix out of her account.

Taking it out in cash was the best way of doing it, which was all well and good, except that meant she'd had to get to Malta and back. With a certain inevitability she'd arrived in Valetta - Malta's ancient walled capital city - just as the banks were closing on Wednesday, so she'd stayed overnight before withdrawing her cash and travelling home.

On her travels she'd had plenty of time to consider what had gone wrong with their plan. In a word, Krantz. If he'd been more patient and come up with a "Plan B" which hadn't involved killing Branigan's family things might have worked out differently. As it was, Krantz unleashed a tiger and, in so doing, had made the whole operation a personal battle which had ended in Krantz's own downfall, injury and arrest.

Still, Roz mused, at least with him locked up he wasn't going to be able to behave as he had at the fetish club and with her afterwards. She still had the bruises to show from her encounter with Greyson's dark side.

As to the mental scars...

Throwing her overnight bag containing a change of clothes and bundles of Euros onto the bed, Roz put on her slippers and went into the kitchen to pour herself a glass of wine. A well-deserved drink to celebrate a satisfactory end to the most unsatisfactory operation of her career.

Opening the fridge, Roz took out a bottle of sauvignon, some tomatoes and a salami. After pouring the wine she placed the salami on a chopping board and reached for a knife. Finding her largest knife missing she selected another and sliced the salami and tomatoes. Placing her glass of cold wine and plate in the living room, Roz headed across the hallway to the bathroom, lowered the toilet seat, pulled down her knickers and squatted.

She examined the bruises on her thighs as she sat, before glancing further down and wondering what the bar of soap was doing on the floor.

Suddenly Roz's heart began to pound and her head whipped up; she never left the toilet seat up and hadn't dropped the soap onto the floor. Hurriedly yanking her knickers back up, she pulled the door open to reveal Greyson Krantz standing millimetres behind it, the missing knife clutched in his left hand.

'Hello Roz,' he whispered, 'have you missed me?'

18:31 Hendon, North London

'What's for supper tonight?' Branigan asked as Chloe began searching the kitchen cupboards.

'It's Thursday,' Chloe said, glancing at a list Alan had taped to the wall, 'so it's spaghetti Bolognese, garlic bread and sticky toffee pudding.'

'Oh yes,' Branigan said, his head shaking as he marched over to the cupboard nearest the door and opening it with a flourish, 'and to think Sally would spend ages making her own from scratch with fresh ingredients, when all she needed to do was buy a tin.'

He plonked three cans on the work surface.

'Didn't we have sticky toffee pudding on Monday?' he continued, crossing to the fridge.

'Yes,' Chloe agreed, trying to be upbeat having seen the glisten in Branigan's eye as he thought about Sally, 'but the puddings are on an entirely different cycle and today's comes with that tinned cream as opposed to the shaving foam stuff we had with it last time.'

Presumably drawn by the sound of tins being opened, Alan appeared wearing a pale blue Mr Spock outfit with his favourite set of pointed ears.

'I'm hungry,' he said, looking round the kitchen and satisfying himself that preparations were underway, 'what with one thing and another I didn't have lunch today.'

Chloe wanted to ask how the seven or eight sausage rolls she'd seen him eating at the golf club fitted in if they weren't lunch, but decided he already looked stressed enough.

'Are you all right, Alan?' she asked.

'Oh, you know,' he said sadly, scratching the pointed tip of his plastic right ear absently, 'I've got quite a lot to do.'

Looking bemused, Branigan excused himself.

'I need to go and clean myself up,' he said before leaving the room.

'What's going on Alan?' Chloe asked gently.

Alan rocked back and forth, his eyes focused on a spot on the floor.

'You know I have to go into work tomorrow because the police IT man doesn't know what he's doing?' he asked.

Chloe nodded.

'During the service he re-launched the programme I wrote

when we started, you remember, the one I wrote when we were hunting for information on Marty and his friends.'

Chloe nodded, she remembered the fruitless search which produced nothing more than the few hundred friend requests Alan received from people with the surname Brown.

'Well this time - without any other traffic on the office network to slow it up, or me to put a brake on it - the algorithm ran away with itself.'

'You've received more friend requests then?' Chloe asked.

'Yes, and no,' Alan said dolefully, 'this time it was the other way around - my system issued friend requests to everyone called Brown it could find.'

Chloe waited, wondering how many people that might be.

'When we came out of the chapel, I had two thousand three hundred and seventy-two new friends, and by the time we got to the golf club and I was able to stop the programme I'd got three thousand four hundred and eighteen.'

'All called Brown?' Chloe asked, trying to suppress a smile.

Alan nodded.

'Almost all, so you can see I've got quite a lot of correspondence to deal with after supper.'

At that moment Branigan came back into the kitchen.

'What's the name for a camel with two humps?' he asked.

Slightly taken aback, Chloe looked at him quizzically.

'Why do you need to know?' she asked.

'Bactrian,' Alan replied.

'Oh yes, that's it,' Branigan said, before replying to Chloe, 'because there's a picture of one on the screen in the hallway - it just set me thinking.'

Chloe frowned.

'Alan?' she said questioningly.

'My search algorithm translates words into different languages you see,' Alan said by way of explanation.

Branigan caught Chloe's eye and mouthed "What's going on?" to her.

'And that has some bearing on the camel does it?' Chloe

said trying with every fibre of her being neither to laugh nor catch Branigan's eye.

'Yes, because the Mongolian for "Brown" translates back into English as "camel-coloured," you see,' he replied shuffling from foot to foot.

'Okay,' Chloe said, beginning to see some light, 'so am I to take it your search found the Bactrian camel on the screen?'

'Yes, he's one of my new friends,' Alan replied, 'he's called Bob and lives in a zoo in America.'

Once the three of them had gone into the hallway and admired Bob's photograph and Chloe explained over supper that he didn't have to write to everyone who became his friend, Alan seemed much happier.

Then, just as they were finishing the sticky toffee pudding, the doorbell rang.

'Are we expecting anyone?' Branigan asked.

'I'd better go,' Alan volunteered, 'because no one is supposed to know you're here.'

Only when he hadn't returned after three or four minutes did Branigan peer down the hallway. Turning to Chloe, he beckoned her over, holding his left forefinger to his lip; tiptoeing forward and peering silently round the door she saw Alan seated on the hallway floor rocking back and forth whilst clutching something to his chest.

'I asked the funeral director to return Alan's rag doll,' he whispered before turning back into the kitchen and picking up one of the carrier bags which he'd brought back from the shopping centre.

'I forgot to give you this Alan,' he said, stepping out into the hallway and proffering the carrier, 'it's a present to say thank you for being so kind to Molly.'

Standing behind Branigan, Chloe burst into tears as she saw Alan's reaction to the new blanket Branigan had bought him.

'I tried to find one which felt the same,' he explained as he sat on the floor next to Alan, 'I hope it's all right?'

The mewing noise Alan made in reply was all the answer he needed.

A while later, with all three of them sitting side by side on the hallway floor, Alan introduced them to the rag doll.

'This is Scruffy,' he said, passing him to each of them in turn before taking him back and holding him and the blanket close to his chest.

'Oh, yes,' Alan said to Branigan as an afterthought, 'I did as you asked and updated the matrix for them at Vauxhall Cross.'

For a moment Branigan was lost for words.

'I'm sorry?' he asked.

'I said I updated the matrix for them like you asked. You know, when you said, "Alan can you look in on the SIS system and fill in any missing bits of information?"'

'I think I used the word surreptitiously in there somewhere; and I was referring to the back-office system where we could correct any errors without them noticing.'

Alan's ears went bright red.

'Did you do something they might notice?' Branigan asked.

Alan's ears went even more red and he had a whispered conversation with Scruffy, then, while Alan stared straight ahead, Scruffy's head turned to Branigan and nodded.

'Yes, it is quite possible they will notice,' Alan said - like a bad ventriloquist - through Scruffy.

'How?'

'They'll probably notice that there's now a great white shark playing with a beach ball on the bottom of their screen.'

Branigan sat in stunned silence.

Then he burst out laughing - a release he needed after the extraordinary emotion he'd been through in the last 24 hours.

'You know what Scruffy,' he said, staring directly into the face of the rag doll, 'I think there is the tiniest chance they'll notice that!'

He turned and looked from Alan to Chloe.

'I'd love to be a fly on the wall to hear the discussions they're having with IT!' he said.

'I can probably arrange that,' Alan said, starting to stand back up, 'all I need to do is find the right PC microphones to turn on.'

In unison Branigan and Chloe pulled Alan back down.

'No!' They exclaimed together.

'I think it's best you stop where you are,' Branigan said, 'and we make changes together in the future.'

Alan and Scruffy nodded.

'There is one other thing,' Alan added.

Branigan waited in bemused silence.

'This morning I saw Peter Winstone had an appointment with Paige, so I posted a question to help him.'

'What did you ask?' Chloe prompted when Alan didn't continue.

Alan turned to Branigan.

'You know you said it had to be Zack that broke into Paige's because all the Black Ops people were either with you in Marty's office or in Sheffield stealing Chloe's phone when the break in happened?'

Branigan nodded, unsure where Alan was heading.

'Well, I gave Peter a question I can't answer - "What was it Zack wanted to steal from Paige when he broke in?"'

Branigan frowned.

'That's not a question we have on our board,' he observed.

'No,' Alan agreed, 'and we didn't have the other question I wrote for him either.'

Branigan waited half a minute before he prompted.

'And what is that Alan?'

'How did he know whatever it is was there in the first place?'

Branigan stayed silent, sitting on the floor with his eyes closed as he thought about Alan's questions.

'You know,' he said to Alan eventually, 'those are very good questions.'

Alan high-fived Scruffy.

'He must've known what he was looking for from your article Chloe,' Branigan said, standing up and touching the screen so Bob-the-Camel's picture disappeared, 'your article is here somewhere.'

He flipped through random screens trying to remember where to look for it.

'You said you had "access to the original journalist's personal files including photographs, a copy of the shipping paperwork and even the false papers Branigan was using."' Alan said, remembering word for word the article he'd read in the hotel in Sheffield.

'How do you do that?' Branigan asked, looking down at Alan who was still sitting on the floor.

'What do you think he was after?' Chloe asked.

'Well, it ties in with what struck me in the chapel,' Branigan said, finally finding Chloe's article and putting it on the screen, 'when that reading came up about walking through the valley of the shadow of death.'

Chloe too got to her feet.

'I saw your head shoot up when that line was read,' she said.

'Yes, because it reminded me what Alan said ages ago which I'd been struggling to remember. He said the container was being shipped through an agent hidden in the shadows,' Branigan said, pausing while Chloe worked out the significance.

Chloe still didn't see it.

'You've lost me Branigan,' she said.

It was Alan's turn to scramble to his feet like an excited child with his hand in the air. Branigan smiled at him.

'Yes Alan?' he said.

'I know the answer,' Alan said, 'he didn't hide his identity behind an agent because he didn't think it mattered.'

'Exactly,' Branigan agreed, 'I think he shipped the consignment under his own name - only when Cressix, or should I say Gregory, agreed to buy the contents of the container did having his name on the paperwork matter.'

'Then how did Paige end up with a copy if it was so sensitive?' Chloe asked.

'Because Zack probably gave Gregory a copy of the shipping document to prove he had title to the goods in the container, and, when he posed as Cressix, Gregory Brown gave a copy to Paige in support of his story without realising it contained anything significant.'

'Okay, I think I get that now,' Chloe continued, 'and I'm probably being really thick here, but how does that help us if Zack's already stolen it?'

Branigan said nothing, while Chloe worked it out.

'In that picture, the one where you were holding all the cash,' she exclaimed excitedly, 'you had another copy in your hand, didn't you?'

Branigan broke into a grin.

'Yes,' he said, 'it's sitting in a box in my attic. You see, they fired me so quickly I never got to hand back in all the documents I still had from Kyrgyzstan.'

20:42

I waited until Branigan appeared and was about to carry Molly inside the chapel; then - just as he, DCI Tenant, Jasper, and the man from MI6 were having their altercation - I picked the card up from under the peach tree.

That was a nice idea, don't you think - a tribute to Sally and Molly only he and I would recognise?

So now I have his telephone number and will call him tomorrow to make the arrangements for our meeting on London Bridge.

In the meantime, I have final preparations to make for what should be an interesting day.

21:01 Hendon, North London

'What's stopping us going over to your house now?' Chloe asked.

'If we go now, we'll need the lights on and that'll attract attention from neighbours and passersby,' Branigan explained, thinking how much Mrs Rutherford and her poodle would be enjoying the gossip surrounding him and, how quickly she would phone the police if she saw activity.

'We need transport,' he continued, nodding towards the front room where Alan was watching television, 'and the pointed-eared one is engrossed in events on the planet Vulcan, plus common sense says we should go in daylight.'

Although seemingly engrossed in the noisy soundtrack to the Star Trek movie, Alan was clearly paying attention.

'It's the planet Qo'noS,' he corrected from the other room.

Branigan shook his head in wonder.

'Alright, Qo'noS,' he said, 'but there's little point in racing over there when I'm scheduled to meet Zack tomorrow anyway. If he's a no-show we can all head over to my house and pick it up.'

'I won't be able to come,' Alan called out, 'because I have to spend the day at work because the police computer man is useless.'

'It looks like I'm the only one at a loose end tomorrow,' Chloe observed, 'why don't I go and get it while you two boys get on with your stuff - it'll give me something to do?'

Branigan shrugged.

'I don't have a problem with that,' he said, 'I'll let Jude know you're dropping by to collect the spare key and then it's really easy to find the box the papers are in.'

He went on to draw a sketch of the house, putting a cross at the point in the attic room where she should hunt.

FRIDAY 5TH NOVEMBER

CHAPTER 33

04:22

Arthur Franks didn't mind being a security guard because the work was easy, even if the hours were antisocial.

His bosses at Strankley Security Services never looked in on him, so he was able to do as he pleased - spending most of his time either dozing in the security hut or watching videos on his phone.

It wasn't like this site was particularly special. No one ever wanted to nick anything from a demolition site - the most they wanted to do was clamber in and have a look around the building which made Arthur's job that much easier.

In fact, Arthur would have been sound asleep right now had it not been for Head Office breaking with tradition and sending someone to shadow him.

'Are you telling me no one contacted you and said I was coming?' The earnest man said when he introduced himself, 'They said they were going to.'

He thrust his ID pass under Arthur's nose.

'They told me you were one of the best and that I'd learn a lot from you.'

Encouraged by these words, Arthur welcomed the younger man.

'I don't know how much there is to show you,' he said modestly, 'but I'll do my best, but first-things-first, let's get that van of yours off the road - you can park it over there next to my motorcycle.'

Arthur indicated a space near the front gate next to an old

motorbike.

With the white van safely parked, it didn't take Arthur long to show the newcomer the ropes; once you'd shown someone how to patrol with a torch, complete a security log and where the kettle was there isn't much more to do.

'I was in the armed forces, you know,' Arthur explained as they waited for the kettle to boil, 'I saw action in the Falklands - there are some stories I could tell you.'

Making their tea, the man feared Arthur was going to start recounting them.

'I have some cake here,' he said, reaching into his small backpack and taking out a metal tin, 'would you like a piece?'

'I don't mind if I do,' Arthur replied, taking the larger of the two slices, 'you know, we'd have loved a bit of cake like this when we were in the Falklands.'

He took a bite, unconcerned as the man reached into his backpack for a second time.

No doubt Arthur could've told the newcomer some stories about 9 mm pistols from his days in the Falklands - unfortunately, Zack didn't give him a chance.

06:34 Hendon, North London

'How long are you expecting to be at work?' Branigan asked as he watched Alan put his packed lunch into his bulging satchel.

'I don't really know,' Alan replied, cutting an extra slice of Battenberg cake and wrapping it in foil, 'so I'm taking some extra provisions just in case.'

Branigan nodded. Based on what he'd seen going into the bag, Alan would be fairly well placed to survive a nuclear winter, let alone a meeting with the police which over-ran a bit. He turned to a sleepy-looking Chloe who was sitting at the kitchen table wrapped in the voluminous pink velour dressing gown.

'You know where you're going and what you're looking for?' he checked.

Chloe waved him away, her right sleeve flapping like a loose sail.

'Yes, we've been through this already,' she said, picking up her coffee and sipping it as if her life depended on it, 'I go to Jude's, pick up the key; go to the top floor and rummage through the boxes - it isn't rocket science Branigan. Now, just go and have your meetings, make sure Zack doesn't try and kill you this time and I'll see you back here later.'

Satisfied that his satchel was packed, Alan opened a cupboard and took out one of the many packets of sugar frosted cornflakes.

'I may not be back until quite late,' he said importantly as he filled a bowl to the brim, 'because the police will probably need me to help them.'

Branigan raised an eyebrow questioningly and stopped himself from commenting.

'At least this time our meeting is out in the open - he's not going to find it easy to plant a landmine on London Bridge,' he said.

'True, but even so, be careful!' Chloe called as he left.

07:12 Hendon, North London

'Buzz Lightyear is on the move,' DC Nick Wills said into his radio, 'he's on foot, heading east towards the station.'

'Copy,' came the reply from one of his colleagues already in position at the far end of the road.

The two were part of a team of six officers briefed earlier by DS Drake.

'Based on intelligence we have received,' Drake had explained, trying to make the mission sound more calculated than a hunch based on Alan disassembling a picture at the previous day's funeral, 'we believe he will make contact with Branigan at some stage during the day.'

He pointed to a photograph of Branigan taking pride of place on the wall behind him.

'We're calling him "Woody" for the purpose of open radio conversations and he is the main focus of the operation. Follow Buzz Lightyear,' he said, using the soubriquet he'd selected for Alan, 'and eventually he will have contact with Branigan.'

'Buzz Lightyear is walking alone and wearing a navy duffel-coat, mustard coloured corduroys, a black and white bobble hat with the Star Ship Enterprise on it and has a school satchel strung across his chest.'

'Copy that,' came the reply with what sounded like muffled laughter in the background, 'it sounds like Mr Lightyear will be difficult to distinguish once he gets into a crowd - you'll need to stay close!'

'Twats!' DC Wills said to himself as he climbed out of the unmarked car and followed Alan.

07:32 London Bridge

David Price stepped out of the back of his black Range Rover, spoke briefly with his driver, pushed open the door of the station café and recoiled slightly as he was assaulted by the smell of grease and frying bacon. Glancing round the room he took in the melamine tables, plastic chairs and tabloid newspapers being studied by the handful of customers, before alighting on Branigan seated towards the back of the room.

He shook Branigan's hand firmly and settled in the chair opposite with his back to the door.

'Hello Branigan,' he said, glancing around at the surroundings, Branigan's jeans and sweatshirt and then down at his suit and striped college tie, 'I fear I'm a little over-dressed.'

'I don't think they have a dress code,' Branigan observed as a burly member of the counter-staff wearing a grease-stained apron brusquely took their drink order.

'This is a little awkward,' David said, 'but I need you to know that I meant what I said yesterday; I'm truly sorry for what you've been through and my part in it.'

Branigan nodded his acknowledgement and bent forward across the table.

'Let's put all that behind us,' he said, his voice soft and low, 'and focus on the big issue - are you any nearer to finding the nuclear material?'

'No. We've conducted thorough searches of Gregory's home and office and found evidence of his involvement, but nothing that points us towards either Zack himself or the whereabouts of the plutonium,' David replied, glancing briefly over his shoulder to make sure there was no one in earshot.

'What did you find?'

'Copies of bank statements, a telephone number in his diary, a mobile phone he used for contacting the Black Ops team and a trail on his office computer that showed he'd made bank payments from there.'

'But nothing of any more use?' Branigan asked, sitting back briefly as their coffees arrived and they each ordered a bacon sandwich.

'No - we've even tried going back to the beginning to establish how he became involved with Zack in Kyrgyzstan.'

'I can help you there,' Branigan replied, before explaining how Ed Khan had made contact with Zack, sent a message to London from an internet café in Jezkazgan and ultimately paid with his life having introduced the pair.

David shook his head.

'I hate to think of Gregory behaving like that,' he said, 'and then keeping Ed's murderer under cover for all of this time. Clearly, we've looked to see if we can find any trace of where he might have been planted, but - aside from identifying where the money went at the outset - we've drawn a blank.'

'You're talking about the bank account funded from the Cayman Islands cash seizure?' Branigan asked.

David Price was clearly surprised.

'You have done your homework, haven't you?' he said, nodding appreciatively, 'Those funds look like they paid Zack, funded the unit in Farnham, and latterly paid the Black Ops team, but we haven't even been able to clarify the link from Gregory to that team other than the probability it stems from a bungled operation in Germany.'

'There is one strange thing,' he continued, 'neither the bank nor we can explain how the money vanished from that account.'

Branigan looked perplexed.

'How do you mean "vanished?"'

'Just that; until recently there was £5.7 million on the account - then it suddenly changed to thirteen pence one day last week without any transaction to alter the balance.'

Branigan went to say something and then checked himself.

08.14 The Strand

Alan's equilibrium was thrown.

Not only had he arrived at the office to find a uniformed policeman in Reception, but also there was blue and white plastic tape stretched strategically around the whole ground floor of the building.

To make matters doubly worse, when he emerged into what was supposed to be the tranquil haven of the top floor, he found it populated by people who weren't supposed to be there.

In fact, it got worse than that, because someone had invaded his space and heaped bunches of cut flowers on his desk.

'Morning Alan,' Andy Meadows called from Branigan's desk, while Hussain and Kelly did the same from Clive's and Adam's.

'Oh, hello Alan,' Anna said, brushing past him on her way

to the kettle, 'would you like a cup of tea?'

By the time he'd found a new home for the cut flowers Alan was visibly distressed.

'Sorry Alan,' Anna called from beside the kettle, 'the police didn't want the flowers well-wishers left cluttering up Reception.'

08:15 Hendon, North London

There were no police watching Alan's house by the time Chloe left on her way to collect the shipping paperwork from Branigan's home. Now revived by two cups of coffee and dressed in her own clothes, she strode purposely down the road to Hendon underground station.

08:18 Vauxhall Cross, London

In the ICR at Vauxhall Cross Michael and Alex conferred ahead of their scheduled 09:30 briefing with David Price.

'We have precious little to report,' Alex said.

Michael glanced at his watch.

'And unless something dramatic happens in the next hour and a quarter, we're going to have to tell David just that.'

08:20 St Thomas' Hospital, Lambeth, London

Peter Winstone had no great desire to be back at St Thomas's Hospital, but as a credible witness to Wednesday's events – or at least the aftermath of those events – he knew he had no choice but to help the new officers in charge of the Krantz case. Besides, from his brief involvement with the events at JJ's and The National Theatre, Peter was well aware that Greyson-fucking-Krantz was much more involved in the action than Branigan; you didn't need to be a rocket scientist to see that. Anything he could do to help the police pursue one of the main protagonists in recent events could only help.

He already knew these two of course - he'd met them at

The Club after Branigan had so magnificently pounced on the six of them having dinner.

Peter stepped round the fabric screens hastily placed across the end of the dental area where the unfortunate Daniel Tyrone had met his end and was greeted by the two policemen.

'Ahh!' DCI Tenant said, 'So good of you to come.'

08:22

It's a lovely day.
Cold, bright and there's a steady breeze blowing from the East.
Passing overhead there is a constant stream of aircraft taking off from Heathrow and I have a magnificent view from my vantage point.
Conditions couldn't be more perfect.

08:25 Wapping, East London

Ken Briers was focused on an article he was editing when he heard the soft "zip-zip" sound of nylon stockings rubbing together and the "tip-tap" of heels on the floor.

'Morning Paige,' he called without looking up.

Teetering on her heels, Paige veered towards his desk.

'Has anyone reacted to yesterday's piece?' she asked, referring to the article she'd written about Branigan appearing at the funeral and making his escape by motorcycle.

'No,' Ken replied, looking up and taking in the faux fur coat and black PVC skirt, 'nothing from anyone suggesting the story contravenes the D-Notice if that's what you mean.'

'Good,' Paige said, 'in which case I'm going to write a follow-up.'

'Based on what?'

'I'm not sure yet.'

'Did you get anything from friends and neighbours at the funeral yesterday – what about writing up their reaction?' Ken proffered.

Paige thought about Jude and her umbrella.

'No,' she replied, 'that's a bit clichéd – I'll see if I can come up with something a bit more interesting.'

08:27 The Strand

DC Nick Wills was standing at a bus stop on The Strand looking back towards the office of Marty Freeman Investigations. He and the team hadn't encountered any problems following Buzz Lightyear - he'd kept his head down and not looked around him once as he'd made his way by foot and underground to work.

08:30 London Bridge

In the café Branigan took a bite from his bacon sandwich.

'You know the police are still after you?' David Price asked.

Branigan finished his mouthful before replying.

'I figured they would be,' he said.

'Alex has been speaking with his contacts – they don't have you down for events at the fetish club, but there's still everything else they want to talk to you about. You know I'll do my best to sort things out if and when they do arrest you, don't you?'

Branigan nodded.

'What about Farnham, has that produced any leads?' he asked.

'No,' David replied, 'Thank you for that incidentally - the bomb disposal people were very complimentary about the job you did there - but forensics have drawn a blank on any fingerprints or evidence leading us back to Zack.'

'I may shortly be able to help you with tracing him,' Branigan said.

David Price stiffened.

'How?'

'He was at the funeral and has invited me to meet with

him today.'

'You're kidding me!'

Branigan shook his head and explained about the peach tree and the message.

'Where are you meeting him?' David asked.

'On London Bridge at 09:00.'

David looked at his watch.

'There should be enough time to get a team here,' he said.

'No,' Branigan insisted, 'he asked me to come alone and I'm not going to spook him by turning up mob-handed.'

'As I'm here already, will you at least let me provide modest back-up from the sidelines?'

'As long as you don't involve anyone else,' Branigan agreed, glancing at his phone which had just buzzed, 'Do you mind if I just deal with this text message?'

David invited Branigan to go ahead while he took the opportunity to go to the toilet. Seated alone at the table, Branigan tried first Chloe and, when that didn't go through, Alan.

'Hello Alan, it's me, Branigan,' he said, raising his eyes heavenwards as he listened to the reply, 'The Branigan who was in your kitchen while you ate your cereal this morning.'

08:32 Marty Freeman Investigations, The Strand

Having identified Branigan to his satisfaction, Alan sought refuge in Marty's office and shut the door.

'Alan, can you get a message to Chloe, only I think she's on the underground and I can't get through.'

'Yes,' Alan replied flatly.

'Tell her Jude has just texted and that she's taken Daniella to nursery school and left the key to my house under the mat.'

'Yes,' Alan said sorting through the pens in Marty's office distractedly.

'And can you also tell her that I've remembered the shipping document is in with a bundle of papers inside a brown envelope labelled "Confidential Information" with the word

Bishkek written on the front,' Branigan continued, unsure whether Alan was listening to anything he was saying.

There was silence on the other end of the phone.

'Have you got that?' Branigan asked.

'Yes, you want me to tell Chloe the key to your house is under the mat and that the shipping documents from Bishkek is in the attic in a brown envelope with the word Bishkek written on the outside,' Alan said testily before hanging up.

08:32

I think it's only fitting that Paige Henderson is the first person I send the announcement to; after all, she was in Bishkek when this started – we even bumped into each other in the hotel when I'd spoken to Cressix on the house phone. She hasn't recognised me since, although I knew her the instant I saw her again 14 days ago; I just don't think she's clever enough to join the dots. On the other hand, Branigan is a real problem, he's even realised that he has the shipping document with my name on it in his attic! How the hell is he still alive? He should be dead after Hampton Court.

I kick myself every time I think of the opportunities I've had to dispose of him – still, that's about to change.

I press the send button on my computer and the message goes to Paige.

08:50 London Bridge

In the café, Branigan and David Price waited while the young waitress cleared their plates.

'What do you think Zack is trying to achieve by meeting with you today – especially after the carnage he caused at Hampton Court?' David asked.

'I've thought hard about that and where the mine was placed,' Branigan replied, 'and don't think I was the intended target; I just happened to be where Zack had the opportunity to murder his handler.'

'But why did Gregory attend the meeting if he thought Zack would kill him?'

'Gregory thought he and Zack were united by a common enemy – me – and that the maze was the perfect place for the attack to happen. I'm sure he lured me there believing Zack would shoot me through the hedge when I called out – there was even an arrow on the ground showing the direction he should fire. Put simply, Gregory thought he was safe and would remain anonymous behind the hedge.'

David Price shook his head.

'I still don't see why Zack wanted to kill him.'

'Because Zack still wants to promote his ISIS cause by going through with the Peach Tree plan and Gregory was the only person who could identify him.'

'All the more reason for us to hope you can identify him after your meeting,' David said, glancing at his watch, 'which reminds me – how did he spell his name on the invite?'

Branigan looked perplexed.

'He simply put a "Z" on it – why do you ask?' Branigan replied.

'It's only that in Gregory's diary he had the name spelled differently, he'd written Zahhāk,' David said, spelling the name out.

Branigan closed his eyes and his head started spinning as he was transported back to the morning of Molly's murder, his little girl snuggled next to him listening to the tale of the serpent king.

'Fuck, fuck, fuck!' Branigan said with such vehemence a number of heads turned in his direction. 'I've only heard the name spoken by a Russian - that name isn't pronounced Zack, it's Zah-hock.'

'And the difference is significant because...?'

'Because Zahhāk is a monster from Persian folklore,' Branigan replied.

Not immediately grasping the significance, David frowned just as Branigan's phone buzzed insistently.

'Speak of the devil,' Branigan said after glancing at the message, 'it appears he's waiting.'

Still pre-occupied with his thoughts, Branigan left the table and headed outside with David Price trailing behind.

After a brief conversation with his driver, David went to watch from the southern end of London Bridge while Branigan walked towards the centre of the span, took his phone out of his pocket, and dialling first Chloe and then Alan when he got no answer.

'Listen I don't have time,' he said when Alan answered and prompted him to identify himself, 'I need you to look up the name Zahhāk for me.'

The sound of passing traffic drowned out the clatter of Alan's keyboard as he searched for the name and read about the mythical character.

'Oh, that's interesting,' Alan said to himself, 'he had two serpent heads - one on each shoulder – and they were both evil.'

08:57

I can see Branigan crossing the bridge now. He's on the phone looking around for me. I told him I was here already, but actually have one more text to send to tell him exactly where to meet.

08:59

Paige opened her email and rubbed her wrists absently as she read a message headed "Operation Peach Tree."

'I suppose this is your idea of a joke,' she called across to Ken Briers.

Ken looked up, clearly confused.

'What the fuck are you talking about?' he asked.

'This email about Operation Peach Tree and an imminent terrorist attack; and all this crap about Bishkek and a land mine called Bouncing Betty?'

Branigan was still waiting for Alan when he received a text telling him to look on the lamppost in the central reservation for instructions on where to meet.

He stepped onto the road and waited to let a double-decker past.

David Price watched as Branigan started to cross the road, pausing to let a bus go past.

'This changes everything...' Alan said just before Branigan's phone went dead.

OPERATION PEACH TREE
Friday 5th November

CHAPTER 34

09:00 onwards

'Have you ever heard of the Persian Liberation Front?' Paige asked Ken.

The News Editor shook his head.

'I assume they want to overthrow the Iranian regime,' he said distractedly, his focus on the next paragraph of the message, 'but what worries me is this bit about needing to evacuate The City and an explosion which will "leave a mark for the next millennium." I have no idea what it means, but we need to get this across to the authorities as soon as possible.'

He scrabbled through the top drawer of his desk until he unearthed a card which bore the legend "Terrorist Threat."

Dialling the number listed, he rapidly found himself speaking with an earnest man in MI5 who seemed to have an immediate grasp both of the significance of the message and the scale of the threat.

'Forward me the email,' the man instructed, 'and wait until we have assessed the content – please don't publish the threat unless we advise you ...' he broke off as a loud thumping sound reverberated through the News Room 'What was that sound?'

'I think it was an explosion nearby,' Ken replied.

I savour the rush of wind as the shockwave from the explosion rushes over me.

In the chaos which follows I can see no sign of Branigan – one moment he was crossing the road towards the bomb, the next there's the tangled wreckage of a double-decker bus, an over-

turned car and lots of people panicking.

I hail a cab and tell the driver where I need to go next. That's the first part of my work done, now I need to address the next issue while my brother orchestrates the main event.

'What was happening on London Bridge?' The cab driver asks.
'I think there was a car accident or something,' I lie in reply.

Alan ignored the sound of the explosion as he climbed into the back of a taxi on the Strand.

'Buzz Lightyear has just left the building and is heading North East on Aldwych towards Kingsway; dressed as before and now carrying a large aluminium case,' DC Nick Wills said breathlessly as he climbed into the unmarked car which had raced to pick him up when Alan emerged - and did anyone else hear that noise coming from somewhere; it sounded like an explosion?'

By the time the shockwave had travelled up the River to St Thomas's Hospital and Vauxhall Cross it had lost sufficient impetus to go unnoticed, leaving Tenant and Drake to continue quizzing Peter Winstone on everything he'd seen.

In the ICR an alarmed Michael Jenkins re-read the flash security-alert email triggered by Ken Briers' conversation with MI5.

'Alex,' he called urgently, beckoning his colleague over and pointing him towards the specific terrorist threat warning, 'this looks like Peach Tree!'

The words were hardly out of his mouth before Alex's mobile started to ring.

'I'm on the South side of London Bridge,' David said before Alex could say anything, 'and there has just been an explosion on the Bridge. I can see casualties; alert all the services - this is a major incident.'

At the scene of the explosion Branigan climbed unsteadily to his feet.

Despite being shielded from the blast by the passing bus, he'd been blown off his feet and left momentarily stunned by the force of the shockwave as it thundered past him.

In the stillness that followed, Branigan absorbed the twisted wreckage of the bus, the screams for help and the stunned and disorientated people caught up in the explosion. Making his way to the bus, he glanced at the tangled remains of the lamppost in which the bomb had been concealed, before climbing through the gaping hole where the bus's rear doors had been blown out of the frame.

In the lower-cabin there were dead and wounded sitting slumped in seats; three wounded and bloodied people stumbling around dazedly; a twisted hole in the side of the vehicle; and a 3ft length of lamppost protruding from the driver's back. Four dead and seven walking wounded he assessed, before climbing the front stairs.

Mercifully the top deck was almost empty - just a mother with two small children at the front and a young couple seated right at the back. Disorientated but surprisingly unharmed, the young couple were scrambling to their feet in an effort to get to the mother who's cries Branigan had heard from outside.

He quickly assessed the three of them. Twin boys about Molly's age sitting in the seat in front of mum, the boy nearest the aisle and mum in the seat behind most obviously in need of help.

Mum was holding both hands to a huge cut on her head and the boy was nursing a left arm which, to judge by the pointed fragment of bone protruding through his anorak had taken a strike from a piece of shrapnel. Although crying, he was surprisingly quiet and beside him his brother was white with shock and sitting still.

'Are you okay?' Branigan asked the quieter of the two boys, who nodded in response.

Turning to the mother, he beckoned over the walking-wounded from the back seat.

'Hold her wound together, there'll be some paramedics along shortly.'

He glanced outside as people woke up to the spectacle that was unfolding. A police car and an emergency response vehicle were coming from the Square Mile of The City towards them, people were checking their own injuries before turning to help those less fortunate than themselves.

People running onto the bridge to help

He pulled off his sweatshirt as he knelt beside the crying boy.

'What's your name?' he asked.

'He's Luke, his brother is Noah,' the distraught mother told him as the young couple began to fuss around her.

Cover the wound and control the bleeding.

'Okay, Luke,' Branigan said calmly as he ripped his top into strips, 'I'm going to tie a piece of this over your arm and try and stop your arm bleeding. Then we'll get a doctor to make it better for you.'

He could feel the bus moving as help arrived, and as he secured the tourniquet around Luke's arm someone stood beside him and passed him a distinctive striped Balliol College tie.

'Use this for a sling,' the wearer said.

'Okay, Luke, can you move to this seat here so I can look at Noah?' Branigan said taking the tie without looking up at his benefactor.

After gently helping the small boy across to the neighbouring seat, his companion knelt down beside him.

'Let me help with Noah,' David Price said, 'while you go and do what you can elsewhere.'

For a moment Branigan was perplexed.

'There's been a message calling for an evacuation before a major blast,' David explained, 'this is Peach Tree.'

Branigan immediately grasped the significance.

'With The City as the target?'

David nodded as he gently felt around Noah's torso for

signs of injury.

'Who claimed responsibility?' Branigan asked.

'Someone we know little about - the Persian Liberation Front.'

Branigan shook his head.

'I should have worked that out,' he said, before stooping to Noah, 'I'm going to leave you with my friend David - he'll look after you.'

I can see the streets below filling up as people run away - the message is getting across.

Picking up the loudhailer and turning up the volume, I prepare to clear the last of the people from around me.

'This is not a drill,' I announce, 'you need to leave the area immediately and stay clear of the Square Mile.'

I keep repeating this and watch with pleasure as workmen come scurrying past on their way into the burgeoning throng on the street.

Peter Winstone's phone rang as he'd been showing Tenant and Drake the vending machine in which Krantz had dumped the scalp.

'I'm sorry, major incident, I have to go,' he said succinctly.

After watching Peter's hurried departure, Tenant was still ruminating on what might be happening, when it was Drake's turn to receive a call.

'The surveillance team,' he said when he put the phone back in his pocket, 'Buzz Lightyear is on the move.'

Back in the financial heartland of London, Branigan's torn jeans and blood-soaked shirt occasioned side-long glances of disapproval from the tide of posh Londoners he was swimming against as he made his way into the area under threat.

As he passed Aldgate Station there was the distant "Whummmp" of another explosion somewhere to the North which reverberated through the throng desperately trying to make their way into the already over-crowded underground.

He scanned over the heads of the people around him, looking at tall buildings, rooftops and tower cranes - somewhere in this skyline there was a bomb hiding in plain sight.

Ignoring the policeman urging him to go the other way, he pushed through to the site entrance to a new building and stopped a man in a yellow hard hat.

'Is there anyone you don't recognise on your site - up on the roof maybe?' he asked.

'Fuck knows,' the man replied, 'but if he's on the roof he'll have to be fucking Spiderman because there's no access.'

Branigan glanced up at the glass and metal structure and realised the impracticability of getting to the roof.

'Where else is there building work,' he pleaded, 'it'll be near here, another site with a tall building on it?'

The man shook his head.

'There's nothing,' he said, threading a chain through the gate and fixing a padlock, 'most other sites are just coming out of the ground, the only other one is the demolition they're doing off Cheapside.'

By the time he'd shut the padlock Branigan had gone.

On the Thames, the river taxi Peter Winstone had boarded at Westminster Pier made its way lazily downstream, its journey seemingly unaffected by the events occurring in London's financial heartland.

Only the little plumes of smoke hanging above the highrise buildings gave any clue as to the chaos into which Peter was heading.

I'm ready to go.

Three of the ten shells I placed in the lamp posts have detonated; which leaves another seven before this one goes off.

The lamp posts are a clever place for the bombs, don't you think? No one batted an eye when I turned up early in the morning opening them one by one and seeming to check the wiring.

Give someone a hi-vis jacket and a flashing light and everyone turns away because no one thinks it's suspicious.

Ten mortar shells wired to cell phones, each with a timer; except the one Branigan ran into earlier - that one was triggered by my sibling, the other Zahhāk - I'm almost sorry Branigan isn't here to get the joke.

One last check.

The sealed tube, the timer ticking away inside, the mercury switch set to stop tampering and just the safety pin stopping it being live.

I pull out the foot-long metal pin and head to the lift.

In under an hour this part of London will be uninhabitable for a thousand years.

David Price reluctantly climbed into the back of his Range Rover.

'Vauxhall Cross - as quick as you can,' he said to his driver.

In the confusion onboard the double-decker, he'd elected to stay with Noah until a paramedic arrived.

'Can you point to where it hurts?' he'd softly asked the pale boy sitting quietly beside the broken window.

Noah looked up at him with the blind faith of a youngster who trusts an adult to make things right; he pointed to his right side where he was leaning against the wall of the bus. Kneeling beside him and edging into the gap where Luke had been sitting, David carefully felt around the trusting child, his left hand working between Noah's anorak and the plastic wall panel.

He'd frozen when he came across the jagged piece of metal propelled through the side of the bus like a javelin, pinning Noah's tiny body to where he was sitting.

'You just stay still,' David whispered soothingly as he felt the wetness and took Noah's left hand in his right, 'and I'll stay with you until we get more help.'

Noah nodded, smiled and squeezed his hand tightly.

David stayed like that. Kneeling on the floor with the

small boy's feet dangling inches in front of him, his left arm draped across the boy's lap and their free hands clasped.

Then Noah's hand went limp and his head fell to one side.

In the back of the Range Rover, David wiped the tears from his eyes, regretting ever starting the conversation which mooted Operation Peach Tree.

'Can't you just drive past this bloody thing?' Tenant said testily.

He and Drake were trying to catch up with the team trailing Alan and their path was blocked by an ambulance on "blues and twos" coming in the opposite direction.

'With the greatest of respect, sir,' Drake said, backing up to give the ambulance enough space to get past, 'his case is probably more urgent than ours.'

Tenant grunted begrudgingly as they moved forward again and the sound of their own siren helped clear the path ahead.

Branigan's heart leaped when he found the half-open gate to the deserted demolition site and saw the white van just inside. Not conclusive given the plethora of such vehicles to be found on building sites, but after scrambling up the scaffolding around the building he was able to see a gouge on the roof he recognised from the CCTV in Farnham.

He craned his neck upwards at the towering concrete structure. Either the staircase or a two-gondola builder's lift strapped temporarily to the outside - candidly, neither looked that promising, but his urgency dictated that he try the lift.

Unlike a conventional lift, this temporary one was designed to carry heavy loads by counter-balancing one gondola against the other. In simple terms, the two lifts were at either end of a cable slung over a pulley at the top - so as one came down, the other went up. He examined the lights and buttons on the control panel and cursed - a green light showed the gondola at ground level was secure, while a similar light for the one at the top was glowing red – the lift was going nowhere. That was when the door at the top was closed, the second light turned green and he began to move upwards.

I start down, surveying the busy street below.

All those people running away unaware of what is about to happen.

Of course, I have my motorcycle in the back of the van so I'll be okay – I'm not sure about the rest.

I wish Cressix and Branigan could be here to witness this. Cressix would be horrified that I've hijacked his precious idea and unleashed it on London.

Branigan would be morally outraged that we've outwitted him in our fight for Persian independence.

I'm halfway down and passing the other lift when it happens.

What is it that the British say – "Be careful what you wish for?"

On the street below, everyone was so intent on getting away from The City that no one looked up and saw the dishevelled Branigan clamber over the metal bar protecting the entrance to the rising lift, haul himself onto the roof of the gondola and swing into the downward heading car as they passed.

'Hello Jasper,' Branigan said to the startled occupant.

'Branigan,' Anna's boyfriend - Jasper Farhad - said, reaching into his toolkit, 'I thought my sister had killed you with the London Bridge explosion.'

Branigan processed this information; Zahhāk's deal with Cressix had seen him bring his family with him! Anna, his sister, not his girlfriend!

'You should have stayed out of this,' Jasper said, pulling a heavy wrench out of the toolkit, 'our fight to liberate Persia never concerned you.'

Branigan moved towards Jasper who jabbed at him with the wrench. A more practiced fighter than Red and his friends.

'You're wrong; you dragged me in the moment you and Cressix messed with me in Bishkek.'

'And rather like now, you were too late on the scene,' Jasper said cuttingly, 'you missed the main delivery in Bishkek, you're too late to stop this device and too far away from my sister to stop her finishing off your new girlfriend.'

Branigan recoiled at this news and rage flooded through him. As Jasper sprung forward once again, he ducked and charged in low, avoiding the spanner in Jasper's right hand but not the twelve inch metal safety pin from the mortar Jasper had in his left. The tent peg-sized pin buried itself in Branigan's right thigh until its agonising passage through his muscle was brought to an abrupt halt by his thigh bone.

Like a wounded animal, Branigan roared in pain and lashed at Jasper's chest with short sharp jabs. In response Jasper pulled Branigan in close and began to wrestle him.

Aware that he had lost any advantage now that he was grappling at close quarters, Branigan manoeuvred himself so that his back was toward the lift controls and slammed his elbow into the "Up" button. The sudden stop threw Jasper off balance and the pair stumbled and then tumbled towards the open side of the lift car.

Were it not for the metal spike protruding from his leg, Branigan would have found it easy to leap to his feet and take the advantage – as it was his right leg buckled underneath him and he fell towards the opening. Scrambling out of the way, Jasper was able to kick out at Branigan's torso as he rolled passed, tipping him over the edge, out of the gondola and into oblivion. Only at the last moment did Branigan's scrabbling fingertips manage to grasp the edge of floor of the open gondola so he hung with his legs dangling ten stories up as the lift rose inexorably back to the top.

'I told you, you were too late,' Jasper said, throwing the

wrench with all the force he could muster at the grasping fingers of Branigan's right hand and watching it bounce high off the metal floor and tumble over the edge as Branigan whipped his fingers away. His luck didn't hold as Jasper kicked out with his feet and the dangling Branigan lost grip with the fingertips of his left hand.

'Harâm-zâde,' Jasper cursed in Farsi as Branigan succumbed to gravity and disappeared.

Inside Branigan's house Chloe was making her way back upstairs carrying a small wind-up torch she'd found in a kitchen drawer - her first effort to search the attic having failed when she found Branigan's DIY project to rewire the house hadn't yet reached that far.

At the top of the narrow second floor staircase was a tiny 3ft square landing with doors on either side into two appropriately named box rooms.

Chloe wound the torch. Thirty whirring turns of the foldout handle and the single bulb sprang into action. It would be unfair to say it didn't work, because it provided a perfectly acceptable beam of light for all of the minute that it lasted.

'Oh shit!' Chloe said, starting to wind the handle again.

Peter Winstone got off the water taxi at Blackfriars Bridge and pushed against the tide of people leaving The City. He didn't know what he was looking for; his was a gut-reaction after he learned from David Price that Branigan had headed off to try and stop the main explosion. When Michael Jenkins had suggested he come in to help man the phones in the ICR, Peter had given a succinct reply.

'Fuck off,' he'd said, 'I'm going to help.'

At Vauxhall Cross there was a collective gasp at the sight of the blood stains on David Price's open shirt when he crashed through the door of the ICR.

'What news?' he asked.

Oblivious to the happenings elsewhere, Alan was seated in the back of the black cab, clutching his aluminium field-kit case to his lap, humming tunelessly and rocking back and forth.

It was quite an ignominious end for Branigan really – after all the heroics he simply lost his grip and fell to his death.
I wonder if they'll need to bury him in a lead-lined coffin - you know, what with what's going to happen? Still, that'll be a funeral I'll happily go to, pay my respects, look all the mourners in the eye and say what a shame it is.
I wonder if the chapel offers a discount for bulk?
They could include Marty Freeman and Herbert Cressix at the same time if that is the case – one big funeral for each of our recent victims.
I press the button to send the lift back down to the ground.

Jasper's hand was on the lift controls when the wrench struck with such force it not only shattered the bones in his hand but also sent sparks flying as it broke the casing of the lift controls.

Like a cobra striking from underfoot, Branigan had reared up through the gap between the lift and the edge of the building and lashed at Jasper's hand. Recoiling from the searing pain, Jasper instinctively clutched his broken hand and doubled over, giving Branigan enough time to haul himself back into the lift.

'Surprise!' Branigan said sardonically.

Jasper tried to use his shoulder to charge at Branigan, who parried with his straight-palm blow and a knee into the underside of Jasper's jaw. As his victim stumbled backwards it was Branigan's turn to use his foot to help him on his journey.

With one deft shove, Jasper disappeared under the safety barrier and screamed for the three seconds it took him to meet his destiny with an upright scaffolding pole.

Not pausing to contemplate Jasper's death, Branigan examined the heavy metal pin protruding from his right thigh and then yanked.

'Fuuuck!' he yelled as a rasping pain shot through him.

Having checked that the resultant bleed wasn't life-threatening, he turned to rifle through the toolkit until he found a spare one of the cheap phones Jasper had used as timers in the pipe bombs. Praying that the phone would work, he powered it up and dragged the toolkit with him as he clambered out of the lift onto the top floor of the building.

'I know you are recording this,' he said having dialled the switchboard at Vauxhall Cross from memory, 'and I need you to pass this to the ICR as a matter of urgency.'

He then went on to describe where he was, alert MI6 to the danger and plead for immediate support for Chloe.

'I'm going to do what I can with the device here,' he concluded, 'and then I'll head to my house.'

The scene which greeted him on the roof sent his pulse racing - a Russian-made field mortar he'd last seen in the back of the lorry in Kyrgyzstan was sitting pointing at the sky. A basic piece of military equipment, the mortar was a modern version of a canon - a heavy steel tube, sealed at the bottom, into which you dropped a self-propelled shell which then shot back out of the muzzle. Throw in a couple of wheels to move the thing around and that was pretty much what he was faced with - except someone had put a steel cap over the open muzzle of this one.

'Oh fuck!' Branigan said as he examined the device.

The bomb was inside the sealed steel barrel. With nowhere to go, it was a pretty fair guess the explosive would try to expand, compress the beads inside the tube to the point they were vaporised and then burst through the heavy steel in which it was encased.

A simple way to dissipate the deadly plutonium as a fine

wind-borne dust which would contaminate the area around the explosion for years to come.

Branigan examined the mortar closely.

The open-end of the barrel had been machined to create a thread, onto which a heavy metal cap was screwed. Like a massive steel bottle-top twisted firmly in place.

Not, he was sure, a manufacturer's modification, but something done in anticipation of the mortar being used as a dirty bomb. A positive was that Jasper had not welded the cap in place, leaving Branigan with one option - he found a mallet from the toolkit, and began to hit the cap with all his might; a move dictated by time, practicality and the same "fuck it" attitude he'd had when tackling the container. The worst that could happen was that the tilt switch triggered and he got to be with Sally and Molly.

In the distance there was the thump of another explosion as he continued to hit the cap for all it was worth. Eventually the cap began to move, not by much - just a millimetre or two – but, buoyed by the fractional shift, he hit harder until it began to turn more freely. Then he was using both his hands, putting all his strength into spinning the cap turn after turn until it came away, the heavy piece of machined steel falling to the ground with a resounding clang.

The first part of his task completed, he did one of those things they told you in training never to do - he peered into the open end of the primed 120 mm mortar. No doubt the advice was the same for what he did next; he put his arm inside the barrel and scrabbled around with his fingers, just managing to pull out three beads which looked like the kind of thing Sally used when she was blind baking. Smooth, round, 1/2 inch in diameter and seemingly innocuous.

Branigan cast around for somewhere to put them, alighting on the empty ammunition containers he presumed they and the explosives had travelled up in.

Unable to reach any more with his scrabbling fingers, he searched the rooftop for an implement until he found a length of aluminium scrap which he fashioned into something like a long-handled ladle; using this he began to scoop the beads out, rolling three or four at a time up the smooth inside of the barrel before dumping them with the others in the ammunition boxes.

In the distance he heard another explosion.

In Branigan's house, Chloe was working her way methodically through the brown cardboard boxes.

Unfortunately, it appeared the police or someone had been through them ahead of her, so the first thing she'd found was that the contents didn't necessarily match the label. This meant she was having to take each box, look through the contents and set it to one side before moving on to the next.

A frustrating process made doubly annoying by repeatedly having to stop to wind the torch. No matter how many times she wound it, the bulb seemed to burn brightly for just one minute before extinguishing itself.

Then, somewhere in the midst of some anthropology text books, she found what she was looking for. A brown envelope labelled "Bishkek" containing a bundle of papers covered with unintelligible Cyrillic script, the top one of which had the words "Bill of Lading" in English next to its Russian counterpart.

Letting out a little whoop of joy, Chloe placed the papers to one side, put the text books back in the box and shut the lid.

As she stood up and prepared to take the documents downstairs, the torch went out again. Winding the handle furiously she was surprised to see the beam from the re-energised torch glint off a pair of shoes right in front of her.

'Oh hello,' Chloe said in surprise as she moved the torch upwards and recognised Anna from the funeral.

Before she could say anything more, her eyes registered another glint, this time off a thin, highly polished, split-bladed knife. A random part of her brain registered it as the type of blade Branigan had described when he explained how Marty and that man in Kazakhstan died.

That was when the blade plunged into her abdomen and the light from the torch went out.

Unaware of Chloe's plight, Branigan continued to remove the ceramic beads using his crudely fashioned ladle. Somewhere in the distance another bomb went off and he realised his could be next.

He thought about tilting the barrel downward so the last of the plutonium rolled out, presumably with much of the plastic explosive; then he heard Sgt Arkwright's voice.

'How lucky are you feeling, Branigan?'

Arkwright was right - it was the easiest thing in the world to put a mercury switch into the device and Jasper had already shown that he liked to set traps in the bombs he made. Resignedly, Branigan continued to scoop the beads out until he could find no more with his crudely fashioned ladle.

He then held his face over the open muzzle of the mortar and waited for his eyes to adjust to the light until he was sure that he was staring at nothing more than a large wad of soft, pliable and deadly plastic explosive.

A helicopter clattered noisily overhead as Branigan shut the ammunition boxes and furiously worked the metal catches shut before grabbing one in each hand and rushing to the lift. Ducking under the safety bar he stared in horror at the shorted-out control panel - the lift was going nowhere.

The giant screen in the ICR was showing images from the helicopter hovering near Branigan.

'What's he doing now?' David Price asked as they watched Branigan secure either end of a length of scrap wire to the two ammunition boxes and drape the cable over his neck so the boxes hung down either side of him.

'I think the lift won't work,' Alex Oldroyd said perceptively.

'And the helicopter can't get to him?' David asked.

'No, air traffic spoke with the pilot for us - there isn't enough room and they don't have any kind of winch,' Alex replied.

They watched in silence as Branigan climbed onto the roof of the stranded gondola, took off his leather belt, doubled it over and lent across to the other lift cable reaching 120ft vertically down to the ground.

'Holy Mother of God!' David Price said, flinching and looking away from the screen as Branigan launched himself off.

Seated comfortably in Roz's living room, Greyson Krantz was watching the news with interest.

'Have you seen this?' he whispered.

'Yes,' Roz replied from the kitchen, 'there have been seven explosions according to the radio.'

'It's all to do with our operation, isn't it?' Krantz said, watching the images from a news helicopter as it showed the thousands of people trying to get away from the Square Mile with thin palls of smoke rising from the scene of the last two explosions.

'Oh Roz,' he called suggestively a few moments later, 'I need you to do something for me.'

Roz appeared from the kitchen, trailing behind her the length of heavy-duty chain he'd bought online for next day delivery. With one end padlocked round her waist and the other locked to the radiator in the kitchen, Roz was able to get around her apartment but no further.

The Herald's newsroom was alive with people watching the TV screens, on their phones, writing copy and trying to cover a story which was moving faster than they were able to respond.

Watching the screen nearest her, Paige Henderson stopped stock-still as a TV helicopter picked up the action from the top of the building and she recognised Branigan.

'Ken,' she called to her harassed News Editor, 'I've just seen Branigan doing something with what looks like a huge gun on top of a derelict building in The City.'

Ken looked perplexed.

'What's he doing there?' he asked.

'I really don't know,' Paige said, 'either he's part of the bomb conspiracy and was caught loading another one, or he's found one and is trying to disarm it - which angle would you like me to write?'

'Do I look like someone who gives a fuck?' Ken said, the strain of the situation sounding in his voice.

In a leap of faith, Branigan was relying on the soles of his shoes and the strength of his belt as he caught the vertical cable between his feet as he began to fall. Then he had to do the most counter-intuitive thing and lean away from the wire rope so his weight created friction between the leather belt and the thread of metal stretching to the ground.

'Shit!' he yelled to himself as he plunged downwards, the rubber of his shoes burning and the leather of his belt abrading as he fell.

By the time he was halfway down, the cable had sawn through one of the two layers of belt wrapped around it and Branigan had to lean in towards the cable to take some of the stress off the thin strip of leather. At the last moment he gripped the cable as tightly as he could with the soles of his shoes and pulled the belt so hard it sawed through completely, jarringly slowing his plummeting descent so he crashed the last six feet onto the roof of the lower gondola. Briefly stunned, he kicked the ammunition boxes off the roof of the lift before jumping down - a move he regretted as soon as his right leg reminded him of the puncture wound from the steel pin.

Having dumped the plutonium into the skip filled with murky water he took hold of the handlebars of the dead night watchman's ancient BSA Bantam motorcycle and studied the controls. There was no ignition key to hot-wire, just a switch with three settings. On, off and emergency. Settling upon "on" as the best option, he flicked the switch, checked the fuel was turned on and primed the carburettor.

Alex Oldroyd was on the phone to Peter Winstone, guiding him towards the tall building on Cheapside.

'I'm a hundred yards away now,' Peter said, 'and there's movement by the gate – I think it's Branigan leaving on a motorcycle.'

As he spoke, there was a flash of light from the top of the building and a deafening "whoomph!" as the mortar detonated, sending the upper lift gondola crashing to the ground followed by dust, debris and pieces of twisted metal which came raining down on the street.

Peter shielded his head from the falling debris and glanced upwards.

'Yes,' he said sardonically, spotting the smoke coming from the top, the twisted body of Jasper impaled like a gargoyle, and the mangled wreckage on the ground, 'it is Branigan on the motorcycle.'

Judith Warde cursed.

Usually well-informed as to the goings on in her street, she'd left a key under the mat at Branigan's house, taken Daniella to nursery and returned to find five police cars, two ambulances, a doctor's car and a fire engine littering the road.

Making her way to the small throng held back by a fresh roll of plastic barrier tape, she turned to the woman beside her.

'What's happened?' she asked.

Before Mrs Rutherford could reply, the poodle clutched in her arms bared its teeth and gave a low grumbling growl.

Ken Briers was unusually complimentary as he read the article Paige had hastily put together.

'I take it there's no foundation for any of this?' he said.

'Well, Ken,' Paige explained, 'there hasn't been any time to check my sources and craft a proper article, but it should serve as a holding piece until we fill in the gaps.'

'I agree,' Ken said, dumbfounding Paige who fully expected him to object to the line she had taken, 'and I particularly like the headline.'

Within moments The Herald's online front page had the banner "Oxy-jobdone!" under which the strap line read, "Hero agent breaks cover to defuse massive chemical weapon threatening London!"

'Hello Jude,' Branigan said to his startled neighbour as he pushed his way through the knot of people gathered behind the plastic tape barrier.

Jude smiled, in stark contrast to Mrs Rutherford who looked disapprovingly at his torn clothes which were streaked with dust, blood, grease and dirt. Ignoring the growling poodle, he marched straight past the barrier tape, through the front door and up the stairs where he looked around quickly, taking in the two people being treated – one in Molly's room and the other on the floor at the foot of the stairs leading to the attic.

Stepping over the recumbent form he took the stairs two at a time in his hurry to get to the top, where he pushed his way past a fireman on his way into the box room on the right which were flooded with the harsh light from an array of battery-powered floodlights.

Chloe was lying on the floor being attended to by two ambulance men and a doctor.

She looked up.

'How's your day been?' she asked.

Branigan looked at the thin chromium-plated shim-like handle of a knife protruding from her stomach and the black patent shoe with chrome toe and heel lying on the floor; a shoe he now recognised as concealing the knife Anna used to murder Ed Khan and Marty.

'I've had better,' Branigan replied, before pointing to the knife, 'and you, are you going to be all right?'

One of the ambulance men answered for Chloe.

'We're just stabilising her, sir,' he said, putting his arm up to stop Branigan encroaching any further, 'she should be okay, but for now if you would like to leave, we need to get on with our job.'

'Alan saved me,' Chloe said as he turned to leave.

On his way out Branigan saw Alan's familiar aluminium case with a huge dent in one end and began to piece things together.

At the bottom of the narrow staircase, DCI Tenant was standing the other side of Anna's recumbent form, a pair of handcuffs dangling from his right hand.

'Mr Branigan,' he said, a satisfied look crossing his face, 'we meet again.'

'You don't need to worry this time,' Branigan said, stepping over Anna and turning his back, 'I'm not going to run off again.'

Hearing his voice Anna opened her eyes.

'I thought I'd killed you,' she said.

'I take it you were somewhere near London Bridge?'

'Yes, you were near the lamppost when I triggered the first explosion,' Anna said, seemingly not caring about confessing in front of the police.

'And in the process killed a number of innocent people on a passing bus.'

Anna shrugged.

'It has put our cause on the map; that was the idea right from the start.'

'From when you agreed your deal with Cressix?'

Anna smiled.

'No – from long before that,' she said, 'Tell me, did my brother succeed?'

Branigan shook his head as Tenant secured the cuffs and read him his rights.

'But he's all right?'

The ambulance men manoeuvred her into a sitting position so they could take her downstairs.

Branigan stayed silent as she repeated her question from halfway down the stairs. Only when she was in the hallway did the significance of Branigan's silence sink in and she let out a wail which echoed round the house.

'May I speak with Alan before we go?' Branigan asked Drake who was holding back while Anna was taken outside.

Drake nodded.

'Hello Alan,' Branigan said, ducking into Molly's room.

'Oh, hello Branigan,' Alan said so weakly the paramedic with him did a double-take to make sure he wasn't losing his patient.

'Are you all right?' Branigan asked.

'They tell me I should pull through,' Alan said in a voice that suggested he was about to breathe his last.

'What happened then Alan?' Branigan asked.

'Oh, you know,' Alan began, 'I worked out the significance of the Zahhāk name and that it meant we were looking for two people. Then I thought about Zahhāk knowing about Farnham and realised Anna could listen into conversations in Marty's office using the pen with the microphone inside I'd placed there.'

'Then I realised Anna had just overheard our conversation about the paperwork and Chloe coming here,' Alan continued, by now in full flight as he excitedly told his story, 'and when I couldn't get hold of you, I came just in time to stop Anna.'

Branigan nodded sympathetically.

'And how were you hurt?' Branigan asked.

'Oh,' Alan said, his voice becoming even weaker as his injuries were mentioned, 'after I'd knocked out Anna, I found a little wind-up torch. When the beam from that fell on

Chloe I saw all the blood and fainted.'

Branigan had to smile.

'So, who found you?' he asked.

Alan pointed to DC Nick Wills in the corner of the room.

'I was following him sir, in the hope he'd lead us to you. I heard Mr Armstrong hit the floor and came up to find the place littered with bodies.'

The hallway now clear, Drake beckoned Branigan out.

As he left the room Branigan turned.

'Thank you, Alan,' he said, before being led away by DS Drake.

When they arrived in the hallway it was clear that DCI Tenant was having a heated debate on the doorstep.

'I understand the urgency,' he said, 'but I can't afford to let him out of my sight – not after his previous performances.'

'Yes, but you'll also understand that some of what I need to discuss with him is sensitive information relating to a terrorist incident.'

'Michael?' Branigan asked.

In reply Michael Jenkins stepped forward and gave a half wave.

'Hello Branigan, David has sent me – I'm just trying to get 5 minutes with you in private so we have your input to the ongoing security situation. David has been called to Downing Street and has a few questions he'd like to ask before he speaks with the PM.'

At the mention of the Prime Minister, DCI Tenant became more co-operative.

'Clearly we don't want to hinder the security services,' he said, 'why don't you keep him cuffed and Drake and I will stand guard while you speak with him in your car?'

Michael acquiesced and the four of them made their way through the knot of people gathered behind the tape towards Michael's dark blue Ford parked ahead of all of the emergency vehicles. Branigan managed a smile at Jude as she encouraged Mrs Rutherford's dog to bite Tenant, an incitement the dog wholly misinterpreted as it turned and snapped at Jude instead.

'I take it this isn't about a debrief?' Branigan said as soon as Michael settled in the driver's seat and locked the doors closed.

'No,' Michael agreed, throwing a glance in the direction of Tenant and Drake who were on the pavement a few feet away, 'David sent me to bring you in.'

Branigan nodded contemplatively and tried to move his cuffed wrists into a more comfortable position.

'What happens now?' he asked.

'We chat long enough for those two to get comfortable and then I drive off,' Michael said, nodding towards the police officers.

'Then what?' Branigan asked.

'We meet up with David and he negotiates your release without you having to be taken into custody.'

Branigan nodded as Michael seized his opportunity, started the car and shot off down the road.

'There is just one thing bothering me...' Branigan began as they hurtled east and Michael checked in his rearview mirror for any sign that they were being followed.

'Which is what?' Michael prompted.

'...how did you persuade Gregory Brown to go to Hampton Court?'

Michael drove on in silence before Branigan continued.

'You see, I don't know whether to call you Michael Jenkins or Herbert Cressix.'

For answer Michael reached down beside him and pulled a heavy pistol out from the driver's door pocket and placed it on his lap.

Branigan recognised the distinctive triangular barrel and huge muzzle of the large caliber Desert Eagle, a fearsomely powerful weapon.

'That's an impressive piece of kit,' Branigan observed, 'I had you down for something more handbag-sized.'

In a surprisingly deft action, Michael dropped his right hand from the wheel, picked up the pistol, clicked off the safety and levelled it steadily at Branigan.

'Just goes to show how wrong you can be,' Michael said calmly, glancing briefly down at the gun, 'it's a trophy from the Middle East and, before you have any ideas, I know exactly what I'm doing with it.'

'Okay,' Branigan said, frowning slightly as he considered the scenario, 'assuming you shoot me with that thing, you'll not only be scraping bits of me off your car for the foreseeable future, but also have some explaining to do.'

Michael changed his voice and became more effete and sing-song.

'Oh no officers, I don't know how it happened. He had a gun tucked in his waistband and managed to point it at me with his cuffed hands,' he began, 'he forced me to drive and then we had a tussle and somehow the pistol went off – it was a terrible accident!'

'Yes, that might work,' Branigan agreed, 'and the purpose of killing me is...?'

'You forget how well I know you and you're the only person out there who isn't going to carry on assuming Gregory Brown was the villain; with you dead this whole chapter closes and life returns to normal,' he paused before continuing, 'What made you guess it was me?'

Branigan was happy to stall for time as Michael turned and manoeuvred through a series of side streets.

'I first had suspicions when I saw you punctuate the Cressix email address so Crescent was properly abbreviated. Then you gave that literary reference to Hampton Court and compounded it by spelling the name Zahhāk in Greg's diary – no one else would have bothered with the accent!'

'But you thought it was Greg at first – that's what you told Marty?'

'Yes, you did well with the alibi of the conference in Manchester. I guess you flew from there and just checked into the hotel without staying?'

Michael nodded.

'It wasn't a spur of the moment dash to Kyrgyzstan after all,' Branigan mused, 'I made the mistake of assuming you only reacted when you saw the contents of the container in the pictures I sent – but it wasn't like that at all; the pictures were your independent verification that you weren't being duped!'

'Well done, go to the top of the class,' Michael said with a mirthless laugh, 'I'd been in contact with Anna since Ed sent his cryptic messages from Kazakhstan and I saw the potential. I tried to buy that consignment, but it was already spoken for, so I stayed in contact with Anna until the right opportunity came along.'

'Why did Ed have to die?'

'Come on Branigan, he'd introduced me to Anna; how could I run her as an asset anonymously if he knew both of us?'

Branigan reasoned this for a moment.

'Which implies Ed knew what you wanted to do with Peach Tree all along and those cryptic emails were directed straight at you.'

'You're on a roll.'

'You agreed to bring Anna and her brother to the UK provided she disposed of Ed - the connection between you - I assume you had some kind of relationship with Ed but were still prepared to sacrifice him to help promote the need for SIS,' he said, 'Was it really worth it?'

'He was just one of the plum trees,' Michael said dispassionately.

Branigan shook his head.

'You waited for Anna to find the right weapon to bring with her,' Branigan surmised, 'and then I was sacrificed once you'd got the verification you needed.'

'The joke is that after all that I didn't need the weapon because terrorist attacks started across the UK and Europe and raised the profile of the security services for me,' Michael added wryly.

'By which time you had Anna and Jasper champing at the bit to promote their Persian cause.'

'Yes,' Michael agreed, 'and I could have continued to contain them if Chloe Travers hadn't written her fucking story.'

'Your solution to Chloe's story was another sacrifice - you contacted Krantz who you'd met in Cologne and asked him to put a team together to kill Chloe and make it look like I did it.'

'I'll admit that was a mistake. He'd royally fucked things up in Cologne but I thought that was a one-off, but you then took that weird computer bloke with you to Sheffield, messed the whole plan up and Krantz over-reacted.'

Branigan took a deep breath.

'That's what you call killing Sally and Molly – an over-reaction?' he said, trying to keep his voice calm.

'And you did nothing to stop Anna and Jasper when you knew they were going ahead with Peach Tree,' he continued when Michael didn't reply.

'What did it matter to me? I'd planted the evidence and everyone believed Gregory was Cressix.'

'How did you get his fingerprints on the phone you'd used?'

'That was easy,' Michael said, now bragging, 'David let slip you'd pointed the finger at Greg, so a few days before he died I "dropped" the phone in his office and later called him, asking him to look for it and check for any messages. With that plastered with his prints, I used his computer to access the bank account and then phoned him and pretended to be you arranging a clandestine meeting at Hampton Court.'

'Gregory, it's me, Branigan,' he continued in a passable imitation of Branigan's voice, 'don't tell anyone you're meeting me – I need to tell you who Cressix is!'

They turned, following a sign for New Spitalfields Market.

'In fact, if you'd only done as you were supposed to – and died in Hampton Court – everything would be neatly tied up by now.'

'I take it you're about to address that issue here and now?' Branigan said, as they pulled to a halt in the car park for the huge fruit and vegetable market, 'I'm surprised you haven't found a lackey to do the job for you.'

Michael turned to him and raised the pistol.

'I lost that luxury when you emptied the bank account.'

Branigan absorbed this information as he scrutinised their surroundings. The car park wasn't overly crowded at this time of day and Michael had chosen a quiet spot away from most of the traders loading their vans. Ahead of them was the huge market building, whilst to their right was a mass of empty car parking, the railway line and a bottled-gas depot. Turning away from Michael slightly he was able to see fencing, a hedgerow, and in the rearview mirror a line of industrial units; even if he could get out of the locked car, there was nowhere obvious to seek cover.

'What do you mean, emptied the account?' Branigan asked.

'Come on Branigan, you can't pretend that you don't know about the £5.7 million missing from the bank.'

Branigan recalled Alan asserting that the Black Ops people had stopped following them - then thought about David's comment that the cash had simply disappeared - and elected not to comment further on the obvious conclusion.

'So now you pull the trigger and pretend we've fought?' Branigan said, twisting in his seat so he faced out of the side window.

'Then how do you explain shooting me in the back?' he continued, glancing down at the wing mirror which had folded in when Michael turned off the ignition.

Michael shuffled nearer, resting his arms on the centre

console.

'He turned around to shoot at me,' he said with his singsong voice, 'I didn't mean for the gun to go off.'

'And it hasn't occurred to you that I told David Price you are Cressix this morning and that Peter Winstone is in the car that followed us?'

Michael instinctively glanced out of the back window to look for a tail, giving Branigan the moment he'd been waiting for; bending suddenly at the waist, he used his cuffed hands to push the centre armrest up so suddenly that Michael was thrown off balance, the gun tilted almost vertically upwards and Michael's finger squeezed on the trigger of the mighty pistol. As the gun punched a hole in the roof of the car, the deafening "Crack!" of the cartridge reverberated in the confined space of the car like a stun-grenade.

Pushing back in his seat, Branigan was able to grab the hot muzzle, twist counter-clockwise and wrench the pistol from the stunned Michael's hand. Realising that despite being cuffed, Branigan had now gained the advantage, Michael didn't wait for him to adjust his grip on the pistol – instead he did what came naturally. He opened the car door and ran.

Branigan didn't try to give chase.

He stayed in the car with the gun held behind him in his cuffed hands and watched in the wing mirror as Michael ran towards the railway line, found the fence there to be impassable and turned to his left.

That was when Branigan fired.

Of course, the bullet missed – he had no chance of hitting a moving target using a gun held behind his back and a mirror to aim – instead the large bullet punched into the pile of gas canisters in the storage yard and sent a huge white cloud into the air. The second bullet also missed the fleeing Michael, instead it sent sparks flying as it pierced a different canister.

In the mirror Branigan watched Michael Jenkins continuing to run through the fireball of exploding gas, his entire body seemingly engulfed in flames as he stumbled on for three more paces before he fell to the ground and his flaming body lay still.

'That's for you Sally and Molly,' Branigan said.

THE EPILOGUE FOLLOWS

Before you go to the next page and start the Epilogue, I'd just like to thank you for reading Scapegoat.
It is my first book and as a self-published author I need as much help as possible to try and publicise it.

If you have enjoyed Scapegoat, please:-
- Leave feedback on Amazon
- Tell your friends

If you have questions or issues with the book, do let me know – I'd love to hear from you - stuart@stuartchampion.com

Finally, do please look up www.stuartchampion.com. There's news of other books there and a growing blog.

Stuart

   Twitter: @stuartchampion
   Instagram: stuartchampion.writer
   Web: www.stuartchampion.com

FRIDAY 4TH MARCH

EPILOGUE

Three Months Late

Fit, lean and tanned, Branigan made his way on foot along Oxford Street in the heart of London's West End. A woman coming in the opposite direction looked at him long and hard, either because she was drawn to his looks, or because she recognised his picture from the newspaper. He shrugged - just like the last time, his celebrity would wane after a few weeks of his being recognised.

The "Guy Fawkes Bombs" as they had become known wouldn't be forgotten and the families of the 23 people who died would probably never be able to come to terms with the event - but, even so, London had largely returned to normal in the 10 weeks he'd been away.

In the City of London there were more police evident on the street and steps had been taken to check anyone seen working on lamp posts, but otherwise there was little to show for the chaos of that day.

Paige had done surprisingly well out of the turn of events.

When Ed Briers gave her carte blanche to write her story that morning, she'd flipped a coin to decide whether to cast Branigan as either the hero or villain and then turned to Chloe's article to give her the basis for her own story. Unashamedly plagiarising great chunks of her friend's work, Paige had trumpeted Branigan's heroism in disarming the po-tentially devastating bomb and suggested that her original article from Bishkek was a de-liberate ruse to help him go undercover.

As it was, her fabricated story was heralded as an incisive piece of news journalism, praised for getting to the heart of the news while it was still happening and earning her a trophy in the "Breaking News" category of the National Journalistic Awards.

With her new-found status as an award-winning journalist, Paige was enjoying more column inches to her name, better pay and greater respect from her colleagues.

Greyson Krantz - the architect of Marta's death - stayed with Roz until the middle of January, by which time his jaw and tendons were all-but healed. He still needed to have work done on his teeth, but he intended to have that done in Europe where he was travel-ling to next.

When he'd finally departed, Greyson waved the keys to the padlocks which still kept Roz chained to the radiator in her kitchen.

'I'll post these on to you,' he said, his eyes glinting with the sadistic malice she'd grown to fear, 'it's been fun.'

When the keys eventually dropped through the letterbox, Roz was surprised by the postmark. The envelope had been posted in Cologne - the place where he'd committed the atrocity which made him persona non grata in the Black Ops world.

From Oxford Street, Branigan turned south and walked to Scott's Restaurant in fash-ionable Mayfair; famed for its high-profile clientele, he thought it hardly the most discrete place to meet.

'But that's the whole point,' David explained when he suggested the restaurant for their meeting, 'there will be far better-known faces there than you and I for the press to look at.'

And he was right.

The press photographer outside looked at Branigan, frowned with distant recognition and kept his camera lowered.

'How are you?' David Price asked, waving his hand to invite Branigan to take a seat.

'Much better, thank you,' Branigan said, sitting opposite, 'the trip gave me a chance to clear my head and come to terms with things.'

'Good,' David replied, pausing to order a bottle of sparkling water and a white Burgun-dy, 'and did you complete the Te Araroa Trail?'

The last time the pair had met - when they'd attended Noah's funeral - Branigan ex-plained that once he had his affairs in order, he was heading off to walk the length of New Zealand.

'Yes, it was amazing, mile upon mile of sand, forests, volcanoes and the most beautiful national parks.'

'You walked it all?' David asked, genuinely impressed.

Branigan half-smiled.

'I treated it as a challenge.'

David nodded.

'And did you do everything you wanted before you left?' he asked tactfully.

'Pretty much, I went down to Devon and scattered most of the girls' ashes on the beach where that large picture at the funeral was taken,' Branigan explained, before pulling out a small platinum heart on a leather thong round his neck, 'although a little bit of them came with me.'

'And I sorted out the house, so when I came back it wouldn't be a constant reminder,' he added.

After they'd ordered crab soufflé and sautéed monkfish starters, David asked Branigan how Chloe was.

'She's fully recovered,' he replied, 'I visited her in hospital before I left and even back then she was much better - now she's spent a couple of months at her mother's and is desperate to do something.'

'I'm pleased,' David replied, genuinely glad to hear the news, 'and I take it she's decided not to carry on with her journalism degree?'

Branigan let out a short laugh.

'Yes, she's realised there's too much hypocrisy in being a journalist - she'd rather do the sort of investigative work she did with Alan and me.'

'Alan is the funny little man I saw at the funeral - the one with the sparkly bowtie?' David asked.

'Yes, even before I went away the three of us decided we should try and do something together,' Branigan explained, pausing for a moment while his soufflé arrived, 'you know, once it became clear Marty's business wasn't going to survive.'

'It was a shame that folded,' David agreed, slicing a piece of his monkfish, 'but it is ev-er-thus with small businesses owned by one person - so how close are you to being open for business?'

'I think we're ready,' Branigan said, 'we've got premises and Alan has been project managing getting those ready. I'm meeting Chloe from the station after this and then we're going to take our first look; then we'll have to start looking for some work!'

David Price nodded.

'I might be able to help you there,' he said, taking a sip of wine.

'There's something I need someone who isn't in the main theatre of The Organisation to look into and I wondered if I could commission you,' he continued, 'the three of you, that is - you seemed to make a good team.'

Branigan looked taken aback.

'I wasn't expecting that,' he said, 'I'll need to speak with the others and, I suppose, we'll need to know what you want us to do and what we'll get paid for it.'

'I won't go into too much detail,' David replied, sitting back while the waiter cleared the table, 'but it carries forward the work you've done so far - let's just say, I think there was more behind the events leading to Peach Tree.'

He took a pen out of his pocket and wrote a number on the

back of his business card in flowing green script.

'That's what I could pay you,' he said.

Branigan's eyebrows twitched - it was more per month than he expected.

'Does that include expenses?' he asked.

'No, that's just the weekly retainer - your expenses would be on top.'

Branigan tried to act as if the sums being mooted were exactly what he expected.

'Good, well, I'll run it by the others and see if they're happy with that,' he said, 'which still leaves the police.'

'Yes,' David Price said grimacing slightly, 'I've spoken with the Home Secretary and the Met Commissioner; I think your name has been removed from all the current files. That doesn't mean you won't get caught up by some of those investigations as they move for-ward, you understand, but we'll have to deal with those as they come up.'

Before they parted, David had one final thing to say.

'I don't do this often,' he began with a wry smile, 'so make the most of it - I apologise for kicking you out of The Organisation - I was wrong.'

Branigan choked slightly. He would have loved Sally to hear that.

After leaving the restaurant, Branigan walked to Paddington Station and waited for Chloe.

Genuinely pleased to see each other they hugged on the platform before climbing in a cab and heading to the new office.

The last discussion Alan, Chloe and Branigan had, took place around Chloe's hospital bed before Branigan went off to New Zealand. Then they'd discussed the failure of Marty's business, how much they'd enjoyed working together and that they'd like to be able to continue to do just that.

'The problem is,' Chloe had said sadly from her bed, 'we need premises, money and, in my case at least, somewhere to live - that's before we even think about getting any business.'

Then Alan's ears had turned bright red as he confessed to taking the money from the Cressix Enterprises account.

'I really don't want it,' he'd explained forlornly, 'I just wanted to stop him spending mon-ey on the people who were chasing you.'

That's when their plan had been hatched.

Chloe would get better.

Branigan would go off to New Zealand and take a break.

Alan would use some of the cash from Cressix to open a new office; when it came to finding an office, Branigan declared his hand.

'I don't want to live with the memory of Sally and Molly, around me,' he said to Alan, 'so we can use my house. Do what you like with the downstairs - as long as the planners are okay with it - but don't touch the upstairs, they're still Molly's and Sally's rooms.'

Alan had accepted the brief and added that he'd also try and find somewhere nearby for Chloe and Branigan to live.

'That's great, Alan,' Chloe had said, 'but whatever you find, I think we'll each need our own front doors.'

In the taxi to find out how Alan had got on, Chloe voiced their shared doubts.

'You know when we said Alan should do whatever he wanted with the new office,' she said, 'do you think that was a good idea?'

'I had the same thought while I was in New Zealand,' Branigan replied, 'but I consoled myself that there's limited scope to change what's there already.'

A few minutes later the taxi drew to a halt outside Branigan's old house.

'Interesting,' he said, stepping out of the taxi and examining the new frontage.

'Yes,' Chloe replied, 'it makes it stand out from the others, don't you think?'

Branigan nodded.

'Did you ever see Marty's office?' he asked.

Chloe shook her head.

'Did it look something like this?' she asked.

'Not something like it,' Branigan said with the hint of a smile, 'exactly like it; even down to the black-panelled front door, the small brass plaque and the metal window blinds.'

He looked up and down the street.

'It's safe to say this is the only house in the road with a Portland stone façade.'

The door was opened by an excited Alan who hopped from foot to foot as he ushered them inside.

'Do you like the outside?' he asked.

'Yes, it's very Marty Freeman Investigations-ish,' Branigan said, looking around the fa-miliar reception with its high-fronted walnut desk and a corporate-grey leather sofa, 'much the same as it is here.'

'It's very nice,' Chloe said, 'but I'm surprised the planners let the changes through.'

'Yes,' Alan said with a slightly squeaky voice, 'when I spoke to them about it, they were quite surprised to find there was an existing permission for change of use and the new fa-çade.'

Both Chloe and Branigan noticed that his ears were bright red.

'The screen is new,' Branigan observed, pointing to the 90-inch television on the wall behind the reception desk which looked into a tranquil aquarium.

'Yes, it's more interactive now,' Alan said, walking nearer the screen and calling Snap-py's name.

Within seconds the giant face of the familiar great white shark appeared, enthusiastical-ly thrashing in the water and biting playfully at Alan's hand whenever he put it near the screen.

'Facial recognition,' he said before leading them through a

door into the main office.

'Wow,' Branigan said, 'this is just like stepping through Marty's old office door into the office we used to share!'

'That's because it is,' Alan said.

'Is what, Alan?' Branigan asked, confused.

'Marty's old office door and the office we used to share,' Alan explained as if it were the most obvious thing in the world.

'Aside from the screens on the wall everything in here came from Marty's office,' he continued, 'I bought the frontage and all the internal fittings from the Administrator.'

Upon closer inspection Branigan could see what he meant.

'This is my old desk,' he said examining the marks on the plain beech desk, 'and that stain on the carpet is where I spilled a cup of coffee.'

Chloe nodded, slightly distracted by the shark swimming past the three 90-inch televi-sions down the left-hand wall which gave the impression they were inside a giant aquarium.

Branigan walked slowly the length of the surreal workspace which had been shoe-horned into his old house, taking in the attention to detail which Alan had used in the transformation - even the coffee cups in the familiar kitchen area were the same.

Shaking his head in wonder, Branigan sat at his old desk with Chloe opposite in what had been Clive's space. Alan padded down to his end of the office and disappeared behind his screens, while Branigan explained the offer of work they'd received from David Price.

Alan cheered.

'We have our first job,' he said.

Branigan looked across to Chloe who nodded.

'Okay,' he said, smiling, 'I'll call David Price and let him know.'

He stepped through the doorway leading to the staircase

and was slightly taken aback to find what appeared to be an entrance into the adjoining building.

'Where does this lead?' he asked.

'Into the house next door,' Alan said simply, 'I bought that so you and Chloe would have somewhere to stay.'

Intrigued, Branigan stepped through the entrance into the living room of the adjoining house.

'You remember when we met up around your hospital bed and you said to Alan, "We'll each need our own front door?"' Branigan called to Chloe as she followed him into the neighbouring building.

Alan came in and stood proudly by the doors as Chloe gasped.

'The red one was easy, because that was yours Branigan and I had that already,' he said enthusiastically, 'but the blue one was more difficult because it was largely destroyed when they bombed your flat Chloe.'

He bent down and used his sleeve to polish the knob on the dark blue door.

'So I salvaged the handle and had a replica door made.'

'My goodness, Alan,' Chloe said, as she examined the handle, 'you did take the brief lit-erally, didn't you?'

Alan beamed.

'Yes,' he said, 'and you've got your own apartments behind each of your doors.'

'You've done an amazing job Alan,' Branigan said, 'you should be very proud, but do you mind if I just go and check on the upstairs of my old house first?'

Taking himself off alone, Branigan found both the bedrooms immaculately restored, so there was no sign of any of the events which had taken place in them. He turned to Molly's bedroom before making his call to David Price and inhaled deeply; the fabric of the room still smelled of his little girl. On the bed Alan had placed identical versions of Puppy and Agadee - Molly's bear and the rag doll - waiting for her should she ever need them.

Branigan stroked Puppy's face and then picked a framed photograph off the bedside table – a small version of the one from the funeral, with a laughing Molly perched on his shoulders as she threw a ball to Sally.

He lightly touched the happy faces.

'I miss you,' he whispered.

Acknowledgements

This book is for Nicola.

Thank you for having the faith in me, putting up with the re-writes and having to re-live some of the more harrowing scenes several times over - without your support this wouldn't have happened.

Then there are the friends who read, critiqued, gave their input and provided inspiration.

Thank you all.

Stuart Champion

20-7-19

Branigan Book 2

Branigan Book 2

I am writing book 2 which starts where this book leaves off.

It features many of the same characters having to grapple with a new series of adventures as they delve deeper into the murky world of espionage, track down Krantz and take on another piece of work found for them by Paige Henderson.

Their new case calls upon Alan to travel to America.

What could possibly go wrong?

Cover photo by John Modder

Printed in Poland
by Amazon Fulfillment
Poland Sp. z o.o., Wrocław